NYPD RED
6

JAMES PATTERSON
AND MARSHALL KARP

D0180020

GC
GRAND CENTRAL
PUBLISHING

New York Boston

Copyright © 2020 by James Patterson
Scott Free copyright © 2017 by JBP Business, LLC
Preview of *Fear No Evil* copyright © 2021 by James Patterson

Hachette Book Group supports the right to free expression and the value of copyright. The purpose of copyright is to encourage writers and artists to produce the creative works that enrich our culture.

The scanning, uploading, and distribution of this book without permission is a theft of the author's intellectual property. If you would like permission to use material from the book (other than for review purposes), please contact permissions@hbgusa.com. Thank you for your support of the author's rights.

Grand Central Publishing
Hachette Book Group
1290 Avenue of the Americas, New York, NY 10104
grandcentralpublishing.com
twitter.com/grandcentralpub

Originally published in trade paperback and ebook in December 2020
First oversize mass market edition: June 2021

Grand Central Publishing is a division of Hachette Book Group, Inc. The Grand Central Publishing name and logo is a trademark of Hachette Book Group, Inc.

The publisher is not responsible for websites (or their content) that are not owned by the publisher.

The Hachette Speakers Bureau provides a wide range of authors for speaking events. To find out more, go to hachettespeakersbureau.com or call (866) 376-6591.

ISBNs: 978-1-5387-3545-9 (oversize mass market), 978-1-5387-1863-6 (ebook)

Printed in the United States of America

OPM

10 9 8 7 6 5 4 3 2 1

In the end, it scarcely matters when a book is this enjoyable." —*Louisville Courier-Journal* (Kentucky)

"Patterson and Karp spare no plot twist in this page-turning thriller...Love triangles, mafia ties, and political entanglements abound, expertly layering this character-driven mystery in such a way that no dull moment ever arises. *NYPD Red 2* is just one more triumph from Patterson's literary empire, and clearly we can't get enough." —*Hampton Sheet* magazine

"Patterson and Karp once again prove that this is one crime series that's not to be missed—the literary equivalent of your favorite summer action movie...Patterson's proficient plotting gives the story its edge-of-your-seat action and suspense, throwing in one clever twist after another...with its entertaining mix of action and wit, *NYPD Red 2* is yet another up-all-night kind of read. Whether you're packing for a poolside getaway or planning a short staycation in your favorite reading chair, it's the perfect pick for literary thrill-seekers." —NightsandWeekends.com

NYPD RED 3

"Patterson and Karp provide plenty of surprises throughout *NYPD Red 3*." —BookReporter.com

NYPD RED 4

"It is equal parts police procedural and caper novel...both loyal and casual readers of this fine series will not want to miss this installment."
—BookReporter.com

RED ALERT

"*Red Alert* is a terrific story, wonderfully told and extremely entertaining, with a captivating beginning, finely paced middle, and satisfying ending…It is the fifth in the NYPD Red series, and the best of the lot."
—20SomethingReads.com

NYPD RED 6

For a complete list of books, visit
JamesPatterson.com.

*For Mel Berger, Bob Beatty, and
Danny Corcoran, who have been there
for me in the best of times and the worst
of times, and for the incomparable,
inspirational Darlene Love
—M. K.*

PROLOGUE

THE WEDDING OF THE CENTURY

ONE

IT TOOK BOBBY a week to decide where to park. It had to be close to the wedding, but not too close. And since he could be sitting in a stolen truck for two, even three hours, it had to be a stretch of real estate where the cops almost never patrolled.

It was a critical decision. Son of Sam had gotten tripped up by a thirty-five-dollar parking ticket.

Learn from the mistakes of others, his father used to tell him. *You can't live long enough to make them all yourself.*

He finally decided on West Twenty-Ninth Street between Eleventh and Twelfth Avenues. The entire block was lined with city sanitation trucks waiting for the next morning's run. The stench alone was enough to keep the street clear, but on the off chance that NYPD did drive by and ask what he was doing there, he'd explain that his alternator had crapped out, and he was waiting for a tow.

He arrived at 16:45. Two-plus hours later, not a single cop had passed by. He killed time reading the papers.

The *Times* didn't give the wedding much ink, just

one piece on page 14 of the Sunday Styles section. But the *Daily News* and the *Post* understood that Erin was American royalty, and they gave her the kind of coverage she deserved. Front page, dozens of pictures, plus detailed diagrams of the Manhattan Center.

Of course, Bobby already had all that information. He'd made three recon runs to the venue in the past three weeks. The first time was strictly to get the lay of the land—two recording studios, a dozen offices, and two spectacular ballrooms, the Hammerstein and the Grand.

The second time, he spent the day working with a catering crew and managed to get what he came for— a master key to almost every lock in the building.

Two days ago he'd set up the live feed. Wearing a baseball cap and a shirt with a logo that said BD RENTALS, he entered the complex through the loading dock and headed upstairs. The Hammerstein was packed with the army of people it would take to get the twelve-thousand-square-foot space perfect for what the network had billed as "the Wedding of the Century." But the Grand was dark, and he made his way to a storage room under the massive stage. At 0100 hours, with the cleaning crew long gone and a lone watchman stationed in the lobby, he'd installed the four wireless pinhole cameras.

The rest of the world wouldn't get to see the wedding footage until ZTV fed it to them one episode at a time, but Bobby now had a live view on his iPad.

The ceremony, which had been scheduled for 1700 hours, did not come off as planned. Which, of course, was part of Erin's plan. She loved to keep the world waiting. And guessing.

By 17:05 the Twitterverse was crackling with rumors, speculation, and general fan mania. She got cold feet. She caught Jamie cheating. She's holding up the network for more money.

And then, at 17:43, a wedding guest posted the tweet Erin's fans were waiting for: Here comes the bride. #TheWeddingIsOn.

The ceremony itself was stomach-turning. Bobby wanted to pummel whoever wrote Erin's vows. *Lifetime of growing. Falling more in love with you every day.* Pure garbage. But he had to admit her last one was kind of funny. *I vow never to keep score—even if I am totally winning.* That was the Erin he loved.

It was now 18:55, and the reception was in full swing. He changed the configuration on the iPad so he could fill the screen with the single image from the ballroom camera. The resolution was excellent, and he watched her dancing with her new husband.

Jamie Gibbs was thirty-two, five years younger than Erin. He had a reputation for being something of a player, but Bobby wasn't impressed. How hard is it to be seen with a beautiful woman on your arm when your mother owns one of the top modeling agencies on the planet? Erin Easton, on the other hand, was completely out of Jamie's league.

"Dude," Bobby said to the smiling image of Gibbs moving around the iPad screen. "You're the heir to a gold mine. Did you think she married you because you're so great in the sack?"

When the dance was over, Jamie and Erin took the stage and made their surprise announcement: Erin was going to change, and then she was coming back to put on a show.

Bobby had watched the dress rehearsal on his iPad last night. Erin didn't have the world's greatest voice, but the network had hired a twelve-piece band, three backup singers, and four dancers. Besides, she was beautiful to watch. All in all, it was a pretty good show. Too bad nobody would ever get to see it.

The crowd applauded, and Jamie stood there looking like he'd died and gone to heaven as Erin walked off the stage to a standing ovation.

"Go time," Bobby said, tossing the iPad onto the passenger seat.

He reached inside his shirt and pulled out the .357 Magnum bullet that was hanging on a chain around his neck. The powder had been replaced by one cubic inch of his father's ashes.

He rubbed his finger gently over the words the old man had had etched into the steel casing: *Succeed, or die trying. Semper Fi.*

Yeah, he thought as he started the truck and tucked the bullet back inside his shirt. That was the plan.

TWO

STANDING IN FRONT of the door to Erin Easton's dressing room, Lenny Ringel felt like one of those guards with the red jackets and the big black furry hats crammed into the sentry box outside Buckingham Palace. Nothing to do, no one to talk to.

It was the ass end of the security detail for the wedding, and Ringel had asked McMaster flat out why he had to protect an empty room for five hours while the other four guards were working the ballroom, listening to the music, ogling the women, and sneaking off to the kitchen to stuff their faces.

"The room's not empty," McMaster informed him. "It's got Erin's wardrobe, her jewelry, and her personal belongings, which, trust me, people would be happy to steal. It has to be secured at all times."

"So why can't we whack it up between us?" Ringel said. "Five guys, we could each take an hour instead of me parked out here like—"

"Ringel," McMaster said, "the place is crawling with important people, and you don't have what I'd call important-people skills. If you don't want the job, just say so, and I'll book another rent-a-cop."

Of course Ringel wanted the job. And not just for the money. When he first told his girlfriend he was working security at the Wedding of the Century, she went batshit, she was so happy.

"Lenny," she said, "you gotta mingle like crazy and come back with as much juicy gossip as you can."

He had to explain that his job was to protect the guests, not stalk them, but at least he'd come back with some cool stories she could tell her friends, and if she wanted to make them sound even cooler, that was fine by him. But now all he could tell her was that McMaster had put him in charge of watching a giant closet full of clothes.

And then, halfway through the gig, Erin showed up, knockers practically popping out of her wedding gown. She gave Ringel a drop-dead-gorgeous smile and said, "Wardrobe change, sweetie. Got a show to do. Don't let anyone in."

He couldn't believe it. Nobody told him about any wardrobe change. "Don't worry, Miss Easton," he said. "Nobody gets past me. Just one thing—my girlfriend, Darcy, is a big fan. She'd kill me if I didn't tell you. I'm Lenny, by the way."

"Well, Lenny, you tell Darcy—hell, don't tell her anything," Erin said. "Let's blow her mind. Where's your camera?"

Five seconds later, Lenny Ringel, the man with no important-people skills, was taking selfies with the most important person at the whole damn wedding. *Suck on that, McMaster.*

"Remember, Lenny," Erin said after he'd clicked off a burst of shots with his cell phone, "don't let anyone in, especially that pain in the ass Brockway, the guy with the camera crew. A girl needs her privacy."

She slipped into the dressing room, snapped the

lock, and left Ringel to dream what it would be like to be on the other side of the door watching Erin Easton change out of her wedding gown.

Forty minutes later Ringel was still reveling in the fact that one of the biggest stars in the world had called him by name. How cool was that?

And then the pain in the ass with the camera crew showed up.

"I'm sorry, sir," Ringel said, every inch the professional. "Miss Easton said no visitors."

"I'm not a visitor," Brockway said. "I'm the guy whose network put up a million dollars to shoot this fiasco, which means I'm paying your salary and hers. She's got a show to put on, and she's late."

Brockway rapped hard on the dressing-room door. "Come on, Erin. Your public is waiting. Time for you to knock 'em dead."

No answer.

He turned to Ringel. "You sure she's in there?"

"Positive, sir, but she said she needed her privacy."

"I'm not paying her to stay private," Brockway said, grabbing the doorknob and rattling it.

"It's locked, sir," Ringel said.

"Not for long," he said, storming off.

Thirty seconds later he was back, this time with McMaster and two of the other guards.

"Ringel, what's going on?" McMaster said. Only it didn't sound like he was asking. It was more like he was blaming Lenny for the fact that Erin apparently didn't want to come out. McMaster banged on the door. "Erin, it's Declan. Are you okay?"

No answer. Within seconds he produced a key, unlocked the door, and swung it open.

"Sweet Jesus," Ringel said. "What the hell happened?"

McMaster didn't know, but after thirty-five years with the NYPD, he knew enough to block the doorway to keep Ringel from charging in and contaminating what was clearly a crime scene.

The chair in front of Erin's dressing table was overturned. A wineglass lay unbroken on the carpet, its contents spilled. On the floor next to it was Erin's wedding gown, the beaded bodice stained a dark red. The wine was white.

McMaster's eyes went to the far end of the dressing room. The clothing racks that had been flush to the rear wall had been pushed aside, revealing a back door. It was closed, but he'd be willing to bet a year's salary that it was no longer locked.

"Stay where you are," he ordered Ringel. Taking the silk square from his breast pocket, he crossed the room; he put the fabric on the doorknob, opened the door, and peered down the hallway that led to the loading dock. "She's gone," he said, storming back. "Lock this place down. I don't care how important these people are. Nobody gets out."

"What about the cops?" Ringel said. "Should we call them?"

"Right behind you," a voice said.

McMaster looked up. The speaker was blond with sparkling green eyes, decked out in a blue cocktail dress and flashing a gold shield. He recognized her even before she identified herself.

"Detective Kylie MacDonald," she said. "NYPD Red."

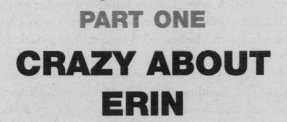

PART ONE

CRAZY ABOUT
ERIN

CHAPTER 1

I REACHED ACROSS the table and handed Cheryl the envelope.

"What's this?" She smiled. Perfect white teeth against flawless caramel skin. "Are you putting me on notice?"

"Hardly," I said. "It's been a year since you seduced me with Chinese food, Italian opera, and your hot Latina body. Happy anniversary."

"Today is June ninth," she said. "Our first date was the twenty-third. Aren't you jumping the gun here, Detective?"

"Open the gift before you judge the giver," I said.

She opened the envelope and took out the reservation confirmation from Bentley's by the Sea, a bed-and-breakfast in Montauk.

"June twenty-first to the twenty-third," she said. "Nicely done, Zach."

"And it's paper, which, according to Wikipedia, is the traditional first-anniversary gift," I said.

"I don't have anything for you," she said.

"We'll be alone for two days and two nights," I said. "I'm sure you'll think of something."

She leaned across the table and kissed me. "Behave yourself, here comes our host."

Cheryl's cousin Shane Talbot made his way from the kitchen to the far end of the restaurant where we were sitting. At six foot two, with a thick crop of red hair, he was easy to track as he zigzagged from table to table, shaking hands, bussing cheeks, and smiling graciously at the bloggers, reviewers, and foodies-with-a-following he'd invited to the opening-night party of his new restaurant.

"They love you," Cheryl said when he finally made it to our booth.

"Of course they love me tonight. I just bought them all a free dinner," Shane said, sliding in next to her. "The question is, will they still love Farm to Fork in the morning when they sit down to blog, Yelp, and tweet about it?"

"This is a tough New York crowd," Cheryl said. "They didn't send those plates back to the kitchen scraped clean because they're polite. You're going to get raves."

"Thank you for your totally unbiased opinion, but let me ask someone who's not a blood relative. How about you, Zach? What'd you think?"

"Fantastic," I said. "Best damn brussels sprouts I ever ate in my life."

He laughed. "Cops are not notorious for their love of leafy green vegetables, so I'm guessing they were also the *first* damn brussels sprouts you ever ate in your life."

"They were the second, but they shot straight to the top. A month from now, this place will be booked solid, and I'll be calling you begging for a table just so I can get more sprouts."

Shane turned to Cheryl. "This guy's a keeper. My

mom will love him. She's coming into town next month once we've got the kinks out of this place. The two of you have to have dinner with us."

"I chatted with your mom last night," Cheryl said. "She already invited us."

"Of course she did. Mom leaves nothing to chance." Shane stood up, gave Cheryl a peck on the cheek, shook my hand, and began working his way back through the crowd.

"He's right," Cheryl said as soon as he was out of earshot. "His mom leaves nothing to chance."

"Meaning what?"

"Meaning I didn't just *chat* with Aunt Janet last night. I had to listen to her whine about Shane for half an hour."

"Listening to people whine is what you do for a living. Aunt Janet was probably just trolling for some free therapy. What's her beef with Shane?"

She squinched up her nose. "'He's thirty-five, Cheryl,'" she said, her voice endearingly whiny. "'The man is not married, and he's too busy with his damn restaurant to give me any grandchildren.'"

"I'm just an amateur shrink," I said, "but if I were you, I'd tell Aunt Janet that she's suffering from a case of meddling motheritis and that her son's marital status is none of her business. He'll get around to having kids in due time."

"*Due time?* Did you hear what Shane said? The woman leaves nothing to chance. She didn't come to me because I'm a therapist, Zach. She played the blood-is-thicker-than-water card, and she recruited me to fix him up with someone who will knock his socks off."

"If she really wants grandchildren, you're going to have to find someone who can get him to take off more than his socks."

"You're not helping, Zach. Most of my friends are married. I need to find someone who is single, smart, and Shane-worthy. Any thoughts?"

My only thoughts were that guys like Shane Talbot didn't need help getting dates and that Cheryl would be wise not to get caught up in the family drama. I was debating whether to say that out loud when my cell vibrated.

Cheryl has a no-phones-at-the-dinner-table rule, but I'm allowed to make sure it's not a work emergency, so I took a quick peek at my caller ID. It was my partner.

"Kylie," I said, explaining why I had to take the call, but that's not how Cheryl took it.

Her eyes sparked. "Kylie," she said. "Interesting. Shane has always been attracted to strong women. Classic mommy complex."

She'd read me wrong. I needed to clear up the misconception, but first I had to answer the phone and let Kylie know that unless it was an emergency, I was too busy to talk to her. "Hey," I said, putting the phone to my ear. "Can I call you back in five?"

"No," she said. "I'm at Erin Easton's wedding, and we've got a shit-storm on our hands, Zach."

"Are you okay?"

"I'm fine, but the bride is missing. It looks like she's been taken. I'm at the Manhattan Center. How soon can you get here?"

"Ten minutes," I said, ending the call and getting out of my seat. "Kidnapping," I said to Cheryl. "I've got to go meet Kylie."

Cheryl was used to my sudden departures. She stood and gave me a quick kiss. "Ask Kylie if she'd be interested in dating a tall, good-looking guy who can cook."

"Sure," I said. But I already knew the answer. Of course she would. Kylie had had a torrid affair with one eleven years ago. Me.

CHAPTER 2

A CAB HAD just dropped people off in front of the restaurant. I jumped in and gave the driver the address.

I was in a hurry, and since not every cabby knows the fastest way between two points, I checked the hack license mounted on the partition. The first two digits were 39. I was in luck. That meant this man had been ferrying people around New York City for at least forty years. He wouldn't be needing a back-seat driver.

"You're late," the cabby said, pulling out.

"Late for what?" I said.

"The Wedding of the Century. Erin and Jamie are getting married in the Hammerstein Ballroom, but it started about three hours ago."

He reached over the front seat and held up a copy of the *New York Post*. A picture of Erin Easton, her plastic boobs and sculpted ass straining the integrity of a string bikini, took up most of the front page. There was a two-inch inset of the other half of the happy couple—the one most people didn't care about—Jamie Gibbs.

"Read all about it," he said.

"Thanks," I said, "but I've got to make a call."

I hit Kylie's number on my speed-dial, and she picked up on the first ring.

"I'm up to my eyeballs in crazy people," she said. "What's your ETA?"

"I was at a restaurant on Bank Street. We're just turning onto Eighth Avenue. I'll be there in less than ten. When did you get the call?"

"I didn't. I was at the wedding. Shelley Trager and the rest of the big guns at Silvercup Studios were invited. Shelley's wife got hit with the stomach flu, so he called me around noon and asked if I'd be his plus-one. I don't have much of a social life these days, so I said what the hell. I was the first one on the scene. I called Captain Cates. She activated a Level One mobilization."

There was a time when cops would hear a Level One come over the air, and it would be a holy-shit moment. These days it's so overused that the sense of urgency is gone. Cops want the details before they drop everything and go. Is it a shooting on a busy street corner? Or did the parents of some Upper East Side high-school kid panic and call 911 because Junior was three hours late coming home from school?

But this was the real deal. When one of the most recognizable people on the planet gets abducted, that's Level One on steroids. Knowing Cates, she'd have called for an army of cops to search the venue, canvass the area, and wrangle the crowd and at least two detectives from every precinct to ID and question the A-list guests, most of whom would probably think they were too damn important to be detained.

I figured by the time I got to the Manhattan Center, it would be a sea of flashing lights and wailing sirens with cops pouring in, guests wanting out, and media trucks clogging the road for blocks.

I told Kylie I'd be there as soon as possible and hung up. "You're not going to be able to get me all the way to Thirty-Fourth," I told the cabby. "Just keep driving till you hit a wall, and I'll jog the rest of the way."

"What's going on?" he said.

"I can't give you the details," I told him, "but let's just say that the Wedding of the Century is now the Clusterfuck of the Century."

CHAPTER 3

YOU'RE A COP in a big hurry, right?" my cabby said.

"Detective," I said. "Affirmative on the big hurry."

"You won't have to jog," he said as he maneuvered around a city bus. "There's always white hats outside of Penn Station keeping traffic moving. I'll drive, you flash your tin, they'll wave us through."

He did, I did, and they did.

I'd clipped my shield to my jacket, and as soon as I got out of the taxi, a uniformed officer spotted me, moved the barrier, and escorted me to the Manhattan Center.

Built as an opera house by Oscar Hammerstein over a hundred years ago, it is now a state-of-the-art production facility catering to film companies, TV networks, and record labels, but much of the old-world elegance and grandeur still lives on in the form of two sprawling event spaces: the Grand Ballroom and the Hammerstein, site of the Easton-Gibbs nuptials.

And now the majestic old building would add a new entry to its star-studded history: crime scene.

The officer led me to the nether regions of the huge

complex, navigating through cinder-block corridors never seen or even imagined by anyone but service people. Kylie and a man in a charcoal-gray suit were waiting for me.

When Kylie dresses for work, she wears pants, a shirt, a jacket, sensible shoes, and minimal makeup. It's the unofficial uniform of the hardworking female detective. It does a fairly adequate job of making her look more like a no-nonsense cop than an incredibly desirable woman. But her outfit today—a sleeveless V-neck blue number that hugged her in all the right places—would jump-start any man's imagination.

"Zach Jordan," she said, introducing me to the man next to her, "this is the head of Erin Easton's security, Declan McMaster. We worked together back when I was assigned to the UN General Assembly."

I knew the name. And the pedigree. McMaster had put in thirty-five years with the department, retiring as a full bird out of Intel. He was a solid block of a man with a salt-and-pepper buzz cut, a square jaw, and a troubled look in his dark eyes. He extended a hand.

"It's a pleasure to finally meet you, Inspector," I said.

"I'm a card-carrying civilian, Zach, so please call me Declan. I wish it were under better circumstances. I've been running security for Erin for three years. Sorry you caught me on the day my post-retirement career officially went in the toilet."

He wasn't looking for sympathy. He was simply stating a cold, hard fact. *Only lost one asset in three years* does not look good on a bodyguard's résumé.

"I know the protocol," McMaster said. "I can't be part of the investigation, but I also don't want to fade into the woodwork. I know Erin Easton's world better than anyone. I know her personal life, her business ventures, her friends, her fans, her wild side, and her dark side. I know everyone who loves her, and everyone she's pissed off. I can help…if you let me."

I could tell by the way he zeroed in on me that Kylie had already heard his pitch. I turned to her, and she gave me a look that captured what I was thinking: *You can't turn this kind of talent and experience down.*

"It'd be an honor to work with you, sir," I said. "Break it down for me."

"This way," he said. We followed him down the corridor to a nondescript wooden door. "This is the back door to Erin's dressing room." It was cracked open, and using his pocket square to avoid contaminating any evidence, he opened it wide enough for me to see our crime scene unit inside. Then he closed it.

"This is a service door," he said. "It's only used to move wardrobe in and out of the dressing room. It was blocked on the inside by a rack of clothes—I don't even know if Erin knew the damn door was here. It was locked from the outside."

"There's not a mark on it," I said. "How many people had a key?"

"Too many to count," Kylie said. "The venue manager told us that most of the doors have universal locks. Master keys are signed out for every event, but not everyone remembers to return them, and nobody in management seems to care. Whoever unlocked this door could have had the key for years."

"I wanted to post a guard out here," McMaster said, "but these cable networks are notoriously cheap. They only paid for five men. I had four watching the crowd. One was assigned to the front of the dressing room."

"Which means whoever took her went out the same way they came in," Kylie said. "This service hallway leads to the loading dock. The good news is there's a surveillance camera out there."

We walked down the corridor to a pair of large metal doors, then stepped outside onto the loading platform. Kylie pointed to a camera mounted two stories above us. "If we've got anything on video, this is our best bet. Benny Diaz arrived about ten minutes ago," she said to me. "Could you ask him to make this area a priority?"

Diaz is with TARU, our Technical Assistance Response Unit. I pulled out my phone and called him.

"Zach," he said. "I'm already at the CCTV terminal pulling video. This place is geek heaven—forty-two cameras."

"You got one that says 'loading dock'?"

"Camera six. I'm looking at you guys on the live feed right now."

"Put a rush on the footage from that camera. This is likely to be where they exited."

"Will do," Diaz said. "And, Zach, can you just confirm one thing for me?"

"What's that?"

"I just zoomed in on your partner, Detective MacDonald. Correct me if I'm wrong, but is she one smoking-hot cop or what?"

I hung up, looked at the camera, and flipped him the bird.

CHAPTER 4

MCMASTER TOOK US to a cordoned-off area in front of Erin's dressing room. Lenny Ringel, the last person to see her, was waiting for us.

"Ringel, tell these detectives what you know," McMaster ordered.

"What I *know*?" Ringel said. "What do you mean, what I know? I don't know anything."

Kylie held up a hand, and McMaster backed off. "I'm Kylie MacDonald," she said. "That's my partner, Zach Jordan. What's your name?"

"Lenny—*Detective* Lenny Ringel. I retired from the job about five—"

"Lenny, when did you last see Erin Easton?"

"About an hour or so ago. She came from the reception area and said she was making a wardrobe change. She had on a wedding gown, but she was going to put on something different for the show."

"What show?"

Ringel shrugged and looked at his boss for an answer.

"She was planning to perform a couple of musical

numbers for the crowd," McMaster said. "It was the network's idea. They wanted to jazz up the special."

Kylie turned back to Ringel. "When you spoke to her, what kind of mood was she in?"

"Great. Happy. I mean, she just got married, and she looked like a million bucks."

"And once she went inside, did anyone try to get in?"

"You mean in the front door, right? Because I wasn't in charge of the back door."

Kylie nodded. "Front door."

"No. I was here the whole time. Nobody tried to get in until that Brockway guy from the network showed up. Erin had told me to keep him out, so I did. Then he left and came back with Inspector McMaster, who had the key. He's the one who unlocked the door."

"Do you remember the exact time Erin went into her dressing room?" Kylie asked.

"The *exact* time?" He looked at Kylie like she had just asked him a trick question and he wasn't falling for it. "No. I wasn't keeping a log. I'm thinking it was probably around seven, maybe seven fifteen—whoa, wait a minute. I *can* tell you the exact time."

He dug his cell phone out of his pocket, hit a few buttons, and flashed us a photo of him and Erin in her wedding gown. "We took selfies," he said. "They're time-stamped. She went into the dressing room at seven oh eight p.m."

McMaster exploded. "You took pictures? Are you out of your goddamn mind?"

"Sir," Kylie said, treading the fine line between I-respect-who-you-are and This-is-my-rodeo. "I just have a few more questions, and then he's all yours."

McMaster deferred to her.

"Let's see what you got, Lenny," Kylie said.

Ringel scrolled through several more pictures—one with the two of them smiling at the camera, one where Erin stuck her tongue out, and finally one where she was planting a kiss on his cheek.

"Pretty kick-ass, right?" Ringel said. "She did it as a favor for my girlfriend, Darcy. Real nice of her. I hope you find the bastard who took her."

"Lenny, I'm going to have to take your phone," Kylie said.

"My phone? Why?"

"Those are the last known photos of Erin Easton before she was kidnapped. They'll be very helpful in our investigation."

"Oh, jeez...you really need my phone?"

"Yes," Kylie said, holding her hand out. "I'm afraid your girlfriend is going to have to wait before she gets to see them."

"She won't have to wait," Ringel said, reluctantly putting the phone in Kylie's hand. "I...I texted them to her as soon as Erin left."

McMaster couldn't hold back. "Damn it, Ringel, you were hired to safeguard these people, not socialize with them. This is why I put you back here, away from a roomful of celebrities. Detective MacDonald, please give this idiot his phone back so he can call his girlfriend and tell her to delete those pictures immediately."

"Boss," Ringel said, not reaching for his phone, "it's too late. By now those pictures are out there."

"Out *where*?" McMaster demanded.

Ringel couldn't bring himself to say the word. Instead he twirled two fingers in the air as if to downplay the size and scope of the worldwide network that would connect billions of people to the pictures of a New York City cop clowning around with the woman he was hired to protect.

I could almost see the headline in tomorrow's *Post*: "Erin Easton Kidnapped While Starstruck NYPD Cop Mugs for Camera."

Somewhere toward the bottom of the story they might get around to saying he was a *retired* cop. But the takeaway would simply be "fuckup cop." The damage-control department at 1PP would be working overtime.

"Out *there*," Ringel finally said. "You know…"

We knew. And there was nothing we could do about it.

CHAPTER 5

MCMASTER FIRED RINGEL on the spot.

It came as no surprise to Kylie or me. Lenny, on the other hand, was predictably blindsided.

"For what? A couple of harmless pictures?" he said as one of the other security guards escorted him out the door.

I knew men like McMaster. He'd take full responsibility for Ringel's failings, but this was not the time to explain or apologize. He went right to the task at hand. He looked at his watch. "She went in there at seven oh eight. If the kidnappers took her early on, they have close to an hour-and-a-half lead on us."

McMaster might have claimed he was just a civilian tagging along with us, but at his core he was a cop who was used to running the show. The time reference was to let us know that he was looking for some quick answers from the crime scene guys. His words and his body language said it all. He did everything but yell, *Let's get this party started.*

Kylie fielded the not-so-subtle hint. "Chuck Dryden is the best criminalist I've ever worked with," she said.

"He's not as fast as some of the others, but he's got eyes like a hawk."

"I know Dryden," McMaster said. "I just wish I could light a fire under him."

"You can't, and I can't," I said. "But the Chuckster is rather fond of my partner here, and I'll bet he's never seen her with this much cleavage. That might generate some heat."

It did. Dryden lit up as soon as he saw his favorite detective standing at his crime scene door.

"Chuck," she said, "I know you haven't dotted your i's and crossed your t's yet, but can you at least give me an idea of what we're looking at here?"

He nodded and walked us to the threshold of the dressing room.

I hadn't been able to see much from the other side, but from this angle I could see an overturned chair, an empty wineglass, and a bloodstained wedding gown on the carpet.

"So the chair toppled, and the glass fell when they grabbed her," I said. "I can't figure out why the dress is on the floor."

"Knowing Erin, she threw it there when she changed," McMaster said. "She never hangs anything up. She has people for that."

"We found this under her dressing table," Dryden said. He held up a piece of orange plastic that I recognized immediately. It was the safety cap from a hypodermic needle.

"There's no trace of the syringe," Dryden said. "They probably took it with them, but they must have dropped this when they uncapped the needle, and they didn't have time to look for it."

He put the cap under my nose. "Smell it," he said.

I took a whiff. Then another. "It smells like liquid dish detergent," I said.

"I have to test it, but I'm pretty sure it's ketamine," he said.

"Special K," Kylie said. "It's a party drug."

"Erin's not a druggie," McMaster said. "She's too smart. That shit ravages your body. She says using drugs would be like buying a store, filling it with all the things you want to sell, then setting fire to it just for kicks. If that's ketamine, then whoever took her used it to knock her out."

"If they drugged her, where did all the blood come from?" Kylie asked, pointing at the red stains on the front of the wedding gown.

Dryden held up a pair of angle-tip forceps. Between the pincers was clamped a tiny sliver of green and gold tinged with blood.

"It's a computer chip," Dryden said. "We'll be able to run a battery of tests on it when we get it back to the lab, but even here in the field, I can tell you that in addition to the blood, we found traces of skin cells snagged on some of the copper ridges, and we can make out the word *Kinjo* engraved on the—"

"Son of a bitch," McMaster said. "The bastards cut her open."

"You know what that chip is?" I said.

"Yeah. It's called a LyfeTracker," he said. "Erin makes only a small percentage of her income from shooting these reality shows. The bulk of it comes from endorsements. It doesn't matter what kind of company; if they offer her enough money, she'll hawk their product. Kinjo is a Korean tech company, and LyfeTracker is like Fitbit in that it tracks your activity, your sleep, your heart rate—all that shit. Only LyfeTracker also has a GPS function like a smartphone. They implant the chip under your skin. It's pretty quick and easy, like getting a piercing. Once it's in your body, the theory is if you're out there hiking in the wilderness, and you get lost, someone who has access to your account can track you down.

"Kinjo signed her to a multiyear, multimillion-dollar deal, and she shot a commercial in a bunch of different locations—the beach, the mountains, a penthouse—and in each scene she's saying, 'You can find me here,' 'You can find me here,' 'You can find me here.' In the last scene she's in the shower looking real sexy, and she says, 'With LyfeTracker, you can find me anywhere.'

"The product worked great for a while, and then about a month ago the damn thing crapped out and stopped transmitting data. The company is working around the clock to resolve the problem before the whole world realizes LyfeTracker can't track shit."

"But whoever took her didn't know that," Kylie said.

McMaster shook his head. "If they did, they'd have known they didn't have to cut her up. We never could have tracked her."

Kylie turned to Chuck. "Thanks. Do you have anything else?"

"Maybe," he said. "I told you I'm not quite ready, but if I'm right, I may have hit the mother lode." He paused, waiting for a reaction. Forensic foreplay.

"What's that?" Kylie asked.

"I think we have the entire abduction on video."

CHAPTER 6

SHE WAS SHOOTING a video when she was abducted," Dryden said. He held up a smartphone. An excellent likeness of Erin's face was etched into the metallic rose-gold case.

"That's her phone," McMaster said. "Now you really know she was taken against her will. She doesn't even go to the bathroom without it."

"We found it under her dressing table attached to a selfie stick when we got here," Dryden said. "The video was still recording. Once we'd dusted and photographed everything, I turned off the camera, removed the phone from the stick, and hooked it up to this laptop so you could view it on a larger screen."

He hit the Play button, and the picture popped on. It was a shot of Erin wearing a low-cut glittery pink top, and from the background details, it was clear that she was sitting at her dressing table looking into both the camera and the mirror as she spoke.

"The deed is done," she said with a giggle. "I am now officially Mrs. Jamie Gibbs." She held up her left hand and flashed a diamond-encrusted wedding band. "I wish I could have invited every single one of

NYPD RED 6 • 33

you to my wedding, but I couldn't, so I decided to do the next best thing. You all know that ZTV is shooting *everything,* and we're putting together a fantastic show that the whole world can watch in September. But this little private video is exclusively for my Twitter followers. I'm in my dressing room, getting ready to sing for my new husband and some of the coolest people in—"

A latex-gloved hand clamped over her mouth, and the picture scrambled as she dropped the selfie stick, leaving the camera pointed at the ceiling. Dryden paused the video.

"From here on in the picture doesn't change until my team arrived and retrieved the camera," he said. "When I get back to the lab I'll be able to analyze the audio track, but for now, you'll have to rely on your own ears."

"Let me drive," Kylie said, putting her fingers on the laptop's trackpad. She hit Rewind and backed the video up about fifteen seconds. As soon as Erin said "coolest people," Kylie froze the picture and then advanced it frame by frame so we could study the hand that came from behind.

It appeared to be male, which came as no surprise. The latex glove was an opaque light blue, which made it impossible to determine his race.

She hit Play, and I closed my eyes so I could focus on the sound. I heard a muffled cry from Erin as the man covered her mouth. It was followed by a yelp. Kylie backed it up and replayed it.

"That was more pain than fear," Kylie said. "I think that's when he stuck her with the needle."

I could make out some faint guttural noises coming from Erin, then the man saying, "Shh, shh, shh, shh, shh," half a dozen times.

"He's trying to keep her calm till the drug knocks her out," I said.

It didn't take long. In less than ten seconds, Erin was completely silent.

For the next three minutes, the sounds were indistinct. Her abductor was doing something, but I didn't know what.

"Declan," Kylie said, letting the tape keep running, "where was that chip implanted?"

"Right about here," he said, tapping a spot under his arm. "It's practically invisible."

"I think what we're listening to is him cutting it out," Kylie said.

Then we heard wheels rolling, followed by the snap of clasps opening. You didn't need to be a detective to put it together. He was getting her out of the building in a trunk.

There were some grunts as he loaded her into the box, then clasps snapping closed, wheels rolling and fading into the distance, and finally the door shutting.

Dryden stopped the video. "I've watched it already," he said. "There's nothing more for about fifteen minutes, and then you can hear the guard outside the door talking to someone. It's followed by loud knocking, and someone yelling…wait, I have an exact quote." He checked his notepad. "'Come on, Erin. Your public is waiting. Time for you to knock 'em dead.'"

"That was Brockway, the network exec," McMaster said. "He came and got me, I unlocked the door, and Kylie was right behind me. How'd you even get on the scene so fast?"

"Your security team was stoic all evening," she said. "All of a sudden, three out of the four of them started running in the same direction. I followed."

"Chuck, do you have a time stamp on the video?" I asked.

His eyes went back to the notepad. "She turned the camera on at seven twenty-eight. The rear door shut at seven thirty-four. End of story."

"Maybe not," Kylie said. "With any luck, the story continues at seven thirty-five on camera six."

CHAPTER 7

I WAS HAPPY that Benny Diaz had caught our case. Of all the computer cops in TARU, Benny is the user-friendliest.

We found him in a room about the size of a Turkish prison cell. There was no sweeping console, no bank of servers, no wall of CCTV screens, just a large wooden table, two racks of DVRs, and a couple of Acer monitors.

"Welcome to the nerve center of your entire case," Benny said. "This security system is everything you could hope for—if you still lived in the second half of the twentieth century." He smiled. "And yet I think I can still tell you the exact minute that Elvis left the building."

"Seven thirty-five," Kylie said.

He looked up at me. "She's not only beautiful, she's clairvoyant."

He plugged a thumb drive into the back of his laptop. "You were spot-on about camera six. I downloaded this. The quality is on par with your average convenience-store videocam."

A picture popped on the screen, and it took me a

few seconds to realize it was the loading dock captured from two stories up by a low-tech camera under the worst possible lighting conditions.

"This is when it all starts," Benny said. He hit Play, and a white box truck came into view and backed up to the dock. The image was so fuzzy, I knew we didn't have a prayer of making out the license plate or the driver's face.

"Hold on," Kylie said. "The time stamp says six twenty-six p.m. Zach and I just saw a video where he grabbed her at seven twenty-eight. Are you telling me he hung around for an hour before he went in?"

"He pulled in at seven twenty-six," Diaz said. "The system clock never got pushed ahead to daylight saving time."

The driver got out. I could tell he was white, male, and about six feet tall; he was wearing tinted glasses and had a baseball cap pulled down low over his face. He opened the rear door of the truck, went inside, and came back out pushing a large box.

"It's a musician's road case," Diaz said. "It's big enough to hold a six-foot-high amp."

"Or Erin," McMaster said. "It's on wheels. It's got those big clasps on the sides. That's what we heard on the tape. That's our guy."

The driver walked out of the frame.

"Do we have any other cameras in the hallway on the other side of the loading dock?" I asked.

"Nada," Diaz said. He fast-forwarded the video until the man reappeared, which was at 6:35 on the video, 7:35 in real time. We watched as he loaded the case into the rear of the truck, closed the door, hopped off the platform, got behind the wheel, and pulled away from the dock.

"So we're looking for a white box truck," Kylie said. "How many of those are there in New York City?"

"Hundreds. Maybe thousands. But this might help narrow it down." Diaz froze the picture. "You see the lettering on the driver's-side door?"

"Barely," she said. "It's a blur, but it looks like Chinese."

"Or Korean. Or Japanese," Diaz said. "Whatever it is, it's not English, and it's enough to help set this one apart from a lot of other white one-ton boxes."

"Call Real Time Crime Center," Kylie said. "Have them pull the photos captured in the past four hours from every single license-plate reader in a twenty-block radius of the Hammerstein, then check to see if any of those plates are registered to a white commercial box truck. If they get a hit, check the truck for Asian lettering on the door."

"I'm on it," Diaz said.

"Finding the truck isn't going to help find Erin," McMaster said. "This was no random snatch-and-grab. The person who did this carefully planned this whole thing. The clock on the security feed may be an hour off, but this guy showed up at the perfect time—when Erin was alone in her dressing room changing out of her wedding gown."

"How could he even know when that was going to happen?" I said.

"All he'd have to do is follow her tweets," McMaster said. "She doesn't eat, sleep, pee, or shop without posting about it on social media." He looked at his watch. "She's been missing almost two hours. By now she's been transferred out of the truck and onto another vehicle or a boat or a plane. Or, if he's totally out of his gourd, she's dead."

"She's not dead," Kylie said. "He's going to need proof of life when he makes the ransom call."

"What makes you so sure he's in it for the money?" McMaster said.

"Because he waited until *after* she'd married a millionaire to take her."

CHAPTER 8

HE WAITED UNTIL *after* she'd married a millionaire," McMaster said, repeating Kylie's logic. "I'd almost forgotten how smart you were."

"Thanks," she said. "Let's go talk to our millionaire husband before the kidnapper gets to him."

We stepped into the hall, where a uniformed cop was going at it with a civilian.

"I don't give a rat's ass who you know," the cop said. "This is a crime scene. Turn off the camera or you're walking out of here in cuffs."

The man, about sixty, wasn't taking orders. "Did you ever hear of the First Amendment? You shut me down, and I'll have your job."

"Declan, do you know that guy?" Kylie asked.

"Harris Brockway. He's a suit with the network. He's a pompous ass, but he's got a lot of footage you're going to want to get your hands on. I'd make nice."

It was a politically savvy suggestion, but Kylie has never been good at making nice, especially with a pompous ass threatening a cop. "Officer," she called out, jumping into the fray. "Can you do me a favor and give them a hand in the ballroom? I got this one. Thanks."

The cop checked out the gold shield clipped to her blue dress, shrugged, and walked off.

Brockway checked out the blonde inside the dress, smiled, and turned on the charm.

"Harris Brockway, vice president of programming at Zephyr Television," he said, waving for his cameraman to move in closer. "My friends call me Brock. And you are?"

"Detective Kylie MacDonald. That's my partner, Zach Jordan. We're investigating the disappearance of Ms. Easton, and you're going to have to turn off that camera."

"Please, Detective, you strike me as an intelligent woman. Do I really have to explain the First Amendment to you?"

"You mean the one where Congress shall make no law abridging the freedom of the press?" Kylie said. "No, I've got that one down. You can broadcast whatever you want. However, there are laws against interfering with a police investigation, which is exactly what you're doing when you bring your camera into an active crime scene. Now, either tell your cameraman to turn it off or prepare to spend the night with him in a holding cell."

The cameraman lowered his camera. "Hey, you work it out with her and the union, Mr. Brockway, but I didn't sign on for no jail time."

Brockway glared at Kylie. "Do you know how much ZTV has invested in this production?"

"I'm not here to help you put on a show, Mr. Brockway. I'll tell you what I can do—I can impound your cameras right now and get a court order giving me access to all the footage you shot today. Or, if you're willing to cooperate and provide me with copies, you can keep on shooting, just as long as you don't point your lens at this side of the yellow tape."

"Fine," Brockway said, spitting out the word. "I'll get you dupes."

"And the script," Kylie said.

"What script?" Brockway demanded.

"Mr. Brockway, I have a boss, and she has a boss, and so it goes, all the way up the chain of command to the police commissioner himself," Kylie said. "Every one of them thinks like a cop, and eventually every one of them is going to ask the same question: 'How do we know this isn't a publicity stunt?'"

"Are you out of your mind?" Brockway said. "This is a reality show. There are no goddamn scripts. How could you even ask such a dumb question?"

"Erin Easton has been around since I was in high school," Kylie said. "She's not exactly the flavor of the week. This kidnapping—real or staged—is going to put her back in the spotlight. When you're a detective investigating her sudden disappearance, the question isn't dumb at all."

"Sorry to disappoint you, Detective, but we're not shooting an episode of *Law and Order*. We have an outline—heartwarming ceremony, over-the-top reception, exclusive interviews with celebrity guests. Basic reality-show fodder. Trust me, none of our writers are creative enough to come up with anything as outrageous as the bride being kidnapped."

"We'll need a copy of the guest list," Kylie said, "along with the names of anyone who accepted the invitation and failed to show."

"Failed to show?" Brockway said with a smirk. "Sweetie, this was the hottest ticket in town. There are two hundred and twenty-four names on that guest

list. Only two people didn't make it. One was Shelley Trager's wife, but of course you know about that one, because you took her spot."

"Who was the other no-show?"

"Veronica Gibbs," he said, the smirk on his face wider and even more irritating. "The groom's mother."

CHAPTER 9

AS SOON AS Declan McMaster realized that Erin was missing, he had his security detail get Jamie Gibbs out of harm's way. The new groom was now locked up in one of the administrative offices on the second floor and was being closely guarded by the NYPD.

"I never even heard of Gibbs until he became the man who was marrying Erin Easton," I said to McMaster as Kylie and I followed him downstairs. "What can you tell us about him?"

"Classic spoiled rich kid, always in the gossip rags, famous for his sexual exploits and his run-ins with the paparazzi, ex-husbands, current husbands, Uber drivers, and just about anyone who got in his way," McMaster said. "Three years ago he woke up with a dead girl in his bed. Not his fault; she OD'd. But according to Erin, it scared him straight. He gave up the blow and the booze and went to work for his mother.

"Veronica Gibbs owns Head Turners, a multi-million-dollar international modeling agency, and she put Jamie in charge of talent development. It's a real job—if Veronica would let him do it. But she's a tyrant. I swear to God, her business card doesn't say *CEO,* it says *BIC*, which, if you ask, she'll tell you stands for 'bitch in charge.' She runs the business and her son's life with an iron fist. Jamie hates living in her shadow, but he doesn't have any real money of his own, so he tolerates her bullshit and cashes the monthly allowance checks."

"Why did Veronica bail on the wedding?" I asked.

"Two weeks ago the new issue of *Vanity Fair* came out. They did a major article on Veronica. Mostly it was about her success running a global company in the cutthroat world of fashion. But eventually the writer asked how she felt about her son marrying one of the most famous women in the world."

"I bet Mama went on a tear when she heard that question," Kylie said.

"Oh yeah. She started with 'Famous for what? Spreading her legs?' I'll spare you the details of the rant, but she went on for three paragraphs—basically called Erin a gold-digging whore. It was less than five percent of the article, but the tabloids and the TV entertainment news shows pounced on it and gave it a life of its own."

"How did Erin deal with it?" I asked.

"She kind of shrugged it off. Or at least she pretended to. But Jamie took it hard. He was really pissed at Veronica. I figured it would all come to a head today, and I was braced for a real catfight the minute the two women came face-to-face, but Veronica never showed."

We arrived at the office where Jamie was secured. Two uniforms were posted outside. A detective from Midtown South was inside. Kylie opened the door and asked the detective to step out.

"How's he doing?" she asked the detective.

"Pretty broken up," he said. "Seems genuine."

"Any phone calls?"

"Nothing incoming. He dialed out once. Nobody picked up, so he left a voice mail. He said, 'Mom, Erin's been kidnapped. Call me back.'"

"Did she?"

"No."

Kylie, McMaster, and I entered the office. Jamie was at the window looking out onto Thirty-Fourth Street. He turned as soon as we walked in. He was about medium height with a puffy face that would have benefited from a more defined jawline.

"Did you find her?" he asked. "Do you know anything?"

"Not yet," Kylie said, "but we have hundreds of cops out there looking. Have you heard from the people who took her—a phone call, e-mail, a text, anything?"

"No." He held up his cell phone. "I'm waiting."

"NYPD will wait with you."

"What does that mean?"

"It means the best chance we have of finding Erin is to be with you when the kidnapper makes contact. Our technical people will monitor all your phones, your e-mail, and your social media accounts. We'll set up a command post in front of your residence, and while we won't stop you from coming and going as you please, we'd prefer if you stay home for the next forty-eight hours.

"Every call you get will be recorded. A detail of uniformed officers and detectives will be assigned to cover your home, both inside and out. And someone from the hostage-negotiation team will be with you at all times. He'll coach you in advance on what to say and what not to say when the call comes."

"I don't need coaching," Gibbs said. "I know what I'm going to say: 'How much? I'll pay. And please don't hurt her.'"

"Jamie, don't be an ass," McMaster said. "These detectives have been through this before. Do what they tell you. Erin's life depends on it. This is Detective Kylie MacDonald and Detective Zach Jordan. You couldn't ask for anybody better to be working this case."

"Sorry," Gibbs said. "This was supposed to be the happiest day of my life. I can't believe what's going on. What do you want me to say when they call?"

"Whatever they ask for, don't agree to it right away," I said. "First thing you want is proof of life. And not just a phone call. You want a video."

"A video takes time. Why drag it out? Why not just pay the ransom and get her back?"

"Because paying the ransom doesn't guarantee that they'll release Erin. And if she's seen the kidnappers, once they have the money, there's no reason to keep her alive. Your job is to keep whoever calls on the phone. Every conversation you have will tell us more about the kidnappers and where your wife may be."

"You think there are more than one?"

"One person took her, but that doesn't mean he's working alone," I said. "Can you think of anybody who might be behind this?"

"No. It's probably just some random maniac who wants money."

"He hasn't asked for money yet, so we have to consider that it's someone who has a grudge, a vendetta, or some other reason to want to hurt her."

"People love Erin. She's super-famous, so of course she has her detractors."

"Do any of them stand out?" Kylie asked.

"Yeah, my mother," Gibbs said with a hint of a smile. "She's taking a lot of heat on social media for Erin's disappearance. But trust me, she had nothing to do with it. If she had, Erin would have been gone long *before* the minister said, 'I now pronounce you man and wife.'"

"We'd like to talk to your mother," I said.

"You and me both, Detective. She hasn't returned any of my calls. On a normal day I wouldn't worry, but…" He choked up and took a few seconds to shake it off. "This isn't a normal day. For all I know, the kidnappers took her too."

CHAPTER 10

THE INVESTIGATION HAD gotten so big so fast that while we were with Jamie, we needed somebody to keep tabs on the dozens of detectives who had been interviewing the guests, the wedding party, the TV production people, and the catering crew.

And there's no one we trust more than Detective Danny Corcoran. We'd recruited him a few months ago, and he quickly became our go-to guy. Give Danny an assignment, and he gets it done, no handholding, no excuses. And the fact that he's also a trained hostage negotiator would be a bonus for this case.

He was waiting for us upstairs.

"Boil it down for us, Danny," I said. "What have you got?"

"Not much. I've never seen so many self-involved people packed into one ballroom. None of them saw anything of any value, but that didn't stop them from offering up theories—especially the actors who play cops on TV. We took names, addresses, and phone numbers, and let them go. The waiters, bartenders, and the rest of the staff were also no help. The inner circle—bridesmaids, groomsmen, best man—were as shocked as everyone else. They all swear that this marriage was the real deal. Jamie loved her; she loved Jamie. And of course they mentioned that the groom's mother hates Erin, but by now I'm guessing you know that."

"Thanks. Anything else?"

"Yeah. Don't be obvious about it, but take a look at that woman on the other side of the yellow tape. The one in the black pants and gray jacket, breathing fire."

I glanced over. The woman was staring straight at us, hands on hips. "Who is she?" I asked.

"Her name's Anna Brockway. Her husband's the network guy. She doesn't like the way the investigation is being handled."

"What did you tell her?"

"She wouldn't talk to me. I'm not high enough on the food chain. She said she wants to talk to 'that blond bitch in the blue dress.'"

Kylie smiled. She'd been called worse. "That would be me. What's her beef?"

"She's pissed because you told her husband that this whole kidnapping business was a big publicity stunt."

"I never said that. Ask Zach."

Danny turned to me.

"Technically, she never *said* it. But if I had to testify in court I'd say she implied it with extreme prejudice."

"Hey, tell me you didn't think of it," Kylie said.

"Of course I thought of it. But you red-flagged it. You asked Brockway if the whole thing was scripted because you caught him harassing a cop and you wanted to get all up in his grille."

Kylie shrugged. "It worked, didn't it?"

"Oh, it worked great. We've been on the case less than two hours, and you've managed to get a network executive's wife complaining about how we're handling it."

"I'd love to stick around and do couples therapy with you," Danny said, "but I've got work to do in the ballroom." He gestured toward Mrs. Brockway. "Can I release the hounds?"

"Do it," Kylie said.

He walked down the hall and lifted the tape, and a short, trim woman in her midforties strode toward us.

"How dare you?" she boomed while she was still twenty feet away.

"Ma'am, there's been a bit of a misunderstanding," Kylie said. It was about as close as she was going to get to the words *I'm sorry.*

"You bet there's been a misunderstanding," the woman said. "Starting with the fact that you don't even know who I am."

"Yes, I do. When I spoke to your husband—"

"You can stop right there. Forget that my last name is Brockway. I've been Erin Easton's manager and publicist for fourteen years. I'm married to the head of programming at ZTV, but that's none of your concern. Erin is my client. I came up with the idea for the *Everything Erin* show, I sold it to the network, and I'm one of the executive producers. So if you're telling people that this horrific kidnapping is scripted, you're accusing me of a crime."

"Not accusing. *Investigating.* It's my job. And when a high-profile celebrity who is a master at manipulating the media suddenly goes missing, my instincts go on point and I have to ask: Is this another one of her Hollywood publicity stunts?"

"The *wedding* is the publicity stunt, you moron! Erin is famous. She earns millions. Do you think I would be stupid enough to fake a kidnapping so she could be more famous and make more money? I know your name, Detective, and if you don't treat this as the crime it is, I'll call the police commissioner and have him assign someone who will."

"And I know your name," Kylie said, "so if it turns out that this *is* a hoax, I'll know who to come looking for."

"Bitch," Brockway said and stormed off.

"I'm not keeping score," I said, "but if I were, I would say that right now it's Mrs. Brockway, one; Detective MacDonald, zero."

"She called me a bitch and a moron," Kylie said. "Believe me, Zach, it's far from over. I'm going to—" Her phone rang. She looked at the caller ID. "It's Cates." She took the call. "Yes, Captain." She listened for a solid twenty seconds, and I watched as her face morphed from pissed to positive. "Let's go," she said as soon as she hung up. "We caught a break. They found the box truck."

CHAPTER 11

WE CALLED MCMASTER, met him in the lobby, and the three of us got in Kylie's car.

"Cates got a call from the Manhattan North duty captain," she said, pulling out and heading east on Thirty-Fourth. "Patrol spotted a white box truck with Asian lettering on the door. It's sitting in the Fairway parking lot at a Hundred and Thirty-Second Street and Twelfth Avenue."

"If we're going to Twelfth Avenue," McMaster said, "why are you headed east?"

"I'm stopping at the precinct to change. This dress is way too low-cut for me to be taken seriously as a crime fighter. When I was interviewing Jamie Gibbs, he barely looked me in the eye. Anyway, patrol found the truck, they ran the plate, and it came back to a VW Jetta registered to an address in Pelham Bay in the Bronx."

"Son of a bitch stole the plates," McMaster said like he was teaching a criminology class to a bunch of rookies at the academy. Like Kylie, he was a micromanager, and I wondered how often they'd butted heads when they worked together.

"Right, sir," Kylie said, a touch of annoyance in her tone. "The plates were stolen, so they ran the VIN on the truck, and it came back to a Korean food-distribution company that had left it parked out at Hunts Point. A detective called them. It's Sunday, so they didn't even know it was missing."

"Damn," McMaster said, "this guy covers all the bases."

"License-plate readers got multiple hits on the truck traveling from Hunts Point to Manhattan," Kylie said. "He went off the grid about four thirty and resurfaced about two and a half hours later on Tenth Avenue a few blocks from the Manhattan Center. Then they tracked him up the West Side Highway to Harlem. Cates wants Chuck Dryden to cover both scenes, so he's on his way up there to check out the truck, and she's pulled in a dozen cops to canvass the neighborhood for witnesses."

Kylie parked in front of the Nineteenth Precinct, ran upstairs, ditched the glamour-girl dress and heels, and came back wearing pants, a T-shirt, a jacket, and flats. On anyone else it might look mannish. On her, it looked fantastic.

She got behind the wheel. "*Now* we're headed west," she said just in case McMaster had any doubt which one of them was in command.

Fairway Market is a New York success story. It started out as a small produce store on the West Side back in the 1930s and has expanded to a chain of upscale supermarkets that caters to millions across the tristate area.

Their store in Harlem is in a sketchy neighborhood, but there's plenty of secure parking, so it's a magnet for high-end shoppers looking for specialty foods and quality produce.

And because the store was open till eleven p.m., the busy lot was a good place to dump a stolen truck.

Chuck Dryden was waiting. "You people certainly have me running around tonight," he said.

"You can thank us for the overtime later," Kylie said. "What have you got?"

He walked us to the rear of the box truck. The road case was in the back. "Blood in the case, blood on the floor," Dryden said. "I just got here, so it will take me a while to see if it matches up with the bloody chip we found in the dressing room. But you love to leap to conclusions, Detective MacDonald, so feel free to make assumptions at will."

"So what you're saying, Dr. Dryden, is that you're ninety-nine percent sure it's Erin's blood," Kylie said.

Dryden laughed and looked away. He loved it when she toyed with him.

"How about prints, hair, DNA?" she said.

"In due time, Detective. However, there are traces of pink glitter in the case. And if you recall, she was wearing a shimmering pink top in the video."

"So now you're a hundred percent sure that this is the vehicle the kidnapper used," Kylie said.

"Not yet, but clearly you are."

"Chuck, you're killing me here. How long do I have to wait before I get something conclusive?"

"Several hours before I can give you anything definitive," Dryden said. "While you're waiting, why don't you talk to that uniformed officer, the one standing next to that squad car?"

"What's he got?" Kylie asked.

For the second time that night Dryden gave her that I-know-more-than-you grin. "He's got an eye-witness in the back seat."

CHAPTER 12

I SIGNALED FOR the officer to step away from the car so we could talk. He introduced himself.

"Mike Koulermos with the Two Six. Your witness is Venetia Jones." He handed me her New York State ID card. "She's a pross. Been at it for years. Knows the game. Never gives us a hard time when we round them up. Her pimp is a weasel named Edgy Randolph, but he won't show his face while we're here."

"What did she see?" I asked.

"That's the thing," Koulermos said. "She won't tell me. I was canvassing the area and asked her if she saw anybody get out of that white truck. She said yes. I said, 'What did you see?' and she says, 'Opportunity.' Whatever she knows, she's saving it for someone with clout."

"Which means she thinks she's got something good, and she wants to barter," I said.

"I think she *knows* she's got something good," Koulermos said. "The word is out that Erin Easton was abducted."

"Bring her over, and let's find out."

The cop went back to the squad car, and I turned

to Kylie. "You want me to take this?" It was more of a statement than a question. Kylie's batting average interviewing hookers was hovering somewhere around .000.

"Good idea. They all hate me."

"Don't take it personally. They just respond better to male authority figures." I turned to McMaster. "You're male, but you've got no authority, so let me do the talking."

He nodded. He was lucky to be along for the ride, and he knew it.

Venetia Jones stepped out of the squad car wearing a purple cocktail dress and fuck-me pumps. Prostitutes in tight short shorts and fishnet stockings are from an era gone by; the women today dress like they're going out for an evening of clubbing.

Her ID card said she was thirty-four, but up close she looked a lot older. She'd probably been on the streets for half her life, and the hazards of her trade had taken their toll. I studied her face and looked into her eyes. I could see the mileage and the battle scars, but if there was ever a fire in her soul, it wasn't there that night.

"The officer tells me you saw someone get out of that truck," I said.

"Yeah. One male, one female, both white."

"Can you describe the woman?"

"Downtown hair, fake-ass titties."

"Come on, Venetia, I need more than that."

She smiled. "I know what you need, baby, but you gotta pay me to care."

On the street, information is currency, and when a hooker has something she thinks a cop can use, she negotiates.

"Do you take gold?" I handed her my card with the

gold detective shield on it. "It's a get-out-of-jail-free card. Call me if you're ever in a jam. It's good for one time only."

She looked at the card and handed it back. "Sorry, Zach. I don't need any juice down the road. I have an ongoing situation that needs tending to immediately. If you want to help me with that, we can talk."

She was playing hardball. She knew she had what I wanted. "Tell me your situation, and we'll take it from there," I said.

"A few weeks ago I met this nice white boy at a bar. We hit it off, went to his hotel room, did a little partying, and he must have been exhausted, because he passed out cold."

"Maybe it was something he drank," I said.

"Well, he don't pay me to fix him breakfast, so I pack up and leave him sprawled on the bed."

"Define *pack up*," I said.

She laughed. "You a damn smart cop. I was in a big hurry, and by accident his Rolex fell into my purse while I was gathering my things."

"Did you run right back and return it?"

"I was gonna, but the next day the cops came down on me. Can you believe it? This pencil-dick rich boy is pressing charges against me, a poor working girl."

"The married ones keep it quiet, so I'm guessing he doesn't have a wife and kids," I said.

"No—just a broom up his ass. Damn fool wants to make a whole federal case out of it. Now, if you know someone at the DA's office who could make it go away, my memory just might come back, and I could tell you about them white folk who got out of that truck."

"How about the Rolex? Can that come back too?"

"You drive a hard bargain, Zach, but hell, why not?"

"I have a friend at eighty Centre Street. *If* what you've got is good."

"Baby, what I got is so good, you gonna tell me to keep the Rolex." She took an iPhone out of her purse, tapped in her password, and pulled up a photo. I leaned over her left shoulder, and Kylie came around the other side. McMaster didn't wait for an invitation. He poked his head above Kylie's.

The picture was dark, but we could see Erin Easton in her sparkling pink top being helped out of the back of the box truck by a man. His face was turned away from the camera, but he was wearing the same baseball cap we had seen in the surveillance video.

"It gets better," Venetia said. She swiped the screen, and this time Erin and her abductor were in close-up, their faces lit by one of the glaring overhead parking-lot lights.

"Shit, shit, shit!" McMaster said. His hand swooped in and grabbed her phone.

Venetia immediately let loose a barrage of F-bombs and tried to wrestle it back. Koulermos jumped in and pulled her off him.

In less than three seconds, I went from the high of catching a break to full-blown rage at a rogue retiree.

I wheeled around. "Phone!" I said.

McMaster handed it over. "I'm sorry, I—"

"Not now!" I turned back to Venetia. "You okay, Ms. Jones?"

"I'm good," she said. "You good?"

"Real good. I'm going to need to keep your phone."

"No problem. I got a backup...or two."

"Did you see where they went?"

"Sorry, honey. I got a business call just then. By the

time I looked up again they was gone. One thing I can tell you—wherever they went, they wasn't walking. That girl was not too steady on them red-bottom stilettos."

"Thanks. Officer Koulermos will take you to the precinct. I want you to write up everything you saw. He'll also take the case number on that little Rolex misunderstanding."

She flashed me a smile that was one part gratitude and three parts victory.

I handed the cop a twenty. "Buy Ms. Jones some dinner."

"There's a real fine sushi-takeout place on Amsterdam," she said, "but it's not cheap."

I handed the cop another twenty. It was a small price to pay for a picture of the kidnapper.

As soon as Koulermos led Venetia to the car, I turned to McMaster and held her phone to his face. "Who is he?" I said. "And where do I find him?"

CHAPTER 13

HIS NAME IS Bobby Dodd," McMaster said. "He's been obsessed with Erin for years. It goes back long before I started working for her. He's broken into her home four times. Once here in New York, another time at her house in Aspen, and twice at her villa in Tuscany."

"Was he ever collared?" I asked.

"No. We knew it was him, but we never had enough proof."

"Erin's doing pretty well for herself if she's got three homes," Kylie said.

"She's got five. It used to be six, but Hurricane Irma destroyed the beach house on Anguilla. Insurance covered less than twenty percent of the loss. Erin is a real estate junkie. As soon as she pulls together four or five million dollars, she starts looking for something new to buy or renovates and redecorates one of the houses she already owns. She makes a lot of money, but she has almost no liquid assets."

"Maybe that's why Dodd waited till after the wedding ceremony before he abducted her," Kylie said. "She doesn't have ransom money. Her new husband does."

McMaster shook his head. "I had the same thought, and now I'm kicking myself for it. As soon as we knew she was kidnapped, my mind jumped to the ransom demands. That's why I didn't immediately think of Dodd. She's got more than one stalker, and Dodd isn't the type to do this for money."

"Then what does he want?"

"Her," McMaster said.

"You don't think he'll ask for ransom money?" Kylie said.

"He might. But that doesn't mean he'll let her go if we pay. The man's got a PhD in crazy. I don't know if God told him this or he just came up with the idea on his own, but he's positive that he and Erin are soul mates and they're destined to be together forever. He's told her that in the letters and e-mails he's sent her and in person every time he's gotten close enough."

"What about an order of protection?"

"If Erin filed an order against every looney tune who stood in the crowd professing his love for her, she'd spend a hell of a lot of time in court. Celebs know they live in a fishbowl. They don't get litigious unless it gets physical or if there are kids involved. They just beef up security and move on with their well-documented lives."

"What else can you tell us about Mr. Dodd?" I said.

"He's forty years old, grew up in Clarksville, Tennessee. His grandfather was a stonemason and started teaching the kid the tricks of the trade when he was only ten. He was quite the craftsman, but his father was a Marine, and Bobby wanted to follow in Daddy's footsteps. He enlisted in the Corps when he was eighteen and served twelve years, so he's well trained in self-defense, weaponry, concealment, and survival techniques. He's smart. Not like *Jeopardy!*

smart; more like Rambo smart. If he decides to go underground and squirrel Erin away in some cabin in Idaho or Montana or God knows where, we'll never find her."

"You have a file on him?" I asked.

"A fat one. I can access it from my phone and send it wherever you want."

"For starters, e-mail it to me and Kylie. We'll open up a case with Real Time Crime and get people down at One PP digging up anything and everything they can find on Dodd. The private correspondence you have from him to Erin won't be on their radar, so thanks—that'll help."

"We should call in the Violent Felony Squad," Kylie said.

The computer cops at Real Time feed us valuable data, but they never leave their desks. The Violent Felony Squad is an elite team that will visit Dodd's known hangouts, comb through his social media activity to track down possible accomplices, check his credit card usage, and try to find him by analyzing dozens of his other daily habits, patterns, and routines.

"I agree," I said. "Violent Felony will give us eyes, ears, and feet on the street."

"Are you sure that's as deep as you want to go?" McMaster said. "We've got Dodd's picture. If you release it to the media, you'll have eight million pairs of eyes looking for—"

Kylie cut him off. "Dodd doesn't know we know who he is. If we release his picture to the media or even just circulate it through the department, he's going to find out. And if he's as cunning as you say he is, once he knows we're onto him, he may drop off the face of the earth completely. Violent Felony is the best way to do an intense search and keep it contained."

"Your call," McMaster said. Clearly he didn't agree. But at least he was finally coming around to the understanding that he didn't get a vote.

Kylie and I had bent the rules by bringing him up here. It had paid off because as Erin's chief of security, he'd recognized the perp. But without that bird on his shoulder anymore, this was as far as he was going to go. I figured it would be easier on him if Kylie cut him loose. I gave her a head nod, and she caught it.

"Thanks for everything, Declan," she said. "I got the e-mail you sent. Zach and I are going to shoot up to the Bronx and check out Dodd's last known address."

"I don't suppose I could come along for the ride," McMaster said. "I'd be willing to take a vow of silence."

"Sure thing," she said. "But since we'll be out there trying to pick up information that will be used in court, I really should give the DA's office a call and see if they still have that pesky rule about not letting civilians tag along on an active investigation."

He laughed. "I'll grab a cab back to the Hammerstein. Keep me in the loop."

"Yes, sir," she said. "As much as I can."

The three of us knew that wouldn't be much, but it was better left unsaid.

CHAPTER 14

THE PELHAM BAY section of the Bronx is a safe, desirable, historically Italian-American neighborhood whose streets are lined with mature trees, moderately priced family cars, and post–World War II architecture.

"Welcome to 1955," Kylie said as she pulled the car onto Zulette Avenue, where many of the homes were red brick with metal awnings and wrought-iron railings. She parked in front of a house that fit the mold, right down to the American flag in the window.

The lights were on in several rooms upstairs, but the downstairs, with its separate entrance to a basement apartment, was dark.

"The landlady is awake, the perp is in the wind," Kylie said as we walked up a flight of brick stairs and rang the doorbell.

"Who is it?" a woman's voice demanded from inside.

"Police," Kylie said as we both held up our shields to the peephole. "We'd like to speak to Lucille Speranza."

"About what?"

"Your tenant."

Most people can't hide the way they feel about cops, and they usually give themselves away immediately. I can break them down into three basic groups: those who are spooked by anyone in law enforcement; those who basically respect us and appreciate what we do; and those who distrust, don't like, or downright hate us on sight.

As soon as Mrs. Speranza opened the door, I could tell she fell squarely into that last group. She was a seventy-seven-year-old widow who stood five-foot-nothing high and weighed in at about two hundred pounds. She had a hawk nose, a mop of Cheetos-colored curly hair that clashed with her red-flowered dress, and a chip on each shoulder.

Instead of a concerned *Is everything okay?*, she hit us with "What's your problem?"

"Do you have a tenant by the name of Bobby Dodd?" Kylie said.

"What kind of stupid question is that?" Speranza said. "You know I do, otherwise why else would you show up here in the middle of the night? What did he do?"

"We'd just like to ask him a few questions."

"I'm not surprised the cops are after him. I never trusted him."

"Is there a reason?"

"He's got no wife, no kids, no girlfriend. I never see him with people. How many more reasons do you need?"

"He rents the apartment downstairs, correct?" I asked.

"Of course he rents the downstairs. You think he lives up here with me?"

"The apartment is dark."

"Then I guess he's not home, and I have no idea where he is. Is that all?"

"No, ma'am. When was the last time you saw him?"

"A few days ago."

"Could you be more specific?"

"Tuesday. No, Wednesday. He was carrying some laundry bags."

"Does he have a car?"

"I don't know. If he does, he doesn't park it in front of the house."

"Do you have any idea where he might have gone?" I asked.

"I already told you. I don't know, and I don't want to know."

"Do you mind if we search his apartment?" Kylie asked.

Speranza thought about it. "And if I say no?"

"We'll be back at three a.m. with a search warrant."

"Wait here. I'll get a key." She closed the door hard.

"The middle of the night?" Kylie said. "It's a quarter to eleven, her lights were on, and she's still dressed."

"The case is only a few hours old," I said, "but clearly she's out of the running for Miss Congeniality."

Speranza returned wearing a lime-green cardigan over her red dress and carrying an oversize purse. We followed her down to the entrance of the basement apartment. She dug into the purse for a key, found it, and unlocked the door.

"Stand back," Kylie said as we entered. I turned on a light.

"I told you he's not there," Speranza said. "The furniture is mine, so don't mess the place up with fingerprint dust and all that crap." She followed us in, and there was no point in trying to keep her out.

The room was a good size, about twenty by twenty-five feet. There was a tiny kitchenette with a breakfast bar, a sofa covered in a pink and green floral fabric, a plush burgundy reclining chair, a walnut dresser from the forties, a chrome and glass coffee table from the sixties, and a Sony TV from a bygone predigital era.

"The couch opens up to a bed," Speranza said. "The toilet is over there." Kylie and I started to open drawers and doors. "What'd he do?" Speranza asked. "Rob a bank?"

"Does he strike you as a bank robber?" Kylie asked.

Speranza muttered something in Italian. I understood enough of it to know that she and Kylie were never going to be besties.

It took us less than ten minutes to search and photograph the place. There was no sign of Dodd, no hint of where he'd gone or what he'd been up to while he was there.

"You done?" Speranza said.

"For now," I said. "We're going to send a forensics team to go over it more thoroughly, but for the moment, it's off-limits."

"No big deal. I don't use it. It's strictly a rental."

"*Off-limits* means you can't rent it," Kylie said.

"Till when?"

"I can't say. It's part of an active police investigation."

"Fine, but it's June. You better be finished investigating by September first."

"What happens then?"

"Dodd's paid up till the end of August. What happens on September first is I either get a new tenant or I start charging the police department rent."

CHAPTER 15

JAMIE GIBBS IS full of shit," Kylie said.

We had just crossed the RFK Bridge from the Bronx into Manhattan and were headed back to the precinct. It didn't matter that it was after midnight; the house would be jumping with detectives digging through notes from the hundreds of interviews they'd done, hoping to find the one nugget that could be a career-changing home run. Breathing down their necks would be a gaggle of anxious bosses demanding immediate answers because they needed immediate answers for their own anxious bosses.

It was the last place on earth I wanted to be.

"Everybody we met tonight is full of shit," I said. "Why single out poor Jamie?"

"When I said we wanted to talk to his mother, he got a little weepy, like maybe whoever took Erin took Mama Bear too. But that's bullshit. Veronica Gibbs is a rock star in her own right. If someone abducted her, one of her many minions would know in a heartbeat and sound the alarm, and TV networks would interrupt their regularly scheduled programming. Jamie knows that better than anyone. So why even suggest that she might have been kidnapped?"

"It was a defense mechanism. He's a mama's boy. Mommy didn't show up at his wedding, and she didn't come running to his side when the band started playing 'There Goes the Bride.' Instead of accepting the fact that the old Mrs. Gibbs doesn't give two shits about the new Mrs. Gibbs, Jamie would rather convince himself that his mother was the victim of foul play."

"Or he was trying to convince *us* that she's a victim so we won't look at her as a suspect."

"Is she a suspect?" I said.

"She has a motive."

"And we have an eyewitness who ID'd Bobby Dodd with Erin," I said.

"What if Bobby and Mom are in this together?"

It didn't make a lot of sense, but when you're trying to solve a crime, logic doesn't always apply. I've seen more than a few preposterous theories turn out to be right. "Okay," I said. "Let's say Mom and Bobby are in cahoots. Make a case for it."

Kylie smiled. Unraveling a mystery was as much a passion as it was her job. "All right," she said. "We know that Bobby is obsessed with Erin. They're soul mates, destined to be together forever. He loves her. He's not going to kill her. So he needs a place to hide her long term. Do you think he's going to chain her to a pipe in some rat-infested basement?"

"I've tried it," I said. "The girls are never impressed, especially the ones, like Erin, who are accustomed to much finer accommodations. Bobby is definitely going to have to step up and spring for a five-star hidey-hole."

The joke fell flat. She kept going, hell-bent on making her point.

"Zach, you read McMaster's file on Dodd. He hasn't had a real job in years. He's got no credit history to speak of. I don't know what kind of cash flow he has, but judging by that rented room he was living in, it can't be much.

"Kidnapping someone like Erin is expensive. Planning it, executing it, keeping her well fed, well taken care of, and under wraps for an undetermined amount of time—you can't run that kind of operation on a shoestring. It takes a lot of money to become invisible. And Dodd is a loner, so it's not like he has a best friend bankrolling his obsession."

"So you're suggesting that he found an *unlikely* friend who saw Bobby as a way to get rid of Erin and who has the resources and motive to do it?"

"Exactly," Kylie said. "Veronica Gibbs."

"Interesting theory. Can I shoot one little dart at it?"

"You can try."

"A lot of people online are pointing fingers at Veronica. Jamie brushed that off, saying that if his mother had orchestrated it, Erin would have been taken long before the wedding. It makes sense."

"Don't you see the brilliance in that?" she said. "That's like Jamie saying, 'My mom couldn't possibly have stolen your Mercedes. She only steals American cars.' We can't ignore Veronica just because the kidnapping didn't go down the way Jamie wants us to think she would do it."

"We're not ignoring her. We may not have a shred of evidence connecting her to the kidnapper, but she's at the top of the list of people who would like to see Erin disappear. We're definitely talking to her."

"No time like the present."

"Fine with me," I said. "I'll call McMaster and find out where she lives."

"Don't bother," Kylie said, pulling up to a hydrant in front of a building at Ninety-Second and Park. "We're there."

CHAPTER 16

"**THAT WAS FAST,**" I said, opening the car door. "It's like you read my mind."

"I figured you really didn't want to go back to the barn and watch a bunch of other cops try to crack this case before we do," Kylie said. "Plus we owe it to Jamie to find out if his mother's been kidnapped."

The doorman assured us that Mrs. Gibbs was alive and well. "She's expecting you," he said.

"She's *expecting* us?" Kylie said.

"Well, yeah. Her assistant rang down and told me the cops would be showing up. I mean, you're here about the whole Erin Easton thing, right?"

"We're in a hurry," Kylie said, not answering the question.

"Right. Mrs. Gibbs is in penthouse A and B. You want to go to A, which is the office. B is her private residence. It's off-limits. Like at the White House," he added in case we didn't get the point. "I'll ring up and let them know you're on the way."

The elevator was manned. The operator nodded politely but said nothing as we rode up. It was a lonely job, especially on the graveyard shift, and I guessed that the absence of small talk was Veronica's idea, not his.

The doors opened up into a vestibule where a highly polished antique table sat on a thick Persian rug. An oversize vase was filled with enough fresh flowers to set me back a week's pay. There were two industrial-strength metal doors, one on either side of the room, and our elevator man pointed at the one marked A.

"Ring the bell and look up at the camera," he said.

We did. We heard an electronic click, and the door unlatched. The operator gestured for us to go through.

"Wait in there," he said.

We stepped in and the door clicked shut. I heard the elevator head back down.

It was well after midnight, but the lights were on, soft music was playing, and the smell of fresh-brewed coffee was in the air. About fifteen feet from the door, a meeting was in progress behind a glass wall. Two men and two women were seated at a table facing a cork wall where six photos, each one of a beautiful woman, were hanging. There was an animated discussion going on, accompanied by head-nodding and some laughter, and finally one of the men pulled a photo from the wall and turned it facedown on the table.

"Another grueling late night at the model agency," Kylie said.

"Sorry to keep you waiting," a voice said. A dark-haired woman in her early thirties walked toward us. "I'm Adriana Stevens, one of Ms. Gibbs's assistants."

We introduced ourselves and gave her our cards.

"We knew somebody from the police would be coming, but we didn't know when," Stevens said.

"I realize it's late," I said, "but clearly we didn't wake anybody up."

"Oh, it's not late. It's Monday morning in Europe, and Veronica is on a videoconference call." She glanced down at her iPad. "How much time do you think you'll need with her?"

"We don't know," Kylie said. "You understand this is a police investigation into the disappearance of her daughter-in-law."

Stevens put a finger to her lips. "Oh God, please don't say that."

"Don't say what?"

"Daughter-in-law," Stevens whispered. "Veronica would go ballistic if she ever heard you refer to that woman as family."

"When can we talk to Mrs. Gibbs?" I said.

"Her calendar is jammed until morning."

"Excuse me? Doesn't she sleep?"

"Not like normal people. She has this remarkable body clock. She naps for a few hours, and she's fine. That's why she has three assistants. We work in shifts." She glanced at her iPad again. "Veronica grabbed about three hours of sleep this afternoon from four to seven, which means she'll be good to go till noon. I can squeeze you in before her breakfast meeting at seven a.m."

"Ms. Stevens," Kylie said, "a woman's life is in danger. We're not here to be squeezed in. Squeeze somebody else out. Now."

"Okay, don't shoot the messenger. I'll tell her. Give me a minute."

As soon as she walked off, Kylie turned to me. "Did you catch that? She *napped* through her son's wedding."

I nodded. That Veronica Gibbs was a piss-poor

mother didn't surprise me. What I was still trying to get past was how she could run a global enterprise on only a few hours of sleep a day.

We watched the meeting on the other side of the glass wall while we waited. One by one, three more pictures were removed from the photo array. There were only two models left, one black, one white.

We never got to see the winner. Veronica Gibbs came marching down the corridor behind her assistant. She was in her midsixties, with perfect hair, the tall, lean, angular body of a model, and the purposeful, angry stride of a pissed-off corporate CEO.

"I have no idea where she is," Veronica called out as she approached, "and I don't give a flying fuck."

She stopped in front of us and held up the cards we'd just given her assistant. "If you have any more questions, Detective Jordan, Detective MacDonald, you can call my attorney. Adriana will give you the number."

The protocol at NYPD Red is that rich-and-famous assholes get treated differently from regular assholes. Essentially that meant the interview was over before it started.

"Just one quick question," Kylie said. "Have you ever seen this man?" She held up her phone with the picture that Venetia Jones had taken of Dodd on the screen.

"Never," Gibbs said. "Is he the one who kidnapped her? You can tell him for me that I'm not going to pay him a nickel."

"Did he contact you?" I asked.

"This guy? No! How would he even get my number? My son, Jamie, called me. He wants me to help him buy back the slut I told him not to get involved with in the first place. Not happening."

She turned and started to walk away.

"Mrs. Gibbs," Kylie called after her.

Gibbs stopped, turned back, and walked toward us. Slowly. A white tigress, her body elegant, her eyes filled with hatred. "I didn't take her," she said. "I didn't pay anyone to take her. I don't know the man who took her, and I have no idea where she is. The only thing I do know is that I hope to God she never comes back. Goodbye."

She turned and walked away again. This time we didn't try to stop her.

CHAPTER 17

WELCOME TO YOUR home away from home," Dodd said as he opened the bedroom door. "It's small, but it's cozy."

He actually smiled. It was pathetic how proud he was.

It was the ugliest room Erin had ever seen. Every inch of the walls and the ceiling were covered with grayish-brown panels. Soundproofing.

The bed was small with no headboard or footboard, but there were clean sheets and, hopefully, no bedbugs. There was no other furniture—just some boxes filled with clothes.

"I can't afford Saks Fifth Avenue," he said, "but I hope you like what I picked out for you."

She hated it. All of it. No-name jeans, vomit-green shorts, underwear that came in packs of three, a bunch of hideous T-shirts, two sweat suits, and a pair of sneakers that were one size too big.

"Bathroom's over here," he said.

There was no door. Just a sink, a shower, a toilet, and a shopping bag from the Dollar Store filled with shampoo, toothpaste, tampons, and other cheap crap.

The lighting was so harsh that she looked like a corpse in the mirror.

"This is where you live," Dodd said. "If I'm in the house, you can sit in the living room or the kitchen with me, but when I'm out, you're in here, and you've got a full-time babysitter. I call her Octomom."

He looked up, and Erin followed his gaze to the dome camera on the ceiling.

"That one is obvious," he said. "The others are not. She's got eight pairs of eyes throughout the house, and she broadcasts everything she sees to my phone or my iPad, so don't think about doing anything stupid. Okay?"

"I won't," she said.

That was the first thing Ari had taught her: *Be compliant.*

Erin was twenty-two years old when *People* magazine put her on the cover and proclaimed her the most desirable woman in the world. A week later, two men grabbed her in the parking lot of a shopping mall in LA and tried to drag her into their van.

They would have succeeded, too, if not for an off-duty cop, a woman who heard Erin's screams and was able to stop the abduction before it happened.

The next day her father hired a bodyguard. Erin had had security people for years, but most of them had been glorified bouncers, musclemen who could wipe the floor with anyone who harassed her, but this one was different. Ari Loeb was a multilingual, combat-trained commando who had served in the Mista'arvim, the elite counterterrorism unit of the Israel Defense Forces.

Early on, Ari had warned her that she was a prime target for another would-be kidnapper.

"I'm not worried," she said. "You'll stop them."

"Yes, but I can't stop a bullet. Let me teach you what to do and what not to do if you're ever held hostage and I'm not there. How do you feel about going back to the mall where they tried to grab you?"

"Fine, if I'm with you."

As soon as they got in the car Erin started asking questions. "Did you ever kill anyone?"

"No talking," he said.

She sulked. "It's a fifteen-minute drive. What am I supposed to do?"

"Pay attention."

"To what?" she said.

"Everything."

He didn't take her to the mall. Five minutes into the drive he pulled over and said, "Being aware of your surroundings can save your life. And if you are released or manage to escape, you want to help law enforcement with as many details as you can remember."

He then asked her five questions about things they'd seen, heard, even smelled on their brief trip. She didn't get a single one right.

"Your brain was already at the mall," he said. "You have to learn to live in the present."

He was so incredibly sexy—jet-black hair, steel-gray eyes, and full lips, and the jacket he wore did little to hide the chiseled body underneath. Erin leaned in to kiss him.

"No," he said, grabbing her wrist. "Not now. Not ever."

"Why? Are you married?"

"No. I am only here to protect you from the insanity of others and your own stupidity. If you don't want to learn, I will look for a job teaching someone who does."

"I'm sorry," Erin said. "Let's start over."

They did, and the next thing Ari told her was never to let her enemy know how well trained she was. He taught her how to stay mentally and physically active. How to capitalize on even the smallest mistake an abductor might make. But most important, he taught her how to deal with a captor: Keep your dignity. It's harder to kill or harm someone who can remain human in his eyes. Establish rapport. Don't antagonize and don't try to convince him that his delusions are unfounded. Above all, comply. You may have to do things you don't want to—including sex. Just do it, because sometimes that's the only way to stay alive.

"Give in," Ari told her over and over and over again during the four years they were together. "But never give up."

CHAPTER 18

IT WAS TWO in the morning when Kylie and I sat down to debrief the bosses. Not just Captain Cates, but all the way up the food chain. Even the mayor showed up for this one.

They asked a lot of questions, some of which we couldn't answer because they were the same questions Kylie and I were still asking ourselves.

"You want to know the difference between the two of us and most of them?" Kylie told me when the session was over. "We're trying to figure out how to solve this, and they're trying to figure out what to do if we don't solve it."

We went back to our desks to crank out paperwork—DD-5s. On a normal case we'd document everything we'd learned to date, and it would go into a file that could be accessed across the department. But this case was a hot potato, and the powers that be were afraid of press leaks, so our reports were restricted to a very short list of people.

It was too late to go home, so at three thirty both of us crashed at the station. I slept till six thirty, showered, and wondered how the hell Veronica Gibbs could exist on so little sleep every day of her life. Kylie was still asleep, so I decided to walk around the corner to Gerri's Diner and bring us back some breakfast.

And that's when my day took a turn for the better.

Cheryl Robinson, the love of my life, was sitting in a booth talking with Gerri Gomperts, the diner owner who will happily unscramble your personal life while she scrambles your eggs.

As soon as I walked through the door, both women stood up. Cheryl ran over and gave me a much-needed hug. Gerri grabbed a coffeepot, poured me a cup, and told me I looked like crap.

I ordered two breakfast burritos and coffee to go, then sat down with Cheryl.

"What's going on with Erin Easton?" she said.

I put an imaginary key to my lips and turned the lock. "Sorry, babe. They're keeping a tight lid on it. Let's talk about something else."

She shrugged. "What did Kylie say about my cousin?"

I knew exactly what she was asking, but I gave her a puzzled look to buy myself some time to come up with an answer.

"My cousin Shane," she said. "You were supposed to ask her about him."

My first impulse was to say, *We were a little busy with this kidnapping thing.* But that was a half-assed excuse, and Cheryl would see right through it. I'd spent the entire night with Kylie. We'd had plenty of downtime in the car. I could easily have told her about the tall, good-looking, ginger-haired, soon-to-be-celebrity chef who'd be perfect for her.

Then it hit me. "You're jumping the gun," I said. "I know *you* think I was supposed to tell Kylie about him, but that's not how guys work. I can't pimp Shane without clearing it with him first. We're going to the restaurant next month to meet your aunt Janet, and I'll ask him then. If he opts in, I'll take the next step."

"We don't have to wait a month," she said. "I was just telling Gerri that after you left, Shane came back to the table, and I told him all about Kylie. He doesn't like fix-ups, but I did such a great presell that he was definitely intrigued."

"Did you tell him she was my partner?"

"And your ex-girlfriend. Full disclosure. At first he thought that might be awkward, but I told him it was your idea to introduce them."

Cheryl's phone chirped. She checked her incoming text and stood up. "Duty calls," she said. "I've got to run. I know you're crazy-busy. So am I. I'll call you later. Let me know what Kylie thinks about Shane."

She leaned over, gave me a quick kiss, and left me sitting there. I drained the coffee in my cup, and Gerri appeared instantly and topped it off.

"Your breakfast is almost ready," she said, "but while we're waiting, I have a question. How much wine did you drink last night to come up with the bright idea of fixing your ex-girlfriend up with your current girlfriend's blood relative?"

"I swear to God, it was a total misunderstanding. I said something, Cheryl heard something else, and now…"

I couldn't finish the sentence, so Gerri finished it for me. "And now you're afraid that if you tell Cheryl that the last thing you want to do is fix Kylie up with a good-looking, successful man who can cook, you will wind up, as the French say, in the *château de bowwow*."

I nodded. "That pretty much sums it up."

Gerri put the coffeepot back on a burner and sat down across from me. I was about to get breakfast with a side order of therapy—whether I wanted it or not.

CHAPTER 19

GARY BANTA WAS a pro. He weaved the ambulance, siren wailing, through the morning traffic on Fifth Avenue with Indy Speedway proficiency. Most vehicles, willingly or grudgingly, pulled over quickly and gave him a wide berth. In a big city like New York, people know that response time to a 911 call can mean the difference between life and death. They also know there's a fat fine if they fail to yield.

The traffic signals are timed so that if a driver maintains the speed limit, the lights in front of him will turn green before he gets to them. But an ambulance clipping along at breakneck speed gets ahead of the sequence, so Gary had to *whoop-whoop* at every corner to run the red lights and avoid barreling into the crosstown traffic.

At Seventy-Fourth and Fifth, he pulled up to the canopy of a stately nineteen-story prewar building.

"Such gross injustice," his partner, Julio, said. "The most beautiful apartment houses in New York, and they're always filled with rich old white ladies."

Gary shook his head. He'd heard Julio on the subject before. He left the lights flashing as they got out.

A uniformed doorman came rushing to the curb. "What's going on?" he said.

Gary checked his iPad. "We got a call for an elderly woman, difficulty breathing. Apartment 8C. The name is Ogden."

"Bunny. Bunny Ogden," the doorman said. "I have her son's cell number. I can call him right now."

"Hang tight, bro," Gary said to the doorman as Julio opened the ambulance's back doors and dropped a gurney to the pavement. "Wait till we get back down. Let's see what's going on before you hit the panic button."

They grabbed their gear, an oxygen tank, and the gurney and headed for the building. The doorman ran ahead, opened the door, and rang for the elevator.

They rode up to the eighth floor in silence and wheeled the gurney down the hall to 8C. Julio rang the doorbell.

It took about twenty seconds before a female voice on the other side responded. "Who is it?"

"Ambulance for Mrs. Ogden. Please let us in."

A lock clicked, and a uniformed nurse opened the door. She looked at the two EMTs, the stretcher on wheels, and the oxygen and tried to take it all in. "I don't understand," she said.

"We got a call that Mrs. Ogden was in respiratory distress," Gary said.

"She's fine. She's watching TV. Who called? Was it her son?"

"Ma'am, please," Gary said. "If you have questions, call our dispatcher, but legally we can't leave the apartment until we check on the patient. Please let us in."

The nurse stepped aside, and the two men entered.

"What's your name, ma'am?" Gary asked.

"Lydia Humphries." She reached into her pocket and took out a cell phone. "I'm calling Mr. Ogden," she said. "Something's not right."

"One more question before you call," Gary said as Julio shut the apartment door behind them. "How long have you been working for Mrs. Ogden?"

"I came here in September, so…nine months."

Gary reached into his equipment bag and pulled out a gun. He held it up to her head and removed the phone from her hand.

"After nine months, I'm sure you know where the old lady keeps the money and the jewelry, Lydia, and if you want to get out of here alive, you'll tell us."

CHAPTER 20

WHEN I GOT back to the station Kylie was still asleep. I walked over to the bed and stared down at her, and my thoughts invariably drifted back to a time a thousand years ago when hers was the face I woke up to every morning.

We were both young, just starting out at the academy, working our tails off night and day to impress our instructors—and each other—with how smart we were. Turns out she was smarter. She graduated at the top of our class, five notches ahead of me. I congratulated her with a gift, a T-shirt with a giant 1 on the front.

The next day she returned the gesture by giving me a T-shirt that said A RESPECTABLE 6.

Our love affair only lasted twenty-eight days, but they were the most unforgettable four weeks of my life. The crushing blow came on the twenty-ninth day, when she told me that her longtime boyfriend, Spence Harrington, had come out of rehab, and she'd decided to give him one last chance.

A year later they were married. Eleven years after that, Spence returned to his coke addiction with a vengeance and wound up in the ICU after a near-fatal overdose. This past January, he completely dropped out of sight. They're still married, but only on paper.

I took one of the breakfast burritos and held it under her nose. It got an immediate response. "Mmmph," she said. "That smells like heaven."

"It's all yours when you wake up, Sleeping Beauty."

She opened her eyes. "That's Detective Sleeping Beauty to you. Did you find Erin yet?"

"No."

She frowned. "Rats."

"Sorry to disappoint you, but how about a little gratitude for the burrito?"

She swung her legs off the bed and took a healthy bite out of the sandwich. "Thanks," she said. "Thanks a lot."

I handed her a cup of coffee. "How you doing there, K-Mac?"

"Is that a rhetorical question?"

"No. You haven't been your regular, annoying pain-in-the-ass self lately, and I'm your partner. I'm genuinely concerned."

"Well, partner, my professional life is aces. I love my job, I love the unit, and I love the people I work with. It's my personal life that kind of sucks. In the five months since Spence disappeared, I've only had one brief relationship—CJ."

"The poker player," I said. "He seems nice enough."

"*Seemed* nice enough. It's all past tense. He moved back to Hawaii. Which leaves me stumbling around my big, beautiful two-bedroom apartment with no husband, no boyfriend, and no desire to download one of those apps where you have a choice of swiping left or swiping right."

"So you're lonely," I said.

She laughed. "Is that a euphemism or are you missing the point? I'm not lonely. I'm horny."

"Aha. I wish I could help you."

"You help me more than you know," she said. "And I'm not just talking about this incredible sausage, egg, and cheese burrito. You were there for me every step of the way when Spence was spiraling out of control. I know there were times when you had to choose between spending the night with Cheryl or holding my hand when I went careening around Harlem, the Bronx, and Atlantic City in search of my drug-addled husband. You're not just my partner, Zach. You're my rock. You're my best friend."

She stood up, wrapped her arms around me, and kissed me on the cheek.

"I'm going to shower and get dressed," she said. "I'll be ready in fifteen minutes."

She left me standing there, my pulse racing, my brain flooded with emotions I had no desire to deal with.

Over the past year I've fallen deeply in love with Cheryl. I can look down the road and see a long, happy future with her. But I've never fallen out of love with Kylie. I keep it under control most of the time, but when I look down the road in the opposite direction, I see a brief, blissful past that I can't let go.

There are times, like this very moment, when I wish that Kylie and I could somehow be friends with benefits.

But I know I have to settle for friends with baggage.

CHAPTER 21

KYLIE AND I couldn't possibly tackle the Easton case on our own, so the borough chief had drafted a small battalion of detectives to back us up. Within hours of the abduction, they descended on the third floor of the precinct and commandeered every inch of workspace that is normally assigned to Community Affairs.

They saved us a lot of legwork, phone work, and grunt work, but they also generated a ton of paperwork. In a criminal investigation, anything and everything connected to the case has to be preserved, cataloged, and available to the court. There was a basket on my desk where they deposited all those reports.

By the time I ate my breakfast and settled in, the basket was buried under a mountain of DD-5s with ripped-out notepad pages stapled to them; computer printouts of background checks of the hundreds of wedding guests, venue employees, and other witnesses; CDs of surveillance videos; and the usual slew of phone messages.

"I hope you brought a broom," Kylie said. "Your desk looks like a subway track after New Year's Eve."

We recruited Danny Corcoran to help us organize it all while we focused on Bobby Dodd.

He didn't own a car, which meant whatever vehicle he'd used to transport Erin after he ditched the box truck could have been stolen. We assigned a team to wade through the stolen-vehicle database, check out any that had been recovered, and see if there were any prints or DNA left behind that could connect it to Erin or Dodd.

Our crime scene team found the wireless cameras Dodd had planted that allowed him to know exactly what was going on during the wedding. It meant that McMaster had been wrong—Dodd hadn't tracked Erin through her tweets.

TARU confirmed that the cameras had been taping everything and that Dodd could have watched it all remotely from around the corner or from halfway around the world.

McMaster had told us that Dodd was more street smart than book smart, but he had stalked Erin Easton with all the cunning and proficiency of a criminal mastermind who knew how to stay ahead of his prey, her security team, and, now, the cops.

The case was still shrouded in secrecy, but by midmorning we knew we had to put Dodd's name into the national criminal database. We also knew we couldn't do it without clearing it with our boss.

We went to her office.

"Captain, we want to put Bobby Dodd's name into the NCIC database," I said. "We won't connect him to the Easton kidnapping. We just want to register him as a criminal wanted for a major felony who should be apprehended on sight."

We watched her consider the suggestion.

"Boss," Kylie said, "don't think about the upside.

We don't expect anything to come of it. Think about the downside. If we don't do it and he gets stopped for a traffic violation in Jersey and let go, all our careers are going to take a sharp nosedive."

She nodded. "Cover Your Ass 101," she said. "Do it."

Her phone rang, and she looked at the caller ID. "Chief of Ds. Don't go away," she told us. "I'm sure he's got questions about the kidnapping." She picked up. "This is Captain Cates. Good morning, Chief." A long pause, then she said, "Yes, sir, they're right here in my office now." She picked up a pen and started writing. Thirty seconds later, she said, "Yes, sir, they're on their way." She hung up. "The chief wants the two of you uptown at a home invasion," she said.

"You're kidding," Kylie said. "Why didn't you tell him that we're neck-deep in this kidnapping, and we're running on fumes as it is?"

"Because I don't question every order that comes down from my commanding officer, MacDonald. You should try it some time."

"Yes, ma'am."

"Do you have a ransom demand?" Cates asked.

"Not yet."

"Then your team can muddle along without you for a few hours."

"Did the chief happen to say why he picked us?"

"He didn't pick you. The order came down from a higher authority."

"The PC?"

"Elected official," Cates said.

"Captain," Kylie said, "I realize it's good politics for the squad that Mayor Sykes has adopted me and Zach as her pet cops, but someone should tell her we can't handle every case that comes down the pike. This should be assigned to a precinct detective. Why does a home invasion need Red?"

"MacDonald, do you really think that nobody along the food chain thought to ask that?" Cates said. "This isn't the mayor's idea. She's just another pawn on the chessboard. The woman who was robbed is Bunny Ogden. Do you know who that is?"

"Never heard of her."

"Perhaps you've heard of her nephew, the governor of the state of New York. It doesn't get any redder than that."

CHAPTER 22

IF WE NEEDED to know just how important Bunny Ogden was, we didn't have to look any farther than the blue-and-yellow New York State Police car parked outside her Fifth Avenue apartment building.

"Really?" Kylie said. "The governor wouldn't send out troopers if Tiffany got robbed, but Aunt Bunny— I guess she rates."

"Jordan, MacDonald."

I looked up and saw the familiar face of Sean Kennedy, a sergeant with the Nineteenth.

"Hey, Sarge," I said. "What have you got?"

"I've got half a dozen cops interviewing tenants and canvassing the neighborhood, but so far nobody remembers seeing anything except for the ambulance."

"What ambulance?"

"Two perps wheeled up in what looked like a legitimate private bus, but we ran its name, and it was a phony," Kennedy said. "They told the doorman they got a 911 call for Mrs. Ogden, went upstairs, tied up the old lady and her nurse, came down fifteen minutes later, told the doorman she was okay, and took off. The nurse managed to get herself loose after an hour, called it in, and once the department found out the vic's connection to the governor, it turned into the crime of the century, which I'm guessing is why you're here instead of looking for Erin Easton."

"What about video surveillance?" Kylie asked.

"You gotta love rich people," Kennedy said. "They have a few cameras in the elevator, the garage, and some of the nooks and crannies where the staff might goof off, but nothing out there on the street where it might do us any good. I talked to a Mr. Paul Aronson, president of the co-op board, and he says they frown on security cameras. Apparently 'they're ugly, they make the building look unsafe, and our residents' comings and goings is none of anybody's business.'"

"Doorman?"

"His name is Ed Carter. Nervous as hell. Already called his union rep. He's afraid the building managers are going to can him. I told him the best way to get back in their good graces is to help with the investigation. I asked him to put together a list of visitors Mrs. Ogden has had in the past three months. I don't know if it'll help, but it's a place to start."

The lobby door opened, and a man wearing a gray uniform and a Stetson with a leather strap and a purple band around it strode out.

"Looks like you guys have a new best friend," Kennedy said. "You deal with him. I'll see you back at the house."

The sergeant walked off as the state cop approached us. "John Hollowell," he said. "You the team from Red?"

He had a pair of gold oak-leaf clusters on his shirt.

"Yes, Major," I said, and we introduced ourselves. "Are you part of the investigation?"

"Only if you ask me to be. Albany wanted me to

stop by, check on Mrs. Ogden, and reach out to local law enforcement." He handed me his card. "If there's anything the state can do for you, call me twenty-four/seven. Have a good day."

He gave us a crisp nod and walked toward his car.

"*Albany* sent him—a major," Kylie said.

"Maybe not all of Albany," I said. "Probably just the one guy who lives in the governor's mansion on Eagle Street. I think it's his subtle way of letting us know that we're on his radar. Let's go see if the doorman can help us find out who robbed Aunt Bunny."

Mr. Carter was ready for us with a list of names going back to January. "Mrs. Ogden doesn't get a lot of visitors," he said. "Family, friends, the physical therapist—that's about it."

"How about deliveries, service people, or anyone else who isn't in the inner circle?"

"All packages go to the concierge, who takes them upstairs personally. If the cable guy comes, the super goes up there with him. He doesn't do that for everyone, but Mrs. Ogden's son pays him extra. She doesn't get any strangers, except maybe for this one guy. He's black, in his forties, well dressed. His name is Maurice. That's all I know. Just Maurice. He comes once a week. He asks for Mrs. Ogden, but my best guess is he's really there for Lydia."

"Who's Lydia?"

"The nurse."

"Why do you think he's there for her?"

"I don't know. She's pretty good-looking. He usually stays an hour. I figure that gives him plenty of time to case the joint and still get in a little afternoon delight."

CHAPTER 23

THE NYPD ORG chart reads like alphabet soup, but those of us in the know can tell a lot about the priority of a case by which letters of the alphabet are assigned to work it.

The Ogden case was a low-level robbery that should have been handled by ECT. The Evidence Collection Team is made up of uniformed cops who, as the name implies, gather evidence and go. No analytical skills are required. But when we got to the apartment, we saw that CSU had been dispatched, and Chuck Dryden, our crime scene unit's most meticulous forensic investigator, was busy at work. He'd changed his shirt and tie since we'd last seen him in the Fairway parking lot, but that didn't necessarily mean he'd gotten a decent night's sleep.

"Good morning, Detectives," Dryden said. "I see that you too have been recruited by the Department of Overkill."

"Once again, politics triumphs over good judgment," Kylie said. "What have you found so far?"

"Cat hair. Mrs. Ogden owns an orange tabby, so we may be looking at an inside job."

Kylie laughed, which I'm sure made Chuck's day.

A woman in pink scrubs entered the living room. "Officers," she said. "I'm Lydia Humphries, Mrs. Ogden's nurse. She's expecting you."

"Why don't you tell us what happened first," I said.

"It was all so fast," she said. "Two men dressed like EMTs came to the door—one white, one brown, probably Latino. They said they got a call that Mrs. Ogden was in distress. I didn't buy it. I was going to call her son, but they pulled a gun. Then they tied us up—both of us. I told them she was ninety-two years old, but they didn't care."

"Can she talk to us?" I said.

Lydia grinned. "Can she talk? Mrs. O. has heart problems, which is why I take care of her. But she can talk a blue streak. The hard part is getting her to stop."

Lydia walked us into a large bedroom that looked like it belonged to Marie Antoinette. A ponderous ivory and gold armoire with two matching dressers lined one wall, cherubs frolicked in the clouds on another, and an ornately carved four-poster canopy bed dominated the center of the room.

Mrs. Ogden was sitting on a tufted love seat facing two windows that had an unobstructed view of Central Park. She stood up when we entered the room and extended a hand. I'd expected a little old lady, but Ogden was big, close to six feet. "I'm Bunny," she said. "You gonna catch these fuckers?" Her language wasn't exactly what Miss Manners would call ladylike.

"Yes, ma'am," Kylie said. "We'll need a little help from you, but we'll catch them."

"Lydia saw their faces, but by the time they got to me, they had put on surgical masks, so all I can tell you is the guy in charge was white, the other was Spanish.

Both had brown eyes. The white guy puts a gun to Lydia's head and tells me I have ten seconds to show him where I keep the money and the jewelry. Hell, I don't need ten seconds. The safe is in the closet, I say, and I give him the combination."

"What did they take?" I asked.

"Fifty thousand in cash. I could have lived with that, but then they saw my jewelry, and they got greedy. I said, 'You take the money, and you'll probably get away with it, but you touch my family heirlooms, and I will hunt you down.' The white bastard laughed and says, 'I'm doing you a favor, lady. You'll be dead soon enough. I'm going to help your heirlooms find a new family.'"

"How much was the jewelry worth?"

"It's insured for one point eight million dollars. But I don't want the money. I want my mother's necklace back, and my grandmother's ring, and the black pearls my husband gave me for our thirtieth wedding anniversary. That's why I called my nephew and told him I want the two of you."

"You asked for us?" I said.

"Damn straight I asked for you. I read the papers, Detective Jordan. You're the rock-star cops in the elite unit. These two sons of bitches are smart. It's not easy getting past the guards at the gate, but they came up with the perfect scam. I need cops that are smarter than they are, and that's you."

"Okay," Kylie said, "this was not a random hit. They targeted you, which means it may be someone you know. So let's start with a question: Who is Maurice?"

"Oh, shit. Who told you about Maurice? Eddie the doorman? Maurice is Lydia's brother. He's a minister. He comes here once a week, and we drink tea while

I bitch and moan about politics and sports and how this city is going into the crapper. And Maurice, who has the voice of an angel and the soul of a philosopher, talks me down off the ledge, and I'm good for another week. Finding him is one of the best things that ever happened to me, so please go back downstairs and tell the doorman to come up with a white suspect, because the black guy didn't have anything to do with it."

"Can we get an itemized list of all the jewelry that was taken?" I asked.

"With pictures," Ogden said. "I'll have my insurance agent messenger it to your office."

"Don't forget about my money," Lydia said.

"He took your money too?" I said.

"No, not really mine. My purse was on the table, but they didn't touch it. The family leaves me two thousand dollars a month for expenses that might come up where I have to pay cash. There was sixteen hundred and eighty-four dollars left in the envelope. They took that."

"Was that in the safe too?" Kylie asked.

"No. It was in a drawer in the dining room," Lydia said. "But it's like they knew. The white guy said, 'Where's the cash they leave for you to take care of the old lady?' I wasn't going to say, but Mrs. O., she told him where it was. Cursed up a storm while she's telling him. They laughed, tied us up, and put tape on our mouths."

My phone rang, and I stepped out of the bedroom to take the call.

"Detective Zach Jordan?" the voice on the other end said.

"Yes. Who's this?"

"It doesn't matter who this is. What matters is I have something you want. Erin Easton. And if you want to see her alive, you have half an hour to get your cell phone to her husband."

"Who is this?" I repeated. I had a pretty good idea, but I didn't want Dodd to know that we'd ID'd him.

"The time is now eleven forty-two, Detective. You have thirty minutes."

The line went dead.

CHAPTER 24

I WENT BACK into the bedroom, stepped behind Kylie, and poked her three times—code for *Let's get out of here.* "You've both been very helpful," I said, giving Mrs. Ogden and her nurse my card. "Call us if you think of anything else."

"You've been through a lot," Kylie said, handing over her card as well. "Are you sure you don't need any medical attention?"

"Positive," Ogden said. "Besides, I think Lydia, the doorman, and I have seen all the EMTs we can handle for one day."

We laughed at her joke, politely declined her offer to stay for tea, and promised her we'd be in touch. As soon as we were in the hallway Kylie pounced. "What's going on?"

"Bobby Dodd just called me."

"He called *you?* At the office?"

"No! On my personal cell phone."

"Well, somebody's popular. First the governor asks for you, now Bobby. What did he want?"

"He's calling back in thirty minutes, at which point he wants my phone in Jamie Gibbs's hand, or else."

We got in the elevator, and I called Benny Diaz at TARU, explained what happened, and told him to trace the last call that came in to my cell. Then I called Rich Koprowski, one of the cops assigned to sit on Jamie Gibbs.

"Rich, it's Zach. Where's Gibbs right now?"

"His apartment, on Riverside, just south of Ninety-Fifth. He's in apartment 10E. I'm outside in the command post."

"Get up there and prep him one more time. He's got a ransom call coming in…" I looked at my watch. "In twenty-five minutes."

"We're ready for him," Koprowski said. "We've got every one of his phones covered."

"Too bad you didn't have mine covered. That's the one the kidnapper called."

"Damn," Koprowski said. "He had a key to the back door of the dressing room, he set up surveillance cameras—this guy is really good."

"You sound like a fanboy. Maybe you can get his autograph when we collar him. Kylie and I are on the way."

We got to the lobby and ran to our car.

"Ninety-Fifth and Riverside," I said.

"You've got to hand it to Dodd," Kylie said. "He knows we're monitoring Jamie's phone, and it's all over the media that we're the lead detectives on the case, so he bribes someone at the phone company, and bingo—he's got your number."

"Hell," I said, "all he has to do is find some millennial at Verizon who needs beer money for the weekend, and he can pull up cell phone numbers for the entire Joint Chiefs of Staff."

My phone rang. It was Diaz calling back. I put it on speaker. "Benny, what have you got?"

"I traced the call," Diaz said. "It came from a computer in Guatemala."

"Thanks. I'll call you later." I jammed my finger into the red disconnect button.

It took a few seconds, then it hit me. "I don't understand," I said to Kylie.

"Dodd's not really in Guatemala, Zach. He's routing the calls."

"Thanks, partner, but I kind of knew that. What I don't get is why he bothered to track down my phone number and call me. I thought it was because my phone wasn't being monitored, but if he can cover his tracks that easily, why didn't he just call Gibbs directly?"

"How many hours of sleep did you get last night?" Kylie asked.

"Less than three. Closer to two if I stop kidding myself."

"We're supposed to be looking for Dodd. Instead, he's got us racing through Central Park delivering your personal phone to the victim's husband. Why do you *think* he's doing that?"

I didn't have to think hard. I knew the answer. "He's fucking with our sleep-deprived brains."

"Yeah," she said, running a red light on Central Park West. "And he's doing a damn good job of it."

CHAPTER 25

WE GOT TO the apartment on Riverside Drive with six minutes to spare.

Koprowski opened the door. "We better talk before you come in," he said, stepping out into the hallway. "Zach, give me your cell phone first."

I gave it to him, and he passed it to the TARU tech who was waiting behind him. Then he pulled the door shut.

"How's Gibbs doing?" I asked.

Koprowski frowned. "So-so. He was okay in the beginning of the morning. I sat with him, and we did a couple of dry runs for the ransom call. Around ten o'clock he started to get squirrelly. He decided that the reason nobody contacted him was because she was dead. After I talked to you, I told him that the kidnapper called you, and you were on the way over. I thought that would calm him down, but no—he got all rattled. He wants to know why the man who took Erin is negotiating with the police instead of her husband. Right now he's a nervous wreck."

"Which I'm sure is just what the kidnapper wants," Kylie said. "Let's see if we can settle him down."

We entered the apartment. The tech who had taken my cell phone was set up at a table with the bank of equipment he needed to monitor, record, and trace any incoming calls.

Jamie was in the living room. He stood up as soon as he saw us.

"How much money does he want?" he asked.

"He didn't say," I said.

"Detective Koprowski told me that the guy who took Erin called you. Why would he do that if he's not going to tell you how much money he's asking for?"

"Because he's not negotiating with me. He wants to talk to you."

"Then why did he call you?"

"Jamie," Kylie said, "sit down."

He sat on the sofa, and she sat next to him.

"Do you know how terrorists work?" she said. "They not only inflict physical damage, they create fear, doubt, and confusion in the minds of their victims. You understand?"

"Yeah. Mind games," he said. "My mother does it all the time."

"This guy's not your mother. You don't have any emotional baggage with him. He's got something you want, and he wants to cut a business deal with you, so you're not going to let him rent space in your head, are you?"

"I hope not."

"Everything is going to be all right," Kylie said. "You're going to get through this. And we're going to help."

"It's been twenty-eight minutes since he called," I said. "If he's true to his word, the phone is going to ring in two minutes." I turned to the tech. "Are you ready?"

"All hooked up," he said. "When you take the call, do *not* put it on speaker or he's going to know he's being broadcast to a roomful of cops. Just talk directly into the phone. You want the conversation to feel like it's personal, one on one. Everybody else can grab a headset and listen in. I'm recording everything. Benny Diaz is tapped in. He's going to trace the call."

Koprowski had set up a large whiteboard in the center of Jamie's living room. Kylie grabbed two markers and handed me one.

"Zach and I are going to talk you through this every step of the way," Kylie said to Gibbs. "Take your time before you respond to anything he says. You good, Jamie?"

He shook his head. "I don't want to screw it up, but right now I don't even know if Erin is alive."

"She is," Kylie said.

"You don't know that for sure."

"Yes, I do. You want to know how I know that?"

He looked at her for the answer.

"Because she's not worth anything to him dead."

He nodded. It made sense. He half smiled.

My cell phone rang.

CHAPTER 26

I ANSWERED THE phone. "Detective Jordan."

"Are you with the husband?" Dodd's voice was unfiltered, unaltered. Apparently he wasn't worried about being identified.

"Yes."

"Good boy. You take orders well."

He paused, waiting for me to come back at him. I didn't take the bait.

"Put him on," he said.

I handed the phone to Jamie.

"This is Jamie Gibbs," he said, his voice modulated, his tone even. As instructed.

"Congratulations, Mr. Gibbs. You're a lucky man. Your wife is beautiful."

"Thank you. Please don't hurt her."

"I have no intention of hurting her. I'm sure you want her back in the same condition she was when you married her. It was a touching ceremony. I watched it on video."

"Can I speak to her?"

"In due time. Don't you want to know what you have to do to get her back?"

"How much do you want?"

"Twenty-five million dollars."

Jamie bolted out of his seat. "Twenty-five million dollars? Are you out of your fucking mind? I don't have that kind of money."

"Mommy does, Jamie. Why don't you call her?"

"*You* call her. See how much you get!"

Jamie was completely off script. Kylie held up both her hands and mouthed the words *Calm down*. Then she put one hand on his abdomen, inhaled deeply, and gestured for him to do the same.

He took a long slow deep breath, and Kylie pointed to the whiteboard, where I had scribbled *Talk to Erin*.

"I need to talk to Erin," he said.

"Hold on," Dodd said.

There was some rustling in the background, and then Dodd said, "Erin, nod your head if you know the rules." A pause. "Good girl. Tell your new hubby what I have in my hand."

"A knife." It was a female voice, and from the look on Jamie's face, it was the one he'd been waiting to hear.

"It's a black straight-edge Ka-Bar, and it's really nasty, isn't it?" Dodd said. "Now, I have Jamie and a couple of dozen cops on the phone who want to know if you're alive. Tell them what I promised I would do to you if you say something stupid or try to talk in code and help them find out where we are."

"Cut me."

Jamie stiffened, and Kylie put her hands on his shoulders.

"Cut you where?" Dodd said.

"My face." The voice was a whimper.

"And then where else will I cut you?" Dodd said.

The words came tumbling out in heaving sobs. "My...my body. I swear...I won't say anything stupid. I just...I just want to talk to Jamie."

"Make it quick."

"Jamie?" she moaned. "Jamie, is that you?"

"Erin, baby, are you okay? What has he done to you?"

"I love you. I want to come home. Please, please, please get me out of here. I'm scared, and I'm—"

"That's enough," Dodd said. "Did you hear that, Gibbs? She's alive. Are you satisfied now?"

Kylie shook her head violently.

"No! I'm not satisfied," Jamie said. "That wasn't a conversation. That was her voice. It could have been a recording or an impersonator. I need"—he looked up at the three new words I'd added to the board—"proof of life. I want a video. I want to see that she's really alive and unharmed."

"Fair enough," Dodd said. "I'll get you your video. You figure out how to get me my twenty-five million."

"I can't get that kind of money overnight. It's going to take a lot of time. Promise me that you'll—"

"He hung up," the tech announced. "The call dropped right after he said, 'You figure out how to get me my twenty-five million.'"

Jamie slumped down onto the sofa and handed me the cell phone.

"You did great, Jamie," Kylie said. "You did really, really well."

"I didn't do shit. My job was to calm Erin down, make her feel like there's hope, and all I did was explode when he asked for twenty-five million. Did you hear her? She's petrified. He's threatening to disfigure her. He's—"

"He's terrorizing her," Kylie said. "And you. You did what we asked you to do. You bought time."

"*Time?* Time for what? I thought he was going to ask for a couple of million. Or maybe five. I don't have nearly that much, but with a little time I could reach out to friends…but twenty-five million? I'll never be able to come up with that kind of money."

"Jamie, it's a negotiation," Kylie said. "He doesn't want to ask for so much that he winds up with nothing. He may only want five million, but he set the bar at twenty-five so that when he finally lowers his price to five, you'll think you're getting a bargain, and he'll get what he wants."

It was complete horseshit. This was not a negotiation. Dodd had all the cards and could demand whatever he wanted. But our job was to keep the hysterical husband from going off the deep end and blowing up the investigation.

It worked. "I might be able to get five," he said.

We didn't care if he could get five million or five dollars. We didn't want him to pay Dodd a cent.

The tech stood up. "Guys, I've got Benny Diaz on the line."

"Put him through," I said.

Benny's voice came over the speaker. "I pinpointed the call," he said. "It came from the Four Seasons Hotel."

"What's the address?" I asked, ready to roll.

"Nile Plaza. Cairo, Egypt."

CHAPTER 27

YOU HAVE NO idea where he's really calling from, do you?" Jamie said. "All this big-deal, high-tech NYPD Red shit, and he can trick you into thinking he's calling from some hotel in Egypt."

"He didn't trick us into anything," I said. "We know he's not there. He could be right next door, but he's got enough techno-savvy to route the call so that it looks like it's coming from anywhere in the world. He's smart. Everything he says and does is part of the subterfuge. Don't take anything at face value."

"*Don't take anything at face value?* Really, Detective?" He bolted up from the sofa. "What about the black straight-edge Ka-Bar knife? Should I not take that at face value?" His fists were clenched, his breathing shallow, his face red.

"Calm down," I said.

"How the hell am I supposed to calm down? Did you hear the fear in my wife's voice? Or am I not supposed to take that at face value either?"

"Jamie, the knife was real," I said. "Erin's fear was very real, but the threat wasn't."

He began pacing the living-room floor. "And how do you know that?"

I knew it based on Bobby Dodd's profile. He had served in the Marines, but nothing led us to believe that he was a violent criminal. He was also in love with Erin and had deluded himself into thinking they would be together for the rest of their lives. I was more concerned that Dodd would take the ransom money and disappear with Erin than I was about him killing her.

But I couldn't share any of that with Jamie.

"All his threats are part of his strategy," I said. "The more he can convince you that Erin's life is in danger, the more likely you are to pay the ransom. He's bluffing. His whole game plan is based on lies and deception."

"Then he and I have something in common," Jamie said.

"I'm not sure what you mean."

"Lies and deception. I'm not only lying to him, I'm lying to you."

"What are you saying, Jamie?" Kylie asked.

"I told you I couldn't pay twenty-five million but that I might be able to drum up five. That was pure bullshit. I couldn't get that either. Hell, I'd be lucky to come up with a lousy million, and we can't buy him off with that." He stopped pacing. "That's why you heard all that fear in Erin's voice. She knows I have no money. Neither of us have any.

"Erin makes millions, but she spends it faster than it comes in. She loves..." He groped for a word, then spit it out. "*Things*. And the more ridiculously overpriced the things are, the more she loves them. She buys these houses a million miles from where she should be living, pours a shitload of money into overhauling them, and then hardly ever lives in them. She owns a twelve-million-dollar boat that she never uses, and even though the designers give her jewelry and clothes to wear on the red carpet, that's like, what—five nights a year? She still has to look like a million bucks the other three hundred and sixty nights, and all that comes out of her pocket."

"And you?" I asked.

"Me?" He laughed. "If you go online to one of those celebrity-net-worth websites, they'll tell you I've got anything from sixty-six million to a hundred and fifty million dollars. I don't know where they come up with numbers like that or how they can get away with saying it, because it's totally bogus. But the kidnapper asked me for twenty-five million, so he must believe everything he reads on the internet."

"I don't think so," Kylie said.

"What do you mean?"

"As soon as he said twenty-five million, you said you didn't have that kind of money, and he didn't even take time to blink. He came right back at you and said, 'Mommy does.'"

Jamie dropped down to the sofa again. "She does—twenty times over. But as she reminds me every chance she gets, it's her money, not mine. And trust me, if I tell her she has the power to save Erin's life, my mother won't part with a nickel."

CHAPTER 28

LET ME DRIVE," I said as soon as we left Gibbs's apartment.

"You need to vent?" Kylie said, tossing me the keys.

I didn't answer. We got in the car, which was parked behind the forty-eight-foot mobile incident command center.

"Millions of dollars' worth of police technology sitting right outside his doorstep," I said, pulling out onto Riverside Drive, "and all he can do is trash our 'big-deal, high-tech NYPD Red shit' because we haven't found his missing wife less than twenty-four hours into the investigation."

Kylie grinned. "So then I was right. You need to vent."

"Damn right I do. Jamie freaking Gibbs knows how to hide behind that pussycat façade—reformed bad boy gone straight. But he can't hide his true colors. The man takes no responsibility for coming up short on the security detail. That's the network's fault. We offer to talk him through a negotiation with the kidnapper, and he says he doesn't need any help—he knows what he's doing. Then the phone call goes south because he loses his shit, so he comes down on me. *'What about the black straight-edge Ka-Bar knife? Should I not take that at face value?'* I wanted to whack him upside the head."

"Cut him some slack," Kylie said. "He's scared shit-less because a maniac kidnapped his wife, he doesn't have the money to rescue her, and his mother, who I'm sure made him as neurotic as he is, won't lift a finger to bail him out."

"I get it. Poor Jamie. That's still no reason to turn on the cops who are busting their humps to help him. And how come you're suddenly so tolerant and forgiving? You usually get off on letting people know when they're behaving badly. You weren't exactly shy about tearing Brockway a new one."

"There's a difference. Harris Brockway is an ass-hole. Jamie Gibbs is damaged goods. And if I had any doubt, our little visit to Cruella de Vil in her fortress in the sky clinched it. Jamie's mother, who can exist with virtually no sleep, made a conscious decision to *nap* through his wedding. The last thing that man needed was a female cop yelling at him because he's not a model victim."

Kylie's phone rang. "It's your girlfriend," she said, looking at the screen. I figured it was Captain Cates, and Kylie was just trying to be cute, but I was wrong. It was my girlfriend.

Kylie answered. "Hey, Cheryl, what's going on?" A pause, then: "CJ? No, that ship has sailed—all the way to Hawaii. He's gone." Another pause. "Your cousin?" She looked at me and grimaced. "I don't know, Cheryl, I've been fixed up with my share of my friends' cousins before, and there's usually a good reason why they're available. What is this guy like?"

She looked back at me to make sure I was paying attention, and then she hunched over, screwed up her face, and did a damn good imitation of Quasimodo. I smiled and looked away—eyes on the road, ears on Kylie's end of the phone call.

But she didn't say a word. Cheryl must have talked for three solid minutes before Kylie said, "He sounds too good to be true. What's the downside? He can't be perfect, or he wouldn't be on the market."

She listened for a few seconds and then said, "Married to his job? That's not a deal breaker for me. In fact, it's a plus. I'm not ready to get serious about—hold on, Cheryl, I've got another call coming in."

She took the second call. This time it really was Captain Cates. I listened as Kylie rattled off a series of "Yes, ma'am"s and then ended the conversation with "We'll be there in ten minutes."

She flashed the phone and went back to the first call. "Cheryl, I've got to go, but what the hell, I'll give it a shot. I'll catch up with you later."

She hung up and turned to me. "Speed it up, Grandma. We may have just caught a break that's going to make the governor of New York a happy man."

"What's going on?"

"Another home invasion, another rich old lady, another ambulance. Same exact MO."

I hit the gas. "Where?"

"Lincoln Towers on West End."

"There are like half a dozen buildings in the complex. Which one are we going to?"

"None of them. We're going back to the precinct. It happened three weeks ago."

CHAPTER 29

MOST COPS WORK within the boundaries of their precincts. Criminals don't. So it's not unusual for detectives from opposite sides of the city to sit down and share information when one of them spots a pattern.

But when those detectives bring a big boss to show-and-tell, it starts to become something of an event.

Kylie, Cates, and I sat on one side of the table. On the opposite side were Detectives Al Devereaux and Paula Moss from the Two Oh and Reuben St. Claire, zone captain for three detective squads in upper Manhattan.

Devereaux kicked it off. "Three weeks ago an ambulance pulls up to a building on West End. The EMTs tell the doorman they got a 911 call, old lady in respiratory distress—Ida Lowenthal. They go upstairs, the private nurse lets them in, the perps zip-tie and gag the two women, then walk off with seventy thou in jewelry plus another fifteen in cash plus six hundred in spending money the family left for the nurse."

"But they didn't touch the nurse's purse or any of her jewelry," Moss said.

"Our guys hit the jackpot—almost two million in jewelry and fifty thousand in cash," I said. "They also took the day-to-day money from the nurse, but nothing that was hers personally."

"They're either the same pair or they're working from the same script," Moss said.

"We ran our nurse's name through the system," Kylie said. "Solid citizen, no history, so far nothing to suggest she was involved. What's the story on yours?"

"Same deal. Clean. But now I'd like to know if these two know each other or work for the same agency."

"The doorman wrote down the name on the bus—NYCC Senior Care," Devereaux said. "He thought the CC might mean Catholic Charities, but it's completely bogus. LPRs got a read on the plates, but they were stolen."

"Ours was Morningside Medical. Also phony," I said. "What about surveillance videos?"

"They knew where the cameras were. They had baseball caps on, and they kept their faces down, looking at the gurney. None of the images are usable. The old lady has dementia, so she was no help, and the best the nurse could give us was two males, one white, one Hispanic, about forty, very efficient—they knew what they were after."

"How about the stolen jewelry?"

"Moss and I have been checking pawnshops plus eBay and a couple of dozen other websites where they might unload it, but so far nothing."

"We're looking at the same MO," Cates said. "The only difference is we're dealing with a high-profile victim, so we have everyone from One PP to the governor's mansion looking over our shoulder. It's going to help a lot that you caught the pattern so fast."

"You can thank the boss for that," Moss said.

Reuben St. Claire was more than a boss. He was a leader. Everyone I knew who had worked under his command said he was the kind of guy who inspired you to be a better cop.

"I caught it in a hurry because I spend more damn time on the computer than I do on the streets," St. Claire said. "And now that the ball is in your court, I drove over to say two things. First is that everything we've got—every interview, every witness, every lead—is yours."

Kylie, Cates, and I knew that St. Claire didn't have to come across town to pledge his cooperation. He was on a mission. We waited to hear what it was.

He leaned forward. "Second is that yours are not the only shoulders being looked over. Everyone in the Bureau of Second-Guessing will be asking why we didn't catch the perps before they started ripping off the governor's blood relatives.

"I know Devereaux and Moss. They're smart, they're thorough, and even though they've got a stack of open cases, this one hit home for both of them. A burglary when nobody is in the house is one thing, but when two assholes break in, brandish weapons, and rip the wedding ring right off Mrs. Lowenthal's finger—that gets all our blood boiling. Bottom line is these guys have been busting their asses on this one. So I'm asking a favor. If you do see anything we missed, I'd appreciate a heads-up."

"You'll be the first one we call, Reuben," Cates said.

And if I knew Cates, it would be the only call. Her mission is to track down bad guys, not help 1PP look for scapegoats.

CHAPTER 30

THE PILE OF leads, tips, background information, and reports of Erin sightings on my desk had grown exponentially since we'd been diverted by the ambulance robbery, and as soon as we said goodbye to Captain St. Claire, we assigned Danny Corcoran to work with Detectives Moss and Devereaux and dived back into the Easton case.

One of the best ways to track someone down is by digging into his financials. No matter how spartan Dodd's lifestyle, he still needed to pay for it. There had to be a trail of money coming in and going out.

"His only reported income is a monthly pension check from the Marine Corps," Kylie said, reading from a confidential file we'd received from the Violent Felony Squad, the only ones on our team who knew Dodd by name. "The checks were direct-deposited to his account at the USAA bank in Clarksville, Tennessee, until March 2018, when the account was closed, and the checks were redirected."

"Is that when he moved to New York?" I asked.

"No. Since then, every check has gone directly to the Wounded Warrior Project."

"He's giving his entire pension to charity?"

"That's what it says."

"Then what is he doing for money?"

"That's what we have to figure out."

It took hours, but we found it buried in the thick file Declan McMaster had given us. Dodd had been stalking Erin for years, but in September of 2017, he fell off the grid. He resurfaced six months later.

McMaster, who is as freakishly thorough as Kylie, figured he'd been doing jail time and decided to track down some of Dodd's cellmates to see what he was planning next.

But he hadn't been locked up. Immediately after two devastating hurricanes hit the Caribbean in 2017, Dodd had signed on with a U.S.-based construction company that had been hired for the rebuilding effort.

"Are you kidding me?" Kylie said, reading the file. "According to this, Dodd earned as much as twenty grand a week."

"Twenty...doing what?"

"Helping the rich and famous restore their ravaged mansions to their former glory. He's a skilled stone-mason, and apparently requests for his services came fast and furious. He could name his own price. And he did."

"Twenty grand a week for six months is half a million dollars," I said. "And assuming he socked it away in a bank somewhere on the islands, it's tax-free. No wonder he gave up his pension to help his fellow veterans."

"And that explains why he has nothing current in his credit-rating profile. Whatever he needs he pays for in cash."

If Dodd had a bank in the U.S., we could stake it out. If he had a go-to ATM or a regular gas station, restaurant, or supermarket where he used his credit card, we could track him. But he had none of those. We'd gone through an exhaustive search, and the only thing we had to show for it was that we were both totally exhausted.

Working a kidnapping case is a race against time, and for us the mission was to find Dodd while Erin was still alive and unharmed. We had the vast resources of the NYPD at our fingertips. All we had to do was pick up the phone and ask, and we could have almost anything we wanted. There was only one thing we couldn't get: sleep.

"We need caffeine," Kylie said. "You want some warm brown beverage from the break room or do you want to head over to Starbucks? I'm buying."

"I never say no to a free triple espresso macchiato," I said. My cell rang. "I don't recognize the number," I said. "It could be Dodd again."

"Put it on speaker."

I did. "Hello, this is Detective Jordan."

"Detective, this is Brock." A pause. "Harris Brockway, vice president of programming at Zephyr Television."

"Yes, sir, I know who you are. What can I do for you?"

"Erin's kidnapper sent us a proof-of-life video."

"Where are you?" I said. "My partner and I will be right over to pick it up."

"You don't have to pick it up. You can see it on ZTV in five minutes. We're broadcasting it."

"Sir, you can't do that!" I said. "It's a violation of—"

"Don't you tell me what I can and can't do. We've been told if we don't air it by eight o'clock tonight, they'll kill her. It's seven fifty-five now."

"Sir, broadcasting that video will jeopardize our—"

"Stop yammerin', Detective, and turn on your goddamn TV set."

He hung up.

"Call Bill Harrison," Kylie said.

Harrison was the assigned ADA for the kidnapping. He knew he was on call 24/7, and he was thrilled to have been handpicked for the biggest case of his career. I dialed his cell, and he answered on the first ring.

"Zach, what's going on?"

I told him. He only interrupted once, yelling, "They can't do that," at the same exact point in the story that I'd exploded at Brockway.

"Bill, he's giving us five minutes. Do you think we can stop them?"

"Hell no, but let me start making some threatening phone calls," Harrison said. "Because it damn well better look like we tried."

CHAPTER 31

CATES LEFT AN hour ago," I said to Kylie. "If this proof-of-life video goes live before we get our hands on it, the wrath of God is going to rain heavily upon this squad, and she's going to get the brunt of it."

"*If?* Zach, we've got four minutes. At this point, NORAD couldn't stop it from going live."

"I know, I know. Just try to find the boss and tell her what's going down."

"I'm on it," she said, cell phone in hand. "And while I'm doing that, why don't you take Brockway's suggestion—stop yammering and turn on your goddamn TV set."

Turning on the TV was easy. There was one right there in the break room. Finding ZTV, the cable channel where Erin Easton was a reality star, was another story. We had a boatload of information about her career, her friends, her enemies, and her private life, but not a single cop had any clue what channel her program aired on. It took another precious three minutes just to come up with the answer.

At least someone in IT had the foresight to make sure that we were hooked up to every cable channel in the city, and by the time I found ZTV, on channel 313, the entire task force was crammed into the break room.

The credits were rolling for the show that had just ended. When they were over, the screen went dark and silent. A few seconds passed, and then it erupted with dramatic music and a spinning graphic that turned into a newspaper with ZTV NEWS BULLETIN on the masthead.

It spun again, and a black-and-white picture of Erin came on the screen with the word ABDUCTED plastered across the bottom.

The camera cut away to a newsroom set with Brockway seated at the anchor desk. "Good evening," he said. "I'm Harris Brockway, vice president of programming here at ZTV. Usually I'm behind the scenes, but as you know, last night at approximately seven thirty, Erin Easton, my dear friend and colleague and a much-adored member of our ZTV family, was abducted."

Five words popped on at the bottom of the screen: TIME SINCE ERIN WAS ABDUCTED. A digital clock appeared next to it. The count was at 1 Day/ 0 Hours / 30 Minutes.

Brockway went on. "She was celebrating the happiest night of her life, and she had just gone into her dressing room, still in her bridal gown."

The camera cut away to pictures of Erin in her wedding dress.

"Oh, shit," some cop called out from the back of the room. "This guy is milking the hell out of this."

The camera cut back to Brockway. "And then, while she was getting changed so she could go to sing for her loved ones, her friends, and her new husband, all of whom were gathered in a ballroom several hundred feet away"—he took a deep breath and visibly composed himself, lest anyone doubt his distress. Composure convincingly regained, he continued—"a madman forced his way into her dressing room and took her by brute force."

The camera cut to a shot of Erin's dressing room after the kidnapping. I knew that Brockway had taken photos of the crime scene before we could stop him. I also knew that every shot he took was a perfect digital image. But the picture on the screen was grainy, black-and-white, doctored to look like one of those lurid photos from the annals of the *National Police Gazette,* the forerunner to today's supermarket tabloids.

Kylie leaned close and whispered angrily in my ear, "That slimy bastard isn't just milking it. He's turning it into a freak show. When the brass sees that, we're screwed."

Again the camera went back to Brockway. "Our network has been besieged by phone calls and e-mails from concerned fans. Many of you have held prayer vigils. The nation—in fact, the world—has been waiting for an answer to those prayers, and tonight I have some news. We just received video footage from someone purporting to be the person who is holding Erin in captivity. I reached Erin's husband, Jamie Gibbs, who confirmed to me personally that he had spoken to the kidnapper earlier today and requested a proof-of-life video. We believe this to be just that."

He took another long dramatic pause. "The good news is Erin is okay. For now. But her life is at great risk. The kidnapper insisted that we air this video or, and I quote, 'You'll never see her alive again.' After careful consideration we've elected to share that footage with the police and the public. The video is being prepared for transmission on air and across all our social media platforms. It will be ready shortly. Please stay with us. Till then, I'm joined by my wife, Anna Brockway, who is Erin's dear friend, trusted confidante, and longtime manager."

The camera pulled back to reveal Mrs. Brockway sitting to her husband's right. I tuned her out and turned to Kylie. "Do you see what's going on here? This prick Brockway is giving people time to call their friends, to tweet, to post it on social media. He's trolling for a bigger audience."

"You and I may hate Brockway and everything he stands for," Kylie said, "but just take a look around you."

There were about twenty cops in the room, some standing, some perched on furniture, some sitting on the floor. At least half of them were either texting or talking on their cell phones.

And then mine chirped. It was a text from Cheryl asking if I knew that the Erin Easton proof-of-life video was about to be broadcast on ZTV. Clearly Brockway's strategy was working.

He had taken a high-profile crime, packaged it as a heartbreaking national tragedy, and was in the process of successfully turning it into a ratings bonanza.

CHAPTER 32

I TURNED MY attention back to the TV. Brockway was now doing the talking.

"Anna, millions of people have been riveted by Erin's ordeal," he said, addressing his wife as if they had just met and not woken up in bed together that morning. "But many of them may not watch her show on a regular basis, and they may only know her as the beautiful woman they see on the covers of magazines."

"Or the woman whose sex tape they whacked off to back in the day," one cop called out.

"You've known Erin for almost twenty years," Brockway went on. "While we're waiting to screen the kidnapper's life-altering videotape, why don't you tell our new viewers a little about the real Erin Easton."

"The *real* one's got small tits, crooked teeth, and no talent," another cop yelled out. "Run the videotape, asshole."

Anna Brockway launched into the story of Erin's meteoric early career. As soon as she started talking, the camera cut away to still photos and film clips that highlighted everything she said.

I had expected the Brockways to vamp aimlessly while they bought time to drum up an audience. But I'd been wrong. They weren't winging it. They were perfectly scripted.

Anna deftly touched on all the hot buttons to win over her audience. She left out the sex tape and Erin's first two marriages, but when she got to the tragedies—Erin's parents killed in a plane crash when she was nineteen and her brother's fatal skiing accident a year later—the camera cut to photos of Erin valiantly coping in her designer mourning couture.

I was hoping that Bill Harrison would get a court order to quash the broadcast, but ten minutes into the production, with #ErinsHostageTape trending, Harris Brockway made the announcement.

His face without expression, his voice somber, he said, "We apologize for the disturbing nature of what you are about to see, but all of us here at ZTV take heart that our brave friend and colleague is still alive and well and that despite all she has been through these past twenty-four-plus hours, her indomitable spirit remains unbroken."

A chorus of profanity was hurled at the screen from every direction. Brockway might be able to con the public, but every cop in the room saw right through him.

The screen went dark and then faded up on a close-up of that morning's edition of the *Daily News*. Erin's picture and the single word TAKEN were on the front page.

The camera pulled back as the newspaper was lowered. And there stood Erin Easton, hair disheveled, no makeup, eyes puffy from crying, wearing a pair of baggy gray sweatpants and a matching sweatshirt.

"She looks like shit," Kylie said.

"I think that's what he's going for," I said. "The worse she looks, the more likely Jamie is to pull the ransom money together."

"I don't know who's watching this," Erin said. "Probably my husband, and the police, and maybe someone at the network. Whoever it is, I want you all to know that I'm…I'm…" She started to sob. "I'm okay."

She put her hands over her eyes, and we watched in silence as her shoulders heaved and her body shook. After about thirty seconds she lowered her hands. "I'm sorry. I'm not okay. I mean, he didn't hurt me, but I want to go home. I have to go home. I'm…"

She looked down at the floor. When she looked back at the camera, she inhaled and stood tall.

"Jamie…sweetheart…I was going to tell you this at the wedding after I performed my song. I'm pregnant."

PART TWO

ERIN IN EXILE

CHAPTER 33

THE CAMERA DRIFTED in on Erin as her eyes welled up, and a tear, glistening like a single pearl, rolled down her cheek. She brushed it away and took a deep breath. She was about to say something else when the screen went dark. Dodd had cut the video. If Jamie Gibbs wanted to see more, he'd have to pay for it.

"And now," Brockway said as the camera cut back to him and his wife, "we learn that the stakes are doubled. The fate of *two* people hangs in the balance—Erin Easton and her unborn child. Anna, what do you have to say about that heartbreaking video we just witnessed?"

I didn't care what either of the Brockways had to say. I headed toward the door and signaled Kylie to follow. She didn't budge. She had her phone to her ear, and she held up her other hand. I waited until she hung up. "We're not going anywhere," she said. "Cates wants us here."

"Doing what?" I asked. "We need to go to the station and get our hands on that video. When did it come in? Who delivered it? Who touched it? If there's any chance there are prints on it—"

"Zach, if there are any prints on it, I'm guessing

they'll belong to Dodd," Kylie said. "Cates told me to send a team to do a follow-up interview with the Brockways and bring the video back to the lab. She wants us to stay right here."

"Why?"

"Snow White is coming."

"That's great," I said. "Because I was starting to worry that there weren't enough bosses with their thumbs in this pie. So glad the chief decided to heap on another one."

There were two deputy chiefs in the Detective Bureau with the same exact name—John White. It was inevitable that they'd get nicknames so people could tell them apart. One was notoriously stingy when it came to approving overtime. He became Tight White. The other was an old-school devout Catholic. He'd been in the department for over thirty years, and no one had ever once heard him utter a single word of profanity. He was christened Snow White.

Chief White arrived twenty minutes after the video had aired, which gave us enough time to catch up with Bill Harrison. By the time we stood face-to-face with Chief White in Captain Cates's office we had some answers—none of them good.

"I've been involved in more kidnappings than I care to count," White said. "But never have I had a case get so far out of my grasp that *a proof-of-life video* was broadcast—in prime time—to a mass audience hungry to wallow in the misery of others. It's ludicrous. It's unthinkable."

Kylie and I stood there. We'd been ordered by Cates not to speak unless it was in direct response to something he asked.

"I just came from the chief of Ds' office," White said. "He had a lot of questions—all of them started with *how*. *How* did a proof-of-life video get on the air? *How* did ZTV have it and not us? *How* did we not know? *How* did we not stop them? And if you've ever been in a room with the chief when he is boiling mad, you know that his phrasing is much more colorful than mine. He says *how* in three words."

He folded his arms across his chest and waited for an answer.

"Sir," I said, "at seven fifty-five this evening, I got a phone call from Harris Brockway at ZTV." I then went on to report the brief conversation I'd had with Brockway that ended with him hanging up on me.

"I then called ADA Bill Harrison. Detective Mac-Donald and I have subsequently talked to Harrison, and he informed us that he immediately tried to call Brockway, but he was redirected to a network attorney. Harrison warned him that ZTV executives were in possession of evidence relating to an ongoing criminal investigation, and the network could be charged with a crime if they disseminated it or tampered with it.

"The network lawyer asked for the name of the judge who signed the order to keep it off the air. There was no judge. We didn't have time. The lawyer said that until they get a ruling from a judge, all they are legally bound to do is give the police an unedited copy along with a narrative as to how it was received. That, he said, put the network in full compliance with the law. By that time it was eight p.m. and Brockway had gone live."

"But the video didn't run at eight," White said. "The ADA had a solid ten minutes to find a judge to shut them down *before* they aired it."

"Yes, sir," I said. "ADA Harrison did reach Judge Charlotte Najarian a few minutes before the video was broadcast, but she refused to stop them from airing it."

"On what grounds?"

"Freedom of the press."

"Hogwash. We didn't ask her to quash the video," White said. "All we did was try to buy some time before it went public."

"That's not how Judge Najarian saw it," I said, wishing I had Bill Harrison in the room to deliver his own bad news. "In fact, she said if the kidnapper sends any future proof-of-life videos directly to the network, she would not deny them the right to air those either. She also said, and the ADA swears this is a direct quote, sir, 'I will not be the judge responsible for Erin Easton's death if the tape *isn't* aired, and she is murdered.'"

Most cops would explode and call the judge every name in the book. Not White. He simply shook his head. "Justice is supposed to be blind, not thinking about how every decision is going to play with the public in an election year."

"Chief," Cates said, "you saw the show Harris Brockway put on. It wasn't slapped together in five minutes. He'd had that video for hours. The network lawyers told him to call Detective Jordan at the last second just to give the appearance of compliance. Please tell the chief of Ds that we deeply regret that the video went public, but we did everything we could to stop it."

"That's all he needs to hear," White said. "The chief doesn't care about network lawyers or self-serving judges. All eyes—around the country and around the world—are on NYPD. And all eyes in this department are on the three of you. Do. Not. Fail."

He turned and left. Cates, Kylie, and I watched him stride out of the office. None of us said a thing, but I was sure that Snow White's three parting words would be echoing in our brains for a long time to come.

CHAPTER 34

RISE AND SHINE, sleepyhead," Bobby Dodd said as he came into the bedroom. "It's a beautiful, bright sunny morning. I wish you could go outside and enjoy it, but what would the neighbors say?"

He laughed, and Erin, who had spent hours lying in bed trying to remember all the rules Ari had taught her fifteen years ago, peered over the covers and did her best to smile at her captor. *Keep your dignity. It's harder to kill or harm someone who can remain human in his eyes.*

"I've got coffee and croissants," Dodd said, setting down a tray. "And a bunch of newspapers, which, of course, are all about us."

There is no us, you maniac. "Thanks. I'll start with the coffee." *Establish rapport. Don't antagonize.* She swung her legs over the side of the bed, and he handed her a Styrofoam cup. She popped the lid and took a sip.

"You like it?" he said.

Lukewarm, god-awful swill. "Perfect," she said.

"I've got a confession to make," he said, spreading grape jelly on a croissant with a plastic knife.

She shrugged. "I'm listening." *I'm a captive audience.*

"Last night was the best night of my life," he said, inhaling half the croissant in a single bite.

She cringed.

"I know you've slept with a lot of guys," he said. "How'd I do?"

You fucking raped me, you animal. "You were very gentle. I appreciate it."

"It'll be even better next time," he said, shoveling in the rest of the croissant.

Above all, comply. You may have to do things that you don't want to—including sex. Just do it, because sometimes that's the only way to stay alive. "Just remember," she said, "you don't have to force me."

"No, no, never. It's got to be natural," Dodd said. "You know I have to tell Jamie that I'm going to kill you if he doesn't pay, but I never would do anything to hurt you. Or our baby. It's going to be so great once we get the money. Just the three of us."

And don't try to convince him that his delusions are unfounded. "Do you mind if I take a shower now?" she asked.

"No, no. Go ahead."

She got out of bed and walked through the open doorway to the bathroom. She knew what would be next.

Dodd waited until he heard the water running.

Then he peeled off his clothes, and, fully aroused, he followed her into the shower.

Erin was waiting for him.

Give in. But never give up.

CHAPTER 35

ABOUT AN HOUR after Erin announced her pregnancy to the world, Kylie and I drove to the mobile incident command post outside Jamie Gibbs's residence to wait for Bobby Dodd's next move.

Cops have a dark sense of humor, and it wasn't long before someone pulled together an impromptu What Time Will the Kidnapper Call? pool, ten bucks for a half-hour box. I, of course, didn't buy in. It doesn't look good when a detective being cross-examined by the defense has to admit he had money riding on how the case would play out. But I had a theory—he'd call in the middle of the night, when Jamie might be at his most vulnerable.

I was wrong. Kylie and I caught a few hours' sleep in shifts, and when I woke up at eight a.m., Dodd still hadn't called. I rang upstairs and asked how Jamie was handling the wait.

"He's crawling the walls, Zach," Detective Koprowski said. "The proof-of-life video is on YouTube, and he keeps going back to the site to see how many people have watched it so far."

"How many?"

"Nineteen million views last time I looked. The number would be a lot lower if they didn't count how many times Gibbs watched it."

Two million YouTube views later, Jamie's home phone rang.

"Incoming on his landline," the tech in the command center said.

I called upstairs to Koprowski. "Does Jamie recognize the number?"

"No."

"Tell him to pick it up."

Jamie took the call. "Hello."

"Jamie…" It was Erin. "Sweetheart, I'm scared."

"Are you okay?"

"Jamie, I'm locked up. He has a knife in his hand. How can I be okay?"

"I mean, has he hurt you? Has he touched you?"

A whimper. But no response.

"Shit," Kylie said. "Bad sign."

"Erin?" Jamie said. "Are you there? Has he touched you?"

"I'm here. He's treated me okay, but I want to come ho—"

Silence.

"Erin? Erin?" The fear and desperation in Gibbs's voice was palpable. "Please…Erin?"

I looked at the tech to see if we'd been disconnected. He shook his head. The abrupt silence on the other end was all part of the psychological warfare. Ten seconds passed before Dodd broke it.

"Time is running out, Jamie. You got your video. You got your phone call. Are you going to pay or do I have to start sending you body parts?"

"I'll pay. I swear."

"Twenty-five million. I've got a bank routing

number. You do this right, and she'll be home in time for dinner."

"It's not that easy," Gibbs said. "I just don't have that kind of money."

"Get it."

"I will. I called my mother, but—"

"No buts! I don't want excuses. I want my money. Now!"

"I'm trying. I left messages. She just hasn't called me back yet."

"I'm trying. I left messages. She just hasn't called me back yet," Dodd said in a high-pitched nasal voice. "Your wife is listening to this, Jamie. You should see the look on her face."

"Tell her I'm sorry. As soon as my mother knows about the baby, I'm sure she'll help."

"Listen, asshole," Dodd said, "your mother knows about the baby. By now, the whole damn world knows about the baby."

"You're right. I know she'll come up with the money. All I need is a little time to convince her."

"You better convince her fast, because a *little* time is all you're going to get—very little. You tell her that the longer she makes me wait, the angrier I get. And if she ever wants to see this baby, she better cough up the money, or she's going to force me to do something I don't want to do."

The phone went dead.

"Disconnect," the tech said.

A second phone on his console rang. "Hold on. It's Benny with a trace." He scribbled something on a piece of paper. "It's a number right here in the city. Let me see who it belongs to."

Kylie picked up the paper as he typed the number into the system.

"Don't bother," she said. "I know the number."

We all looked at her.

"The son of a bitch routed the call through my cell phone."

CHAPTER 36

LESS THAN FORTY-EIGHT hours after her wedding, Mrs. Jamie Gibbs picked up her coffee mug, flung it at the stone fireplace, and cursed out her new husband. "Asshole," she screamed as glass shards scattered across the living-room rug.

"Hey," Bobby said. "Take it easy. It's the maid's day off."

She wheeled around and gave him the finger. "That hag has half a billion dollars, but she hates me so much that she won't pay a nickel to save her own grandchild."

"I guess you picked the wrong mother-in-law. Don't worry. Jamie will come up with the money."

"Jamie? I'm more pissed at him than I am at her."

Dodd grinned. "So then I guess the honeymoon is over."

"Screw you," she said, both middle fingers in the air this time. "Jamie is a people pleaser. He'll tell you whatever he thinks you want to hear. He's really good at making promises. But ask me if he delivers."

"I'm gathering he doesn't."

"Not when he has to go through her. He's like an

indentured servant. You heard what he said. *She just hasn't called me back yet.* What man waits for a return phone call when his wife's life is on the line? Why isn't he pounding on Veronica's front door with a baseball bat demanding that she help?"

"Why did you marry him?" Bobby said.

She plopped down on the sofa and gave him the finger yet again, but this time she didn't put any heart into it.

"Come on, Erin," Bobby said, trying to keep it playful. "Everybody knows why you married him. He's rich. No shame in that."

"He's not rich. She is. He may be heir to the throne but as long as she's the queen, all he gets is an allowance." She picked up the *Daily News* and waved it in his face. "Millions of people are praying for me, but not Veronica Gibbs. She's praying that you kill me."

"You know I'm not going to hurt you," Bobby said.

"You say that now. But what happens tomorrow or the next day or the day after that when you finally realize Jamie can't come up with the money?" She put her hands to her face and started to sob.

Bobby leaned over and tried to put his arm around her, but she shrugged him off. "Don't touch me," she said. She stood up and stormed off to her room.

Bobby didn't know what to say. The two of them had had such a great morning. It was like a dream come true. First the sex in the shower, then they got dressed and had breakfast together. She passed on the croissants, but he'd stocked the fridge with yogurt, and even though he'd bought the wrong kind, it couldn't have been that bad, because she ate the whole thing.

Then he made a fresh pot of strong hot coffee, because he could tell she didn't like the stuff he'd brought from the deli. After that they went to the living room, read the papers, and he told her what she could and could not say when they made the phone call.

It all went well until Jamie dropped the bomb and told them that half a day after the proof-of-life video went live, Veronica Gibbs had not lifted a finger to do anything to help her unborn grandchild.

Erin was right. Veronica was a tight-fisted bitch, but Jamie was the real roadblock. He had no balls.

It was a problem Bobby hadn't planned on, and he wasn't sure how to solve it.

He reached inside his shirt, tugged at the chain around his neck, pulled out the .357 Magnum bullet, and closed his eyes.

The answer would come.

CHAPTER 37

SPENDING HALF MY waking life with my ex-girlfriend can be a double-edged sword.

On the upside, I get to be with her, work with her, eat with her, laugh with her, argue with her, and occasionally I get to bail her out of a jam or be a shoulder for her to lean on. It's like being married, only without the sex, the in-laws, or the mortgage.

Kylie had summed it all up yesterday morning: *You're not just my partner, Zach. You're my rock. You're my best friend.*

I *was* her best friend. And she was definitely mine. That was the good part. The downside was that when you're in close quarters with someone for hours on end it's impossible to escape her private life. Even when you're trying hard to avoid it.

I knew Cheryl's cousin Shane would be calling Kylie, and I was hoping it would be when we were off duty or at least when we were in the office, so I could walk out of the room.

No such luck. We were on the Sixty-Fifth Street transverse on our way back to the precinct. Kylie was driving when her phone rang. She checked the caller ID, shrugged, plugged in an earbud, and took the call.

"This is Detective MacDonald. Who's this?" A beat, then: "Oh, Cheryl warned me you might call." She laughed. The "warned me" bit must have gone over well with him. "I didn't recognize the phone number," she said. "Where's area code 832?"

Houston. He just moved from there.

"How do you like New York?" she asked.

I picked up my phone and started scrolling through my e-mails. I hadn't wanted to be around when Shane called, but now that I was a captive audience, the best I could do was shift my body to look like I wasn't interested while my ears homed in on every word.

"No, really, you're not interrupting anything," she said. "My partner and I are just driving back to the office. Oh, right...of course you know him—Zach. He had dinner at your place a few nights ago. He says you're a pretty decent cook."

She looked over at me to see if I'd react to hearing my name, but I was tapping away furiously, a man hell-bent on responding to an e-mail.

The call didn't last more than a few minutes, but I recognized the dance. It was that giddy first-time meet-and-greet before there was any drama, any craziness, any baggage.

I remembered back when I was in Shane's shoes. It was my first day at the academy. I was sizing up the other recruits when the door opened, and Kylie MacDonald breezed in—blond, tan, with the face of an angel and the body of a sinner.

Heads turned. Conversations stopped. Testosterone surged.

"Excuse me while I go introduce myself to my new partner," one guy said, heading straight toward her. Half a dozen others followed. Not me. I decided that this girl knew she was a magnet, and she'd flirt with the herd but wonder about the guy who showed no interest.

It was my first bit of profiling as a wannabe cop, and I was spot-on. A week later she came up to me after class and introduced herself.

And that's where Mr. Shane Talbot was right now—that first conversation, the banter light and playful, the possibilities endless.

Laugh it up, I thought as she cracked up at something he said. *If sparks fly, and their relationship goes somewhere, so be it.* The irony of it all was that I'd be the one who got the credit for suggesting that the two of them should meet.

Kylie hung up the phone and, still smiling, exited the transverse at Fifth Avenue and headed for the precinct a few blocks away.

She didn't look over at me to tell me who'd called.

And I, of course, didn't ask.

CHAPTER 38

DANNY CORCORAN WAS waiting for us back at the station. He looked like he hadn't slept since we'd assigned him to work with Detectives Moss and Devereaux on the phony-ambulance home invasions.

"We could use some good news," Kylie said.

"The governor, the mayor, and the PC all think you're the lead dogs on this investigation," Corcoran said, "and so far they have no idea that you haven't done jackshit."

"Anything else?"

"For one thing, I'm cleaning up on overtime. Also, we might have found a connection between the two cases, but we have nothing solid as of yet."

"Walk us through it."

"The MO is identical for both robberies, so we've been looking for the nexus between them," Corcoran said. "Find a common thread, and we might be able to tie it to the perps.

"We started with the two buildings, one on the East Side, one on the West. Different owners, different management companies, different staff. No connection. Then we looked at who from the outside was getting inside—exterminators, window washers, dog walkers, cable guys—but there's no overlap. In fact, with these two old ladies, not many people gain entry at all. The staff intercepts all deliveries, and they're happy to do it because the families take good care of them, not just at Christmas but all year round."

"How about the nurses?" I asked.

"Same thing," Corcoran said. "They come from two different agencies that aren't connected to each other. Neither woman has worked for the other one's agency, they've never worked together, don't live in the same neighborhood, weren't born in the same country, and don't go to the same church."

"Get to the part where you may have found a connection."

"You know the old saying 'Follow the money'?" Corcoran said. "These private agencies are staffed with people who are trained to vet the nurses, interface with the clients, plus do a whole bunch of other crap related to the day-to-day operation. What the agencies hate doing is medical billing, so most of them farm it out. The accounts for both of our victims are handled by the same company: ZSK Medical Billing on East Seventy-Ninth Street."

"What does ZSK know about Mrs. Lowenthal and Aunt Bunny?" Kylie said.

"I can't answer that just yet, but I can tell you what they know in general. They handle the billing for twenty-six different nursing agencies, so they have records for tens of thousands of clients. They know which ones are covered by insurance, because those companies cover part of the bill and the clients are only responsible for the balance. But in some cases, the clients pay it *all* out of pocket, and let me tell you, those pockets have to be deep. Bunny Ogden's family is shelling out over a quarter of a million dollars a year for nurses, and Mrs. Lowenthal has more medical issues, so her family pays even more."

"You think someone at the billing company is targeting the obviously wealthy victims?" I asked.

"Look, Zach," Danny said, "these guys didn't come racing up to random buildings and ask the doormen who's old, rich, and sick. They knew exactly where to hit, and they made off with a fortune both times. That takes planning. That takes insider information. And right now, ZSK feels like their most likely source."

"How many people work at ZSK?"

"A hundred and forty-three. I got that from the COO, but that's all I'm going to get without a court order. He won't give me a list of the employees' names or tell me which ones have access to the client database unless I get a subpoena. And he definitely won't tell me what information they have on the two victims without written consent from the families that pay the freight."

"It sounds promising," Kylie said. "What about the bogus ambulances?"

"It's probably the same ambulance. None have been reported missing, but it's not hard to get your hands on one that's been retired. We think they dress it up with a new name and a new logo each time they go on a run. We could alert doormen in the city to look out for NYCC Senior Care and Morningside Medical, but they're more likely to just slap on another decal."

"What about alerting the doormen to be suspicious of any ambulance that shows up?" Kylie said.

"Fat chance getting that past zone captain St. Claire. He made it clear that we are forbidden to tip off a single building employee to the possibility that an ambulance that shows up at their door might not be legitimate. Ninety-nine point nine, nine, nine percent of these emergency calls will be real emergencies, and St. Claire said if one doorman stops one paramedic for one minute and that causes one person to die, we can all look for new careers."

"Good job, Danny," I said.

"Ditto," Kylie said. "Thanks."

"I didn't do all the heavy lifting," Corcoran said. "Moss and Devereaux from the Two Oh put in just as many hours."

"Well, tell them we both said—" Kylie stopped and looked up. Cheryl was walking toward us. "Keep us posted," Kylie said. "I've got to run." She left me standing there with Corcoran and hustled down the hall to talk to Cheryl.

"What's going on with those two?" Danny asked.

I shook my head. "You don't want to know."

At this point, neither did I.

CHAPTER 39

DETECTIVE RICH KOPROWSKI pulled up to the hydrant on the corner of Ninety-Second and Park. "This is your *office?*" he said, looking up at the towering red-brick building. "I didn't think any of these Park Avenue co-ops were zoned for commercial."

"They're not," Jamie said, "but it takes more than a zoning law to stop my mother from getting what she wants." He opened the car door. "Thanks for the ride. See you later."

"I'd be more comfortable going up there with you."

"Not a chance. I'm blindsiding my mother, so unless you have a trick for getting her to part with twenty-five million, you can leave. I'll find a ride home."

"*I'm* your ride. Here's my cell number," Koprowski said, handing Jamie his card. "I'll wait right here."

Jamie pocketed the card, marched past the doorman, strode into the elevator, and stared straight ahead as he rode up to the penthouse. He'd squared off with his mother before, and he had a perfect record: It never went well. Ever.

But this time he was no longer a spoiled rich kid pissing away his life and her money on sex, drugs, and defense lawyers. He was a married man. He had a baby on the way. How could she say no to helping her own grandchild?

He stepped into the vestibule and pulled the key card from his wallet. Would it even work? By now she might have deactivated it as punishment for his marrying the woman she called "that gold-digging whore."

He swiped the card and heard the familiar electronic click. He opened the door and spotted her immediately. She was sitting at the table in the glass-walled conference room, flanked by a casting director, a stylist, and a photographer. They were contemplating the relative merits of three male models who were standing at the far end of the room, chests bare and bronzed, abs tight as fists, eyes as vacant as the dark side of the moon.

Jamie swung the door open. "Out! All of you!" Nobody moved. "Now!" Jamie said.

All eyes were on Veronica. Without even looking at her son, she slowly lifted her right hand and flicked it in the air. The casting director jumped up and shooed the models out of the room, and the others followed.

"*This* is what you were so busy with that you couldn't return any of my phone calls?" Jamie said.

"Why bother returning them?" Veronica said. "You wouldn't have liked what I had to say."

"Say it now."

"The kidnapper did you a favor. Good riddance."

"She's pregnant with my child!"

"How do you even know it's your baby? You dodged a bullet, Jamie. And now you want me to pay money to bring back the one person I told you to stay away from?"

"She's my wife. I love her."

"And do you think she married you because she loves you?"

"Trust me, Erin knows my financial situation. She didn't marry me for my money."

"Of course she didn't. She married you for *my* money. I've worked my ass off for thirty years, made a fortune, and someday it will all be yours, and you'll have barely lifted a finger."

"I don't want it all. All I'm asking for is twenty-five million dollars. You can take the rest and build a monument to your empire and your ego."

"Twenty-five million dollars?" Veronica said. "For that trailer trash? Never."

"All my life, Mom, everything I ever wanted, every goal I ever pursued, every dream I ever followed—none of it was ever good enough for you."

"Oh, please, Jamie, save the my-mother-is-a-heartless-bitch-who-never-loved-me sob story for your shrink. And while you're at it, tell him that I didn't get where I am today by negotiating bad business deals."

"What are you talking about?"

"I'm talking about giving some maniac twenty-five million dollars and *hoping* that he won't murder the only person who can possibly identify him after the money is in his bank account. Of course he's going to kill her—and I'm not going to pay him just to prove I was right."

"You're heartless."

"I'm a businesswoman, and in case you've forgotten, you still work for me. The Young Designers Fashion Show is at the Brooklyn Army Terminal tomorrow. I will be in the front row, and I expect you to be sitting next to me." She stood up and left the room.

Jamie lowered himself into a chair. His mouth was dry. His head was pounding. *Of course that maniac is going to kill Erin,* he thought. His mother was right. She was always right. He rested his elbows on the table and buried his face in his hands. He sat there for almost a minute before his phone vibrated in his pocket.

He didn't recognize the number. *The kidnapper? So soon?* His hands were trembling as he answered. "Hello."

"Don't say a word," the man on the other end said. "I know they've tapped your phone."

Jamie knew the caller's voice. "Don't worry," he said. "They can't listen in on the conversation. They can just monitor that I got an incoming—"

"Which part of 'Don't say a word' did you not understand? Forget what the cops tell you. Don't trust them for a minute. They're not on your side. They're just like your mother. They don't want you to pay the ransom. It's the only way you can possibly save Erin, and nobody wants you to do it.

"Nobody except me," the voice said. "I can get you the money. I want you to meet me in the same place where we cracked open that seven-hundred-dollar bottle of Jack Daniel's Monogram. And don't let the cops follow you."

The line went dead.

Jamie stood up and took a deep breath. A hint of a smile formed on his lips. *There was hope.*

CHAPTER 40

JAMIE TOOK THE elevator to the basement and left through the service entrance on Ninety-Second Street. The plan was to get back in an hour or two, reenter through the side door, and exit through the lobby. With any luck, Koprowski would still be waiting for him in front of the building.

NYPD had been babysitting him since Sunday night, and it felt good to be able to make his own decisions without a bunch of helicopter cops telling him what to do and how to do it. He didn't care how much experience they had. They were on a mission to catch a criminal. His only goal was to bring Erin and the baby home safely.

He walked to Madison and flagged a cab. Harris and Anna Brockway lived in Connecticut, but they had a pied-à-terre on West Forty-Eighth. That's where Brock had introduced him to that ridiculously expensive 94-proof bottle of Jack.

The Brockways were not to be trusted. He knew that. Erin knew that. They took good care of her, but only because there was something in it for them.

"I can get you the money," Harris had said.

Maybe you can, Jamie thought. *But what's in it for you?*

The answer became clear as soon as he entered the Brockways' apartment. "Erin's ratings were through the roof last night," Brock said.

"She's a megahit," Anna added. "Mega, mega, mega. And the pregnancy bomb was the capper."

"We want to do more shows," Brock said. "We want you on camera. This thing can be the biggest hit that ZTV ever had."

"This *thing?*" Jamie said. "The *pregnancy bomb?* A madman is deciding whether my wife lives or dies, I don't have any idea how to save her, and all you can talk about is how well this insanity is playing with your television audience?"

"Hey, hey, calm down," Brock said. "We both love Erin."

"She's like a daughter to us," Anna said.

"We called you over here because you're trying to pull together the ransom money, and we have a solution."

"A deal," Anna corrected. "ZTV is willing to pay for more Erin videos."

"You want more *hostage* videos?" Jamie yelled. "One wasn't enough? You think people haven't gotten their fill of watching her suffer?"

"That's the point," Brock said. "The whole god-damn world is emotionally invested in what happens to her next. Do you understand what kind of a magnet that is? Sponsors will pay through the nose to be part of this."

"Now you've gotten to the heart of it!" Jamie said, pounding a fist into the palm of his hand. "It's all about money, isn't it?"

"You're damn straight it's about money!" Brock

yelled. "And instead of shitting all over the idea, you should be thanking us, because you sure as hell aren't going to come up with twenty-five million dollars by groveling to your mother."

The words hit Jamie like a gut punch. He put both hands on the back of a chair to steady himself. "What did you say?"

"You heard me. Your mother didn't show up at the wedding. She's made no bones about the fact that she hates Erin, and she—"

"No! Not that. How did you come up with twenty-five million dollars? That's exactly what the kidnapper is demanding, and the only people who know that number besides me are the kidnapper, my mother, and the cops. Where the hell did you get it from?"

Brockway looked at his wife. Anna folded her arms across her chest and scowled at him.

Jamie pulled the phone from his pocket. "Answer the fucking question or I will have a platoon of cops here in five minutes."

"Erin called me," Anna said.

Jamie sat down. "Erin...called you? When?"

"About an hour ago. I didn't talk to whoever is holding her, but she said he was listening in. She told me how much money he wanted. I couldn't believe it. And then she told me that you'd reached out to Veronica for help, and the bitch hadn't even returned your calls. Is that true?"

Jamie looked down at the floor. He didn't say a word, but Anna Brockway had her answer.

"Erin convinced the kidnapper that there was another way to get the money," she said, "and that would be for me to negotiate a long-term contract with ZTV and ask for twenty-five million in advance.

I said I would try, but I knew there was no way that would happen.

"As soon as I hung up, I talked to Brock. He came up with the idea of a series of specials. The centerpiece of each would be a new video from Erin. We'd inter-cut that with interviews from celebrities, commentary from police experts, a little bit of fan hysteria, and, of course, the anguished husband desperate to rescue his wife and their unborn child."

"It would be appointment television," Brock said. "Plus it's right in Erin's wheelhouse. It's almost like a continuation of every reality show she's ever done."

"Right," Jamie said. "Only instead of shopping for shoes on Rodeo Drive, she'd be chained to a radiator, sobbing her heart out."

"Oh, Jamie, if you think that's all she's going to give us, you don't know Erin Easton," Anna said. "That girl can work an audience as if her life depended on it. And in this case, it does."

"And you'd pay twenty-five million for a few videos like that?" Jamie said, looking at Brock.

"Are you crazy?" Brock said. "That's the all-in price for the series. Twenty-five episodes. A million a pop."

"Twenty-five videos? How are you going to handle the cops? That first video came in unannounced. The next time you'd be in collusion with the kidnapper. Aiding and abetting."

"Oh, so now you're a lawyer?" Brock said. "Listen to me, Jamie. Your mother's not going to save Erin. The cops are not going to save Erin. You're down to your last option. Yes or no?"

Ten minutes later Jamie Gibbs walked out of the building wondering if he'd made the right decision. He looked at his watch. He'd been gone less than an hour. Koprowski would still be parked outside his mother's place.

He stepped to the curb to see if he could spot a cab.

"You need a ride?" a female voice said.

There was a car parked in front of the Brockways' building. He looked in the window. Detective Kylie MacDonald was sitting behind the wheel. Her partner, Detective Jordan, came around the back of the car.

"Sir," he said, opening the rear door. He smiled politely. But he didn't look happy.

CHAPTER 41

IT WAS MY phone, wasn't it?" Jamie said from the back seat. "That's how you found me, right?"

Kylie made a left onto Eighth Avenue and headed uptown. Both of us stared straight ahead, neither of us saying a word.

Of course it was his phone. He knew we'd been monitoring it. He just didn't know how well.

As soon as the call from Brockway came in to Jamie's phone, TARU traced it. Had Brockway used his own cell phone, his number would have come up as one of Jamie's regular callers. But Brockway wanted to go under the radar, so he'd used a burner.

Big mistake. That sent up a giant red flag. An incoming call from a throwaway phone practically screamed *kidnapper*. TARU immediately alerted me, and I called Koprowski, who told me Jamie was visiting his mother.

A minute later TARU called back to say Jamie— or at least his cell phone—was on the move.

Koprowski raced into the building to get eyes on his subject. By then, the elevator operator had taken Jamie to the basement, and he was on the run.

TARU tracked him as easily as air traffic control watches a jumbo jet cross the country. As soon as Jamie stopped moving, Benny Diaz gave us the address on West Forty-Eighth, and by the time Kylie and I got there, we had a printout of every tenant in the building.

The list was alphabetical. We stopped at B. *Brockway, Harris and Anna*.

Kylie waited in the car while I checked with the doorman.

"Yes, Officer," he said. "Mr. Gibbs went upstairs to see Mr. Brockway about five minutes ago. Shall I ring up?"

"Don't ring, and don't say a word to him when he comes down," I said. "I'll take it from here."

Ten minutes later Jamie came down, and I ushered him into the back seat of our car. He had every right to resist, but he didn't. He was scared, confused, and so shocked to see us that he followed orders without a whimper.

Kylie drove north on Central Park West, then turned onto the Eighty-Sixth Street transverse. About halfway to the East Side, she did something very few motorists crossing the park ever do.

She turned into the parking lot of the Central Park Police Precinct and pulled into a space. The lot was filled with cop cars, and uniformed officers were walking in and out of the landmark nineteenth-century station house like extras on a movie set.

Jamie had probably figured we'd drive him back to his apartment or maybe take him into the Nineteenth Precinct to interview him. But this strange place threw him into a tailspin—which was exactly why we'd picked it.

He panicked. "Where are we? What the hell is going on?"

Kylie and I both turned around in our seats, and for the first time since we picked him up, I broke the silence.

"That's precisely what I was going to ask, Jamie. What the hell is going on?"

"Harris Brockway called me. I went to talk to him. Is there anything wrong with that?"

"Everything is wrong with that," Kylie said. "What is Harris Brockway going to do if it turns out you're next on the kidnapper's list?"

He gawked at us. "I don't understand."

"You told the kidnapper that you couldn't afford to pay the ransom and that your mother wasn't responding to your calls to save Erin and the baby. By now he could be thinking, *I kidnapped the wrong person. Veronica hates the daughter-in-law. Maybe I'll do better if I grab the son.*"

"That's insane."

"Everything that has gone down in the past forty-eight hours has been insane," Kylie said. "Have you counted the number of cops who are watching you? Do you think they're all there to monitor your phone calls? You're a target, and our job is to protect you."

"I didn't ask for protection."

"Jamie, this is New York City," I said. "If there's a bomb scare at the bus terminal, we don't wait for a phone call from Penn Station or LaGuardia to ramp up security. From the minute Erin Easton was abducted, everyone connected to her was in danger, and you are at the top of that list. Now, what did Brockway want?"

"Nothing."

"He didn't call you from a burner phone to talk about nothing."

"He wants me to go on TV."

"To what end?"

"I don't know. He's a network guy. I guess he figures people will watch."

"And how will that help Erin?" I said. "In fact, you might say something that pisses the kidnapper off. Don't you think it might backfire?"

"I don't know what to think. Am I under arrest?"

"Absolutely not."

"Then we're done here. Open the door."

"We'll drive you home," Kylie said.

"No! Just let me out."

I got out of the car and opened the rear door.

"Stop fucking protecting me," he said, getting out. "Nobody's going to kidnap me. And if they do, at least I'll get to be with Erin."

Without looking back, he crossed the parking lot and, shoulders slumped, trudged west along the transverse.

He looked like a beaten man—his world turned upside down, his mother abandoning him, the network sharks exploiting him.

Kylie and I were still in his corner. He just didn't know it.

CHAPTER 42

TWO HOURS LATER, after a hot shower and a mani-pedi, Kylie put on a pair of cropped white jeans, a navy off-the-shoulder top, and her favorite Tory Burch wedges. From the back seat of her Uber, she took out her cell phone and flipped the camera into selfie mode. She wasn't taking a picture—she just wanted one last look at herself before she got to the restaurant.

Kylie tried to think of the last time she'd gone on a blind date.

College. *God, I am so out of practice.*

She reminded herself of why she was doing this. For one thing, she was doing her friend Cheryl a favor. Plus Zach, of all people, thought it was a good idea. And hell, it was a free dinner.

The Uber pulled up to the restaurant, and she got out. She recognized the tall red-haired man standing at the front desk from her Google image search, only he'd traded his chef's whites for a blazer, a tattersall shirt, and a tie.

She smiled. "Kylie MacDonald."

He returned the smile and extended a hand. "Shane Talbot. Your table is ready."

He escorted her to a booth in the rear. "What kind of wine would you like?" he asked as they sat down.

"Surprise me," she said.

He held up three fingers. A waiter appeared with a platter of appetizers while another set a loaf of warm fresh-baked bread and a small stone crock of butter on the table. A minute later the sommelier arrived with a chilled bottle of rosé.

The wine was poured, and Shane raised his glass. "To my meddling mother and my complicit cousin, who came up with this brilliant idea."

Kylie touched her glass to his and sipped the wine. "Oh my God. This is…I'm not good at wine words. How about *darn tasty?*"

He laughed. "The guy who sold it to me said it has a crisp palate of strawberry and crunchy apple gorgeously rounded out by light toasty undertones. But I like your description better. It kind of captures our philosophy of locally sourced fresh food, a range of fine but affordable wines, and minimal pretensions."

"*Minimal* pretensions?"

"Yes. That means I will now attempt to give you the grand tour of the seven different appetizers on this platter without once saying, 'La-di-da.'"

His descriptions were funny, and the food was every bit as good as Cheryl and Zach had promised it would be.

"This is about the point where I would normally say, 'Tell me about yourself,'" Shane said as they dug into the appetizers. "But Dr. Cheryl gave me a complete dossier on you, so I already know the answers to most of the traditional first-date questions—where you're from, where you went to school, what you do for a living. So how about you tell me something Cheryl might have left out?"

"Let's see," Kylie said. "Did she tell you my favorite action movie?"

"No."

"How about my favorite Christmas movie?"

"No."

"They're the same movie," Kylie said.

"Really? Which one is it?"

"Back off, pal," Kylie said. "That's a second-date question."

Shane laughed. "Okay, what did Cheryl tell you about me?"

"She gave me a list of culinary schools you went to, all of which I'd heard of, and she told me you were an apprentice to some famous chef in Switzerland, and I was duly impressed even though I'd never heard of the guy."

"That's terrible profiling," he said. "It makes me sound like I've spent my entire life in the kitchen."

"Haven't you?"

"Heck no. When I was twenty-three I didn't see the inside of a kitchen for eight solid months," Shane said.

"Sounds like jail time."

"You think like a cop. No, I hiked the Appalachian Trail—all two thousand one hundred and ninety miles of it—with my friend Pat."

"Pat-rick? Or Pat-ricia?"

"Back off, pal," he said. "That's definitely a second-date question."

Three courses followed the appetizers, each paired with a different wine, and by the time they were finished, Kylie had decided that Shane Talbot was too much fun and too damn sexy to be one-and-done.

The restaurant was bustling, but he never once turned to look at the crowd. She'd been married to Spence for eleven years, and she couldn't remember a single dinner when he'd spent an entire evening completely focused on her.

"I hope you saved room for dessert," Shane said.

"Dessert, singular? I got through seven appetizers because I was starved, but I couldn't possibly handle a heaping platter of multiple desserts."

"Just one, I promise." He twirled his fingers in the air, and a waiter arrived with two bowls and set one in front of each of them.

Kylie looked at it, leaned down and inhaled the sweet aroma, then finally picked up a spoon and tasted it.

"Butterscotch *budino* with salted caramel sauce," she said. "You're not going to believe this, but this is hands-down my favorite dessert."

"No kidding," Shane said, straight-faced.

"You knew that, didn't you?" she said. "But how? It doesn't sound like something Cheryl would put in her dossier."

"You're right. I had to call her up and ask. You like it?"

"Darn tasty," Kylie said, taking another spoonful.

"I'll make you a deal," he said. "You tell me your favorite action movie slash Christmas movie now, and I will tell you a deep dark secret that nobody knows—not Cheryl, not my mother, no one."

"Deal," Kylie said. "*Die Hard*. It's also my favorite Bruce Willis movie, so it's actually a cinematic trifecta. What's your deep dark secret?"

"I had two desserts waiting in the wings," he said. "I signaled for the *budino* because I'm hoping for a second date."

"Your meddling mother and your complicit cousin will take all the credit," she said. "But absolutely."

She took another spoonful of the creamy dessert, and the sugar shot straight to her wine-mellowed brain.

Damn, she thought. *A girl could get used to this.*

CHAPTER 43

IT'S BEEN SAID that if Gerri Gomperts ever closes her diner, she should go work for Internal Affairs. That woman knows more about the private lives of cops than anybody at IAB.

"Would you like to know how your partner's date went last night?" she said as soon as I walked through the door.

"Do I *look* like I want to know?" I asked.

"You *look* like a guy who's trying to act like he doesn't care," she said. "But who are we kidding, Zach? You can't wait for me to tell you."

"Why do I get the feeling that I'm not going to get breakfast until I let you tell me something? How about you just give me the top line. No details."

Gerri turned on a grandmotherly smile. "It went well."

"Great. I'm happy for her."

The smile broadened. "Very, very, *verrrrrry* well."

"I said no details."

"That's not a detail. It barely qualifies as color commentary. I've got more. Are you sure you're not even just a little bit curious?"

"The only thing I'm curious about is how the hell you managed to dig up so much dirt on Kylie's date this early in the morning."

"Cheryl is in a booth in the back. Women talk, Zach. She told me everything she knows."

"She told you or you pumped it out of her?"

"Is there a difference?"

I ordered breakfast and walked to the rear of the diner. I gave Cheryl a morning kiss and plopped down in the booth across from her.

"Kylie and Shane really hit it off."

"So I heard."

"She called early this morning to thank me for fixing them up. I told her she should be thanking you. It was your idea."

I shrugged. It hadn't been my idea, but we'd come too far for me to undo that misconception.

"He asked her out on a second date," Cheryl said.

"I'm sure that's going to make Aunt Janet very happy," I said.

"Speak of the devil," Cheryl said, looking over my shoulder.

I turned around, half expecting to see Shane's mother. But of course it was Kylie.

"Good morning," she said. She sat down next to Cheryl and stared across the table at me. "You've got a future as a matchmaker, partner. Last night was a home run."

I responded with a lame smile, but the baseball reference made me think of my high-school days when *first base, second base, third base,* and *home run* were metaphors for levels of sexual activity. I shook the thought out of my head.

"Tell him the best part—the dessert story," Cheryl said.

I didn't know if I wanted to hear about any of the parts, much less the highlight of the evening. I was thinking about how to exit gracefully when Gerri came to my rescue.

"Your breakfast is ready," she said. "You said to go, right? It's at the register."

"Where are you going?" Kylie said. "Why don't you stay and eat with us?"

Left unsaid: *And hear all about my fabulous night with Shane Talbot.*

I thought about it. The past nine months had been hell for Kylie. Her husband started popping Percocets like gummy bears, then graduated to a full-blown heroin addiction, and finally dropped off the grid completely.

Kylie had put in a lot of hours since Sunday, and she'd looked beat when she left work last night. But this morning she was totally pumped.

"Zach," Gerri said, rolling her eyes at me as if I were missing the fact that she was there to bail me out. "To go or not to go? That is the question."

"Thanks, but on second thought, can you please unwrap it and bring it to the table? I'm going to stick around for a while." Gerri gave me a nod of approval and left without another word.

"So," I said, "tell me the dessert story."

Kylie smiled. She looked happier than I'd seen her in a long time. Glowing, actually.

I sat back and basked in the glow.

CHAPTER 44

WE WERE JUST finishing breakfast when I got a call from Jamie Gibbs.

"I'm tired of sneaking around like some teenage kid breaking curfew," he said. "I've got a crazy schedule today—a morning meeting at the network, lunch with my biggest cosmetics client, then I'm joining my mother at a fashion show in Brooklyn, after which we will be hosting a dinner in a private room at a restaurant on the East Side."

"Thank you for keeping me informed," I said. "It makes it easier on us."

"You don't get it, Detective. I'm not trying to make it easy for you. I'm giving you fair warning to back the hell off. I don't want to be tripping over a bunch of nanny cops, especially when I'm with my mother. Understood?"

Before I could answer, he hung up. I filled Kylie in on what had just transpired, then I called Rich Koprowski and told him to keep the phone tap on Gibbs but to give him a wide berth—even wider if Veronica was around.

"So Jamie is calling the shots now?" Rich said.

"He's laying down the ground rules on how we should be doing our job?"

"Kylie and I don't like it any more than you do," I said, "but he's our main conduit to the kidnapper. If he feels like we've got him under a microscope, we risk alienating him entirely. Give him some space. Some cooperation is better than none at all."

Our day didn't get any better once we were upstairs. Benny Diaz and his crew at TARU had combed the proof-of-life video looking for a clue and listening for a sound that might help us identify where it was recorded, but they'd come up empty. Dodd had been smart enough not to shoot the video with a cell phone, which would have given us GPS tracking coordinates. Instead, he'd shot it with a GoPro camera.

Then we checked in with Bill Harrison at the DA's office. He didn't have any good news either.

"The network lawyers know we're trying to prevent them from airing any more hostage videos," he said, "so they're screaming 'freedom of the press' to anyone who will listen. I might just as well be trying to shut down an NRA convention by telling the court, 'Those guys have got guns, Your Honor.' No judge wants to fly in the face of the Second Amendment. Or, in this case, the First."

And just when we thought our morning couldn't get any worse, it did. It started with a tweet. ZTV had a fresh-from-the-oven-new Erin Easton video, and they turned to social media to drum up an audience.

By ten that morning about thirty cops were gathered around the TV set in our break room and millions of people were tuned in across the country and around the world.

This episode started just like the previous one—the spinning graphic that turned into a newspaper with

ZTV NEWS BULLETIN on the masthead. It spun again and morphed into a picture of Erin, but this time the producers outdid themselves on the headline.

ERIN IN EXILE, it said.

There were a few groans from the cops in the room. But they weren't the jeers of ridicule for an opponent who'd played dirty. They were more like those involuntary sounds of frustration you make when you realize that you've underestimated your adversary, and he's at the top of his game.

The camera cut to the newsroom set, but the anchor desk had been replaced by a sweeping arc of a Lucite table and five chairs. Brockway was on the far left, and he introduced himself and then the other four members of his panel: a psychologist, a forensic accountant, a special agent with the FBI, and, of course, at center stage, looking drawn and tired, Jamie Gibbs.

"You think we gave him too much space?" Kylie asked.

"Short of cuffing him to a radiator pipe, do you think we could have stopped him?" I said.

The digital clock at the bottom of the screen was still keeping track of the time since Erin was abducted. It was now at 2 DAYS / 14 HOURS / 26 MINUTES.

Another five minutes passed while Brockway lied to the world about how ZTV had come to be in possession of the video he was about to show.

"The outcry from Erin's fans was so overwhelming that the kidnapper wanted to assure her supporters that she was safe and unharmed," Brockway said. "He made the latest tape and sent it to ZTV trusting that we would air it, knowing that public opinion and the Constitution of the United States of America were on our side." Brockway left out God, but he took a long pause after "public opinion" and cast his eyes heavenward. Any idiot could fill in the blank.

The video was a little shy of three minutes long. Erin looked as drawn and tired as Jamie. There were no bombshells like the one announcing the pregnancy. She just thanked her fans for their devotion, praised the network for its support, and begged her husband to do everything he could to bring her home.

The raw meat of this episode was the panel. Brockway started out by asking the psychologist what Erin was going through emotionally. The man clearly had no idea, and his answer rang as hollow as a Miss America contestant promising to do all she could to bring about world peace during her reign.

Next, Brockway turned to Sam Dobin, the federal agent, and asked him what hidden clues he saw in Erin's body language or speech patterns. Dobin rehashed a case he'd worked on ten years ago, but he never really came up with a straight answer.

"Agent Dobin," Brockway said, "our viewers are submitting questions on social media, and here's one that has come up often. Why isn't the FBI handling this case?"

It felt as if everyone in the break room collectively leaned forward. "Yeah, asshole," one cop yelled. "Why aren't you bailing us out?"

"Excellent question, Mr. Brockway," the agent said. "And one I'm sure the powers that be in Washington have posed to the director of the Bureau. The simple reason is that, from the outset, the kidnapper has been communicating with the NYPD. We were willing to watch that play out. But when that communication breaks down— and believe me, it will—we'll be stepping in."

"Hopefully," Brockway said, his tone somber, "it won't be too late."

He then turned his attention to Jamie. "I'm assuming there have been ransom demands. Can you tell us how much they're asking for?"

"I can't comment on that," Jamie said.

"Can't comment? Or can't afford?" Brockway said.

Jamie sat back in his chair, looking like he'd been blindsided.

Brockway raised a hand. "Please don't take offense. I'm here to help. There's a lot of public pressure on you to pay whatever the kidnapper asks. Roger Levenson here is a forensic accountant, and we've asked him to do an analysis of the Gibbs family fortune. Roger?"

"There's a lot of false information online," Levenson said. "Websites that know nothing about Mr. Gibbs will claim to reveal his net worth just to generate viewer interest. But I know where to look, and from what I can tell, most of the wealth is held by Jamie's mother, Veronica Gibbs."

"Interesting," Brockway said. "Jamie, have you talked to your mother about paying for Erin's release?"

Jamie looked lost. Whatever he'd been promised would happen, this wasn't it. Each panelist had a glass of water in front of him, and Jamie, stalling for time, took a sip from his. "I don't know...I...if I feel I need help from my mother, I'll ask her."

"Save your breath." It was the psychologist.

"Dr. Goodman," Brockway said. "Strong words. Are you suggesting that just because there's bad blood between Jamie's mother and his new wife, Veronica won't come to the aid of her son's unborn child?"

"No. I'm saying that the only child Veronica Gibbs cares about is her boy Jamie. Erin Easton stole him away from her, and now that Mama's got him back again, why does she need Erin and the baby?"

"Fuck you!" Jamie screamed, and he tossed the entire glass of water in the TV doc's face. Then he lunged at the man, and the two of them went down to the floor. The FBI agent jumped in to try to break it up, the accountant backed away from the table, and the director cut to a close-up of Brockway.

"Heated moments. Trying times," he said. "We'll be right back after these important messages."

They cut to a commercial, but Kylie and I didn't wait for Brockway to come back. We left the room, ran downstairs to the car, and made a beeline for the arrogant bastard's office.

CHAPTER 45

DON'T SAY A word," Kylie said. She flipped on the lights, hit the siren, and barreled through the red on Lexington.

"Why would I say a word?" I responded, buckling my seat belt. "Oh, do you mean because running hot to a nonemergency is a flagrant violation of traffic safety, departmental policy, and common sense?"

"Who's to say this isn't a life-threatening emergency?" she yelled over the high/low wail of the siren. "Clearly that TV asshole is playing fast and loose with Erin's."

"I love your logic. Save it for the inquest after you bowl over a couple of pedestrians."

She slowed down, turned off the siren, hesitated, then killed the flashing lights. "You feel better now, Zach?"

"Much better. And much, much safer."

"That whole bit with the psychologist was a setup," she said. "Brockway baited Jamie, and then the shrink moved in for the kill."

"I'm in violent agreement," I said.

My phone rang. It was Koprowski with an update on Jamie. "Elvis has left the building," he said.

"Just stay with him," I said. "We're on the way to the studio to get our hands on the new video."

"Why bother?" Koprowski said. "I heard on TV that the feds are taking over the case."

"That would be funny if you and I were the only ones who heard it, but I bet everyone at One PP was watching, and none of them are laughing."

It took us fifteen minutes to get to the network headquarters, storm the reception area, and demand to see Harris Brockway.

"He's still on the air," the receptionist said. "But he's expecting you."

"I'll bet he is," Kylie said. "Get him out here. Now."

"Yes, ma'am."

A production assistant escorted us to the green-room, which I've come to learn is almost never painted green. It's just a big cozy lounge with comfortable furniture and plenty of refreshments where guests can relax while they're waiting to go on-air.

"Can I get you anything?" the PA asked.

I waved him off.

"Just water," Kylie said.

He handed her a bottle of Poland Spring and left. Kylie sat down. I paced. We knew better than to talk. The room was wired for sound.

I looked at my watch. I figured Brockway would let us stew for a while, but I was wrong. I looked through the glass wall and saw him approaching quickly, his camera and sound crew behind him. I looked up at the monitor. I was on TV.

"Detective Jordan," Brockway said, bursting into the room. "I'm guessing you saw our exclusive, and you're here to pick up the original of the latest video of *Erin in Exile*. ZTV is always honored to be working side by side with the NYPD."

He turned to Kylie, who was still holding the bottle of water. "Detective MacDonald, I see you've helped yourself to some refreshments. What's the latest on your search for Erin? What can you tell our viewers?"

Kylie set the water down and stood. She's got a hair-trigger temper, but she's not stupid. She was not about to be sucker-punched on national television.

"I can't comment on an ongoing investigation," she said. "But if you turn off the camera, there's something we'd like to share with you."

Brockway turned to his cameraman. "You heard it here, ladies and gentlemen," he said to his audience. "The bond between yours truly and the police continues to get stronger as we work together to find Erin Easton's kidnapper and return her home safely. This concludes our live broadcast. We now return you to our regularly scheduled programming. But don't go far. We'll be back with breaking news as soon as it happens."

He stood there in silence, his smug face filling the screen, until a woman with a headset yelled, "And we're out."

"My office," Brockway said. "It's totally private."

We followed him to a large office suite, entered his inner sanctum, and closed the door.

Brockway's face lit up. He actually believed the three of us were now on the same side. He sat down at his desk, rolled his mouse, and stared at his computer. "Just checking my Twitter feed," he said. "Holy shit—twelve thousand retweets and counting. Are we trending or what?" He leaned forward and clasped his hands in front of him. "So...what can you tell me?"

"Just this," Kylie said. "I have made it my personal mission to put you behind bars for obstruction of justice."

"Christ, lighten up, will you, Detective?" he said, leaning back in his chair. "I'm the press. The press doesn't obstruct. We inform."

"Then your first mistake was not informing us as soon as you got the video from the kidnapper," Kylie said.

"Oh, really?" He opened his desk drawer and removed a Ziploc bag. Inside was a handwritten note. "This came with the video. It says, 'Air this and do not call the cops or she will die.' I did what I had to do to protect a member of our family."

"Bullshit," Kylie said. "You had a responsibility to call us."

"Wrong, missy. My only responsibility is to keep Erin's loyal fans informed. That's why we're doing a two-hour special tonight, and we will continue to report on this vital news story whether you like it or not."

"You're not *reporting*. You grabbed lightning in a bottle, and all you're doing is cashing in on these videos."

"Tell it to the judge, Detective," Brockway said. "Oh, wait...you did, and the judge told you to back off."

CHAPTER 46

DUMBEST DAMN PLACE in the world for a fashion show, Bobby thought as he looked through the scope of his Winchester 70 at the abandoned railroad bed four stories below.

The goddamn Brooklyn Army Terminal. Skinny-ass models parading up and down a runway that was built on a bunch of rotting old train tracks. How the hell is that supposed to sell clothes?

He inched the long gun across the crowd of spectators until the puffy face of Jamie Gibbs filled the crosshairs. He was sitting in the front row, smiling at models as they strolled down the runway.

What are you smiling at, asshole? I've got your wife. Where's the rest of my money?

Three hours ago the network had wired a million dollars to Bobby's offshore account. It was more money than he'd ever had in his life, but it wasn't enough. He needed the whole twenty-five million to support a woman like Erin. The network was willing to pay, but only in installments of a million bucks.

"I'll be damned if I'm going to make twenty-four

more of those videos because you can't come up with the goods," Bobby said to the image of Jamie in his scope. "How dumb do you think I am?"

And then, out of nowhere, Oswald popped into his head.

Well, maybe it didn't come out of nowhere. Bobby was hunkered down in a sniper's nest, and not only was Lee Harvey Oswald the most famous sniper he knew, he was also his father's favorite example of piss-poor planning.

"Oswald was the dumbest Marine that ever was," Bobby's father had told him. "He worked at the Texas School Book Depository. He shoots Kennedy from the sixth floor of where he works, drops the rifle, and leaves the building. How long do you think it takes for them to do a roll call and realize he's the only one missing? And then, does he have an exit plan? No, he runs home, picks up a pistol, and starts walking the streets until a cop stops him. He shoots the cop, then hides in a movie theater until the Dallas PD drags him out and arrests him. Dumb, dumb, dumb."

Whenever the subject came up, there was never any discussion about what had possessed an honorably discharged U.S. Marine to shoot and kill the commander in chief. His father always seemed to obsess over how incompetent Oswald was.

Bobby wouldn't make any of the same mistakes. Getting into the sprawling former military complex had been easy. He blended in with the swarm of journalists, photographers, and invited guests as they entered the venue. His rifle was in a tripod bag, and when others headed for the atrium to gawk at the runway, Bobby made his way across a skywalk to a secluded parapet on the fourth floor of Building B.

The plan was to take his shot and be gone before

anyone knew what had happened. All he needed was the right soundtrack.

The show had kicked off with "Eye of the Tiger." Corny, but the crowd didn't seem to mind. Then came Elton John belting out "The Bitch Is Back," followed by Springsteen singing "Born to Run." Good one, but not good enough.

Two more tracks. *Not yet,* he told himself. *Not yet.*

And then he heard it—the opening notes to his father's favorite AC/DC song, "Highway to Hell."

Karma, he thought.

He repositioned himself, laid his cheek on the stock, and looked through the scope.

And then came the thrum, thrum, thrum of the guitars and the driving beat of the drums as the music kicked into high gear.

Bam. Boom. Boom. Boom.

The sound was pulsing, echoing through the canyon below.

Bam. Boom. Boom. Boom.

He squeezed the trigger.

Bam. Boom. Boom. Boom.

It was deafening as the crowd picked up the energy and added to the chaos.

Bam. Boom. Boom. Bang.

Perfect shot.

He didn't watch Jamie drop to the floor.

He packed up the rifle quickly, and with the models still strutting down the runway and the crowd still keeping time to the music, he made his way downstairs to the parking lot and headed home to the woman he loved.

CHAPTER 47

ADA BILL HARRISON had spent the morning tied up in court, so by the time we got a face-to-face with him it was midafternoon. At that point Kylie was fed up with the justice system, and of course, she did nothing to keep it a secret.

"They're not just airing these videos, Bill," she said, pointing a finger at Harrison. "They're tampering with evidence."

"And you can prove that, Detective?" Harrison said.

"Oh, give me a break. They got an envelope from the kidnapper. I'll give them the benefit of the doubt and say that they opened it in good faith. But once they knew what was on that flash drive, they passed it up the food chain. If there were any prints or traceable DNA on that drive, they're gone. That's tampering. Not to mention that they didn't call us the minute they got it. Zach and I didn't see the video till we tuned in with the rest of the world. And you're telling me you can't stop them?"

"I talked with Mick Wilson," Harrison said. "He's sympathetic to the issue."

"But?"

"But he's the district attorney, not the Gestapo. ZTV is standing behind the First Amendment."

"You mean *hiding* behind it. They're a reality-TV network. They don't care about freedom of the press. Their stock-in-trade is exploiting the human condition. Surely you can find a judge who isn't afraid to come down on them for that."

"I watched a video of the show when I got back to my office. You're right. ZTV is milking this kidnapping for all it's worth. But I also saw the note that came with the video. 'Air this and do not call the cops or she will die.' That's the bigger issue. I have no problem finding a judge who is willing to tangle with the media. But finding one who is willing to silence the network and take the fall if Erin is murdered is impossible."

"Thanks for nothing."

"Hey, I haven't exactly been doing nothing," Harrison said. "So don't take it out on me because Brockway is making the police department look bad. I saw that FBI agent he put on camera. I'm sure that crack about the feds stepping in and taking over is going to reverb throughout One PP."

"Well, at least Agent Dobin fired a warning shot," Kylie said.

"What is that supposed to mean?" Harrison said.

"It means that a friend of mine works for the Southern District, and she told me that the U.S. attorney would love nothing more than to sink his teeth into a high-profile case of a kidnapped actress and a multimillionaire mother-in-law who won't lift a finger to help her."

"You're telling me that the U.S. attorney thinks he can step in and take this case?"

"He didn't go on national TV and announce it

like that idiot from the FBI, but he's talking about it behind closed doors."

"Son of a bitch," Harrison said.

My cell phone rang. It was Rich Koprowski.

"I need you and MacDonald at the Brooklyn Army Terminal forthwith," he said.

"What's going on?" I said, hitting the speaker button.

"We tailed Jamie to a fashion show at the Brooklyn Army Terminal. There was a shooting. A sniper killed Veronica Gibbs. ESU is searching the venue for the shooter, but so far we've got nothing."

"What about Jamie?"

"He's okay. Nobody heard the gunshot, but he was sitting right next to her when she dropped like a stone. He went to help her up, but she was already dead."

"We're on the way," I said and hung up.

Koprowski had used the word *forthwith*, which is cop-speak for "immediately, without delay." But Kylie wasn't quite ready to leave. She turned on Harrison.

"This morning ZTV broadcast a show to millions making Veronica Gibbs the heavy—the person who wouldn't cough up the money to save her daughter-in-law and her unborn grandchild. Somebody saw that show and decided things would work out better if Jamie inherited the money in a hurry, so that person killed her."

"You don't know that for a fact," Harrison said.

"Here's what I do know, and you can pass it on to Mick Wilson," Kylie said. "Harris Brockway and ZTV may not have Erin's blood on their hands, but they sure as hell have Veronica's."

CHAPTER 48

SINCE WHEN DO you have a *friend* who works at the U.S. Attorney's Office?" I said to Kylie as we merged onto the Brooklyn Bridge.

"*Imaginary* friend. I was trying to light a fire under Bill. I guarantee he went straight to his boss's office and warned Mick Wilson that the feds are threatening to take over the case. The first thing Wilson will want to do is reassure his millionaire donors that if they ever get kidnapped, he'll do the right thing by them. He's probably on the phone right now trying to find a judge willing to come down hard on ZTV." She grinned. "Win-win."

"In what universe is flat-out lying to the district attorney a win?"

"Come on, Zach. It's more like I was fertilizing the seed that the FBI guy already planted."

"Fertilizing the seed sounds a lot like shoveling shit to me."

We got to the Brooklyn Army Terminal in twenty minutes. Rich Koprowski was waiting for us.

"No sign of the shooter," he said. "We looked at the security videos. It's an old system, basically useless. CSU pinpointed where the shot came from. It was a fourth-floor balcony. We found a single two-twenty-three shell. Veronica has a single bullet hole through her forehead. It's over two hundred yards. The shooter was a pro."

And Dodd was a marksman in the Marines. I exchanged a look with Kylie. I was sure she was thinking the same thing.

"Any witnesses?" I asked.

"We have the whole show on video, but all eyes were on the girls. One of Veronica's models saw her go down. But she said people pass out at these extravaganzas all the time—drugs, alcohol, anorexia, strobe lights—so she just kept walking, didn't break stride once. The music was blasting, so nobody heard the shot, and it was so chaotic you couldn't even hear Jamie yelling for help. By the time we figured out we had a murder on our hands, the shooter was probably driving home on the BQE."

"We should talk to Jamie," Kylie said. "Where is he?"

"There are some trailers in the parking lot where the models did their hair and changed clothes. Brooklyn Homicide is talking to him in one of those."

He led us to the trailer and asked the two Brooklyn cops inside to step out. We didn't have to identify ourselves. They knew who we were.

"You caught the Easton kidnapping," the older one said.

"You guys might have caught a piece of it yourselves," I said. "Our kidnapper may be your shooter."

We filled them in on everything. They didn't bat an eye until we told them we'd ID'd Bobby Dodd within hours of the abduction.

"Holy shit," the younger one said. "I'm amazed that never leaked to the media."

"We kept a tight lid on it. If he'd known we were looking for him, he might have panicked and cut off all communication. But this shooting changes everything. As soon as we clear it with our boss, we'll release Dodd's name and picture to the press."

"Starting with every single network that competes with ZTV," Kylie said.

"And you think Dodd is our shooter?" the older one said.

"He has the motive, and he certainly has the talent," I said.

We traded phone numbers and agreed to stay in touch. Then Kylie and I went inside the trailer. Jamie was sitting in a makeup chair staring at himself in the mirror. "We're sorry for your loss," I said. "Can you tell us what you saw?"

"You know how people always say, 'It happened so fast'? It really did. I was sitting right next to her. She was enjoying the show, and then all of a sudden she jerked back and fell from her chair to the floor. I bent down to help her, and that's when I saw the blood. She was already dead."

"I have to ask, Jamie," I said. "I know you hated being cooped up with a bunch of cops watching you, but why did you come here?"

"This is one of the biggest shows of the season. Mom wanted me here. I figured it was just some more time I would have with her to try to convince her to give me the twenty-five million. She had a good heart, but people didn't understand her. You know how many death threats she got on Twitter from Erin's crazy fans because she wouldn't pay the ransom money? And now one of those bastards actually killed her, thinking I'd get her money."

"What makes you think it was a fan of Erin's?" I asked.

He shook his head. "I don't know. Do you think it was the kidnapper?"

"It turns out the kidnapper is a fan. Have you ever heard of a man named Bobby Dodd?"

"Dodd? He's not a fan. He's a stalker. Is he the one who took Erin?"

"We're pretty convinced he is."

"How long have you known it was him?"

"We've known for a while, but it's not the kind of information we can share with the public."

"I'm not the public. I'm her husband. Why couldn't you have told me?"

"Jamie, you spoke to him on the phone. We couldn't take a chance on you blurting out his name. He might have killed Erin on the spot."

Jamie thought about it. The look on his face made me think our explanation actually made sense to him.

"Well, the next time I talk to Mr. Dodd, I'm going to let him know that he's a total idiot. When my mother was alive, I might have had a chance to change her mind and convince her to give me the money, but now that she's dead, her estate will be tied up for years before I ever see a dime."

"Is there anything else you can think of that might help us?" I asked.

"Just that I never should have gone into cahoots with the network. They said they were going to help me, but all they did was vilify my mother on national TV. Dodd might have killed my mother, but Harris Brockway painted a target on her head. It's his fault that she was murdered."

I gave him an understanding nod, but I wondered

if Kylie and I shared some of the blame. Would the security guards who were scanning the crowd at the Brooklyn Army Terminal have spotted Dodd if we had released his identity?

I shook the thought out of my head. If there's one thing I've learned over the years, it's never to second-guess your decisions. I wasn't about to start now.

CHAPTER 49

HONEY, I'M HOME," Bobby called out as he came through the front door. A wide smile crossed his face. She couldn't hear him, of course. She was locked in a soundproof room. But one day, he thought, one day, this is the way it would be.

The travel websites had painted the picture of white sands, golden skies, and turquoise water. Bobby could picture the rest: Erin, wearing something sexy, greets him at the door when he comes home from an afternoon on his fishing boat. The baby, playing on the floor, reaches up to him, and she gurgles and giggles as he lifts her high in the air. A glass of chilled white wine. The heady smell of bread baking in the oven.

Soon, he thought. *Soon.*

He unlocked her door. "I have good news," he said. She sat up in bed.

"I just solved our problems," he said, sitting down on the bed beside her. "Mama's money is now Jamie's money. All of it. Every penny."

"What are you talking about?"

"Veronica is dead."

She threw her legs off the side of the bed and stood. "How did she—oh God, no! You killed her. Did you? Did you kill her?"

Bobby stared at her, confused. "I thought that's what you wanted."

"You thought I wanted you to commit murder? Are you insane?"

"But she was evil. You hated her."

"I hated how she treated me. I hated that she wouldn't help Jamie pay the ransom. But who in their right mind kills someone just because you don't like them?"

She buried her face in her hands and began to sob. "Why would you do this to Jamie? She was his *mother*. He never understood her, but he loved her."

"I'm sorry," Bobby said, kissing the top of her shoulders.

"Get away from me. You're disgusting." She pulled away hard and ran into the bathroom.

There was no door, and he watched as she tore off her clothes and flung them to the floor. She turned on the shower and stepped inside.

They all get crazy, his father had taught him. *Your job is to do whatever it takes to make them happy again.*

Bobby stood there watching the steam fill up the bathroom. The hot water would calm her down. Plus he knew how to make her feel good. Real good.

He peeled off his clothes and stepped into the shower. She didn't say a word. He took the soap and washed her back. Then he lathered up his hands and ran them over her breasts. Her nipples responded, and she arched her back and moaned.

"Turn around," she said. "Let me do you."

He turned, and she ran her nails up and down his back.

He was rock hard. She reached down between his legs, and he thrust himself into her soft, slippery palm and gyrated his hips as she licked his ear.

"Oh, Bobby," she said, her hand expertly sliding up and down the length of his shaft. "I love you. I love you so much."

The words exploded in his ears. He couldn't hold back. He spasmed once, twice, again, and then she felt his body go limp.

"Feel the water on your skin," she said, tipping his face up and massaging his scalp. "Let it relax you."

He let out a long slow moan. Without warning, she clutched a fistful of his hair, snapped his head back, and, in one swift stroke, raked the blade she held across his neck. Just like Ari had taught her fifteen years before.

His fingers clutched at his throat, but all he could feel was the flap of severed skin and the warm blood. He threw himself backward, bringing them both down hard on the tile floor, her body beneath his.

Bobby Dodd was a combat-trained Marine. He knew what she had done. He knew he was about to die. What he didn't understand was why.

Air bubbled through the blood that was spilling from his neck as he exhaled. He gasped and tried desperately to inhale, which only caused him to choke.

Forty-seven seconds after Erin Easton drew the makeshift blade across her captor's neck, he died.

She crawled out from under his body and slowly stood, the water still beating down hard. Then she stumbled from the shower, threw on a pair of shorts and a sweatshirt, and ran out the front door to freedom.

PART THREE

THE BOBBY DIARIES

CHAPTER 50

SNIPER SHOOTS FASHION Mogul" was more than just a local headline. It was breaking news from Paris to Milan to Tokyo. And with the eyes and ears of the world focused on its biggest case in years, Brooklyn Homicide pulled out all the stops.

By the time Kylie and I finished talking to Jamie, the terminal was packed with detectives, patrol, ESU, CSU, EMS, and whatever other letters of the alphabet Brooklyn could throw at the case. They certainly didn't need us. But we couldn't leave.

Our bosses in Manhattan would be asking who, what, when, where, and why. And despite the fact that they had all signed off on our strategy not to release Bobby Dodd's identity across the department, every one of them would be demanding to know how the hell the most wanted man in the city could get past a detail of twelve tactically trained police officers who were assigned to secure an event that Erin Easton's husband was attending.

They'd bombard us with questions, and we couldn't exactly respond by saying, *We'll call Brooklyn and see if they know.* So we stuck around for a few more hours and gathered our own data.

Jamie didn't leave either. "My mother would never want me to abandon her at a time like this," he said. "I'm not going anywhere until her body is removed from the area."

He said it reverentially, as if he expected two attendants in black suits to carefully place Veronica on a gurney and silently wheel her into the back of a white-curtained hearse. But the reality was that this was a crime scene, and when the techs were finished, someone was likely to yell, *Bag her and throw her in the meat wagon.*

I gave the medical examiner's team a heads-up that the next of kin was watching their every move and to keep it toned down. Just to be sure, Kylie and I decided to wait with Jamie.

So, as luck would have it, we were standing at his side when the phone call came.

He stiffened, looked at the caller ID, and shook his head. "I don't recognize the number. Area code 713," he said.

"Houston, Texas," I said. "Put it on speaker when you pick up. TARU will be on the other end tracking it. Keep him on as long as you can, and whatever you do, don't call him by name."

He hit the green button, and his entire life changed. "Jamie...it's me."

"Erin, baby, I love you. Are you okay?"

"I...I..." And then she wailed, "Oh God, Jamie."

"Is he hurting you?"

"No, no. Not anymore. I...I made a razor blade. He followed me into the shower, and I...oh God...I cut his throat. He fell down bleeding, and..."

"And what, baby, what?"

"I escaped." With that, the dam broke. She began sobbing hysterically.

A man's voice came on the phone. "Hello. Hello."

"Who's this?" Jamie demanded.

"Hello. My name is Hector Gonzalez. My wife and I see this woman on the road, and she's waving hands, and she say, 'Help, help,' so we stop, and we help."

"Is she hurt? Is she okay?"

"She's crying very much, but I think she's crying happy now that we find her. We are waiting for police."

Kylie grabbed Jamie's arm. "Where are you?" she yelled into the phone.

The man turned away from the phone and yelled something in Spanish. A woman, probably his wife, responded, "¿Quién es?"

That I understood. But in case I hadn't, he asked again, in English, "Who is this, please?"

"Detective Kylie MacDonald. I'm with the New York City Police Department. Where are you now?"

"Es la policía," he informed his wife. "Apple farm," he said to Kylie.

"What apple farm? Where? Texas?"

"No, no. New York." His accent was so thick it came out "Noo Jork."

And then we heard the sirens in the background.

"I no speak such good English," Gonzalez said. "You a police. You talk to other police."

The sirens got closer and then died away. We could hear voices as cops came on the scene.

And then my phone rang. Benny Diaz from TARU.

"Zach, the phone belongs to Hector Gonzalez, Galena Park, Texas. The call is coming from Ball Road in Warwick, New York."

I thanked him, then called Captain Cates and told her

what was happening. With cops on the scene, anyone with a scanner would know that Erin Easton was alive and safe. The word would go out on Twitter within seconds. I had to make sure my boss called her boss with the news, rather than the other way around.

For the next five minutes all Kylie and I could do was listen to the background commotion of first responders coming onto a crime scene and trying to put the pieces together in a hurry. We knew the drill. Victim first.

We waited until Jamie's phone came alive again. "Hello, this is Officer Georgene Fredericks, Warwick PD. Who is this?"

"This is Detective Kylie MacDonald, NYPD. My partner and I—"

Jamie wrenched the phone away. "This is Jamie Gibbs. Do you see my wife, Erin Easton? Is she okay?"

"Yes, sir. I recognized her. She's in shock right now, but she's okay. We have her in custody. We'll be taking her to the hospital. Please put the detective back on the phone."

Jamie handed his cell back to Kylie. "Officer Fredericks, Ms. Easton was abducted by a white male named Bobby Dodd. I can text you a photo with his pedigree. In the few seconds that we had Ms. Easton on the phone, she said she cut his throat before she escaped. I have no idea where she was being held or how badly she hurt him."

The Warwick cop's answer was quick and confident. "We'll find him."

"Officer, be advised that we're also looking at Dodd for the murder of Ms. Easton's mother-in-law. He's ex-military, combat-trained, and incredibly dangerous. Please be careful."

"Don't you worry, Detective," Fredericks said. "We're on it." Her voice was eager. Too eager. I could picture a bunch of country cops champing at the bit to get on with the biggest adventure of their careers.

Kylie caught it too. "My partner and I will be in Warwick in thirty minutes," she said.

"Thirty? Where are you now?"

"Brooklyn."

"You're a good two hours away, Detective. More like two and a half with rush-hour traffic."

"Don't *you* worry, Officer. We won't be sitting in traffic."

CHAPTER 51

YOU HAVE A helicopter?" Jamie said as soon as Kylie hung up.

Kylie nodded, knowing what was coming.

"I'm going with you," he announced.

By all rights we should have said yes. The man was a victim; his wife had been abducted, his mother murdered, and his life turned into a living nightmare. But the last thing we needed when we were trying to interview Erin Easton was her loose cannon of a husband getting in our way.

"That's not a good idea, Jamie," Kylie said.

"Why not?"

"Because first and foremost, Erin needs medical attention. If you get there before the doctors are finished, you'll either distract them from the job at hand or you'll wind up pacing the hospital waiting room for two hours. You just told us your mother wouldn't want you to abandon her at a time like this. Don't leave her alone. When you're done here, Detective Koprowski will drive you to Warwick."

Jamie nodded. Once again Kylie's cop logic made sense to him. It also worked for us. We'd have Erin for a few hours without interruption, and Koprowski could drive us back to New York.

The chopper set down in the parking lot of the vast complex, and we were picked up by none other than the chief of detectives himself, Harlan Doyle. No surprise. Our mission was to work the case. His was to work the media.

We landed at the Hickory Hill Golf Course and were greeted by Patrick Brown, the Warwick chief of police.

Our chief of Ds is not big on foreplay. "Where's Easton?" Doyle asked, skipping the introductions.

"St. Anthony Community Hospital," Brown said. "Two guards at her door, four more covering the entrances and exits."

"And the perp?"

A small smile crossed Brown's face, and he took a deep breath. I doubt if he realized he was puffing out his chest, but I knew he was feeling good about the news he was about to drop.

"We were able to determine where she was held, a house on Ball Road, not far from where she was found. The front door was wide open. We did a tactical entry, and we found one white male, naked, deceased on the shower floor. His throat was slashed from the right ear to the left jugular. The ME wasn't on the scene, but the paramedic from the volunteer ambulance corps said he must've bled out. I didn't see much blood, but then the shower was still on, so I figure most of it went down the drain."

"ID?"

"We found a wallet in his jacket pocket. Tennessee license issued to Robert Allen Dodd. Photo matched the dead guy, but I figured you might want to see for yourself, so I took a quick pic of the body."

He handed Doyle his cell phone. The chief took a look and passed it over to Kylie and me.

"That's the man we're looking for," I said. "Brooklyn Homicide is looking for him too. Great work, Chief Brown."

The chief of Ds picked up on my lead. "Absolutely. Top-notch. I think I have all I need to deal with the press."

"There's a slew of them gathering at the hospital," Brown said. "I'll have one of my officers drive you."

"Excellent. I'd like you personally to take my two lead detectives to meet with the victim. NYPD will be sending a crime scene unit to go over every inch of the house where she was held. Until then, secure it and leave the body where it dropped until they get there."

And with that, Harlan Doyle was done. Wham-bam. He headed toward a waiting cop car.

"Wow," Brown said as he watched him walk away. "I can see why he's in charge."

Kylie and I followed Brown to his radio car. She got in front; I sat in back. Chief Brown drove. He was in his midforties, born and raised in Warwick, and clearly taken by the big-city cops that had descended on his quiet little community.

"Who owns the house where Erin was held captive?" Kylie asked.

"Blanche and Stanley Katz. Nice folks—I'm guessing they're in their midfifties. They moved up here from the city about ten years ago. They write these books that nobody reads. Something about art history. They're working on another one, and they're hopping around Europe for a year, so they rented the house out. They've done it before. They left their itinerary with us at the station in case of emergency. I guess I better contact them."

"Please don't," Kylie said. "Not until we're sure they're not involved."

Chief Brown looked at her. "Involved? Them? Hell no."

"I'm sure you're right," Kylie said, "but until we are one hundred percent sure that there is no other connection between them and Dodd besides unsuspecting landlord and homicidal tenant, we're not giving them a heads-up."

"Son of a gun," he said. "You're right. I never would've thought of that. I guess I could learn a lot about police work from you folks. If you ever want to come up to Warwick and teach a class to the troops one of these nights, I'll buy the pizza."

"That just may be the best offer we've had all day," Kylie said and flashed him a warm smile.

Brown returned the smile and held on to it as he turned his face back toward the road and drove to the hospital. Clearly he was in awe, and I'd bet anything that this was the single biggest day of his career.

For us, it was just another Wednesday.

CHAPTER 52

LESS THAN AN hour after Erin's escape, St. Anthony Community Hospital was surrounded by TV trucks, fervent fans, and local lookie-loos.

The state police and the volunteer fire department were out in force, redirecting traffic and doing their best to clear the roadways. Chief Brown detoured off the main drag, navigated onto a side street, and dropped us off at the emergency room entrance in the rear of the building.

We met with Sarah Paris, the doctor heading up Erin's medical team. Dr. Paris turned out to be a straight talker and a good listener whose only concern was her patient's well-being, not her celebrity status.

Small-town docs can be put off by the in-your-face directness of big-city cops, so I eased into the interview. "Dr. Paris, we're familiar with the HIPAA regulations about patient privacy, but this is a criminal investigation, and—"

The doc held up her hand. "I did my residency at Lincoln Hospital in the Bronx. It had the busiest ED in the entire city—shootings, stabbings, gang violence.

There were some nights I talked to more cops than patients. Ask anything."

"For starters, how is she?" I said.

"Physically she's okay. A few cuts and bruises, nothing major. She's also fourteen weeks along in her pregnancy, and the baby is fine. The real damage is psychological. Beyond the ordeal of being abducted, she was raped repeatedly."

"You know that for a fact?"

"I know that because she told me several times, and I believed her. We have an ob-gyn on the way to the hospital, and of course we used a rape kit to gather the physical evidence. But even more traumatizing than her captivity was her escape. She said she managed to get away by luring her abductor into the shower, then slitting his throat. She's in fear that all she did was wound him, and despite the fact that there are two policemen outside her door, she's deathly afraid that he will come for her."

"He won't," Kylie said. "He can't. He's dead."

"That's good news and bad news at the same time. I'm sure she'll be relieved, but knowing she killed another human being will undoubtedly add to the PTSD. She's going to need a lot of therapy."

"Can we see her now?" I said.

"See her? Yes. Interrogate her? No. I'll give you five minutes, ten max. I'm admitting her for a day or two. If you're going to make her relive what she's been through, at least let her get some rest first."

She escorted us to a corner room on the top floor. Erin was lying in bed, tubes coming out of her arms, a bank of glowing screens monitoring her vital signs. Her face was pale and blotchy, her eyes vacant, her hair still damp from her life-changing shower with Bobby Dodd.

Kylie took the lead. "I'm Detective Kylie Mac-Donald. This is my partner, Detective Zach Jordan. We've been looking all over for you. Nice to finally meet you."

Erin managed a half smile. "I know your names. He told me who you were. He talked to you on the phone." She didn't have to tell us who *he* was. "And I recognize you," she said to Kylie. "You were at my wedding. Blue dress. Am I right?" She didn't wait for an answer. "Did you catch him? He's insane. You have to catch him."

"We didn't have to catch him. He was found dead on the shower floor. He can never, ever hurt you again."

I could see the relief spread across her face. "Is it true? About Veronica? When he came back this afternoon, he told me…" She started sobbing. "I'm sorry."

"I'm afraid that Veronica Gibbs was shot," Kylie said. "She died instantly."

"Oh, poor Jamie. Where is he? I can't wait to be with him."

"And he can't wait to be with you. He's on his way. Police escort, so he'll be here soon. But first we'd like to ask you a few questions. We won't take long. Are you up to it?"

She shrugged. "Sure."

"Do you mind if we sit down?" I asked. It was a simple request, basically unnecessary, but when you're dealing with people who have been stripped of all their power, you give them back as much control as you possibly can.

"Please," she said. "Sit."

We sat.

"Let me just start by saying that we are in awe of

your strength," Kylie said. "You're a fighter, and you came out a winner."

"I was trained. Ari was an Israeli commando. My father hired him just in case something like this ever happened. I told my dad it was stupid, but Ari was so cute and sexy I didn't want him to leave." She looked up at the ceiling and waved. "Thanks, Daddy."

"You can thank Ari too," I said. "He taught you well."

"One night, years ago, he brought me into a room and said, 'You've been kidnapped. The bad guys will be back in an hour, and they're going to kill you. You better have a weapon when they get here. Find one.' Then he locked the door. I think I spent most of the time crying because there were no weapons in that room. He came back an hour later and showed me how to make five."

"Amazing," Kylie said. "Where did you find the blade?"

"It took me a while to figure it out. Nothing in the room looked lethal. Nothing. And then that first night he came in, he wanted sex. I never tried to fight him off. I knew better. I just lay there on the bed, breathing hard, and pretending I was enjoying it. My eyes were always closed. I couldn't look at him but I could hear him moaning and groaning and telling me he loved me. I tried to tune him out until all I could hear was the sound of the bedsprings creaking, creaking, creaking. And all of a sudden, I knew the answer.

"I waited for him to leave and lock me up for the night. I pulled the mattress off the bed. It was one of those old-fashioned kinds where the springs are held together by metal straps. It took me hours to pry one of the springs off. Then every time I knew he was out of the house, I honed it against a metal pipe that was under the sink in the bathroom until it was razor-sharp. I never wanted to…to do what I did, but when he told me he killed Veronica, I knew he wouldn't stop. If he didn't get what he wanted, I was next."

The door opened, and Dr. Paris came in. "Time's up, Detectives," she said. "Excuse us."

She drew the privacy curtain around the bed and asked us to step out of the room. We stood in the doorway. A few minutes later she pulled the curtain back, and we stepped back in.

"She needs to rest," the doc said. "She should be released by Friday. Why don't you pick it up with her then?"

"Just one more question," I said. "Please."

"*One* more? Sure. Go ahead."

"Erin, did he have any accomplices?" I asked.

"He's the only one I ever saw. The only one I ever heard. The room was soundproofed. If he had a partner, I never saw him or heard him. But I don't think so. I mean, why would he?"

"What do you mean?" I said, asking another question.

"He thought we'd have this life together. He was never going to let me go." She laid her head back on the pillow and closed her eyes. "He thought he'd get the money." Her speech was fuzzy, slurred. "We'd leave the country and…" She let out a long sigh.

"And what?"

"We'd live…hap…" She fought to stay awake. "Hap'ly…"

And then she was out like a light.

"Happily ever after," Dr. Paris said. "I think that's what she was going for."

"You gave her something to knock her out, didn't you?" I said.

"I'd have given her an Ambien if I could have," Dr. Paris said. "But she's pregnant. The only thing I did when I went behind that curtain was hold her hand and tell her that she was safe and that the man who had turned her life into a living hell was dead and gone forever. I told her that she was brave, that now it was time to let us take care of her, and that her baby needed her to sleep more than the police needed her to stay awake. Sorry, Detectives, but this woman is mentally and physically exhausted, and she needs to recover before she can be subjected to a police interrogation."

The doc was right. We had a lot of unanswered questions, but the answers would have to wait.

CHAPTER 53

LIKE MANY COMBAT-TRAINED Marines, Bobby Dodd had known how to hide in plain sight. The white clapboard two-story farmhouse with the wraparound porch sat at the end of a seven-hundred-foot driveway and was practically invisible to anyone driving or walking along Ball Road. It was just far enough off the beaten path to be ignored, yet it was only a short drive from the heart of Warwick. He could have holed up there for months.

By the time Kylie and I arrived, the place was crawling with law enforcement—local, state, and the NYPD Crime Scene Unit. Chief Brown parked on the road, and the three of us walked to the garage, where a crime scene tech was collecting evidence from an aging Volvo wagon.

"That's Mrs. Katz's car," Brown said. "In case you were wondering how your perp got around, the engine was warm when the first responders arrived."

Chuck Dryden, our go-to criminalist, stepped out of the house and greeted us. "Detectives," he said, more chipper than usual, "I must admit I've never truly understood Ms. Easton's appeal as a so-called entertainer, but she certainly makes one hell of a ninja. Her abductor, Robert Dodd, was six foot three and over two hundred pounds, most of it muscle. She's half a foot shorter and about sixty pounds lighter, and yet she shanked him in the shower like a hard-core lifer at Attica."

"We heard," Kylie said. "She told us she Mac-Gyvered the weapon out of a bedspring."

"Aha," Dryden said. "You saved me some time. I haven't been here long enough to figure that out."

"Show us what you've got so far," I said.

"From the outside, the house looks normal," Dryden said. "The curtains are drawn and the shades are down, and if anyone rang the bell and Dodd opened the front door, all they'd see is a cozy little farmhouse living room. What they wouldn't see is the prison cell he fashioned for her."

He led us down the hallway past several polished-pine doors until we got to the bedroom farthest from the front of the house.

"This was reserved for the guest of honor," he said, opening a metal fire door.

We went inside. The walls, windows, and ceiling were covered with twelve-by-twelve acoustic foam soundproofing panels. "The odds were slim to none that anyone would even get close to this room, but if someone did, Erin wouldn't have heard anything, and no one would have heard her.

"After the first 911 call, the house was tactically swept by the locals. They found the body. White male, supine in the shower, water still running, naked except for a bullet on a chain that he wore around his neck, his jugular severed."

Kylie and I stepped into the bathroom where Bobby Dodd was still lying where he had taken his final breath. We didn't stay with him long. Like Erin, all we cared about was that he was dead.

We went back to Erin's bedroom.

"Look at this crap," Kylie said, poking through the box of bargain-basement clothes that had been Erin's wardrobe. "It makes you wonder."

"About what?" Dryden said.

"It looks like whoever bought these clothes had absolutely no idea how to shop for the woman who would be wearing them," Kylie said.

"Most men," Chief Brown said, "that ain't exactly their strong suit."

"Dodd wasn't like most men," Kylie said. "He idolized Erin. He knew everything about her. And yet he dressed her in clothes she normally wouldn't be caught dead in. I think he did it to humiliate her. Knowing how much emphasis Erin places on exteriors, I bet he handpicked this junk to make her feel less than."

I watched Chief Brown's face as he took it all in. I was pretty sure he'd decided that Kylie was the smartest cop he'd ever encountered.

We followed Dryden into a second bedroom. "Dodd's prints were all over Erin's bedroom, but hers aren't in here," Dryden said. "This was his man cave. We found an assortment of disguises, half a dozen burner phones, and a laptop. The search history appears to be intact."

"How about guns?" Kylie said.

Dryden smiled. As usual, he was saving the best for last. He opened a closet door. Inside was a small arsenal—handguns, rifles, and semiautomatics.

"The man had more guns than my aunt Martha has Hummel figurines," Dryden said. "But I think this is the one you're looking for."

He picked up a soft case, about three feet in length, with the brand name *Berlebach* sewn into the black canvas.

"I'll bet half the photographers at that fashion show brought in bags that looked like this. But they were bringing in tripods. This, on the other hand..." He unzipped the case. Inside was a rifle. "It's a Winchester Seventy," he said, carefully picking up the gun with his gloved right hand. "And there's a box of jacketed hollow-point cartridges at the bottom of the bag."

"What caliber is the ammo?" I asked.

"Two-twenty-three."

"That's the same caliber bullet that killed Veronica Gibbs."

"Give me a few hours, and I'll let you know if this is the same gun."

My cell phone rang. It was the chief of detectives. "Jordan," he said.

That was it. Just my name. But the way he said it sounded more like he'd been chewing on it, hated the taste, and was spitting it out.

"Yes, sir."

"Meet me at the golf course where we put down the chopper. You and MacDonald. Now." He didn't wait for a response. He hung up.

I turned to my partner. "The old man wants to see us."

"About what?"

"He didn't say." I headed toward the door. "But the phrase *dead man walking* comes to mind."

CHAPTER 54

THE COP WHO had been assigned to drive Chief of Detectives Doyle met us at the golf course.

"They set up a temporary office for your boss inside the clubhouse," he said. "He told me to have you wait for him there."

We followed him into the building. "The manager apologized for the lousy accommodations," he said, "but they're in the middle of painting the place."

As we approached Doyle's loaner office, I could smell the fresh paint. And then the cop opened the door and flipped on the light.

"I can't believe it," Kylie said as soon as the cop left.

Neither could I.

There's a running joke in the department: if your boss calls you into his office, and there's plastic on the floor, the odds are you're going to get whacked.

The first thing Kylie and I saw when we entered the room was the plastic tarp on the floor.

"Hey—they're painting the place," I said.

"I don't care what they're doing, Zach. It's a bad omen. A really bad omen."

The only seat in the room was a desk chair. We remained standing.

Five minutes later Doyle walked in.

"So, Detectives," he said. "How is your day going?"

"Fine, sir," I said.

"I'm so glad to hear that," he said. "Funny thing…when I heard that Ms. Easton was safe and in custody, I thought my day would go well too. But, alas, I was sadly mistaken." He slid into the chair and rested his arms on the desktop. "Would you like to know why my day is going so badly, Detectives?"

"Yes, sir."

"My day went into the crapper—in public, mind you—because you, Detective Jordan, and you, Detective MacDonald, fucked up royally."

Some bosses are screamers. When they're angry, they want every cop in the borough to feel their wrath. Doyle's voice was calm, devoid of emotion. In fact, he spoke so softly I had to strain to hear every punishing word.

Very passive-aggressive. Very effective.

"You were the leads on this case," he said. "You made the call to keep Dodd's identity under wraps. I believe the argument you used was something like 'We want him to think it's safe to walk among us.' Your captain signed off on it. Her boss signed off on it. We all signed off on it. Why? Because we had faith that you knew what you were doing, and you'd catch the bastard.

"Well, he did walk among us. He brought his assassin's rifle into our city and walked past God knows how many of our smartest cops, none of whom were looking for him, and then he shot and killed one of our most influential citizens. Only then did you release his name and picture. Is that correct?"

"Yes, sir," Kylie said.

"A few hours later, he was dead, and the press put two and two together and asked how long we'd known Dodd was our primary suspect. I sidestepped with the usual 'I can't comment on an ongoing investigation,' but they didn't let up. They asked how I felt about the fact that this…this *celebrity*…this woman who is famous for what she wears, where she shops, and who she bangs was able to save herself when the elite NYPD Red Squad couldn't. I assured them that everyone in the department was relieved to know that Ms. Easton was safe and sound, and that was all that mattered.

"And as I looked across the room, I could see that every one of them was thinking the same thing: *Doyle is full of shit*."

He sat back in his chair. "But enough about my day," he said. "Tell me about yours. Did you determine if Dodd had any accomplices?"

"It doesn't appear that way, sir," I said, "but we can't yet rule it out."

"So then the answer to my question is: 'We haven't solved that one either.' Maybe you should get some help from Ms. Easton. She seems to be good at bailing you out."

"We spoke to her briefly, sir, but she was too drained to go on. We'll be interviewing her as soon as the doctors allow it."

"You do that. Do you have anything else to say, Detectives?"

We should have said, "No, sir," and backed out of the room. But Kylie doesn't walk away from any confrontation without getting in a few choice words.

"We made a judgment call, sir," she said. "If it turned out to be wrong—"

"*If* it turned out to be wrong?" Doyle said, his voice getting edgier, his tone angrier. "Don't delude yourself, Detective MacDonald. It turned out to be spectacularly wrong. I understand that cops working under pressure can make a bad call. But the rich and powerful people who grease the wheels of this city don't want to be at the mercy of your average cop. That's why we created Red. You are supposed to represent the finest of New York's Finest. But as tomorrow's newspapers will undoubtedly point out"— he stood up, put his palms on the desk, and leaned into us—"you and your partner *did not live up to the hype*."

CHAPTER 55

IT'S NONE OF my business," Rich Koprowski said, "but the chief of Ds has got some pair of balls blaming the two of you for Veronica Gibbs's murder. You might have made the call to keep Dodd's identity under wraps, but everyone up the chain of command—including him—signed off on it."

"You're right, Rich," Kylie said. "It's none of your business. It's mine and Zach's, and we don't want to talk about it."

"Fine," Koprowski said. "He's still a dick because of what he did to me."

The three of us were in Koprowski's car driving back to the city.

"He didn't do anything to you except tell you to drive Jamie Gibbs up to Warwick," Kylie said.

"I did. I drove him to the edge of town, and then what? Doyle tells me to turn him over to the local cops so they can drive him the last mile to the hospital. What the hell is that about? It made me feel like a goddamn delivery boy."

"Rich, I hate to break the news to you, but as far as Doyle is concerned, you *are* a delivery boy. You drove

Jamie up, and now you're driving Zach and me back to New York. We didn't exactly cover ourselves with glory in this case, and the chief of Ds doesn't want it to look like the only thing NYPD is capable of is chauffeuring the victim's husband to her bedside. But if it's any consolation, we really appreciate the lift."

She tipped her seat back and closed her eyes. I was aching to talk to Cheryl and dump some of the day's misery on her, but I didn't want an audience, so I curled up against the door in the back and drifted off to sleep. The rest of the trip was blessedly silent.

I got home at ten p.m. and called Cheryl as soon as I got in the door.

"Hello," she said, her voice groggy with sleep.

"Damn, did I wake you up?"

"S'okay...I know you had a tough day...how ya doin'?" she mumbled.

"I'd be a lot better if I were in bed with you."

"Good idea...bad timing...hostage negotiators' conference...Rochester...have to be...LaGuardia... five in the morning," she said, fighting to stay awake.

I'd forgotten all about it.

"Back Saturday...love you." She hung up.

"Love you too," I said, too late for her to hear.

No girlfriend, I thought. *A perfect ending to a perfectly rotten day.*

I reheated some leftover Thai food, opened a cold beer, turned on the TV, and sat down to watch *The Shawshank Redemption* for the umpteenth time.

I think I've figured out why it's my favorite movie. My job forces me to see the world in black and white. Cops versus crooks. Good guys versus bad guys. But in *Shawshank,* I root for the prisoners. I hate the warden. The lines are blurrier, and sometimes I take comfort in blurry.

The nap I took in the car threw off my sleep rhythm, and I wasn't tired enough to go to bed until three a.m. I slept through the alarm and didn't get to the office till eight thirty.

"Glad you showed up," Kylie said. "I was afraid you'd miss all the fun."

"What's going on?"

"Good news, bad news, and worse news," she said.

"I usually start with the worst, but I desperately need some good news."

"The lab ran ballistics on the bullet that killed Veronica Gibbs. It definitely came from the rifle that's covered with Dodd's prints."

"So Brooklyn Homicide gets credit for closing *our* high-profile murder," I said. "How is that good news?"

"They're celebrating with a steak dinner at Peter Luger's. They called to invite us." She grinned.

"Screw them. What's the bad news?"

"Dr. Paris called. Our star witness spiked a fever last night and will not be available to talk to us today or tomorrow. Saturday is a maybe. No guarantees."

"Great. Let's call Chief Doyle and tell him he can count on at least two more days of zero progress."

"I don't think the chief will be taking any of our phone calls," she said, picking up a copy of the *New York Post* from her desk and handing it to me.

There on the front page was a picture of Chief of Detectives Harlan Doyle taken at yesterday's press conference. It must have been snapped just as a reporter threw him a tough question, because Doyle's lips were pursed and his eyes were squinting. Clearly he was straining to come up with a good answer.

The headline above the photo read: "Top Cop at NYPD Clueless in Erin Kidnapping."

"I'll spare you the pain of reading the article. It's a heartwarming saga about how the plucky little media star overpowered her abductor and did 'what the elite NYPD Red Squad couldn't.' Save her own ass."

I sat there, stunned. "When I went to bed last night, I thought I'd hit a low point in my career," I said. "Turns out I was wrong. There is something worse than looking bad to your boss."

I stared at the picture of Doyle caught like a deer in the headlights. "And that's making *him* look bad to the rest of the world."

CHAPTER 56

THURSDAY AND FRIDAY passed without us making any real headway on our two biggest cases. Saturday was our day off, but we were ready to go to work if we could talk to Erin. I didn't want to risk another rejection from Dr. Paris, so I called Jamie.

"She's getting out in a few hours," he said, more excited than I had ever heard him. "We're going home."

"When can we talk to her?"

"Definitely not today. She'll be exhausted from the press conference."

"Jamie, please," I said. "She really should talk to the police before she talks to the press."

"You try telling that to Anna Brockway," he said. "You have no idea what's been going on since Erin escaped. The offers are pouring in. Everybody wants a piece of her."

"Including the NYPD," I said. "Jamie, your wife murdered Bobby Dodd. The Orange County district attorney will classify it as a homicide."

"It was self-defense."

"You know that. We know that. But our job is to get a detailed statement from Erin so the DA can close this out as justifiable."

"Okay, okay, gotcha. And I know she really wants to talk to you. She appreciates all you..." He groped for the right words. "You know...all you and Kylie *tried* to do. How about tomorrow morning at eleven? My apartment."

"We'll be there," I said.

That afternoon Cheryl flew back from Rochester. As soon as she came through the front door, I wrapped my arms around her. "God, I'm glad you're back," I said.

"I know. You sounded so bummed over the phone that I decided to come straight from the airport. Let's talk."

Talking was not what I had in mind. True, I had called her half a dozen times while she was out of town, but now that she was back, I needed a girlfriend more than I needed talk therapy.

"I'm feeling better now," I said, pulling her closer. "We can talk later."

She backed off. My intentions were transparent, and Cheryl was a professional on a mission—a trained psychologist making a house call. Romance was off the table until she helped me resolve my issues.

I sat down on the sofa. She remained standing. I looked up and gave her my best happy-to-see-you smile. "Go ahead, Dr. Robinson."

She didn't smile back. "Fair warning, Zach. I'm not going to sugarcoat it."

She was serious. I got an uneasy feeling in my stomach.

"Let's start with the most troubling thing you said to me on the phone," she said. "'I made the wrong decision and got a woman killed.' Do you really believe that?"

"I believe if we had released Dodd's picture—even internally—there's a good chance he might not have been able to shoot Veronica Gibbs."

"A good chance. So what is that? Ninety percent? No, wait…he was a sniper-trained combat Marine. How about fifty-fifty?"

I shrugged. "Whatever. She would have had some kind of chance."

"Or…" Cheryl let the word hang there for a few seconds. "She could have had a one hundred percent chance of not getting shot. All she had to do was not go."

"She wasn't the type to put her life on hold. It was an important show."

"I'm sure it was. But then something more important happened. Her daughter-in-law was kidnapped. Her son wanted to pay the ransom, but he couldn't. Veronica Gibbs was a smart businesswoman. She knew that she was the only one that stood in the way of Jamie getting the money. She had to at least *think* that she might be a target. But she decided she'd be damned if she publicly admitted that this kidnapping had anything to do with her. She's the one who made the wrong call, Zach. So stop blaming yourself for her death. You did not put Veronica Gibbs in harm's way."

"You know we offered her police protection," I said. "She flat-out turned us down. We didn't want Jamie to go out in public either, but we couldn't stop him."

"Zach, the best police department in the world can't protect people from themselves."

The words struck a familiar chord. "I knew that,"

I said. "But sometimes I forget. Thanks. That helps."
I stood up.

"Sit down," she said. "I'm not done."

I sat.

"Zach, I see unhappy cops every day. Sometimes they're depressed because they can't crack a case they're desperate to solve. Or because a case they thought they'd nailed got thrown out of court on a technicality and some lowlife who should be doing serious prison time is walking around free. And sometimes it's not about the casework. They're ready to quit because someone who is better at politics than they are got a promotion, and they didn't."

"Okay," I said, not exactly sure where she was going with this.

"It's not easy being a cop. It can be a frustrating, thankless job. But you've had a damn good run. You were still in your early thirties when you got promoted to detective first grade. Then you were drafted for Red. You and Kylie have become the go-to cops for the most prestigious unit in the department, and you've closed every big case they've ever assigned you."

"True."

"And that's your problem," she said.

"What's my problem?"

"You're spoiled."

I did a double take. "What's that supposed to mean?"

"You've been riding the wave so long, you forgot what it's like to crash and burn. I can't tell you if you made the right call or the wrong one, but after hearing thousands of sob stories from cops of every rank, race, and responsibility, I can tell you this: Shit happens. Don't wallow in it."

I laughed. "Shit happens? Don't wallow in it? They taught you that in shrink school?"

"Actually, my father taught it to me when I was a little girl, only he used more kid-friendly words."

"Lay them on me."

She sat down next to me on the sofa, put her hand on my cheek, and whispered softly in my ear, "Suck it up, buttercup."

I pulled her close. "You're a good psychologist," I said, "but I really miss my girlfriend."

"In that case," she said, lying back and pulling me on top of her, "this session is over."

CHAPTER 57

BY SUNDAY MORNING, hordes of fans and paparazzi had flocked to Ninety-Fifth Street and Riverside Drive in hopes of getting a firsthand look at the most Googled, most talked-about, most sought-after celebrity on the planet.

NYPD had cordoned off the area in front of Jamie's building and corralled the crowd behind makeshift barriers on Riverside.

Kylie and I arrived just before eleven. In addition to the doorman, two of Declan McMaster's security team were stationed in the lobby. They recognized us but still checked our IDs.

We took the elevator upstairs. McMaster let us in. "Did you see the crowd out there?" he said. "They loved her before this, but now it's out of control."

"She shanked her kidnapper," Kylie said. "That's cult-hero status."

"Meanwhile the poor woman is freaked. She can't shake the fact that she snuffed out a man's life. I have to warn you, she's not herself, so when you question her—"

"Declan," Kylie said, "we question victims all the

time. We don't expect someone who's been kidnapped, raped, and living in fear for her life to *be herself*. All she's got to do is give us some straightforward, honest answers."

"Relax. I'm just offering you some insight here. It's not like I'm telling you how to do your job," he said, having just tried to tell us how to do our job. He led us to the living room, where Erin and Jamie were sitting on the sofa.

She was wearing gray sweatpants and a black I LOVE NY T-shirt. There was a bandage wrapped around her left forearm. "Hello again," she said. "Can Jamie stay while we do this?"

"I'm afraid not," I said.

"What do you want to know?" she asked as soon as Jamie and McMaster had left the room.

"Whatever you remember. Start with the abduction."

She shook her head. "I slept through the abduction. One minute I was making a video for my fans, and the next thing I knew I was in this house I'd never seen before, and *he* was there."

"You knew him," Kylie said. It was a statement, not a question.

"He's been stalking me forever. My bodyguards carry his picture. Three different judges have signed orders of protection against him. So, yeah...I knew Bobby Dodd."

"What happened once you woke up in the house?"

"The first thing I remember is that my arm hurt like hell, and it was a bloody mess. I had this health-tracker chip implant that he cut out while I was drugged." She peeled back the bandage on her left forearm and showed us the wound. "He apologized, but he said he had to do it so no one would find us. I didn't tell him that the damn thing stopped working, and it was a piece of crap. One thing I learned from my friend Ari—never volunteer any information."

"Once you were in the house, were you locked up in your bedroom the entire time?"

"No. Sometimes we'd eat together in the kitchen. Ari trained me to look for signs of another person— a second coffee cup in the sink, a cigarette butt in the garbage—but I never saw a trace of anyone but Bobby. It made sense. Why would he need a partner? He was convinced that I wanted to be with him and that I only married Jamie so I'd have enough money to run away with him. He told me that as soon as he got the money, he was going to take me to Belize."

"Belize?" I said.

"I know what you're thinking," she said, reading the look on my face. "How was he going to get me through airport security? He wasn't stupid. His plan was to go by car. He showed me the route on Google Maps. We'd cross the border at Brownsville, Texas, and then head back east across Mexico for a couple of days until we got to Belize. It's insane, but he had it all planned. He said we could be happy together. Just me, him, and the baby."

We kept asking questions, and she didn't hesitate or hold back on anything—including the details of the constant sexual abuse she had to endure. She turned out to be an ideal witness, much smarter and a lot stronger than her public image.

"Can I ask you a question?" she said two hours into the session. "Am I going to be charged with murder?"

"Erin, our job is to get the facts," I said. "You confessed to killing a man, so his death is classified as a homicide. But if the DA finds that your actions were justifiable, it's a pretty good bet that there won't be any charges."

"I didn't plan on killing him."

"You put together a pretty deadly weapon."

"It was only for self-defense."

"Were you defending yourself when you killed him?" Kylie asked.

She shook her head.

"We need a verbal answer. Were you defending yourself when you killed him?"

"I was trained by an Israeli commando. I know how to read the signs," she said, her voice louder, more defensive. "He was going off the deep end. I had to kill him before he killed me."

"What do you mean, he was going off the deep end?" Kylie said.

"After Bobby made the deal with the network, he became unhinged. I think that's why he killed Veronica."

After Bobby made the deal with the network? It was one of those rare cop moments when you've tapped into a mother lode of new information and you want to jump up and scream, *Eureka!*

But we didn't jump. Or scream. In fact, I don't think either of us blinked.

CHAPTER 58

ELABORATE," KYLIE SAID, as if we were already privy to Bobby's deal with the network and just needed to flesh out a few details.

"Take your time, Erin," I added. "Try to remember as much as you can."

"I don't think Bobby ever really wanted twenty-five million dollars," Erin said. "He would have been happy with a lot less. But he didn't want me to think that *I* was worth less. So somewhere along the way, twenty-five million became the magic number.

"The first time he talked to Jamie, it went the way Bobby expected it to. He knew Jamie would ask for proof of life. But after the second call, Bobby was furious. He couldn't believe that Jamie had reached out to his mother, and she hadn't even returned his phone call.

"Bobby was pissed at Veronica. He started to get nervous that he'd never get any money. That's when he came up with the idea to get the network to pay the ransom. He asked me who he should talk to, and I said Harris Brockway but that the best way to get to him was to call his wife, Anna, who is my manager."

"And did he call Anna?"

"He had me make the call. God, she was so happy to hear from me, and then she put Brock on the phone, and he negotiated with Bobby."

"Did you hear the conversation?"

"Every word. Bobby had it on speaker. He wanted five million for another video, but Brock said he could only authorize a million on his own. Anything more than that, and he'd have to ask his bosses, but he didn't think they'd go for it. So Bobby took the deal."

"Did Brockway pay the million?"

"Oh yeah. Otherwise Bobby wouldn't have made the second video. He had one of those offshore banking accounts in Belize, and Brock wired him the money. Then ZTV did that horrible *Erin in Exile* show with that asshole psychologist who said I stole Jamie from Veronica and now that she had him back, why did she need me and the baby?

"Bobby and I watched it together. I think that's when buyer's remorse set in. He hated the network for only paying him a million. He said Brock was jerking him around. He didn't want the money in small increments. He said he knew how to fix everything. He locked me up and left the house. I think that must have been when he decided to eliminate Veronica."

"Did he tell you he was going to kill her?"

"Oh God, no. I would have tried to talk him out of it. I didn't like her, but Jamie loved her. It's so sad. He blames himself for her death."

"What happened when Bobby came back to the house?"

"He told me our problems were over. He said Veronica was dead, and Jamie had plenty of money to pay the ransom. But I knew better. It could be months, maybe years before Jamie sees a dime of his inheritance, and I knew that once Bobby found that out, he would go berserk. I didn't know if he would kill Brock or Jamie or me or all of us. That's when I got my blade and went to the shower. I swear on my baby's life that I didn't want to kill him, but I..."

"But you what?" I said.

She looked at me, reluctant to go on.

"Erin, this is important. It explains your state of mind."

She nodded. "I didn't want to kill him, but...I gave up hope that you would ever find me."

She wasn't trying to be hurtful, but the statement still felt like a stake through my heart. Another reminder that we had failed. But this time I didn't retreat into doubt and self-pity. I remembered the words of wisdom passed on to me the night before by my psychologist/girlfriend: *Suck it up, buttercup*.

I stood. Kylie wanted to get out as much as I did and was on her feet a second later.

"Erin, I wish we had been able to do more for you," I said, "but you're a brave and resourceful woman, and we appreciate your taking the time to relive your ordeal with us. I think we have what we need, but can we give you a call if anything comes up?"

It's our standard exit line, and people are so happy to see us leave that they always say yes.

"Of course," she said. "Anytime."

Kylie and I didn't say a word till we got to the car. Then I dialed ADA Bill Harrison and put him on speaker.

"Bill, it's Kylie and Zach," I said. "I know it's Sunday, but this can't wait."

"Go for it."

"Harris Brockway told us that the kidnapper sent

him that second proof-of-life video with a warning to air it or he'd kill Erin."

"Right."

"We just got a statement from Erin that Brockway negotiated a deal for the video with Dodd and wired him a million dollars to an offshore account."

"So what you're saying is that you can prove a network executive is a liar."

"I'm saying he colluded with the kidnapper. What can you get him on?"

"Not much. He didn't collude. He forked over the ransom money. There's no law against it."

Kylie grabbed the phone out of my hand. "But he lied to the police about an ongoing investigation," she said. "And then he hid behind the First Amendment."

"And the high-priced legal team at the network will say he didn't lie. He withheld the facts because he was fearful that telling the cops any of his private conversations with the kidnapper would put Erin's life at risk."

"Are you telling me he can pull all that shit and just walk?" she said.

"He won't exactly *walk*. If the DA decided to go after him, which I can promise you is not going to happen, the case would wind up in some misdemeanor proceeding, the judge would slap him with a small fine, Brockway would promise to be a good boy, and the records would be sealed."

"Bill, have you met this guy?" Kylie said. "He's a total asshole."

"Kylie, don't shoot the messenger, but may I remind you that being a total asshole is also not a crime. In fact, in Brockway's business, it's probably regarded as an asset."

"Thanks a lot," she said. "Sorry to ruin your Sunday."

"No problem. I was just sitting here reading the *Times*. You didn't ruin my Sunday."

"Well, you ruined ours."

She hung up, handed me the phone, and spit out those three little words I've heard from her many times before. "I hate lawyers."

CHAPTER 59

MONDAY MORNING ARRIVED dreary and drizzly. Kylie and I had a mountain of DD-5s to crank out on the Easton kidnapping, and yet I was borderline happy to be at work. I figured if we could get it done by midweek, then we could finally put the case behind us. On Friday, Cheryl and I were driving to Montauk to celebrate our one-year anniversary. I couldn't wait.

By eleven a.m. Kylie and I had conference-called the Warwick PD and finished our report to the Orange County DA. We couldn't make any promises to Erin, but I was confident he'd decide in her favor.

"We need coffee," Kylie said.

I didn't, but I followed her to the break room anyway.

"Guess where I'm going this weekend," she said.

Somewhere special with Shane, I'll bet. "I have no idea," I said. "Tell me."

"Orlando."

"Really? Are you—"

"Jordan! MacDonald!" It was Cates. "Suit up. Sutton Place at Fifty-Eighth Street. Another ambulance robbery, only this time we don't just have an angry governor. We've got a dead old lady."

We headed for the stairs. The coffee and Kylie's travel plans would have to wait.

Sutton Place is a small stretch of expensive real estate in the Fifties between First Avenue and the East River. Even driving the speed limit, we got to the imposing red-brick prewar building in only seven minutes.

We started by interviewing the doorman. It was a familiar story: An ambulance races up, two EMS techs tell him they have an emergency call, a woman in distress, Edith Shotwell, apartment 7B. The doorman sends them straight up. Fifteen minutes later they come down, tell him the patient is fine, and take off.

Same MO, same pattern we'd seen before—with one exception. Witnesses in the first two robberies said one of the perps was white, the other was Hispanic. This time, according to the doorman, one was white, the other was African American.

"Light- or dark-skinned?" I asked.

"Medium," the doorman said. "Pretty much the same color as me."

"I hate to ask, but are you sure he was African American?"

That got a laugh. "Detective, they had their hats pulled down low when they came in, and they were wearing them paper masks when they left, but trust me—he was black. I know a brother when I see one."

We talked to one of the first cops on the scene.

"The ambulance arrived at eight oh eight," he said. "Doorman wrote it down in his logbook. The name on the side of the bus was Prestige Medical Transport. He clocked them out at eight twenty-two. Two hours later Mrs. Shotwell's daughter gets here, goes upstairs, and finds the mother and her nurse zip-tied and gagged. She rips the duct tape off her mom, but the old lady is dead. The nurse is okay, just shook up. She and the daughter are waiting for you in a neighbor's apartment, seven A. CSU just arrived. They're up there with the DOA."

Kylie and I took the elevator up to the seventh floor. CSU was just getting started, but we didn't need an expert to tell us the cause of death. There were petechial hemorrhages in Mrs. Shotwell's eyes where the blood vessels had burst, and there were traces of glue from the duct tape on her mouth. She'd suffocated.

We went across the hall to the neighbor's apartment. The daughter introduced herself. "I'm Bethany Geller," she said. "Those animals murdered my mother."

"We're sorry for your loss," I said. "I promise we will do everything we can to find them."

"Thank you." She rested her hand on the shoulder of a woman, about sixty, who was sitting on the sofa. "This is Paloma Hernandez. She's been with the family for three years."

Paloma barely looked up. "It's my fault," she said. "I shouldn't have let them in."

"Don't blame yourself," Kylie said. "They fooled the doorman, and they fooled you. You let them in because you thought they were there to help."

"I beg them not to put the tape on her mouth. I say she has breathing problems from the COPD. But the one, he just said, 'She can breathe through her nose.' Ten minutes after they left Mrs. Edith started to choke. I think maybe she aspirated on her own vomit. I don't know. I'm not a doctor, but if I wasn't tied up, I could have helped."

"Can you describe the two men who entered the apartment?"

"One was a white guy—he was maybe six feet tall. The other was black, a little shorter. They both have brown eyes, but the rest of their face was covered with a surgical mask."

I didn't bother asking her if the second perp may have been Hispanic rather than white. Ms. Hernandez knew the difference.

I turned to the daughter. "Ms. Geller, the drawers in your mother's room were pulled out and emptied. It would help if we knew what they took."

"Things. Nothing worth killing someone for."

"I understand, but they are going to try to sell those things. The more details you can give us, the better the chance we have of finding your mother's killers and bringing them to justice."

"It was the jade," Paloma volunteered.

Geller nodded. "Of course. Ever since she was a girl, my mother loved jade jewelry—green, black, red, all colors."

"Do you think you can describe what they took and give us an approximate value?" I asked.

"I pay the insurance premium, so I can get you a list. Her favorite was a lavender jade oval set in a cluster of diamonds. That was appraised at forty thousand dollars. The entire collection was worth maybe five or six hundred thousand dollars."

"They take the envelope with the money too," Paloma said.

"What money?" I said.

"I leave an envelope with cash for Paloma," Geller said. "It's for household expenses or for when they go out on their excursions."

"What excursions?" I asked the nurse.

"Mrs. Edith, she didn't like to be cooped up in the apartment, and she loved riding the subway, so in the nice weather we would take the train to places like the Bronx Zoo or the Brooklyn Museum or, her favorite, Coney Island. We were just there last Sunday. She loved to sit on the boardwalk and eat an ice cream cone."

"And how much was in the envelope?"

"Six hundred and forty-two dollars," Paloma said. "I keep a good count. Also Mrs. Edith's MetroCard, but that had only like twenty dollars left on it."

"Detectives."

I looked up. It was Benny Diaz from TARU. Kylie and I thanked Geller and Hernandez, told them we'd be in touch, and walked over to where Benny was waiting.

"The good news is that the surveillance system in this building was state-of-the-art when they installed it," he said. "The bad news is they installed it fifteen years ago."

"Do you have anything we can use?" I asked.

"If you're looking for blurs and blobs, you're in luck. But if you're hoping for facial features, you're going to have to ask your perps to start robbing buildings with better security cams."

He opened his laptop and showed us half a dozen screen-grabs. The photos wouldn't help us identify the suspects, but they definitely settled one issue. Our eyewitnesses had been right: One of the phony EMTs was white; the other was black.

"So there are at least three of them," Kylie said. "And if the white guy from today isn't the same one from the previous robberies, we're up to four."

Our dynamic duo was turning into a gang.

CHAPTER 60

"THEY CAN HIDE their faces, but they can't hide their wheels," Kylie said. "If you were driving a fake ambulance to a fake emergency call, what would you do to look authentic?"

"Run the lights."

We called the NYC Department of Transportation and had them check the traffic cameras from lower Manhattan to Harlem. Sure enough, a red-light camera had caught the ambulance blowing through the intersection at Sixty-Third Street and First Avenue.

"Can you give me the plate number?" I asked the tech. Even if it had been stolen we might be able to pick it up on license-plate readers and see where the ambulance had come from.

"Sorry," the tech said, "but it's unreadable. They put a reflector cover on the plate. They're not legal, but people do it all the time."

"Right," I said. "If we catch them, we'll slap them with a summons."

"Give me your e-mail, and I'll send you the photos," he said. "You can't make out the driver's face, but the logo on the vehicle is clear as a bell. Prestige Medical Transport."

"The name is phony," I said, "but the pictures of the ambulance will help us pinpoint the model and year." I thanked him and hung up.

"These guys scope out each victim in advance," Kylie said. "They know whose apartment they're going to hit before they get there, and so far they've only targeted buildings where they can avoid getting picked up by security cameras. They're getting their insider information from somewhere."

The question was, from where? We ran Paloma Hernandez's name through the system, and she came up clean, just like the first two home attendants had. And each of the three had been placed by a different agency. There had to be a common denominator. We just couldn't figure out what it was.

We stuck around while CSU combed through the apartment, but they couldn't come up with any prints or DNA that could help us identify the two intruders. We were about to leave when Kylie stopped dead in her tracks.

"The MetroCard," she said. "The one they stole from Mrs. Shotwell."

"What about it?"

"Moss and Devereaux have been checking pawnshops and dozens of sites online where the perps might sell the jewelry. But these crooks are too smart for that. They must have a fence taking the pricey stuff off their hands, so good luck tracing any of Mrs. Shotwell's jade. But there's one thing that a fence wouldn't be interested in, and it's traceable: her MetroCard."

"It's a long shot," I said, "but it's a great idea."

We called Bethany Geller and asked if she knew

how her mother had paid for her MetroCard. She gave us the answer we were hoping for.

"I bought it for her. I put it on my credit card a year ago, and it refills automatically."

"Did you cancel the auto payments yet?" I asked.

"I didn't think of it, but I better do it now, otherwise those bastards will keep riding the subway on my credit card."

"Don't. Please," I said. "Do *not* cancel your mother's MetroCard."

"Why not?"

I told her. Two minutes later Kylie and I called the NYPD Transit Bureau's special investigations unit. We gave the detective who took the call Geller's Visa card number and asked him to pull the usage file. Within seconds, he linked the credit card to one of the city's millions of MetroCards.

"Can you tell us when it was last used?" I asked.

"I can tell you when and where, and if you give me a minute to scan the video, I can give you a description of the person who used it."

A few minutes later he had an answer. "It was used a week ago Sunday at eleven fifty-three a.m. at the Fifty-First Street station by an elderly white woman. She was with a younger woman, Hispanic, probably her caretaker. They had one of those rolling portable oxygen tanks. The card was used again at two fifty-nine p.m. at the Stillwell Avenue station in Brooklyn."

"Coney Island," Kylie said. "That jibes with Paloma's description of their last excursion."

"Do us a favor," I said to the Transit cop. "Can you put an alert on that MetroCard and call me or my partner as soon as you get a hit?"

"Whatever you need."

"It's still a long shot," I said to Kylie after I hung up. "These guys have done everything right every step of the way. Do you think they'll be stupid enough to use a stolen MetroCard?"

"Hey, they were stupid enough to turn a robbery into a homicide with a piece of duct tape," she said. "Anyway, what New Yorker can resist a free ride on the subway?"

CHAPTER 61

THE TEXT POPPED up on my phone and Kylie's at the same time. It was a short cryptic message written in the inimitable style of Detective Danny Corcoran.

Your dead guy is still writing checks.

It was the most promising news I'd heard in days. We knew that Bobby Dodd had spent six months in the Caribbean working as a stonemason. We figured he had amassed as much as half a million dollars in hurricane money. The question was: Where did it go? The easy answer: an offshore account. But he couldn't have stashed it all.

Kidnapping costs money. We contacted the people who owned the house in Warwick, and they told us he'd paid them thirty thousand dollars in cash to rent the place for a year. Then there was his food, travel, and other day-to-day expenses. Bobby needed ready cash, and that had to be someplace more convenient than a bank in Belize.

The Violent Felony Squad had been looking for any financial bread crumbs Bobby might have dropped, but they'd come up empty, and as soon as

Erin was safe and Bobby was dead, they'd moved on to their next top-priority case. That left us with a skeleton crew. Danny Corcoran was the backbone of the skeleton.

He was waiting for us at the precinct, a stack of spreadsheets on his desk, a smile on his face.

"The late Mr. Dodd has sixty-eight thousand dollars in a checking account at Chase Bank," he said.

"How'd you find it?" I asked.

"I went back to the security footage at the Hammerstein Ballroom. Two days before the wedding, he was in the building, probably to set up the live-feed cameras. He was wearing a work shirt that said BD RENTALS. That's when the light bulb lit up. I'd been searching for personal accounts, but Bobby was smarter than that."

"He ran the money through a corporation," Kylie said.

Danny nodded. "It's called BD Rentals, just like the shirt."

"Your text said he's still writing checks."

"There was an electronic transfer from that account over the weekend—a thousand dollars—the same auto-disbursement that's been going out on the fifteenth of the month since January. It went to the bank account of a lawyer in Pelham Bay."

"That's where Bobby was living. Who's the lawyer?"

"His name is Dominic Bruno. He's an old-school neighborhood lawyer who's not afraid to dabble in new technology. He's got a website. He's had a storefront law office on Crosby Avenue for fifty years. He's Italian American, bilingual, and 'a pillar of the community'—that's a quote."

"Forget what it says on his website. What do you hear on the street?"

"I called the local precinct. According to the

community affairs sergeant, Bruno is all that and more. The locals call him the Mayor of Crosby Avenue. He runs the St. Theresa festival every year, he's president of the Forty-Fifth Precinct Community Council, he pays for the holiday lights along Tremont—the list goes on. Bottom line, he's a churchgoing, straight-shooting gentleman, beloved by one and all."

"Great job, Danny," I said. I turned to Kylie. "Let's pay Mr. Bruno a visit and find out what Bobby loved about him."

CHAPTER 62

GOSH," KYLIE SAID as we drove past the low-rise red-brick buildings that housed the shops along Crosby Avenue, "the neighborhood hasn't changed much since we were here last week."

I laughed. It had barely changed since Eisenhower was president.

The office of Dominic F. Bruno, attorney-at-law, was in the heart of the business district, nestled neatly between a pizza parlor and an eyebrow-threading salon. We parked and went inside.

The woman at the front desk was impeccably dressed, all smiles, and at least a decade past retirement age. "Can I help you?" she chirped.

"Detectives MacDonald and Jordan, NYPD," Kylie said, showing her shield. "We'd like to speak to Mr. Bruno."

"Can I tell him what this is in reference to?"

"It's a police matter."

"Oh, you can tell me, honey. I'm not just the receptionist. I'm his sister, Rosemary Polito." She gave Kylie a big smile.

"How about we tell him first, and then he can tell you?"

Rosemary lost the smile and picked up her phone. "Two NYPD detectives to see you."

Within seconds a door in the rear opened, and Dominic Bruno stepped out. He had to be one of the most handsome septuagenarians on all of Crosby Avenue—six feet tall, olive complexion, thick salt-and-pepper hair, and a warm, engaging Crest Whitestrips smile.

"Dom Bruno," he said as he strode to the reception desk. He gripped my hand and shook it firmly. Then he reached for Kylie and gently cupped her hand in both of his. "To what do I owe the pleasure?"

"Can we talk in private?" Kylie asked.

"Say no more." He escorted us to his office. The walls were covered with awards and photos, some dating back decades: Bruno with Mario Cuomo, Bruno with Mayor Koch, Bruno with Cardinal O'Connor.

"Rosemary can make you a nice cup of espresso," he said as the three of us sat down at a conference table.

"No, thank you," Kylie said. "We just have a few questions about one of your clients, BD Rentals."

"I may not have the answers. I never even met them. One brief phone call about six months ago, and since then everything is handled electronically."

"They've been wiring you money every month," Kylie said. "Can you tell us what it is they're paying you for?"

"Detectives, I love the NYPD," he said, gesturing to a picture of himself with the CO of the Forty-Fifth Precinct. "But surely you know I'm bound by lawyer-client confidentiality."

"Your client is dead. Does that unbind you or do we need to get a subpoena?"

"Subpoena? There's no call for that. How do you know my client is dead?"

"It was in all the papers. BD Rentals was owned by Bobby Dodd."

He sat back in his chair. "The kidnapper?"

"Yes, sir. Can you tell us where the money is going?"

He nodded. "It's a very simple transaction. BD would send me the check every month, and I would then deposit it into a 529 college savings fund for three children."

"Do you know if they're Dodd's children?"

"They're not. They're the grandchildren of a woman I know from my church."

"What's her name?" I asked.

He put his fingertips to his head and rubbed his temples. "This woman is very much alive, Detective, so I'm afraid we're back to lawyer-client confidentiality again."

"Counselor, your client is doing business with a man who kidnapped, raped, and murdered," I said. "Do you really want to—"

"Wait a second. What am I thinking? She asked me to be the go-between as a favor. I didn't charge a fee. She's not a client." He lowered his voice. "Her name is Lucille Speranza."

"Dodd's landlady?"

"I guess you know her," Bruno said. "Ever since it got out that he lived in her basement, she's been all over the television and the newspapers."

"We met her before she was famous," Kylie said. "But she told us Dodd had paid up through the end of August. So what are the thousand-dollar checks for?"

"I told you. It's for a college fund for her grandkids—Samantha, Nina, and Ryan."

"That's not my question. If the rent was paid, what else is she doing for Dodd that nets her a thousand dollars a month?"

"That's none of my business. You'd have to ask Lucille. Do you need her address?"

"No, sir, we don't. Thank you for your time, Mr. Bruno."

We stood up and started to leave.

"Detectives," he said, "I shared Lucille's information with you because I don't think she and I have a lawyer-client relationship. But she may see it differently, and to be honest, she can be sort of a...a difficult person."

"That would be putting it mildly, sir," Kylie said.

"Maybe you can do me a favor, then. Even though it's after the fact, maybe you could issue me a subpoena. Then I'd have no choice but to tell you what I told you."

"Understood," Kylie said. "We'd be happy to do it, sir."

He flashed us a victory smile. "Thank you."

The Mayor of Crosby Avenue may well have been beloved by all, but he was also smart enough to cover his ass.

CHAPTER 63

LIFE FOR LUCILLE SPERANZA had changed dramatically since we'd last seen her. Newspapers printed her picture. TV networks ran her sound bites. Magazine editors wanted her story. Overnight, she had become to Bobby Dodd what Kato Kaelin had been to O.J. Simpson.

Even now, five days after she'd become known around the world as the Kidnapper's Landlady, several news vans were parked outside her home.

"She's quite the celebrity," Kylie said as we walked up the stairs. She rang the bell. "You think she'll still remember her old friends Jordan and MacDonald?"

I barely recognized the woman who opened the door. Gone was the mop of unruly orange hair. It was now a soft brown and styled. Gone was the baggy red-flowered dress. She now wore one that was navy and tailored. Someone—probably a TV producer— had gone to the trouble of getting her camera-ready. But of course, no makeover artist in the world could change Lucille's unique brand of charm.

"What the fuck are you two doing back here?" she said. "I thought this case was closed."

"That's fake news," Kylie said. "Don't repeat it next time you're on TV."

She turned away from Kylie and squared off with me. "How the hell do you put up with her?" she said.

"She's an acquired taste," I said. "We need to talk to you. Can we come in?"

"No. I have nothing more to say. I told you everything I know."

"You may have left out a few things. Like why the man you said you barely knew is sending a thousand dollars a month to Samantha, Nina, and Ryan's college fund."

That blindsided her.

"Your silence speaks volumes," Kylie said. "Now, can we come in, or would you rather the TV cameras filmed us escorting you to our place?"

Speranza opened the door, and we followed her to the living room.

"I don't know why you damn cops keep hounding me about this Bobby Dodd shit," she said.

"Let's get back to the question about the money he'd been sending you every month," Kylie said.

"He was a tenant. It was rent money."

"You told us he was paid up through the end of August," I said. "Why was he sending more money in June?"

"It must be a mistake. I'll send it back."

"Do you care about your grandchildren, Mrs. Speranza?" Kylie said.

"My grandchildren? Why the hell would you drag them into this?"

"Why the hell would you have a psycho killer funding their college education? We didn't drag them into this. You did. And if you'll start spitting out answers instead of venom, maybe they won't get to see their names in the morning paper."

Any other seventy-seven-year-old granny probably would have started cooperating to avoid bringing shame to innocent family members, but Lucille Speranza was determined to go down swinging.

"You cops are all alike. You're all on the take, and you're all bigots. What do you think, just because I'm Italian, I'm a criminal?"

"It doesn't matter what *we* think. But you might want to worry about what your friends who watch the six o'clock news think," Kylie said, pulling out her cuffs. "Hands behind your back."

Speranza threw her hands up in the air and backed away. "All right, all right. It wasn't the rent. That was paid. We had a separate deal."

"What kind of deal?"

"He paid me extra for storage."

"What do you mean, *storage*?"

"What do you think *storage* means? I kept shit for him."

"In the basement?"

"No. I keep it here. He paid extra because he knew it would be safe in my house."

"And what did you keep for him?"

Speranza took a deep breath and looked at us with eyes that were brimming with contempt. The woman who had called us bigots hated cops. She probably always had and definitely always would.

She spit out the answer to the question. "He had a box."

CHAPTER 64

THE BOX WAS an olive-drab metal footlocker with Bobby Dodd's name and serial number stenciled on it.

"He didn't leave me no key," Speranza said.

Kylie bent down and examined the padlock. "Core-hardened steel," she said. "It looks brand-new except for the scratches on the shank." She looked up at Speranza. "I hope you didn't break a nail trying to get it open."

Speranza responded with her middle finger.

It was unlikely that Dodd had left it booby-trapped, but protocol and good sense dictated that we evacuate Speranza's house as well as the two homes that flanked hers, cordon off the entire block, and bring in the bomb squad.

That's not easy to do without attracting attention, and by the time the men in the moon suits lumbered down Zulette Avenue toward the house, the streets on the other side of the barricades had become a sea of news vans.

The entire operation took less than forty-five minutes from discovery to all-clear, but the media circus was just getting started. And in the center ring stood Mrs. Speranza. Her fifteen minutes of fame was going into overtime.

Kylie and I went back to the house. ESU broke the padlock while CSU documented it all on film.

"Now comes the fun part," Kylie said as a tech lifted the lid.

The inside looked like a survivalist's wish list, everything a trained Marine would need to bug out and stay gone: guns, knives, ammo, a bulletproof vest, camping gear, fake IDs, even paper maps, because you can't use a GPS when half a dozen law enforcement agencies are trying to hunt you down.

One by one, the items were photographed, cataloged, and laid out for inspection. Under the weapons was a fat manila folder that was crammed with all things Erin. Magazine covers, feature stories, videotapes, CDs, and hundreds of pictures, some clipped from fan books, but many of them candid shots, most likely taken while he stalked her.

The biggest surprise was the diaries—handwritten journals dating back fifteen years. I picked one up and opened it to a random page.

October 12, 2014

Erin and I drove up to the Berkshires for the weekend partly just to look at the fall foliage but mostly to find a house for us. Not that we're going to live up in Massachusetts. She'd rather be where it's warm all year round. It doesn't matter anyway because none of the places we looked at were right for us. It's Sunday and she's got a rerun on tonight. We'll watch it but I keep telling her that the damn network should be making new shows

*instead of just repeating the old ones over and over.
I sent them fourteen e-mails about it but so far they
haven't written back. What do you expect from a
bunch of idiots.*

I flipped to another page, then another. It was all
the same. Bobby Dodd was in love with someone who
wasn't there, and he had journaled their life together
as if they actually had one.

Kylie had a second volume, and I watched her face
as she flipped through it, waiting for her expression to
turn from cold to compassionate as she read a few of
the entries. But it never did.

"Well, this sucks," she said, finally putting the
diary down.

"Granted, it's not Shakespeare," I said.

"I'm not talking about the writing. I'm talking
about the fact that it's all fiction. Our job is to read
everything Bobby wrote and find out how he planned
all the crimes he committed. Was he a loner, or did
he have accomplices? What if we read for a week,
and we finally get to the part where he says he was
in cahoots with Mrs. Speranza? Or the Brockways?
Or the Rockettes? How do we know what's real and
what's crazy? How do we know what to believe, what
to follow up on?"

They were smart questions, but I had no answers.

"Zach, you and I have great bullshit detectors when
we're sitting across the table from a suspect, studying his word choices, watching his body language.
But it's hard to find the truth when you're wading
through a thousand pages written by a delusional
man."

And then the answer came to me. "You're right,"
I said. "We're going to need professional help, and I

just happen to know someone who's extremely adept at deciphering the thoughts of a delusional man."

Kylie tapped herself on the forehead, that classic gesture you make when someone else comes up with the obvious answer before you do.

"I know Dr. Robinson too," she said. "In fact, I know her so well, I think she might actually enjoy reading this crap."

CHAPTER 65

AS SOON AS I got back to the station I went directly to Cheryl's office. "Please tell me you're free tonight," I said.

"I could be," she said, giving me one of those seductive smiles that made me wish I had more than police work to offer her. "What did you have in mind?"

"A foursome—you, me, Kylie, and the insane ramblings of a psycho stalker-rapist-kidnapper-murderer-badass. Bobby Dodd left behind his diaries. Kylie and I have to make sense out of them. We thought it might be more productive if we brought along a trained psychologist. For the record, you were our first choice."

"I'm flattered."

"But wait, there's more," I said. "If you act now, we'll throw in an all-expenses-paid dinner from the Chinese takeout joint of your choice."

"It's hard to say no to an evening of insane ramblings and General Tso's chicken. Sign me up."

Twenty minutes later, Kylie, Cheryl, and I were sitting in a conference room with the diaries.

"Logic might dictate that each of us start from the

beginning," Cheryl said. "But we're not going to be able to read it all in one night, and it's better to get at least one pair of eyes on every page. So let's break it up into thirds. I'll take the first third, Kylie the next, and Zach the last."

The time flew as I got sucked into the strange world of Robert Allen Dodd. Kylie had been wrong. It wasn't all fiction. It was filled with fantasies about Erin, but there was also page after page about his father, all of which sounded heartbreakingly genuine. Bobby, at least the way he told the story, was a good son, and when his father was dying of cancer, Bobby was at his bedside around the clock. And then I turned to a page that punched me in the gut.

"Hey, guys," I said, "can you take five? I want to read you something."

They put their books down, grateful for the break. I read it word for word, just as Bobby had written it.

September 8, 2014

Two days ago my father, Jody Elias Dodd, died peacefully in his sleep. When the funeral director brought me the urn from the crematorium, he also gave me this little box that he said was from Dad.

There was a note. It said, Dear Bobby, Being your father is the best thing that ever happened to me. I'm sorry I won't be around to watch your six, but keep this close, and I will always be with you. Love, Dad.

Inside the box was a .357 Magnum bullet on a gold chain and inside the bullet were some of Dad's ashes. Then I read the engraving on the back: Succeed, or die trying. Semper Fi.

I could barely breathe and as soon as the funeral guy left I bawled like a baby. I love you, Dad. Miss you. And don't you worry. I'm not going to fail.

"That's not delusional," I said. "That's not a fantasy. The date matches up with the date of his father's death in McMaster's file. And the bullet—we saw the bullet. It was around his neck when he died."

Kylie and Cheryl had also found pockets of truth throughout Bobby's prose and had marked each one with a Post-it note. We decided to transcribe the important points onto a large whiteboard. We drew a line down the middle and labeled one side RANTS, the other REALITIES.

After four hours we'd gone through less than half of the journal entries, some of them real, most of them make-believe, none of them helping us come up with the answers Chief Doyle was looking for.

Cheryl had an early-morning meeting and left at about ten. Kylie and I plugged away at it, determined to work as long into the night as our brains and bodies would allow.

I was back in Bobby's world when the call came in from the NYPD Transit special investigations unit.

"Detective Jordan, I've got a hit on the MetroCard you're tracking," the cop on the other end said. "It was swiped at nine forty-seven at the Sixty-First Street Woodside station in Queens. Video shows a white female, blond hair, midthirties, wearing lavender hospital scrubs."

"You clocked her at *nine forty-seven?*" I said. "Jesus, man, it's ten fifty-three. What part of *priority* did we not make clear?"

"Take it easy. Ninety percent of the requests we get are stamped *priority*."

"How many of them are connected to a homicide? If the card gets swiped again, I need to know it real time. I also need a screenshot of the blonde in the lavender scrubs."

"You'll have it in two minutes," he said.

We ran the picture through facial-recognition software. No hit. Meaning the woman with Edith Shotwell's stolen MetroCard had no arrest history in New York City.

Kylie and I went back to the diaries and stayed at it until three a.m. We found nothing of value. All in all, it was not a great night for the good guys.

CHAPTER 66

I SLEPT AT the station house. Soundly, but not long. My cell rang and jarred me awake at 6:50. I answered and *mmph*ed some semblance of my name into the phone.

It was the same cop from Transit, the one I'd chewed out the night before. "Sorry to wake you, Detective," he said, not sounding remotely apologetic, "but you said you wanted this in real time."

"No problem. What've you got?"

By now, Kylie, who had been sleeping in the next bed, was sitting up. I put the call on speaker.

"I've got another hit on your stolen MetroCard," Transit said. "It was swiped at booth four eighty-two on the downtown six line at Seventy-Seventh Street and Lexington three minutes ago. I just pulled the video. Same woman as yesterday, same lavender scrubs."

"Shoot me the best screenshots you've got. And thanks."

"Any time, Detective," he said. "Transit is always happy to come to the assistance of the elite Red Squad."

His voice was rife with the attitude of someone who feels like he's just won a pissing contest, but I didn't care. We were closing in on a suspect.

Last night, all we knew about the woman using the MetroCard was that she was wearing scrubs. The obvious conclusion was that she was a hospital worker, but since all three robberies involved in-home caretakers, she also might have been on her way to or from a private nursing job.

This morning she was wearing the same lavender scrubs and was catching a train about a hundred feet from the entrance of one of New York's major hospitals.

"She's catching the train at Seventy-Seventh and Lex," Kylie said. "What do you bet she works at Lenox Hill? She's probably a nurse or a tech pulling a night shift."

"I know their head of security," I said. "Let me track him down. I bet he can search the employee database and ID her."

"Screw the head of security," Kylie said. "We don't have to ID her. We know what she looks like, and I'll bet you twenty bucks I know where she's going."

"The Sixty-First Street Woodside station in Queens," I said.

"Right. Which means she has to take the six train to Grand Central, walk over to the Flushing line, and catch the seven train to Queens. Even if every train was waiting for her when she got to the platform, it would still take her at least twenty-five minutes to get there. More, if we're lucky. Let's go."

She bolted out the door. I followed. Not because it was the way I would have handled it, but because my partner is a heat-seeking missile, and when she's on a mission, I know enough to either back her 100 percent or get the hell out of her way. And I've never done anything but back her.

"How long do you think it'll take us to get to Woodside?" I yelled, following her down the stairs.

"With you behind the wheel, Grandma? About an hour and a half. With me driving, we could stop for coffee, and we'd still be there in plenty of time to collar Blondie."

CHAPTER 67

THANK YOU," KYLIE said as I buckled up and braced myself for the ride.

"For what?"

"I know how you think. If it were up to you, you'd radio ahead for backup."

"The thought crossed my mind."

"Would you like to know what thought crossed my mind? Erin got credit for taking down Dodd, Brooklyn is throwing a steak dinner to celebrate closing the Veronica Gibbs homicide, and I'll be damned if I'm going to let a bunch of Queens marines steal our collar."

"You're welcome," Kylie said.

She made a hard right onto Second Avenue, which was just on the cusp of rush hour but still moving. There's a traffic cop on most corners in the low Sixties. One by one, the cops spotted our flashing lights and waved us onto the Ed Koch Bridge.

"We've practically got eyes on her now," Kylie said when we got to Queensboro Plaza on the other side of the East River.

It was an overstatement. We were directly under

the elevated tracks where the number 7 train to Flushing ran. But there was no train in sight.

Kylie weaved in and out of the traffic along Queens Boulevard, then followed the tracks when they jogged to the left on Roosevelt Avenue.

We had just passed the Fifty-Second Street station when we saw the train about a quarter of a mile in the distance. Kylie hit the gas, ran a few reds, and skidded to a stop just as a train from Manhattan pulled into the Woodside station.

We jumped out of the car and ran up the stairs, our eyes darting left, right, and center as the early-morning commuters spilled onto the platform and headed for the exits.

Our suspect wasn't there.

"NYPD runs faster than the MTA," Kylie said, looking at her watch. "I guarantee she'll be on the next one."

Seven minutes later another train rumbled into the station. We stood in the middle of the platform and flashed our shields at the conductor.

"You can let them out of the forward cars, but don't open the back half," I said.

The doors slid open in the first five cars, and about thirty people got off.

"You see your man?" the conductor asked as we watched the passengers head toward the exit.

"Our man is a woman," I said. "Turn the rest of them loose, and keep it parked till I give you the green light."

The remaining doors opened, and I immediately spotted our lady in lavender getting off. I released the train, and Kylie and I followed her through the turnstiles.

"Ma'am," Kylie said.

The woman turned around.

"NYPD," Kylie said, holding up her ID. "We'd like to ask you a few questions."

"About what?"

"About the MetroCard you're using. Where did you get it?"

She looked confused. "Where does anybody get a MetroCard? I bought it from the machine."

"Ma'am, that's not what I'm asking. I'm asking where you got the MetroCard you used last night at this station and then again this morning at Seventy-Seventh and Lexington Avenue."

I watched her eyes. The panic set in as the answer came to her. She knew exactly where she'd gotten the card, and she wasn't eager to tell us.

"I don't remember," she said. "Is that a crime?"

Kylie was stone-faced. "Let me see some identification, please."

The woman's hands trembled as she dug into her purse and pulled out a driver's license that ID'd her as Catherine Leicester.

"This picture looks like it was taken a few years ago, Catherine," Kylie said, looking at the license. "The one I've got of you is more recent."

Kylie produced one of the screenshots Transit had sent us and held it close to Leicester's face. "Now, where did you get the MetroCard?"

Being accosted by two cops who shove a time-stamped mug shot of you in your face can be intimidating. And if you're a basic law-abiding citizen, like Catherine Leicester turned out to be, it can be downright terrifying.

She blurted out the truth. "I didn't do anything wrong. My boyfriend gave it to me."

"What's his name?"

"Gary. Gary Banta. Is he in trouble?"

Kylie pressed hard. "Where is Gary right now?"

Leicester was shaking now. "He's at work."

"Where? Where does he work?"

"He's FDNY."

"So he's a firefighter? What engine company?" Kylie demanded.

"No," Leicester said.

"No what?"

"Gary's not a firefighter. He's an EMT."

CHAPTER 68

WE TOOK CATHERINE LEICESTER'S phone, drove her to the station, and arrested her for possession of stolen property. It was a bullshit charge. Her real crime was being Gary Banta's girlfriend, but we needed a legal excuse to lock her up so she didn't tip him off that we were looking for him.

Since Banta worked for the fire department, logic might dictate that we ask for their help in tracking him down. But the FDNY is a tight-knit organization, and we knew from experience that if we reached out to them, they would immediately circle the wagons to protect their own.

So we called the DOI. All governments have their share of crooks, and in New York City, the job of weeding out the bad apples falls to the Department of Investigation. The name is deceptively innocuous. In reality, it's an all-powerful agency with the authority to investigate any city department, elected official, or employee.

There were six NYPD detectives working at the DOI. Any one of them could have helped us track down Banta, but when you're investigating a uniformed member of the FDNY, you want a detective who will ask very few questions. That was Joe Donahue.

Five years ago Joe had been shot in the line of duty. At least a dozen detectives were assigned to look for the shooter, but I'm the one who collared him. I remember the day I walked into Joe's hospital room and gave him the good news. He never said, *I owe you one.* He didn't have to. The gratitude was in his eyes, and the bond was formed. After Joe recovered, the PC offered him a safe spot at DOI, and he grabbed it.

I dialed his direct line. As usual, he was happy to hear from me. I did about ten seconds of the usual long-time-no-see foreplay, and then I asked if he could run a check on EMS tech Gary Banta.

I listened as his fingers tapped away on the keyboard.

"Got him," he said. "He's with division two out of the Bronx. Been on the job sixteen years. Decorated twice, once for rescuing a woman and two kids from a submerged vehicle after a flash flood."

"You got a photo ID and maybe a home address?" I said.

There was only so far I could push before Donahue did his job and pushed back.

"Zach, every keystroke I make on this computer is recorded. I didn't have a problem with searching for a name, but I start digging deeper, and I've got to justify it to my boss. What are you looking at him for?"

I told Joe about the home invasions that had led to a homicide and the stolen MetroCard that had led us to Banta.

"Shit, man," Donahue said. "This guy's a hero. Are you positive it's him?"

"The only thing I'm positive of is that if word gets out that NYPD is looking to question a decorated member of FDNY, this whole thing will turn into an intramural shit-show. Look, Joe, I don't want to jam you up with your bosses, but if we don't keep this tight…"

I let the possible consequences hang in the air unspoken.

I heard the clack of Donahue's keyboard.

"Today is his day off, but he signed up to work the day game at Yankee Stadium," Donahue said. "They're playing the Red Sox, which is always a clusterfuck, so they heavy up on cops to deal with the drunks and double up on buses to cart away the bleeders."

"When does he start?"

"A few hours before the game, so he should be out there now. Hold on. All these units have GPS." A brief pause, and then he was back. "I've got three buses parked at the corner of One Hundred Sixty-First Street and River. They're probably having coffee and shooting the shit, waiting for batting practice to start."

"Joe, we're on the way up to the Bronx now. I know Banta's name is on his uniform, but anything else you could mention to help us…"

Again, I left it open-ended.

"He's driving bus number three fourteen. I'll shoot you a copy of his ID."

"Thanks," I said. "I owe you one."

He came back fast. "No, you don't. Good luck. And Zach, one more thing—for Banta's sake, I hope that you're wrong."

"I know, Joe. And for your sake, I hope that I'm right."

CHAPTER 69

WHY?" KYLIE SAID as we barreled along the FDR Drive toward the Willis Avenue Bridge. "Why would a public servant with a stellar track record suddenly start robbing old ladies? Gambling debts? Drug addiction? Medical expenses for his family?"

"If it were just Banta I would say any one of those could drive him to that kind of desperation," I said. "But he's not alone. He's got two partners that we know of. Three EMTs can't all be drowning in gambling debts or have kids who need kidney transplants. They've got to be in some serious financial shit together, and they decided that this is the only way to dig themselves out."

We hopped on the Deegan and headed north to the Bronx.

"There are three buses at the stadium," Kylie said. "Guaranteed that Banta is with at least one of his partners in crime. The problem is FDNY won't have a record of who he was riding with because he pulled the robberies on his days off using a phony ambulance."

"Don't think about the others," I said. "Focus on Banta. DOI will pull their cell numbers and tell us who pinged off the towers in the robbery locations. All we have to do is get Banta, and we'll get them all."

We got off the Deegan at Jerome Avenue, turned right on East 161st Street, and pulled up to Babe Ruth Plaza where two EMS buses were parked. Four uniformed technicians were hanging out, having coffee. None of them looked like the picture of Banta that our man at DOI had sent us.

We were in an unmarked car, but these guys could have spotted a Crown Vic Interceptor in a crowded parking lot. We could almost see their antennas go up.

"You think they made us for cops?" Kylie said, a big grin on her face.

"I don't know. Why don't you go over there and try to sell them some Girl Scout cookies? See if they fall for it."

"The four of them are just staring, waiting for us to make a move," she said. "If we both get out of the car, they'll know we're here on business and get spooked, and one of them will radio Gary. One cop is a lot less intimidating than two."

"Be my guest," I said.

"I'd do it, but Gary already has a girlfriend. Besides, you're not nearly as intimidating as I am."

I opened the car door, but I didn't get out. "Laugh it up," I said. "Like I'm telling you a story about my old pal Gary."

"Zach, we're running a scam here, not putting on a show. Just go, and try not to screw it up." And then she laughed.

I laughed back and sauntered over to where the four EMTs were hanging.

"What's up, Detective?" one of them asked. He was

white. The name on his shirt said HUNTER. "Are we in a no-parking zone or something?"

His buddies laughed. I laughed with them and held up both hands. "Trust me," I said, "I come in peace. I saw a couple of buses parked out here, and I thought I'd see if a friend of mine was working the game today. But I guess he's not."

"What's his name?" Hunter said.

"Banta. Gary Banta."

"Gary's around."

"I can't stay long. My partner's all antsy about getting back, but I'd love to catch him for a few minutes. I haven't seen him in a while. I used to run into him all the time when I was at the Five Two."

"Well, then, you know he never drinks coffee," Hunter said. "He took a run over to the juice bar to pick up a spinach smoothie or some healthy crap like that."

"That's Gary," I said. "He's going to outlive us all."

"What's your name? I can raise him up on the radio for you."

"I'm Zach. But do me a favor, don't radio him. Do you know which juice bar? I want to see the look on his face when I surprise him."

"It's the one over on Gerard Ave. next to the Foodtown. There'll be a big red and white bus in front of it with *FDNY* plastered across the side. You think you can find it, Detective?"

The other three laughed again. "You guys are bigger ballbusters than Gary," I said, laughing with them.

I thanked the EMTs, walked back to the car, and got in. "Gary's at a juice bar," I said, pulling up Google Maps. "Go straight and make a left on Gerard. At least we get to arrest him without the four of them giving us a hard time."

Thirty seconds later Kylie made the turn onto Gerard, and I could see the Foodtown. What I didn't see was a juice bar. Or an FDNY ambulance.

"Shit," I said. "I've been suckered."

I was about to call Joe Donahue at DOI, but my cell rang. He'd beat me to it.

"Zach," he said, "did you make it to the Bronx yet?"

"Yeah, but Banta's crew sent me on a wild-goose chase. By now, I'm sure they radioed him and told him we're coming."

"That would explain why he left the stadium and is headed north on the Deegan doing eighty miles an hour."

CHAPTER 70

THEY SAY THAT police work, like war, is hours of boredom punctuated by moments of sheer terror. The monotony of filling out DD-5s and sifting through surveillance videos was suddenly behind us, and while the prospect of a high-speed chase produced more adrenaline than terror for me, knowing that Kylie was behind the wheel was not without its sense of dread.

"Buckle up," she said, firing up the light bar and hopping onto the sidewalk to make a U-turn. She gave the siren a couple of *whoop-whoop*s, yelled, "Out of my way, people," to pedestrians and drivers who needed no verbal warning, and barreled the wrong way down a crowded one-way street.

By the time I grabbed the radio and turned it to a citywide channel, we were tearing across Jerome Avenue toward the service road to the Deegan.

I keyed the mic. "Central, this is Red One. Be advised we are in pursuit of a homicide suspect driving an FDNY ambulance. He's headed north on the Deegan from Yankee Stadium."

Some calls bear repeating. Central didn't disappoint.

"Unit," she said, "you are advising me that you are chasing an *FDNY ambulance,* and that it is being driven by a *homicide suspect*."

"Affirmative. Notify aviation. The bus number is three-one-four."

I still had Joe Donahue at DOI on my cell. "Joe, I need an update."

"He just passed Van Cortlandt. He's heading into Westchester."

There's a confounding rule about pursuing a vehicle outside of our jurisdiction. Technically we couldn't chase him unless we had him in sight. We weren't close enough to see him, but I wasn't exactly about to broadcast that.

"Central, notify state, county, and local that we are crossing into Westchester."

"Ten-four, Red One. Will notify them immediately."

Immediately in dispatcher-speak doesn't mean "instantaneously." It takes a while for one dispatcher to contact the other, and then it takes another while for the second dispatcher to get the word out to her troops.

While that was going on, Kylie was eating up the distance between us and Banta. He had a head start, but city ambulances aren't as fast as people might think. They get where they're going in a hurry because they can break traffic laws and clear a path for themselves. But on a drag strip, a cop car would leave Banta's bus in the dust.

A new voice came over the radio. Male, deep, with a Jamaican lilt. "Bronx Auto Crime, Central. Get me a current location on Red One."

Kylie's eyes were glued to the road, but I could see the grin spread across her face. Some bored-out-of-his-gourd detective who had been cruising the streets of the Bronx on a stolen-car detail just hit the high-speed-chase lottery.

"Red One, Central. We are north through Van Cortlandt Park."

"Auto Crime, Central. Show us responding toward that location."

When something big breaks on citywide, any cop who picks it up is going to radio his buddies and tell them to roll over to that channel. Within minutes half the cops in the city would be tuned in to the drama on the Deegan and hoping it would come their way.

The radio lit up, and by the time we crossed the city line into Yonkers, Bronx Narcotics and Highway One had signed on for the ride. And by the time we passed the Empire Casino, three more cars and an ESU truck were en route to join the posse.

"No shortage of volunteers," I said.

"NYPD chasing FDNY. Who wouldn't want a piece of that?" Kylie said. "At best, these cops figure they have a shot at being on the six o'clock news. At worst, they've got a war story to spin at the bar tonight. I bet for most of them, it's better than sex."

I checked in with DOI. "Joe, what do you got?"

"He jumped off the Deegan. He's on the off-ramp to the Sprain."

"We are about a mile shy of the Sprain," I said. "We're gaining on him."

"Hold on, he didn't get on the Sprain. He took a right on Tuckahoe Road."

"He had a clear shot to the thruway," I said. "Siren or no siren, how does he expect to outrun us if he's taking local streets?"

"He's not getting on the highway. He just turned onto East Grassy Sprain Road."

"I never heard of it. Where the hell does it go?"

"It runs parallel to the parkway. It goes through Yonkers, past a bunch of businesses, private homes, a golf course, a school—makes no sense."

"We're on East Grassy Sprain now," I said. "I have eyes on him."

I called our location in to Central, which was still getting units responding left, right, and center. Wherever Banta was going, there was a shitload of cops going with him.

We were less than two city blocks behind him when I saw the big green and white sign: SPRAIN LAKE GOLF COURSE.

There was a red-brick guardhouse with a flimsy wooden barrier at the front gate. Banta could have easily crashed through it, but his siren worked its magic. The guard lifted the gate just as he sailed through. Kylie gave him a *whoop-whoop*, and he wisely kept it open.

If I'd thought Gary Banta were stupid, I might've assumed he'd just driven himself into a dead end. But Gary was a planner. He knew where he was going, and clearly, he had played this course before.

I scanned the fairway. The grass was lush—soft, green, and wet. Emphasis on wet. The golfers were either carrying their bags or pulling them along with two-wheelers. The course was too soggy for motorized golf carts.

That didn't stop Gary from turning his five-ton beast off the road and powering it onto the perfectly manicured green carpet.

Kylie followed.

Clods of mud as big as basketballs flew up and pelted our windshield. She goosed her washers and turned on the wipers, but that only made it worse. We were driving blind.

By the time Kylie saw the sprinkler head, it was too late. It chewed up our left front tire, and we came to a sudden hard stop.

I jumped out of the car. The EMS bus was at least two football fields away. And then I heard it.

Helicopter.

But it wasn't one of ours. It was Gary Banta's ride out.

CHAPTER 71

WE CAN DO IT," Kylie said. She got out of the car and broke into a run.

And then we heard the howl. Siren.

We both turned. A chocolate-brown Chevy Impala, strobe lights white-hot and flashing in the windshield, was tearing up the fairway, regurgitating mud-caked green divots, thick as yesterday's porridge, onto the already ravaged hallowed grounds.

"Cavalry," Kylie said.

The back door flew open, the car slowed, and Kylie and I piled in.

There were three of them in the car, one white, one black, one brown—young, lean, and undercover. They had the requisite tats on their arms and seven-day stubble on their faces; their shirts and jeans were just ratty enough to be urban cool. They looked more like a boy band than the cavalry.

"Are you the Red team who needs help catching a bus?" the guy in the front passenger seat said. "Sorry to keep you waiting." His buddies laughed.

"You Bronx Auto?" Kylie said, picking up on the

Jamaican accent. "I thought they were sending real detectives."

Bigger laugh. Cops busting cops' balls, even at a time like this.

"Son of a bitch," the driver said as we skidded into a ninety-degree turn. "This wreck fits right in at the Webster Projects, but it ain't worth shit on the golf course."

He jammed the gearshift into low, got traction, and righted the car. "What'd they do?" he said. "Kill somebody and steal a bus?"

"Home invasions. One old lady died. And they're legit EMTs," Kylie said.

Brothers under the same blanket. A sobering detail. Head shakes all around.

"Armed?" the Jamaican asked.

"Presumed," I said, my eyes glued to the chopper that had just settled onto a putting green. The bus tried to barrel through a sand trap. Big mistake. Wheels spinning, kicking up a sandstorm, it ground to a halt.

Doors were flung open. The driver, white, and his partner, black, scrambled out and headed for the helicopter, which was a solid fifty yards away. The black guy was fast, agile, but the driver, Banta—I was sure of it—was slow navigating his way out of the wet sand.

We weren't doing that well ourselves as the car went slip-sliding across the slick turf. And then another spinout as the Impala did a complete one-eighty.

"Faster on foot," Kylie said. She bailed out of the back door and ran toward the chopper. I jumped out after her.

The chopper was small, a single-engine, no markings except for a tail number. NYPD Aviation would be able to outrun it—if they were here. But they were still minutes away, and that's all the time Banta needed to lift off and fly in any direction on the compass, land in a secluded spot, and drive off to parts unknown. That was Gary—always planning ahead.

The pilot must have been one of his EMS cohorts, because less than thirty minutes after Banta got the call that we were on to him, this guy showed up with the getaway plane, no questions asked.

I was a hundred feet away when the black EMS tech climbed into the chopper. Kylie was closer, but not by much.

Gary was going to outrun her. He knew it. I knew it. And Kylie knew it. Which was probably why she reached down to her right hip.

"Don't shoot," I screamed, my voice drowned out by the *whump-whump* of the rotors.

Kylie breaks a lot of rules and bends even more. She's got a reputation as a maverick, and she's proud of it. But there's one rule that will cost her her job if she violated it. A cop cannot—repeat, *cannot*—shoot at a moving vehicle unless he or she is returning gunfire.

That means if a car is coming at me at seventy miles an hour, I have two choices: get hit or get the hell out of the way. Firing my gun is not an option.

There are no loopholes, no excuses. And in this case, there was no justification for shooting. Kylie's life wasn't in danger, just her pride. She was determined not to lose Banta.

He clambered into the helicopter and pulled the door shut. The engine whined, the blades spun faster, but Kylie didn't stop. Just as the pilot pulled on the lever to create more lift, she jumped onto the landing-gear skid, brought her right hand up from her hip, shook it hard, and jammed it through the narrow vent window.

It wasn't a gun. You don't shake your gun. You shake your department-issued can of mace. It's not much bigger than a tube of lipstick, but it packs more than enough wallop to incapacitate a cockpit full of bad guys.

The chopper smacked down hard as Kylie yanked her arm out of the window and pirouetted off the skid like one of the Flying Wallendas coming down from the high wire, ready to take a bow.

The chopper doors burst open, and the occupants spilled out, choking, wheezing, and dropping to the ground.

Kylie went directly to the fallen hero, cuffed him, and yanked him to his feet.

The boy band, guns in hand, joined the action and helped me take care of the other two in short order.

The rotors on the chopper eased to a stop, the last echo of the siren died out, and the civilians who had been watching—and recording—the action burst into applause.

Except for one man—one very, very angry man. He came running toward us yelling something about crazy bastards having to pay.

Hard to blame him. He was the groundskeeper.

CHAPTER 72

WE SEPARATED GARY BANTA from the others and poured him into the back of a squad car. He didn't say a word for the entire forty-five-minute ride back to Manhattan. He didn't have to. Guilt, shame, and remorse were etched on his face.

We got to the precinct just at the change of tour, so the place was humming with the energy of a big-city police station. Kylie and I walked through the door, our pants and shoes caked with mud, and all the cops in the room stopped what they were doing. But they weren't looking at us.

They were staring at one of their own, still in uniform, wrists shackled, head hung low, eyes unable to meet theirs. I gave the desk sergeant a quick nod. Paperwork later. We rushed Banta upstairs and out of the line of fire before some wiseass cop said something that would send him into a tailspin.

"That was rough," I said as soon as we got him into a chair in the interrogation room. "You okay?"

He gave me a stoic nod. But I knew the stony façade couldn't last long. Everyone has a breaking point, and for Gary Banta, all it took for the dam to burst were seven words.

You have the right to remain silent.

Translation: *Life as you know it is over.*

His body heaved; he slumped in his chair and wept uncontrollably.

I put a hand on his shoulder and said, "We'll help you get through this, brother."

Brother. It wasn't a sign of respect. It was a tactic. When you want someone to talk, treat him like gold.

We gave him water, tissues, and time to cry it out. He declined a lawyer. He had too much he needed to get off his chest.

"Gary," I said in my best father-confessor voice, "you have a record anyone would be proud of. This isn't you."

He looked up, grateful that I had a hint of the man he used to be.

"Tell them that," he said, his voice barely above a whisper. "The family. Tell them how sorry I am. It was supposed to be a victimless crime. Insurance was going to reimburse them. We never meant for anyone to die."

"We?" I said.

"Me, Diggs, and Ramos. It was just the three of us."

"What about the crew at Yankee Stadium?"

He cracked half a smile. "They're clean. The only thing they're guilty of is giving me a heads-up that a cop was lying about knowing me. Hunter made you when he said I don't drink coffee and you bought it. I drink it by the gallon."

I returned the smile and shrugged. "FDNY, one; NYPD, zero." I put my hand on his shoulder a second time. "I saw a picture of the fire commissioner pinning a medal on you," I said. "It was only two years ago. How'd you get from there to here?"

He closed his eyes for about ten seconds as he reconstructed a life gone wrong. "I'm a single dad," he said when he opened them. "Two years ago I was on top of the world. My daughter finished college, she got a great job, and I had some money in my pocket. Same with the other two guys. So we bought a house in Peekskill, worked on it on our days off, and flipped it six months later. We cleared fifty-seven grand, and we were hooked.

"We bought another house. Bigger, much more money, but we were like addicts. We were going to get rich flipping houses. And then Murphy's Law kicked us in the balls. First it turned out the electric wasn't up to code, then we had to spend ten grand on a truss to support the second floor, and finally, the crusher—mold.

"The place was a money pit. We were in over our heads, and we couldn't scrape together enough to get out. And then one day Diggsy and I catch a call, a guy hit by a car on Bainbridge Avenue. We pick him up in the bus, and we're cutting his shirt off, and we see them. Bags of coke taped to his chest. Turned out to be five kilos—street value was like eighty, ninety grand.

"The guy says to us, 'Don't rat me out to the cops. Just hang on to the blow for me for a few days, and there's fifteen grand in it for you.' Diggs and me, we're straight shooters, but we're hemorrhaging money on this house, and we can't say no to fifteen large. Two days later, the guy—we named him Mr. Bainbridge—calls and tells us to drop the coke off at a Sunoco station on East Tremont. We do, and the guy gives us a bag with fifteen Gs in it."

He looked up at us. "You know where this is going, don't you?"

"Bainbridge called again," I said. "Any drug dealer would be happy to have two upstanding citizens with EMS badges on his payroll."

"The next run was to Jersey. A week later, it's Norfolk, Virginia. That's a long haul. So we call Ramos. He was in the toilet with us on the house-flipping, plus he's a pilot. Why drive across five state lines when you can fly?

"We did seven runs in all, some by car, some by plane. Then Bainbridge says he needs us to bring twenty keys to Baltimore. It's a half-a-million-dollar payload, and he'll pay us fifty grand for a two-hundred-mile drive. The three of us are giddy like little kids, because this is all we need to finally get out of the hole. We decide to make a weekend out of it. Drop the coke, collect the cash for Bainbridge, then celebrate with hard-shell crabs and enough beer to float a battleship."

I looked at Kylie. We both knew what was coming next.

"The handoff is in the parking lot of a renovated warehouse in a decent part of town. Three dudes pull up in an Escalade. One gets out and shows us the money, five hundred grand. We give him the coke, and the other two get out of the car, both with AK-47s. One says, 'Live or die. Either way, we get the money.' We vote live."

"Do you think Bainbridge set you up?"

"Doesn't matter. We can't go to the cops, and we owe him half a million. We spend the weekend in Baltimore anyway, and that's where we hatch the plan for the home invasions."

"Your targets weren't random," Kylie said. "How did you know who to hit?"

"Diggs has a kid brother, Tyreese. He works nights cleaning offices at a company that does the billing for a bunch of nursing agencies in the city. Ty is mentally challenged, but he's a whiz with computers. We tell him what we need, and he shows up the next morning with a printout. He has no idea what he's doing. He just wants to make his big brother happy."

"And what about Bainbridge?" she said.

He stiffened. "What about him?"

"What's his real name? You help us land a drug dealer, and I'm sure the DA will be willing to knock some time off your sentence."

"Detective, you don't need me to give up his name. You can go to my log and come up with the accident victim I picked up on Bainbridge Avenue. But that won't do you any good. You need me to testify, and if I do, it doesn't matter if the DA sends me to prison for only a day and a half, I'll never get out alive."

He was right. All we could do was tell Narcotics the story and let them figure out what to do about Bainbridge. Kylie and I had bigger problems to deal with. And at the top of that list was Chief of Detectives Harlan Doyle.

CHAPTER 73

MAYBE IT WAS the gardenias that helped us crack the code of Bobby Dodd's diaries. Or maybe it was the moon earrings. Or the birthday gift. It didn't matter. Cheryl found them all.

It was Wednesday morning and Cheryl, Kylie, and I were back in our war room still trying to deconstruct Dodd's ramblings of his imagined life with Erin.

"Zach, Kylie, listen to this," Cheryl said. "It's dated June third of this year. 'Erin and I met in our secret place. Her hair was pulled up under the hat, and the shades covered her eyes, but she still looked beautiful, and she smelled all summery, like gardenias.

"'She said she was sorry she couldn't be with me on her birthday tomorrow but she's got plans with Jamie. I said I understood, and I was happy enough to have her to myself the day before.

"'She was wearing tiny gold crescent earrings, and I said that the moons on her ears went real good with the stars in her eyes. She laughed and said I was sweet. Then we talked about our plans to be together. I can't wait.

"'Before she left I gave her the birthday present I

bought her. A little metal case she can keep in her purse to carry her credit cards and maybe a picture of me (ha-ha). The design on the outside has these cool silver-and-black Japanese fans. The note I wrote said, *With love from your biggest fan*. She said she simply adored it. And I said I simply adored her.

" 'She asked me when my birthday is and I told her that it was on March thirteenth, and she said she was sorry she missed it but next year she was going to buy me something special. I told her not to worry, that I'd get my real present on June ninth.' "

"What do you think?" Cheryl asked.

"He kidnapped her on June ninth," Kylie said. "No surprise that he was obsessed with it on June third."

"I mean what do you think about the gardenias and the stars in her eyes and the moons on her ears?"

Kylie shrugged. "I think some love letters should come with barf bags."

"Zach, help me out here."

"Cheryl, I'm not sure where you're going with this," I said. "Clearly you didn't flag it because you hoped I could be half as romantic. What do you see that we're missing?"

"Details, Detective. Details. There are some very specific facts in this diary entry that we can check."

" 'Erin and I met in our secret place'?" Kylie said. "How is that specific?"

"It's not, but we may be able to find out if Erin smelled like gardenias, wore gold crescent-moon earrings, and brought home a Japanese-fan-motif credit card holder on June third."

"So what if Dodd managed to get a few details right?" Kylie said. "No surprise. He's been stalking her for years. Somewhere along the way he smelled her perfume. He saw her with those earrings."

"What about the gift, the credit card holder he says he gave her?" Cheryl said.

"She may have one. That doesn't mean she got it from him."

Cheryl stood up and went to the whiteboard. "If that's the case, we'll put the diary entry here," she said, pointing to the RANTS side of the board. "But if some of the little nuances hold up under scrutiny..." She tapped the REALITY side of the board.

"I'm not sure what you mean by 'hold up under scrutiny,'" Kylie said.

"Erin's security chief used to be NYPD. He'd know what's real."

"Careful, Doc. If you show McMaster a diary entry about Bobby and Erin meeting in a secret place and planning to run away together, he's never going to say it happened. He doesn't work for the cops anymore. His allegiance is to her."

"Good advice," she said. "Luckily, I'm not a cop. I'm a psychologist, and one of my main concerns is Erin's well-being."

"That's bullshit."

Cheryl smiled. "You know that. I know that. But McMaster doesn't. Ask him to stop by. I want to pick his brain."

CHAPTER 74

MCMASTER SHOT CHERYL'S theories full of holes.

"Gucci's 'Gorgeous Gardenia' is one of the perfumes she pimps on her show," he said. "All her fans know that. As for the earrings, she wore them on the cover of *People* magazine about a year ago. Not everyone will remember that, but a man like Dodd would. It's chapter one in the basic stalker handbook."

"What about the gift?" Cheryl asked. "If she has it, we could dust it for prints and—"

"Dr. Robinson," McMaster said, "do you know how many gifts Erin gets every week? From men, from women, from kids. She has a separate closet to store them all. Ninety-nine point nine percent of them come through the U.S. mail. So if I dig through the closet and find the case with the Japanese fans, and you find Dodd's prints on it, what does that prove? He bought it, put it in an envelope, and dropped it in a mailbox."

Cheryl frowned. "Thanks. I guess that's why I'm a shrink and not a cop."

"No problem," McMaster said. "I appreciate that

it's your job to analyze all these wacko fairy tales in Dodd's diaries." He turned to me and Kylie. "But you guys *are* cops. Why are you wasting your time on this crap?"

"You were a cop too, Declan," Kylie said. "You of all people should know that it can take longer to wrap up a case than it does to solve it. And the chief of Ds doesn't think we're wasting our time. He wants to know if the man who kidnapped Erin Easton worked alone. Zach and I *think* he did, but Chief Doyle doesn't want us to *think*. He wants us to *find out*."

"And those *fairy tales* that the three of us have been reading," Cheryl said, "allow us to rummage through the twisted mind of Bobby Dodd. And if he did have an accomplice, I would think you'd want to know about it as much as we do."

McMaster exhaled hard. "You're right," he said. "My priorities have been a little screwed up. A few days ago I was positive that this kidnapping was a career-ender for me. But Erin wants me to stay on. I've been so desperate to get this nightmare behind me that I stopped thinking like a cop and started acting like a man with a business to save and a reputation to protect. I'm really sorry. Tell me what I can do to help."

"For starters, can you find out where Erin was on June third?" Kylie asked.

"I can tell you where she was every day for the past couple of years. June third is the day before her birthday. What's the significance?"

"Dodd says he was with Erin that day. Which probably means that wherever she was, he was close enough to watch her. If we know where Erin was, we can figure out where Dodd was, and with any luck we might be able to find out if he was alone or with someone."

"Give me a sec." He pulled an iPad out of his brief-case and began tapping on it. His face screwed up in a scowl. "Shit. It was one of her WAN days."

"Meaning what?"

"Meaning every now and then, she puts on the standard celebrity disguise—sunglasses, baseball cap, baggy sweats—and she goes out into the real world to WAN, 'walk around normal.' I'm not allowed to follow."

"But knowing you," Kylie said, "you have."

He grinned. "Not me, and don't ever repeat this, but a couple of years ago I hired someone she'd never met to tail her on those days. The first time, she took a cab to the Cloisters museum up at Fort Tryon Park. The next time, it was the Bronx botanical gardens. She really was *walking around normal*. I don't like it, but I get it. The poor woman has spent most of her life in a goldfish bowl. Sometimes she just needs to totally escape and be by herself. Bottom line: I have no idea where she was on June third."

"We could ask her. Will she remember?"

He shook his head. "After what she's been through? I seriously doubt it."

"What about the GPS chip?" I said. "The one that Bobby cut out of her arm. The one that was supposed to keep tabs on her whereabouts."

"The Korean company's LyfeTracker," McMaster said. "Good call, Zach—if it was working. But like I told you, it crapped out about a month ago. Middle of May or so. They're still trying to figure out how to fix the problem."

"I'm not an engineer," I said, "but a better battery might do the trick."

"It doesn't take a battery," McMaster said. "The chip runs on kinetic energy, like a self-winding watch.

The more you move, the more juice it produces. When it stopped working I spoke to one of the engineers in Korea. He said maybe Erin wasn't active enough to get it charged. I said bullshit. The woman is a human dynamo. A week later he calls me back and tells me I'm right. It's a product flaw. Erin generates plenty of energy. The damn chip was just not storing enough to transmit the data. It's like having a GPS in your car, but it won't tell you where you are."

"But…" Kylie said, working the thought out in her head as she was talking. "But just because your car doesn't tell you where you are doesn't mean it doesn't know where you've been."

"You lost me," McMaster said.

"Something was sapping the energy from the LyfeTracker, which kept it from transmitting Erin's whereabouts," Kylie said. "But did it at least have enough juice in it to *record and store* the data?"

"I have no idea," McMaster said. "It was just another one of Erin's crazy product endorsements. I didn't really ask the engineer too many questions."

"Well, I've got a few questions for you," Kylie said.

"Go for it," McMaster said.

"What's the engineer's phone number, and what time is it in Korea?"

CHAPTER 75

MCMASTER LOOKED AT his watch. "It's one in the morning in Seoul. Nobody at Kinjo Technology is going to pick up the phone for at least six more hours."

"Do you have a home number for the engineer?" I said.

"No, but I'll bet Peter Woon has it. He's the head of their New York office. At least, he was when he came to see me last week."

"He came to see you? Why?"

"To apologize on behalf of Kinjo. They signed one of the most recognizable people on the planet to be the spokeswoman for their new product. She did a commercial saying, 'With LyfeTracker, you can find me anywhere.' Then she goes missing, and nobody can find her. Zach, the man was embarrassed beyond belief, but to his credit, he took full responsibility for the product failure."

"And you think he's going to be the fall guy?"

"Let me put it this way. Kinjo had big plans to roll LyfeTracker out around the world. Now it's in the scrap heap, and the only thing that's going to roll are heads. The smart money is on Peter's. Corporate culture is a bitch."

Thirty minutes later we were in a conference room in Kinjo's Fifth Avenue office sitting around a massive rosewood table with six men in suits. On an eight-foot screen that dominated the far wall was Kang Woo Ki, sitting in front of a laptop in his home seven thousand miles and thirteen time zones away. His eyes were bleary, his hair looked like he'd combed it with an eggbeater, and he was definitely not wearing a suit. He was in close-up, so for all I knew, he was sitting in his boxer shorts. Clearly, he was trying to figure out what the hell was going on.

Woon opened the session by exchanging a few remarks with Mr. Kang. It was in Korean, so I could only guess what was said. Woon might have simply been explaining why the man had been dragged out of bed. Or, since Kang was the company's senior engineer, the two of them might have been making plans to get stinking drunk after their first trip to the unemployment line.

Introductions were made, and finally, Kang, speaking in perfect English, said, "How can I help you, Detectives?"

"The chip that Ms. Easton was wearing stopped transmitting data over a month ago," I said.

He winced and gave a slight head bow.

"The question is, was it still recording her movements?"

He pondered that briefly. "In theory. The satellite connection was flawless. The problem was that the elements we used for the transmitter—"

I had no time for a science lesson or a mea culpa. "Sorry to interrupt," I said. "You are saying that *in theory,* the chip was gathering data. If that's true, then her whereabouts—even after the transmitter failed—would be embedded in the LyfeTracker."

"Forget *in theory*," he said, his voice stronger as he cleared the cobwebs from his head. "Most definitely."

Magic words. Kylie and McMaster sat forward in their chairs.

"How do we retrieve it?" I said.

"I'm afraid you can't do that."

Kylie dropped the flat of her fist onto the table and blew the exasperation from her lungs.

And then…

"Correction," Kang said. "You *could* retrieve the information, but not without Ms. Easton's permission."

"Why do we need her permission?" Kylie called out to the giant screen.

"The chip is in her body," Kang said. "You can't just rip it out of the woman. It's a violation of her—"

"It's already been ripped," Kylie said, standing up. "I have it right here."

She held up the evidence bag that we'd picked up before we left the precinct. A loud, long "Ohhhh" came from the men around the table. We hadn't told anybody, them included, that Dodd had cut the chip out of Erin's arm.

This seemed like a good time to fill them in.

"So if the chip was removed, it wasn't a failure on the part of LyfeTracker that the police couldn't find her," Peter Woon said, his Wharton-educated brain rewriting history to save his corporate ass. "Detective, can you make a public statement to that effect?"

We're all whores in one way or another. We get into bed with strangers because we have something they want, and they have something we need.

"Once this case has been resolved," I said, "the department would be happy to tell the press that the kidnapper removed your tracker from Erin's arm because he was concerned that we would use it to find her." *And I will leave out the fact that the damn thing was broken anyway, so it was a wasted effort on Dodd's part.*

Wide smiles and animated Korean chatter around the room as the suits realized that their company's reputation could be salvaged.

"Mr. Kang," Kylie said, cutting through the din. "Now that we have the chip, can you help us figure out where it's been since it stopped transmitting? And no more theories, please."

"Yes, I can. All we need is a power source." He barked some orders in his native language, and the youngest two suits bolted from the room.

Twenty minutes later the chip was hooked up to a contraption that was linked to Mr. Kang's laptop in Seoul.

"Give me a date and time," he said.

"Sunday, June ninth, at five p.m.," Kylie said.

"The chip was at three-eleven West Thirty-Fourth Street in New York City," Kang said, the address of the Hammerstein Ballroom.

"The damn thing was recording the whole time," McMaster said.

"Last night at eight p.m.," Kylie said.

"It was at one fifty-three East Sixty-Seventh Street, also in New York."

And we knew for sure that was exactly where it had been—tucked away for safekeeping in the evidence room at the Nineteenth Precinct.

More than a month after it had stopped transmitting, and a week and a half after Dodd had dug it out of Erin's arm, the damn thing was *still* recording.

There were ten of us in the meeting—nine in New York, one in Korea—all with one thing in common.

Big, wide, shit-eating grins.

CHAPTER 76

ERIN EASTON HAD a brand-new stalker, and she had no idea that he was tracking her every move.

It was my old friend Benny Diaz from our Technical Assistance Response Unit.

We gave Benny the LyfeTracker, the power source that Peter Woon graciously donated to help us gather evidence that might help wipe some of the egg off his corporate face, and Declan McMaster's detailed log of Erin's comings and goings over the past year.

"One question," Benny said. "Erin's security people know exactly where she was ninety, ninety-five percent of the time. Shouldn't I just focus on the times when she went off on her own?"

"No," I said. "I know it's a lot more work, but if Declan has her shopping at Fifty-Ninth and Third, and the LyfeTracker says she was at Fifty-Eighth and Park, then none of the data will hold up, and the DA will kick us out of his office."

"Benny," Kylie said, "if we're going to use this technology to prove where Erin was when McMaster wasn't watching, then it better be spot-on for all the times when he *was*."

"You got it," Diaz said. "But it's going to take me a few days. I'm crushed with other work."

"Take all the time you need," Kylie said. "We'll tell the chief of Ds you're busy with stuff that he *doesn't* give a shit about."

"Come back tomorrow morning at eight," he said. "I like my coffee black and my bagels buttered."

The next morning we were back with coffee, bagels, and high hopes.

"I'll start with the good news," Benny said. "I know they had transmission problems, but the GPS in that little sucker is as good as anything on the market. Maybe better. It was pinpoint accurate across the board. There was one time when McMaster's log said Erin was on a photo shoot in front of the Alice in Wonderland statue in Central Park, and LyfeTracker practically had her sitting in Alice's lap. I'd testify in court that the damn thing knew where Erin was every step of the way."

"Good news is usually followed by bad," I said. "Drop the other shoe."

"Ye of little faith," Diaz said. "This time the good news is followed by even better news. Listen to this— over the past year there were eleven separate days when Erin went off on her own. I cross-checked them with Bobby's diary. On five of those days, he didn't post anything. That leaves six days when she's off the grid, and he writes that he was with her.

"I eliminated three of them right away because his description of where they were is completely different from where the GPS says she was. For instance, one entry said they took a romantic sunset cruise to the Statue of Liberty, but I know for a fact that she was in an apartment building near Tompkins Square from four in the afternoon till ten at night. There might have been romance in the air, but I doubt if she saw the sun set."

"So we're down to three days when they might have been together," I said.

"May nineteenth, May twenty-seventh, and June third," he said. "According to McMaster the tracker stopped transmitting on May twelfth, so as far as Erin was concerned, she was untraceable on those three days. But once I powered up the chip I knew exactly where she was—Pelham Bay Park all three times."

"Dodd lived in Pelham Bay. Does he mention that park in his diary?"

"Not in so many words. On May nineteenth he writes, 'Erin and I had our secret rendezvous down by the water.' I tracked her walking through the park to the Long Island Sound."

"How many cameras do we have in the park?" I said.

"Not a one. Sorry. It's Pelham Bay, Zach, not Central Park."

"Then why are you getting my hopes up?"

"Because on May twenty-seventh, Bobby writes about walking through the park and smelling the horses."

"I read that," Kylie said. "I figured he was talking about the hansom cabs in Central Park."

"NYPD mounted troop D has its stables in Pelham Bay Park," Diaz said. "Maybe those are the horses he smelled."

"*Maybe* won't cut it with the DA," Kylie said. "Even if you can put Dodd in the same location as Erin, that doesn't prove anything. He stalked her wherever she went. Unless you get us hard evidence that they were together, the only thing that tells us is that Erin Easton was being followed by a crazy person. And without any cameras in the park—"

"That's what I thought," Diaz said, cutting her off. "And then it dawned on me—those stables are a department asset, and like every NYPD facility, it's on camera twenty-four/seven. I called the desk sergeant this morning, and he verified it. I sent one of my guys over there to download the footage from May twenty-seventh. He should be back here in an hour."

"Benny," I said, "if you can find proof of Erin and Bobby together, it's going to blow her story out of the water and turn this case on its ear."

"I think maybe I can," he said. "And if I do, it's going to cost you guys a lot more than a bagel."

CHAPTER 77

KYLIE AND I had Erin's cell phone records on file. We dug them out and tracked back to the days and times that Benny had zeroed in on.

In all three cases, Erin's phone was off. It didn't prove a thing, but it was highly coincidental that the woman who almost never pulled the plug on her cell had rendered it untraceable during the exact times that we suspected she and Bobby were together.

An hour went by. And then another. And then Benny called and said three words that would change Erin Easton's life forever.

"We got her."

Minutes later, Kylie and I were in Benny's office. "Most of the cameras are pointed at the stables," he said. "But this one is mounted above the stalls, and it picks up a nice wide swath of the park. I cued it up at a minute before we see them just so you can get the feel of things."

He rolled the footage. It hardly seemed like we were watching a crime surveillance video. The day was sunny, the resolution was excellent, and the park was lush and green.

And then they appeared. Erin was in what McMaster had jokingly called the standard celebrity disguise. It was about as effective as putting a Groucho Marx mustache on George Clooney. She was entirely recognizable.

Next to her, as big as life, was her stalker, the man three judges had ordered to stay away from her—Bobby Dodd. Not only were he and Erin in the same frame, but they were talking, laughing, and holding hands.

Benny froze the image, and I could imagine it splashed across every front page around the world.

"She's playing him," Kylie said, practically yelling at the screen.

Diaz smiled, proud of his contribution.

"Good police work, Benny," I said. "But it doesn't prove a thing."

The smile faded fast. "Why not? It's two weeks before the kidnapping, and I just showed you a picture of the two of them together."

"And I can show you pictures of Trump and Hillary together," I said.

"But not holding hands and frolicking in the park," Kylie said.

Diaz laughed out loud. "So you agree with me," he said to Kylie.

"No. Unfortunately, I have to agree with Zach. It sure as hell *looks* like she's prepping him, plotting out the kidnapping and everything else that came down the pike, but any first-year law student could get up in front of a jury and fill their heads with reasonable doubt."

Diaz looked at the image on the screen and then turned back at Kylie. "I don't know," he said. "It looks pretty damning to me."

Kylie cleared her throat. "Ladies and gentlemen of the jury," she said, her eyes drilling into Diaz. "Erin Easton was an international media star who was about to marry an incredibly successful, powerful, and wealthy man. Why would she suddenly throw that all away to team up with a lowlife who had preyed on her for more than a decade?"

"The ransom money?" Diaz said meekly.

"Twenty-five million?" Kylie said. "Chump change. Jamie was heir to half a billion."

Benny's head nodded as he processed what she was saying.

"I sense reasonable doubt creeping in," Kylie said.

"Look, I'm a computer cop. I watched the video. It hasn't been doctored, and my takeaway is that Erin is hiring Bobby to kidnap her. But you make a pretty good lawyer. I'm starting to think I could be wrong."

"You're half wrong. She wasn't *hiring* him. She was seducing him. Telling him all the things he wanted to hear, spinning the same pipe dreams he'd written about for years. I think somewhere along the way Erin must have found out that Jamie *wasn't* as rich as she'd thought. His mother had all the money, and the only way Erin would ever see a nickel of it would be over Veronica's dead body.

"Erin knew Jamie wouldn't be able to come up with the ransom money. She also knew that Veronica wouldn't cough up a cent. It all played out just as she'd scripted it, and by then Bobby was in so deep, the only way he could get enough money to keep the woman he loved was to kill the woman she hated. And as soon as he did that, Erin killed him."

Benny's mouth hung open. He looked at me. "Where are you on all this?"

"She's right. Chief Doyle always suspected Bobby had an accomplice. It just didn't occur to us that it could be Erin. The problem is, we still don't have what we need to prove anything."

"So how do you stop her from getting away with it?"

"Give us a minute," Kylie said. "We just cracked the code. Zach and I haven't come up with a game plan yet."

"Whatever we do," I said, "we've got to do it fast."

"Why's that?" Benny said.

"Because Jamie Gibbs just inherited half a billion dollars. If anything should happen to him, that money goes to Erin. Even if Jamie leaves some of it to his unborn child, for the next eighteen years, Erin Easton will call the shots on how every penny of Veronica's fortune is spent."

CHAPTER 78

INCREDIBLE," CAPTAIN CATES said after we'd caught her up. "The woman's gone from victim to hero to suspect in less than a week."

"That's show business," Kylie said. "One minute you're riding high, the next minute you're in the back of a patrol car on your way to Central Booking."

"From your lips," Cates said, "but right now you don't have enough to charge her."

"Not yet. But she's coming in at noon. We'll give her a shovel and hope she buries herself."

"I'll be watching on the monitor," Cates said. "With my finger hovering over the chief of Ds' direct line."

Erin's version of noon turned out to be three forty-five.

"You look fantastic," Kylie said, gushing like a fangirl and giving her a big hug. Next came the outpouring of love and concern: *How are you? How is the baby? How are you sleeping? It must be so comforting to have a strong man like Jamie at your side. And how is he doing? His mother's death was such a blow. It's so good that you can be there for each other.*

My turn next: *So sorry to drag you in after all you've been through. One final interview so we can tie it up in a bow for our boss. We all want to put it behind us.*

Erin responded as if she were doing a late-night talk-show interview. She opened up immediately, thrilled to fill us in on her favorite subject—herself.

"So tell us when you first met Bobby Dodd," Kylie said, easing into the interview.

We'd already heard every detail from McMaster, but we listened intently as Erin recounted a time when she truly was a victim.

"Prior to your wedding day," I said, "when was the last time you'd seen or heard from Dodd?"

"Oh God, it must have been at least a year—maybe more," she lied. "I was finally starting to think he was gone for good."

"Prior to June ninth, did he ever hurt you?"

"No."

"Touch you?"

"No. He couldn't get close. I always had my security people."

"Were you *ever* alone with him?"

"Never."

"Did he ever manage to get past security and talk to you directly?"

"Not until he kidnapped me."

"We were told he broke into your house in Aspen," I said.

"And my apartment in New York. And the villa in Tuscany, twice. Four separate times, but I was never at home."

"Why do you think he was so interested in seeing where you live?" I asked.

"He was obsessed. He was a voyeur."

"Any other reason?"

"The man was batshit-crazy, Detective. I'm not sure what you're getting at."

"This is going to sound strange," I said, "but I have to ask—did you and Bobby Dodd ever go house-hunting in the Berkshires?"

"House-hunt—no! How could you people even come up with such a ridiculous idea?"

"Erin," I said, "we didn't come up with it. We read about it in Bobby's diary."

Her eyes screamed in panic: *What diary?* But she managed to keep her voice under control. "I'm sorry. I don't understand. What diary are you talking about?"

"Let me explain," Kylie said. "You're right about Bobby being obsessed with you. In fact, he was so obsessed that he kept a detailed diary of your life together."

"He kidnapped me on a Sunday, Detective. I escaped on Wednesday. It was all of seventy-two hours. I wouldn't exactly call that a *life together*."

"I'm talking about the fifteen years before he kidnapped you," Kylie said, reaching to the floor and hauling up a large carton. She stacked Bobby's diaries on the table.

She handed one to Erin and opened it to the house-hunting entry. "Read this, and you'll understand."

We watched as she read it. At first she was horrified. And then she burst out laughing. "Well, he's right about one thing. He calls the network a bunch of idiots. But the rest is all in his head."

"Thanks," Kylie said. "We needed your answer for the record. I'm sorry, but there are several more entries we were hoping you could either confirm or deny."

She shrugged. Clearly this was a waste of her time and ours. Then she gave us a smile and a nod. *Noblesse oblige*—the privileged generously accommodating the wishes of the masses.

"Did you and Bobby go skiing in Vermont?" I asked.

"Oh God, no. Everyone knows I despise the cold."

We rattled off several more places that we'd had on our RANTS side of the whiteboard. She dismissed each one with a snarky comment and a wave of her hand. By the time we got to the Tower of London, she was totally relaxed. The diary entries were now more of a parlor game than a threat.

"Here's one that supposedly took place close to home," Kylie said. "I know you said you hadn't seen him for a year before he kidnapped you, but he has the two of you holding hands and walking in Pelham Bay Park a few weeks before your wedding."

Erin's jaw tightened, but she coasted smoothly into the lie. "No. I don't even know where Pelham Bay Park is."

"It's in the Bronx," I said. "You should visit it sometime. It's the largest park in New York. Three times bigger than Central Park."

"Funny thing about Pelham Bay Park," Kylie said. "As big as it is, it's basically a camera-free zone."

By now I was standing on Erin's left side, Kylie on her right, both of us ping-ponging comments back and forth, making her work hard to figure out exactly what we knew.

"It's the perfect place to go if you don't want to be videotaped," I said, and I could see her jaw unclench. "Of course, someone like Bobby would know that."

"There's one thing Bobby didn't know," Kylie said. "Our mounted police unit has a stable there."

"And…" I said, waiting for Erin's head to snap back toward me. "It's got a state-of-the-art surveillance system."

"I'm sure that's lovely for the horses," she said, "but I really don't see what that has to do with me."

"You tell us," I said, and I slid the image of her and Bobby across the table.

"That's not me," she said, barely looking at it. "It's fake."

"No, Erin," Kylie said. "This is an official NYPD photo. There's nothing fake about it. What you see is exactly what the camera saw."

Erin picked up the picture and stared at it hard. Then she put it down, leaned back in her chair, smiled at us both, and said the one thing we didn't want to hear.

CHAPTER 79

DO I NEED a lawyer?" she asked.

She'd said the L-word—the one that can bring an interview to a crashing halt. Kylie and I hadn't charged Erin with a crime, so we weren't obligated to Mirandize her. But Miranda warning or not, as soon as a suspect asks for a lawyer, it's over—no more questions.

But of course, Erin hadn't *asked* for a lawyer. Her exact words were "Do I need a lawyer?" And she'd sort of chirped it more than said it.

Some people called her Airhead Easton, but I'd come to understand how damn smart she was. She knew the rules of the game as well as anyone. She knew she could shut down the interview in a heartbeat.

But she didn't. I wondered if she thought that asking for an attorney would make her look guilty. Or maybe she didn't want to have to deal with TMZ and the gossip-rag headlines screaming "Erin Lawyers Up." And then I looked at the smirk on her face, and I knew.

She was dicking with us.

She didn't think this was a fight she could lose.

"I can't tell you if you need a lawyer," I said, "but it's totally within your rights to contact one."

"I'll keep that in mind," she said, "but I think I can clear up the misconception, and we can tie this up in a bow for your boss, just like you wanted."

Another smirk. The Ping-Pong match had now become a game of cat and mouse, and Erin was positive that she was the cat.

"Please," I said. "Clear it up for us."

"That's not me in the picture with Dodd," she said. "I know it *looks* like me. But a lot of women try to look like me. And a few of them are so good at it that they make a fabulous living doing shows and corporate events and all kinds of private parties. Trump has impersonators, Elvis has impersonators, and so do I."

And just like that, she was as famous as the president of the United States and the king of rock and roll. *Nicely done. Except for one small detail.*

"So it might be you or it might not be you," I said. "Knowing you have all these impersonators would certainly create reasonable doubt in my mind."

"Exactly," she purred.

"Good thing you had that chip under your skin," Kylie said. "That ought to help us sort it out."

"Correct me if I'm wrong, Detective, but I thought I heard you say the picture was taken a few weeks before the wedding."

"May twenty-seventh, to be exact," Kylie said.

"Unfortunately, the chip stopped working weeks before that, so I'm afraid we're right back to reasonable doubt."

"Maybe not," I said. "It turns out someone made a mistake. The chip didn't stop working. It just stopped transmitting data. The GPS kept a record of your every move right up until the day you had Bobby cut it out of your arm."

"We took the liberty of downloading your itinerary," Kylie said, producing the report from TARU. "If you look at May twenty-seventh, you'll see that LyfeTracker has you in Pelham Bay Park at the exact moment the NYPD cameras picked up you and Bobby Dodd working out how to murder your mother-in-law."

Erin bolted up. "I had nothing to do with Veronica's death! That was all Bobby's idea."

"Bullshit!" Kylie said, pounding the table for effect. "Do you expect anyone to believe that you teamed up with a maniac just to get a mere twenty-five million dollars in ransom? I don't buy it, my partner doesn't buy it, and I guarantee you a jury won't buy it. You had your eye on Veronica's money from the get-go."

"Not true," Erin said, slumping back into her chair. "Not true."

"Then why would you have yourself kidnapped?"

"You wouldn't understand. This Red cop shit sounds good on paper—a big fancy police force that caters to the high-rollers. But then it falls apart because you're all nickel-and-dime players. You have no idea what it's like to be me."

"Enlighten us."

"I've been world-fucking-famous for twenty years, but I've got a clock on me, and it's ticking louder and louder. It's saying, 'Erin, your fan base is aging out, the new fans have found a dozen younger idols, and your TV show is about to tank.' I'm not an actress. I'm not a performer. I'm a personality. I'm a brand, and my brand was starting to circle the drain.

"I've seen it happen to other women, and it's not pretty. One day you're an A-list superstar with money pouring in and then all of a sudden you're a face in the where-are-they-now montage on BuzzFeed. The money's not coming in anymore, but it never stops going out, and I could see myself in five years doing game shows, showing up with my tits half out at insurance conventions in Vegas, and starring in cosmetics infomercials aimed at a bunch of desperate women who think their lives would be better if they looked like me.

"My career was on life support. And then I found Jamie. He's not the best-looking man I ever met, or the best in bed, or the best anything, but he had money—or at least I thought he did—so what the hell? I started dating him. Exclusively. Every night. Every weekend. The paparazzi tracked us wherever we went, and it drove Veronica crazy. She knew why I was with her precious little boy, so she began trashing me something fierce, and now she was not only his boss at work, she was trying to run his love life. So he figured out the one thing he could do to show Mommy who's really in charge—*marry the bitch*.

"The media loved the feud, and then the Brock-ways came up with this Wedding of the Century fiasco. Suddenly I was getting talk shows again, and magazine covers, and five-minute pieces on *Access Hollywood*, and I didn't want it all to end on June ninth. So yes, I came up with the idea for the kid-napping. But I didn't do it for the money. I did it to keep my brand from dying. And I swear to God, I never planned to kill Veronica Gibbs."

"Just Bobby Dodd," Kylie said.

Erin froze. She'd been so glorified in the media for overpowering her captor that she'd convinced herself she was every bit the heroine they said she was. But in reality she was nothing more than a stone-cold, commando-trained killer.

"I'm going to read you your rights," Kylie said. Then she paused. I doubted if it was to give Erin a moment to process it all. Knowing Kylie, she was giving Captain Cates enough time to dial up the chief of Ds and let him savor the arrest in real time.

"You have the right to remain silent," Kylie began.

I tuned out the rest of it as my brain kicked into another gear, and I was able to reflect on the irony of it all.

After years of enjoying fame she'd done nothing to earn, Erin Easton was finally going to be world-famous for something she'd actually done.

CHAPTER 80

IT WAS SURELY the single worst day of Erin Easton's life, but for Chief of Detectives Harlan Doyle, it was shaping up to be one of the best.

The man and his entire command had been skewered in the press for failing to save Erin. But then Doyle found out that she'd had no desire to be saved, and he was not going to let this humiliating piece of departmental history remain uncorrected. So he did what anyone in his shoes would do when he smelled redemption. He broke out the heavy artillery.

Within minutes of Erin being charged, Doyle and his old buddy Mason Bachner, the deputy commissioner of public information, put together an operation to make sure that the news of her arrest broke big.

And, boy, did it ever.

It started with the perp walk.

Most people think that the suspect's brief journey from the bowels of the precinct to the confines of a patrol car is a haphazard affair, just a handful of random cops moving their prisoner from one spot to another like so many baggage handlers while the cameras record it for posterity.

Not true. If the perp is high profile enough to generate media frenzy, then the walk has to be a brilliantly choreographed piece of theater.

And nobody put on a better show than Matthew Diamond.

Lieutenant Diamond was one of Doyle's go-to guys at DCPI Bachner's office. Cates gave us the heads-up that he was on his way, and we were downstairs when he arrived.

He went straight for the front desk. "Good afternoon, Sergeant McGrath," he said. "And how has your day been going?"

"Just fine, sir."

"I'm about to change all that," Diamond said, the upbeat tone gone. "In less than an hour the cameras will be rolling, and the eyes of the world are going to be on your precinct. My job is to ensure they see exactly what the chief of Ds wants them to see."

McGrath didn't have to ask what *his* job was. "Yes, sir. What can I do to make that happen?"

Diamond started with casting. "I want three of your sharpest officers at the front door, another dozen on the street. And McGrath, we're not shooting a sequel to the mall-cop movies. I want New York's Finest, not New York's fattest."

McGrath, a large-boned fellow and proud of it, laughed. "Yes, sir."

A half an hour later, the stage was set. Sixty-Seventh Street from Third to Lex was locked down, the entire block cleared except for the prisoner-transport vehicles. The members of the press were clustered behind barricades with a lean, mean cop stationed every five feet. NYPD choppers circled overhead, and a heavily armed team from the Strategic Response Group patrolled the ground, on the lookout for international terrorists or local nutjobs.

Spielberg might have been able to mount a more elaborate production, but not in thirty minutes.

At 5:45, on the cusp of the evening news cycle, the precinct doors swung open and Erin Easton stepped into the light. I was at one elbow, Kylie at the other. A roar erupted as the media horde screamed her name.

Erin instinctively moved her right arm to wave to the crowd, but her wrists were shackled behind her back. She stopped and stared them down as tape rolled, shutters clicked, and scores of reporters shelled her with questions. Most of them were unintelligible, but the ones I could make out all started with *why*.

And then she turned and kept walking, eyes straight ahead, lips pursed tight, head held high.

It lasted all of eighteen seconds, but it was a perp walk for the ages, one that would live on not just in pop culture, but in department lore. NYPD Red parading the most famous criminal on the planet in front of a global audience. I could just picture Chief Doyle, who must have watched the live feed at 1PP along with DCPI Bachner, the police commissioner, and the mayor. Doyle would remain stone-faced on the outside, but inside he'd be laughing his ass off.

And he'd only just begun.

I'd driven from the precinct to Central Booking hundreds of times. When you've got just a single prisoner, all it takes is one car. But this was Doyle's big show, and Diamond had ordered up five gleaming black Escalades and eight motorcycle cops from Highway Unit 1 to clear the way.

The Harleys pulled out, and a minute later the

rest of us followed. Dozens of TV stations—local, national, and international—filmed the convoy as we made the six-mile run from Sixty-Seventh Street to FDR Drive to Centre Street. It was the best coverage of a cop-car caravan since LAPD chased O.J.'s Bronco down the 405.

Kylie and I escorted Erin to the basement of the vast detention complex and handed her over to a corrections officer who searched her and processed her paperwork.

Then we watched as Erin was led toward a cell that held thirty women.

But the guard was only taunting her. A door thunked, and Erin was shoved into a private cell—gray walls, steel toilet, and no escape from the cat-calling women directly across from her. As I left, the last thing I heard was "You're one of us now, bitch."

And that ended act two.

Kylie and I walked next door to One Police Plaza, where Chief Doyle was about to raise the curtain on act three, a carefully orchestrated press conference.

"Congratulations, Detectives," he said, shaking our hands. "You finally lived up to the hype."

He took the stage. His boss, the police commissioner, stood a step behind him and to his right. Kylie and I were positioned to the left.

Doyle leaned into the sea of microphones. "In the course of investigating the kidnapping of Erin Easton and the murder of Veronica Gibbs, the two lead detectives from NYPD Red—Zach Jordan and Kylie MacDonald—uncovered evidence that Ms. Easton was a coconspirator in her own kidnapping.

"There is incontestable proof of her colluding with her kidnapper, Bobby Dodd—the man who killed Mrs. Gibbs and who was subsequently murdered by

Ms. Easton. She has made a statement and has been booked. She will be arraigned tomorrow morning. That's all I have for now, but I'll take questions."

Damn right he would take questions. Starting with the one he'd planted. He pointed to a female reporter in the front row. She stood up.

"Peg O'Ryan, *Eyewitness News*. Chief Doyle, now that you've discovered that this kidnapping was a conspiracy and nothing like what it appeared to be on the surface, can you tell us if anyone else was involved?"

"That's a good question, Peg." Doyle hesitated as if he were wrestling with an answer. But knowing the man, I figured he had rehearsed it with her an hour ago. "As you're aware, this is still an ongoing investigation, so I'm limited in what I can say." Another pause. "But I will tell you this: we have information that a person or persons at Ms. Easton's network, ZTV, may have provided money—a million dollars, in fact—to the kidnapper, Bobby Dodd, in exchange for a video of Ms. Easton in captivity."

"Did the network know that the video was staged?"

"I can't say, but when you go behind the backs of the NYPD during an active criminal investigation, it doesn't matter if you're colluding or aiding and abetting. You're breaking the law, and if you're a television network, you're violating the public's trust. Someone at ZTV has a lot of explaining to do."

O'Ryan fired off another question. "Would that someone be Harris Brockway?"

"Peg, you know I can't confirm that."

"Can you deny it?"

The chief shook his head as if he'd been placed in an uncomfortable position. But the three people behind him knew he was relishing the moment.

"No," he finally said. "I can't stand here and honestly deny it."

The crowd erupted. Nothing had been said, but the conclusion was clear: Brockway had paid Dodd a million dollars for the video.

ADA Bill Harrison had told us that Brockway would probably not go to jail for what he'd done. But one thing was sure: his career in television was over.

I knew it, Kylie knew it, and, judging from the Cheshire-cat grin on Harlan Doyle's face, he not only knew it but was proud as hell to be the man who'd made it happen.

KYLIE AND SHANE, ZACH AND CHERYL

CHAPTER 81

Friday, June 21
Delta Flight 2786

WE'RE FLYING FIRST CLASS?" Kylie said as she sat down in seat 1A.

"That's what happens when you plan a trip at the eleventh hour," Shane said, sitting down next to her. "All the cheap seats are gone."

"Nice try, but you knew you were going to Orlando months ago."

"Okay, I lied. I'm tall. I bought a first-class ticket back in February. I had to buy you one a few days ago because it's always so awkward to tell your last-minute date that she's sitting in coach. But if you're having trouble adjusting to all this legroom and the free champagne, I'll ask the flight attendant if she can find someone in the back of the plane to change seats with you."

"I'll muddle through," Kylie said. "But you see what happens when you try to lie to a detective."

"Yes, and I'm very impressed with your interrogation skills. Now, if you'd like to pat me down and frisk me, I think we have time to sneak into the bathroom before takeoff."

Kylie laughed. *Good-looking, cooks up a storm, and he can make me laugh,* she thought. *Triple threat.*

He rested his hand on hers, and she inhaled sharply as her body responded to his touch. Shane Talbot was gifted with large, strong, magical hands. And not just in the kitchen. She smiled, remembering the first time they'd made love. Then she silently corrected her earlier thought. *Quadruple threat.*

"Hey," he said, "I spoke to Cheryl this afternoon. You'll never guess what she said just before she hung up."

"She probably said, 'Don't be lying to Kylie MacDonald. She's one smart cop, and she'll trip you up every time.'"

"No. She said, 'Have fun in Disney World.' I straightened her out. I said we were going to the Southeast Food Expo. And she said, 'But Kylie told Zach that you were going to Disney.'"

"Not true. I told Zach that we were going to *Orlando* for the weekend. I can't help it if his mind jumped to talking mice and fairy-tale princesses. If he wanted to know specifics, he should have asked."

"Kylie, if you tell your old boyfriend that you're going to Orlando with your new boyfriend, he's never going to ask for specifics."

"At what point did we establish that you're my new boyfriend?"

"My cousin the shrink is so right. You love to mess with Zach's head. And I think I should be flattered that you're starting to enjoy messing with mine."

He leaned over and kissed her, lingering just long enough for Kylie to wish she'd taken him up on his offer to pat him down in the bathroom.

There was something about Shane Talbot that was unfathomable. The physical attraction was intense, but it was more than that.

It was…no, it definitely wasn't love. Too soon.

You can't decide that you love someone just because he dazzles you with dinner, and the sex is good. Okay, better than good—incredible. But love? That takes time.

Or maybe it doesn't. She'd only loved two men in her life, and she'd fallen for each of them hard and fast.

With Spence, it was date him, dump him, take him back, marry him, walk out on him eleven years later, and now…

Now? Good question. She hadn't seen or heard from him since January. It was strange to be technically married and not know whether your husband was alive or dead. But one thing she knew for sure: she didn't love him anymore.

It was different with Zach. Their affair had lasted all of four weeks. The only reason she'd ended it was to give Spence one more chance. But she'd never stopped loving Zach. Never would.

And now there was Shane Talbot with his first-class seats and his butterscotch *budino* and his—

"Hey! Ground Control to Major Tom."

She looked up. *That handsome face, that thick red hair, those incredible hands…*

"I can almost hear the wheels inside your head turning a mile a minute," Shane said. "What's going on in there?"

"Nothing much. I was just mulling over this new-boyfriend concept."

"How am I doing?"

"You're in the lead," Kylie said. "But don't let it go to your head. It's still only a one-man race."

"Excuse me, sir." It was the flight attendant.

Shane looked up. "Yes?"

"You're going to have to buckle your seat belt."

A wide smile spread across Shane's face, and he leaned over and whispered in Kylie's ear, "Funny…that's the same advice Cheryl gave me when I told her you and I were going away for the weekend."

CHAPTER 82

Sunday, June 23
Bentley's by the Sea, Montauk, New York

HAPPY ANNIVERSARY," Cheryl whispered in my ear.

"It's the middle of the night," I slurred, hugging my pillow closer to my cheek.

"No, it's not. It's five o'clock in the morning, and I want you to see your anniversary present before it's too late."

I half rolled over. "Bring it here."

"No can do. It's on the beach. Get up. We're running out of time."

I'd rather have celebrated our anniversary over a late brunch, but when you're a man in a relationship, you learn that some things are not debatable.

We threw on some clothes, grabbed a couple of blankets, left the warmth of our cozy little cottage, and trekked out past the dunes. We spread one blanket on the cold damp sand and wrapped ourselves in the other.

"I'm ready for my present," I said.

Cheryl checked her watch. "Three more minutes."

I rested my head on her shoulder, closed my eyes, and drifted right back to the land of Nod. A few minutes later she elbowed me awake.

"There it is," she said, pointing toward the horizon.

The sun was just cracking through the shroud of darkness, spreading soft blues and vivid pinks across the sky.

"You don't even have to unwrap it," Cheryl said. She had her camera in her hand and was aiming it at the rising sun.

As the sky bloomed orange, and shafts of gold sliced into the Atlantic, the fog in my brain finally lifted, and I realized—*that* was my gift.

"It's the dawn of a brand-new year together," she said, "and I wanted to share it with you."

Words failed me. I pulled her closer, and as I sat there huddled under the blanket soaking up the majesty of the moment with the woman I loved, my life of the past two weeks felt distant and surreal. This was where I belonged.

Twenty minutes later we walked back to the bed-and-breakfast, stripped off our damp clothes, buried ourselves under a thick down comforter, and slept for another four hours.

We made love before we got out of bed, then made love again under a high-pressure rainfall showerhead that pelted us with fat droplets of steamy hot water.

We had just finished dressing when Cheryl's phone rang. She looked at the caller ID. "Zach, I've got to take this. I'll meet you in a few minutes for breakfast."

The dining room was wood and stone with an eclectic mix of brightly colored Persian throw rugs underfoot and a wall of glass looking out toward the ocean. There was a large groaning board laden with berries, breads, jams, cheeses, and sterling chafing dishes filled with stick-to-the-ribs, clog-up-the-arteries options. The coffee was dark roast and smelled like nirvana.

I poured two cups, toasted two thick slices of raisin pumpernickel to tide me over till Cheryl got there, and found a quiet table. Ten minutes later, she arrived, her jet-black hair pulled back in a ponytail, her honey-bronze skin glowing against a yellow tank top. Heads turned. They always did.

"Sorry," she said. "Some phone calls just can't be ignored."

"Troubled patient?" I said.

"No. It was Aunt Janet. She talked to Shane this morning."

"What a sweet boy," I said. "He called his mommy to say how much fun he was having at the Magic Kingdom."

She gave me a look that was half a frown, to let me know that she didn't appreciate me making fun of her cousin, and half a smile, because I was so damned adorable when I did it.

"You know they didn't go to Disney World, and Shane doesn't have to call Aunt Janet. She calls him incessantly."

"And how is his devoted mother these days?" I said.

"Deliriously happy. She said she's never heard him talk like this about a woman before. She thinks he's smitten with Kylie."

I nodded. Kylie could smite mightily. I should know.

"Aunt Janet has been waiting a long time for Shane to find someone. She thinks Kylie may be the one."

As did I.

"She has high hopes," Cheryl said.

"For what?"

"Grandchildren."

"You may want to tell Aunt Janet that Kylie isn't

exactly the maternal type. Also, she's still very married to Spence, which could throw a monkey wrench into those granny dreams."

"She knows about Spence, but Shane told her that Kylie said it's over. It doesn't matter if he comes back. She's done with him."

That's exactly what she told me back at the academy. "I'm done with him." Twenty-eight days later he came back, and I became history,

But Spence is Shane's problem, not mine. The last thing I need to do is get involved in Kylie's love life. Especially now, when mine is going so—

"Zach, what are you thinking?"

"Nothing. I mean, nothing except what a great weekend this has been."

The waitress came and bailed me out. She set two glasses of champagne down on the table. "Congratulations on your anniversary," she said, her voice as bubbly as the wine.

"I wonder how she knew," Cheryl said once the waitress was gone.

I shrugged. "I may have let it slip when we checked in."

"A toast," she said, lifting her glass. "This past year has been..." She stared at me, groping for a word. Finally, she settled on one. *"Interesting."*

I would have gone with *rocky.* Over the past year, we'd tried living together, but that failed. Then there was the time I almost blew the relationship by acting like a jerk because Cheryl spent days on end with her ex when his mother died. And of course she was none too happy about how invested I was in Kylie's personal life, especially after Spence disappeared, and she caught me digging into the past of Kylie's poker-playing boyfriend.

"You're right about that," I said, raising my glass. "Cheers." I started to drink.

"I'm not finished," she said.

I lowered my glass.

She smiled. "Let me take it from the top. This past year has been *extremely* interesting. Here's to next year. Let's hope it's a *lot less* interesting."

I laughed so hard I almost spilled my champagne.

"I know, I know," Cheryl said, touching her glass to mine. "But I can dream, can't I?"

ACKNOWLEDGMENTS

The authors would like to thank the following people for their help in making this work of fiction ring true: NYPD Detective Danny Corcoran, Senior Assistant Prosecutor Jessica Gomperts (Bergen County, NJ), Dr. Jon Madek, Lily Karp, Matthew Diamond, Gabe Diamond, Dan Fennessy, Bill Harrison, David Hinds, Mel Berger, and Bob Beatty.

ABOUT THE AUTHORS

JAMES PATTERSON is the world's bestselling author and most trusted storyteller. He has created many enduring fictional characters and series, including Alex Cross, the Women's Murder Club, Michael Bennett, Maximum Ride, Middle School, and I Funny. Among his notable literary collaborations are *The President Is Missing,* with President Bill Clinton, and the Max Einstein series, produced in partnership with the Albert Einstein estate. Patterson's writing career is characterized by a single mission: to prove that there is no such thing as a person who "doesn't like to read," only people who haven't found the right book. He's given over three million books to schoolkids and the military, donated more than seventy million dollars to support education, and endowed over five thousand college scholarships for teachers. For his prodigious imagination and championship of literacy in America, Patterson was awarded the 2019 National Humanities Medal. The National Book Foundation recently presented him with the Literarian Award for Outstanding Service to the American Literary Community, and he is also the recipient of an Edgar

Award and nine Emmy Awards. He lives in Florida with his family.

MARSHALL KARP has written for stage, screen, and TV and is the author of *The Rabbit Factory*. He is also the coauthor of the NYPD Red series with James Patterson.

AN ACCUSED MURDERER
FACES A REVENGE PLOT AND A
STRONG-WILLED DETECTIVE
ON A QUEST FOR THE
TRUTH...BUT DID HE DO IT?

PLEASE TURN THE PAGE FOR
THIS LIGHTNING-FAST
THRILLER
BY JAMES PATTERSON WITH
ROB HART.

SCOTT FREE

CHAPTER 1

Staten Island Register
Breaking news update
Playground Killer suspect to be released

Thomas Scott, the man arrested in connection with the Playground Killer slayings, is due to be released from custody this afternoon. According to law enforcement sources, key evidence in the case has been dismissed by a judge.

About forty members of the press are waiting outside the front doors of Richmond County Supreme Court. Extra police officers are being called in to help contain the crowd.

The reign of the Playground Killer began in June, when Billy Taylor, 5, was discovered in the early morning hours, laid out on a slide in a playground on the South Shore of Staten Island. Two more victims followed, arranged in a similar fashion: Mei Zhou, 4, in September, and just a few weeks ago, John Kennelly Junior, 5.

All three children had attended the same day care center, Happy Times, in Westerleigh. Suspicion quickly fell on Thomas Scott, 37, who is a part-time custodian at Happy Times.

Police were unable to obtain a warrant to search his home—a small, one-bedroom apartment in Eltingville. Scott reportedly lives alone and has no known immediate family.

A few days ago, an anonymous source turned over to police evidence found in Scott's apartment. While police will not confirm, sources have told the Register that it was a collection of photographs of the young victims.

But in a shocking twist, emails uncovered by Scott's lawyer reveal that Detective Rex Hanlon, the lead investigator on the case, collaborated with one of the victims' parents to break into Scott's home to search for evidence.

Judge Kelly Reyes ruled that the evidence was obtained in violation of Scott's constitutional right to privacy. With the only hard evidence against him suppressed, Scott is due to be released.

Detective Hanlon has been suspended with pay. Law enforcement sources say they're still pursuing Scott as a suspect.

But many fear a killer may be back on the streets.

"I don't feel safe with him out there," said Julie Rodriguez, a mother of two who was playing with her children in Silver Lake Park. "I think I'm just going to take my kids home now."

Keep an eye on the Register website for up-to-the-minute updates from the scene.

CHAPTER 2
THOMAS SCOTT

THOMAS SCOTT STEPPED out of the glass doors of the Richmond County Courthouse, squinting in the harsh sunlight. He was greeted by a cavalcade of clicking cameras. The shiny bulbs made the press look like a horde of insects, advancing and ready to devour him. That's pretty much how it felt, too.

He should have asked if there was another exit out of the building. His lawyer had warned him there would be reporters, but he didn't think it would be this bad. He'd never seen so many people who wanted his attention at one time.

His heart slammed in his chest and he felt light-headed. He looked behind him, hoping he could retreat to the safety of the courthouse, but saw only a line of stone-faced cops blocking the glass doors.

The reporters kept hurling questions at him, yelling over each other to be heard. Each question cut like a knife.

"How do you feel?"

"What did the judge say?"

"What do you plan to do next?"

"Did you kill those children?"

Thomas felt a hand on his arm and turned to find his lawyer, Mark Amato. The handsome young man didn't betray any concern or nervousness, just smiled that hundred-watt smile of his and whispered, "Don't say anything."

Amato ran his hand through his brown hair—like it was a ploy to draw attention to his artfully sculpted haircut—and put a finger up in the air. The questions stopped and the cameras turned toward him.

"We're very pleased the judge agreed that the police violated my client's Fourth Amendment right to privacy with their illegal search," Amato said. "Mr. Scott is innocent of these heinous crimes. He looks forward to returning to his routine, as well as seeing the real killer brought to justice. We have no further statement at this time."

Thomas couldn't help but smile, even though he had been concentrating on looking neutral. Amato warned him that every newspaper tomorrow would run a picture of his face on the front page, and his expression would be endlessly analyzed. Plus, he knew how he looked. His nickname in high school was "Caveman," thanks to his heavy brow and big hands.

Losing most of his hair in the last few years hadn't helped anything.

He wasn't handsome like Amato. The guy was young, probably no more than 30, but he was confident and smooth. He looked like the kind of lawyer you saw on television. When Thomas was first arrested, he got a dozen offers from attorneys looking to represent him. Amato was the only one who made him feel comfortable. It helped that Amato offered to take the case pro bono, too.

But while he was good, he wasn't that good. The press didn't want to hear that there'd be no further statement. They continued to shout questions, pushing closer. Beyond them were people screaming "monster" and "murderer" and "psychopath." Thomas felt like if the press wasn't in between him and them, the crowd would tear him apart.

Amato gripped Thomas's arm and pulled him through the crowd. One of the reporters grabbed his other arm, trying to get his attention, and Thomas yanked it away. Anger and fear and confusion were buzzing in his head like a swarm of flies. He tried to distract himself as they pushed through the crowd. *Focus on something good.*

He thought about home. He wondered if it had gotten dusty in the five days that he was gone. Probably did. He'd have to sweep, but then he'd have to mop, too. Just to be sure. That's the thing about dirt— it's a constant battle just to keep it at bay.

He thought about his bathroom, too. His *clean* bathroom. It would be a welcome sight, after the cold metal toilet bolted to the wall in his cell. It looked like it hadn't been cleaned since it was installed. Thomas couldn't bring himself to sit on it. He had to hover over it, his legs aching and cramped because of the awkward angle.

Early on, Amato had been hopeful the judge would set bail, but given the high profile nature of the case and the clear and present danger to the community, Thomas was remanded to Rikers Island. Amato warned him it wasn't going to be a pleasant visit, that anyone who was believed to have perpetrated violence against children wasn't safe in a prison setting. There was a hierarchy, and an alleged child-murderer would be at the bottom.

That became clear on the first day. Thomas was waiting to use the phone to call Amato when a young man called him a kiddie-killer and cracked him in the jaw. He went tumbling to the floor and a group of inmates surrounded him. Through their kicking feet he could see one guard rushing to help him—and another guard step in his way, to make him wait. To give the inmates a few minutes to beat on him.

After a doctor who wouldn't look Thomas in the eye confirmed he didn't have any cracked ribs or internal bleeding, the guards decided to put him in solitary confinement. "The Bing," people called it.

It was a small room with a cot, a thin foam mattress, and a toilet/sink combo. He was alone for twenty-three hours a day. That lone hour of freedom was for the shower, or walking around in a circle in a small activity room.

In the beginning it wasn't so bad, outside of the pain. He would roll over in his sleep and a jolt would travel through his torso and he'd wake up. But Thomas didn't mind the rest. The solitary part. He was used to being alone.

It was the filth that got to him. Being locked in a place where dirt had won the war, it was pretty much his worst nightmare come true.

The grimy window and the crud on the toilet. The dirt in the corners that he couldn't quite wipe away with a wad of wet toilet paper. The occasional roach that would scurry across the floor. He could never figure out where they came from. They just appeared. He asked a corrections officer for a bucket of cleaning supplies, figuring that cleaning would help pass the time. The officer just laughed at him. Thomas didn't understand why. He wanted to help.

All he ever wanted to do was help.

It turned out, though, he wasn't safe just because he was alone. The guards would push him, yell at him. One guard in particular would shove his food tray hard enough through the slot that it would clatter to the floor, the contents spilling across the concrete. Thomas would do his best to clean it up but couldn't bring himself to eat any of the spoiled food.

By the fourth night, he was crying himself to sleep, his sobs drowned out by the sounds of the men screaming and yelling in the cells next to him. If there is a Hell, that was what it is like.

But that didn't matter anymore, because he was out.

As Thomas and Amato approached the curb, where a shiny black car Amato had arranged was waiting, they were peppered with more questions.

"What do you think about the judge's decision?"

"Do you still trust the police?"

"Do you have anything to say to the parents?"

And then, a yell cut through the crowd.

"You son of a bitch!"

The press parted, turning their clicking cameras and outstretched recorders toward the man barreling Thomas's way.

He was a big guy, heavy around the midsection, sandy hair thinning, meaty fists balled up. The kind of guy who'd played football in college and could still do some damage. And damage seemed to be his goal.

Thomas recognized him. John Junior's father.

John Junior was—*had been*—smart and funny and energetic. Always said hello to Thomas, asked him how his day was. Always said *please* and *thank you*. He was a good kid.

His father didn't look nearly as amiable.

John launched himself into Thomas, hitting him in the midsection, and the two of them tumbled to the ground. Thomas felt his head smack off the pavement, pain radiating through his skull and his still-bruised torso. He tried to roll over. Some reporters were caught in the scuffle and knocked down with them. Others were throwing elbows and swinging cameras, jockeying for position, trying to get the best view of the melee. And as a result, more of them ended up falling into the tangle of limbs.

Thomas tried to extricate himself from the scrum and felt a fist bounce off his chin. He looked up and saw John Junior's dad, rearing back to hit him again. So completely consumed by anger, he looked like a wild animal. Two cops appeared and pulled him away, his feet kicking into the air.

Thomas climbed to his feet and stood there, numb, as Amato dusted him off and said, "Let's get to the car. Now."

Thomas turned to his right and found a cop staring at him. An older, lanky guy with a bushy mustache. The cop leaned in, getting so close to Thomas's ear that Thomas could feel his hot breath. He grabbed Thomas's elbow, digging his thumb into the funny bone nerve. Thomas tried to twist away and found he couldn't, pain throbbing from his hand to his shoulder.

"I had my way, I'd lock you in a room with that guy and let him rip you apart," the cop said, nearly whispering. "You're lucky there are so many cameras here."

The cop let go, leaned back, smiled, and winked.

Thomas was struck by a wave of terror and looked around, hoping one of the reporters might have heard it, but of course, no one had. He turned and leapt for the car, yanking the door open and climbing across the seat. Amato followed and pulled the door shut.

The reporters descended, some of them pressing the cameras directly onto the window, but the sound of their questions was muffled by the glass.

"Are you okay?" Amato asked.

"No," Thomas said.

"We can press charges..."

"No."

"He tried to kill you."

"I just want to go home."

Amato nodded and fell back into the plush leather seat, unbuttoning his navy suit jacket. The driver inched the car forward, careful not to run over any of the reporters blocking their path.

"What about this Detective Hanlon?" Amato asked. "I can start the paperwork to file a civil suit. The city likes to settle. They'll throw a few hundred thousand at you, easy, just to get it to go away. We make a little noise, maybe they throw in a little more."

"I just want this to be over," Thomas said, putting more emphasis on the words, annoyed that he had to. For a smart guy, Amato didn't always seem to be good at listening.

"That bastard was intent on seeing you spend the rest of your life in jail," Amato said. "And for what? So he could say he closed a case?"

Thomas turned toward Amato and looked him in the eye, hoping that would convey how serious he was. "I want this to be over."

Amato recoiled in the seat a little. It made Thomas wonder what Amato thought of him. If the lawyer was just as scared as most other people seemed to be. He thought maybe he should apologize, but he just turned and looked out the rear window of the car as the driver pulled forward and made a hard left toward Bay Street.

As the assembly of press disappeared from view, Thomas thought about the quiet sanctuary of his empty apartment.

And the clean bathroom.

CHAPTER 3

JOHN KENNELLY

THOMAS SCOTT'S APARTMENT hadn't accumulated any dust.

The surfaces were so cleanly polished they seemed to glow, even in the dim light. It had the quality of a magazine catalogue—the design sparse and minimalistic, everything carefully arranged, so tidy that dust would fear to tread.

John Kennelly wasn't sure what to expect from the apartment of his son's killer, but he knew it wasn't sterile neatness.

Scott's shirts, even his t-shirts, were ironed and hanging in the closet. The socks in the dresser were folded into pairs. In the pantry, boxes of cereal and pasta were lined up in size order. As John opened the cabinets and checked in the closets, the word that kept coming to him was *meticulous*.

It wasn't until he got to the DVD rack, sitting on the floor next to a small flat-screen television mounted to the wall, that he paused, dread rolling in like an oncoming storm.

The rack was completely filled with stuff for kids. Disney movies, from the old cartoon stuff like *The Little Mermaid* up through the newer Pixar films. Box sets of the Batman and Superman cartoons. The entire *SpongeBob SquarePants* series.

No movies for adults. Nothing that wasn't animated. And Scott didn't have any kids.

A chill traveled up John's spine. The apartment suddenly took on a sinister tone. What kind of man was so devoted to cleanliness and kids' movies? What kind of weird combination was that?

At the kitchen counter, he eyed the knife block. Grasped the black handles, sliding the knives out one by one, wondering which was sharpest. He pulled out the biggest and touched his thumb to it. He felt a tiny jolt of pain and a thin red sliver appeared on his skin. He put the knife back and stuck his finger into his mouth.

No, he thought. No knife. He'd do it with his hands.

He moved to the bathroom. The room glowed orange from a small nightlight. The room smelled like bleach. There was a toothbrush in a holder, a tube of toothpaste, and a bar of soap in a soapdish, all placed neatly on the counter. John stepped inside and sat on the closed toilet, his knee twinging from when he'd slammed it into the pavement earlier.

It was so stupid to attack Scott in public like that, but he couldn't help himself. The second he saw Scott, the whole world went red.

At least here he'd have some privacy. Nobody to pull him off.

More important than that, he'd have time. All the time he wanted.

In an hour, he was supposed to be at the Friends of Compassion meeting, in the basement of St. Francis Church, down the block from his house. He was supposed to take comfort in the support group for parents who had lost young children. He was supposed to sit and drink bad coffee and listen to parents who were completely lost, unsure of what to do with themselves in the face of such cataclysmic loss.

John wouldn't be attending. He wasn't lost. He knew what he wanted. What he *needed*.

He moved the shower curtain aside. There wasn't a hint of mold or mildew. The tub looked brand new. He ran his hand across it and found the surface was smooth and cold.

He wondered if that was where John Junior died.

Drowned in the tub, struggling to breathe, and that son of a bitch holding him down under the water until the life was gone from the most perfect thing John had ever made.

He was breathing faster, his vision blurring. He could never tell which memory was going to smack into the side of his head like a fist. They just came at random. This one was from the Staten Island Ferry. Eight months ago? It was a clear spring day, and they were headed to their first Yankees game.

"Just the boys!" John Junior proclaimed for days, marching around the house in his brand-new Yankees cap. It was a few sizes too big and came down over his ears. John wanted it to be something John Junior could wear for the rest of his life. It would fit one day.

The boy loved the hat. He wouldn't take it off, not even when he got into bed.

When they got on the boat, John sat his son on the rail. They watched as the boat approached the Manhattan skyline, the buildings sparkling in the sunlight. John had taken that boat five days a week for years, to his brokerage firm on Vesey Street. That day, seeing it through his son's eyes, the wonder and the excitement, it was like seeing the majesty and grandeur of the city for the first time.

John reached up and adjusted the cap on his head. It was a little too small for him, but he hated to take it off. When he wore it, he felt like he could live inside that memory. And that memory was preferable to this hollow, hateful reality.

It was his fault. All his fault. He dropped John Junior off at school one morning, and somehow the boy went missing between the front door and his first activity of the day. No one noticed for four hours. After getting the call and chewing out the administrators for their foolish lack of responsibility, John combed the neighborhood around the school, thinking the boy had wandered off—John Junior had a habit of wandering.

He wouldn't allow himself to let in that primal fear, the fear every parent has. Refusing to believe that the worst could have happened.

And then the worst did happen.

A jogger found John Junior in Hamilton Park. Laid out on a slide, his clothes damp, arms folded across his chest. The third victim of the Playground Killer.

No. The third victim of *Scott*. It was Scott who did this.

John slipped off the toilet and folded over the lip of the tub, running his hands across the bottom of it, wishing with everything he had to be struck dead in that moment, if it could somehow bring back his son.

He'd lived a good life. Long enough. He'd trade it in, trade everything in, to give John Junior a second chance.

A pair of hands ran over his shoulders, and he felt Susan kneeling behind him, wrapping her arms around his stomach. Her long blond hair tickled the back of his neck as she pressed herself against him.

"We need to go," she said. "We shouldn't be here."

John sniffled and cleared his throat. "No."

"Do you really think he's coming back?"

"He has to come back eventually."

"And what if he's with someone?" Susan asked, her voice gentle. "You're not thinking this through, John."

"Damnit!" John slammed his fist on the lip of the tub. A jolt of pain shot through his arm and he cried out, cradling the fist in his stomach. The pain broke down the wall he'd been building, and he cried so hard he shook.

Susan hugged him tighter, but she also seemed to be pulling him up and away.

After a few moments, John was able to compose himself.

"It's not right, Susan," he said. "He was five. He had a whole life. And that monster gets to go on? I won't let it." He felt tears rising to his eyes again. "I can't let that be, Susan. I can't. I won't live in a world where something like that can happen."

"John—" Susan said, running her hand through his hair.

She placed her hands on his cheeks and turned him around so he was facing her. She pressed her face to his, and he felt tears on her face, mixing with his. They sat there like that, holding each other. John had no idea how long. After a little while she stood and pulled him up. He felt like a puppet. The tension gone from his limbs, his chest wooden and empty. It was dark outside now, and they moved toward the front of the apartment.

Maybe he would attend that Friends of Compassion meeting after all. It was probably better than what he planned to do now: Go home and drink whiskey until the bottle was empty or he passed out. The only way he was able to sleep through the night anymore.

When they were within ten feet of the door, the knob jiggled.

John and Susan stopped and watched the door crack. John set his feet and put his arm across Susan, herding her behind him.

"John, think about this," Susan said.

"I have thought about it."

His heart raced. This was the moment he'd been waiting for. This was his chance to bring some order back to the universe. It was the most excited and happy he had been in weeks.

The door swung open.

The figure in the doorway was backlit by the harsh lights in the hallway. But immediately John knew something was off. Scott was tall and lean, built for labor. This person was shorter and stockier. Older. Definitely not Scott.

"I thought I might find you here," the figure said.

And then John recognized the voice, along with the gray curly hair and the thin mustache.

Detective Rex Hanlon.

The man whose idiotic mistake freed his son's killer.

John found that the inferno of anger raging in his chest didn't discriminate. A target was a target. He screamed and launched himself at Hanlon.

CHAPTER 4

THOMAS SCOTT

THOMAS STOOD IN line behind a woman in impossibly tight jeans, chunky green heels, and a sheer white tank top. A leopard-print bra peeked out from underneath. With long fingernails, she peeled twenty-dollar bills off a thick roll, placing them, one at a time, in the slot at the bottom of the scratched glass partition that separated the clerk from the rest of the lobby.

Actually, "lobby" was too strong a word. It was a small room with two small chairs, a couple of cracked and faded magazines piled on a small coffee table.

The clerk, a scruffy man in his forties, wore an indifferent expression as he watched the small pile of money grow. Once the woman was done, he put a key hanging from a diamond-shaped piece of plastic into the slot.

The woman turned, her lips a deep brown, the corners of her eyes pointed into cat's eyes with liner and mascara. She winked at Thomas and said, "Room 4 if you get bored later, tough guy."

Thomas didn't acknowledge her. Didn't even look her way, lest it be mistaken for some level of interest. The thought that he could just go over like *nothing* and just pay for it? He had a hard enough time talking to women as it was. That was somehow much scarier.

He didn't want to think about it. He had other things to worry about.

Like staying alive.

He couldn't stop thinking about that cop who threatened him. And the look on the face of John Junior's dad.

He thought about Amato's parting words, too. What the young lawyer said when the car dropped him off at the Staten Island Express Suites, a run-down motel off the expressway, not too far south of the Verrazano-Narrows Bridge.

"I'm sorry to do this," Amato said. "At a bigger hotel, you're going to get recognized. Place like this, nobody makes eye contact. That's going to help right now, because you need to be anonymous. Do you understand?"

Thomas didn't, not really. He had already planned his perfect night: ordering in Chinese food—sesame chicken and a wonton soup with extra wontons. He'd eat while marathon-watching the *Toy Story* movies. His favorite meal and his favorite movies, to erase the stress and horror of the last week.

But Amato seemed to know what he was doing—Thomas wasn't in jail anymore, after all—so he figured it was best to listen. Given how many people knew his address, it probably wasn't safe.

At least Amato was willing to pay. He handed Thomas a stack of bills and said, "Take a shower, get some rest. Watch some TV and order in. I'll show up in two days with some fresh clothes and we'll figure out the next steps, okay?"

"Why not tomorrow?" Thomas asked.

"There's a lot of work still to be done. Just think of it like a little vacation. It's rare that a man gets two days with nothing to worry about. Try to enjoy it."

"Okay," said Thomas, accepting the money, still feeling like he was being dumped on the side of the road. Which, essentially, he was.

There wasn't much to enjoy about this.

As he approached the clerk, he thought about the pile of money in his pocket, and the cheapness of the rooms, and the fact that he was hungry. He didn't want to go looking for an ATM, so he figured it would be better to just pay for the room on his credit card, hold onto the cash for now. He slid his card through the slot.

The clerk took it and stared at the name for a few seconds before he jabbed at his keyboard. If he recognized Thomas, he didn't betray it. He behaved with the same level of indifference as he had toward the woman before Thomas.

"Can I get a room far away from the woman that came in before me?" Thomas asked.

The clerk, who was reaching for a key hung up on the pegs on the wall, shrugged and moved his arm, reaching for another one—room 12.

Thomas took the key, nodded to the clerk, and made his way outside and down the sidewalk, circling the parking lot. His room was the last one on the far end.

The room was dark and musty inside, with an ancient smell of cigarette smoke permeating the carpet and blinds. He turned on the light next to the door and did a quick inventory. There was a small dresser with a television on it. Not even a flat-screen, just a chunky old tube television.

There was one bed that sagged in the middle, with

a floral spread that reminded him a little of his grandmother's couch. The wallpaper, peeling in the corners, matched the bedspread. Inside the bathroom, there was a shower and a toilet and a window. The sink was outside the bathroom door, in the closet area.

It was not a nice room.

And it certainly wasn't clean.

There were no visible bugs or vermin. That much he could count as a victory. The first thing he did was take a big wad of toilet paper, soak it, and wipe down the top of the dresser and the nightstand and the toilet. Then he took a dry wad and followed the same path.

It wasn't much, but it would do.

Then he sat on the corner of the bed and tried not to think about the kinds of things these rooms were typically used for. He really hoped the sheets were laundered between guests.

The walls seemed to be closing in on him. Even though he was free to walk outside, even though he could stand up and spread his arms and not touch the walls, he suddenly felt like he was back in his cell on Rikers.

Trapped, alone, and everyone outside these four walls wanting to kill him.

What he needed was a drink. He didn't usually drink, but isn't that what people turned to, in situations like this? Hopefully it would dull him enough so he'd be able to get through the night without tossing and turning too much.

Without thinking about the children.

Their soft, sweet faces, and the life that had been drowned out of them. The way they looked after they were dead, placid and serene....

When he closed his eyes, he saw their faces. Didn't

matter the time of day. Didn't matter the circumstance. It's what he saw. They haunted him, and sometimes he wondered if they would ever go away.

He wondered if there was a bar nearby. A liquor store. Something.

First things first: He needed a shower. A real shower, in private, not in a room full of other men.

He stripped his clothes off, hanging up the suit jacket Amato had gotten for him, balling up his socks and placing them into his dress shoes. The rest he neatly folded and placed on the edge of the bed. Then he stepped into the bathroom and turned on the shower, letting the weak stream of water get as hot as possible.

And like he did every time, he held his breath, counted to five, and climbed in, careful to keep the spray out of his face, getting nervous even at the thought of feeling water enter his nose.

CHAPTER 5

REX HANLON

HANLON COULDN'T SIDESTEP; the hallway was too narrow. John Kennelly was a big man, which made him dangerous when he was in a *good* mood. And now he was furious.

The way Hanlon figured it, he probably deserved what happened next.

He braced for the impact when he felt something brush past him. Kat Taylor, swimming in her oversized white sweater, black hair pulled into a tight ponytail, stepped in front of him, blocking John's path.

She was half the size of John, and yet stood between the two without fear. Probably because she knew what would happen next: John stopped, almost falling forward from his momentum, not wanting to hurt her.

That didn't stop him from trying to get to Hanlon. He tried to step around her but she kept moving to block his path.

Hanlon was relieved that he'd brought Kat. After having her break into the apartment, he thought it might be best not to involve her with anything else.

But she raised the issue. She said they needed to do something about Scott—and that she would do whatever she could to help.

Without her, this would have turned out very differently.

And probably much bloodier.

"Everyone, please, just stop," Hanlon said, flicking on the wall switch. The blast of light made everyone squint, and his hand instinctively moved toward his belt, so he could jerk it up into his jacket and come out with his gun.

Not that he wanted to shoot John. But just in case. He'd seen people at their worst, at that point where unspeakable acts of violence became very speakable, and John was well past that point.

John finally gave up trying to get past Kat and stuck a finger toward Hanlon.

"What are you doing here?" he asked.

"Let's go in the living room, Mr. Kennelly," he said.

"Don't 'Mr. Kennelly' me. My son's killer is free because of you."

"And I'm here to make that right."

That made John stop and listen. His eyes went wide, and he suddenly looked a lot less likely to tear out Hanlon's throat with his bare hands. That was a good start.

John retreated toward the living room, backing up slowly, not taking his eyes off Hanlon. He sat back onto the couch, perched on the edge of it. Susan sat down beside him, while Kat stood off against the wall, her arms folded.

Kat already knew what was coming. They'd talked on the walk over from the shopping plaza a few blocks away where they parked. Now it was time to get the Kennellys on board. It would be a tough job, and an

376 • JAMES PATTERSON

extra set of hands—strong hands especially—would make the whole thing easier.

Hanlon could feel retirement hiding right around the corner, waiting to pounce. He wasn't a young man anymore. There was strength in numbers.

And this, to his mind, would help make things right. He knew how it felt, to see justice not get done. He knew the pain and the ache that lived in your soul because of it. And he didn't want them to go through that. More than that, he wanted to close what he was pretty sure was going to be his final case.

He'd spent years watching an imperfect system let guilty men go.

And he was tired of it.

So he got ready to talk. The whole ride there, Hanlon had been rehearsing. Talking to the empty, rainy roadway. Trying to figure out the right combination of words. By the time he parked, he was feeling pretty good. He'd developed an apology that respected the parents and their loss, and put his own actions in the appropriate light, with a promise to fix it.

But standing in front of such blatant fury and sadness, John and Susan perched on the couch and shaking with anticipation, he forgot everything he came up with. So he decided to wing it.

"I can never apologize enough for what happened," he said. Turning to Kat, he added, "I never should have put you in that position. Asking you to sneak in here—that was wrong. It was an act of desperation. But I knew—I *know*. Thomas Scott is the man who did this, and goddamn any system that would leave kids in danger."

Hanlon turned to John and Susan.

"Before we move forward, I want you to know something." He paused, looked at the floor. "I lost my son in a car accident years ago. He was eight. I don't want you to think I know the exact kind of pain you're feeling right now. I can't. How you lost your kid and how I lost mine, they're very different things. But I know that feeling of emptiness, of…"

He caught himself. The memory was choking him up already. The thought of Chris, and the way he laughed, and how he was showing an interest in music and talked about wanting to learn guitar—it suddenly became too much. He closed his eyes, focused on the task at hand.

"There's a kind of hurt that only a parent who lost a child knows," Hanlon said.

John seemed to soften. "What is this?" he asked.

"The system failed," Hanlon said. "I failed. A killer is back on the street. I propose we take him off it."

"You mean kill him," John said, his face lighting up a little.

Hanlon nodded.

"How did you even know we would be here?" John asked.

"After that display at the courthouse today, I figured there was no stopping you," Hanlon said. "Despite what you may think, I'm actually pretty good at my job."

"This is a lot to take in," Susan said, pressing a hand to her chest.

"It is," Hanlon said. "And we don't have to do it. We can end this conversation right here, right now, and all go our separate ways. But if we do follow through on this, we need to make a promise to each other. What's discussed and decided stays in this room. Just between us. No one else."

There was a sniffle behind them.

Hanlon froze.

Someone else was in the room.

His hand went to the inside of his jacket. His age was catching up with him. He should have been paying more attention. Listening more closely. He'd pushed the front door closed, but he should have locked it.

He turned to find Paul and Daisy Zhou, the parents of Mei, the second victim, standing in the hallway. The two of them so small in the hallway, standing apart from each other.

He didn't need to ask how much they had heard.

Their wide-eyed expressions of shock made that pretty clear.

CHAPTER 6

THOMAS SCOTT

THOMAS STOOD BEFORE the glittering rainbow of liquor bottles. He didn't usually like liquor. Being in the cramped aisles of the store made him feel like a kid. Small. He kept his arms at his side, for fear of knocking something over and getting yelled at. He wished he could have stopped into a deli for some beer, but he had a beer every now and again, and he knew he needed something stronger.

He remembered when he was younger, doing a shot of tequila forced on him by some older kids at a party, and expelling the contents of his stomach across a table. Everyone laughed at him, and the girl who lived in the house forced him to clean it up in his stumbling, drunken state. Mopping up his vomit while a group of people stared and laughed—it was the only time in his life he *wasn't* happy to be cleaning something.

No tequila.

He came across the rums, which seemed like a safe bet. Rum was made from sugar, so it would be a little sweet. He picked the cheapest bottle he could find off the shelf and hefted it, looked around to see if there was any soda, something to mix it with.

Finding nothing, he approached the counter and placed the bottle down next to the register. A young Korean woman with glasses and long black hair picked up the bottle and scanned it, said, "Nineteen ninety-five."

Thomas pulled a twenty-dollar bill out of his wallet and placed it on the counter. The woman picked it up and furrowed an eyebrow at him. "You look really familiar, you know that?"

Thomas panicked, tried to say something, but found his mouth had gone dry, like he'd been sucking on a wad of cotton. He looked down and away, trying to hide his face. Wishing there was a hole in the floor he could crawl into.

"You're the guy from the news," she said. "You're that guy who killed those kids!" She looked past Scott and yelled, "Hey, Reggie, get out here!"

"Ma'am, I just want to—"

"No, you get out of here, right now," she said. "Reggie! Get this guy out of here."

Thomas turned and saw that the other customers in the store were staring now, looking at him with a mix of fear and revulsion. Some of them pulled out smartphones and held them up in his direction, taking pictures or filming him.

Then he saw a big black guy, built like a refrigerator with muscles, cutting through the aisles and headed in his direction.

Thomas figured he wasn't getting his change. He gripped the neck of the bottle and ran for the door, flinging it open into an older woman in a puffy black coat. The door hit her with a loud *bang* and the glass cracked. She cried out as she was thrown back onto the pavement. Thomas stooped to help her, trying to apologize. He felt terrible. He should have been paying attention.

"Get the hell off her!" someone yelled.

Thomas looked back and saw that Reggie was almost outside now. He didn't look like he was in the mood for a polite conversation. The woman on the ground was screaming and scrambling to get away from him, more afraid than anything else.

So Thomas ran.

He tried to outrun the feeling, but couldn't: he wasn't safe anywhere.

Couldn't even go out to the store without being recognized. And while that thought should have made him upset, that the place he'd called home his whole life would suddenly turn on him, it just made him angry.

He'd only ever been nice, tried to help, and this was his reward.

As he pumped his legs, throwing himself forward into the night, raindrops pelting his face, all he wanted to do was hurt someone. Channel that anger into something. The thought of that impulse filled him with shame, but he couldn't help how he felt.

Some things, you just can't help.

CHAPTER 7

DAISY ZHOU

DAISY COULDN'T BELIEVE what she was hearing.

She could feel Paul's apprehension, the way he reached over and gripped her hand. But she was glad they'd come here. Glad the door was ajar and they'd come in at this exact moment.

Making that bastard pay. The idea alone was exhilarating. Ever since Mei had died, Daisy had felt like she was treading water. Just struggling to stay afloat, and constantly exhausted. Sometimes she'd doze off at her desk, head jerking forward and bumping her computer monitor.

And as much as she hated to admit it, she felt herself drifting away from her husband. The death of their daughter cast their relationship in a new, unflattering light. She looked at a man like John Kennelly and saw someone who was broken, but at least trying to put the pieces back together.

Paul just sat on his chair in the den, staring off into space. Barely checking in at the Forest Avenue coffee shop they owned, never lifting a hand to help around the house. It was like he'd given up. They still had another child, and she was exhausting herself keeping the household together.

Thinking about Scott dead filled her with energy.

It was the best she had felt in months.

She imagined what it would be like. How they would do it. If she would get to contribute. Fire a bullet or plunge a knife. She was shocked at how little she cared about the consequences.

Because it would be for Mei, and that would make it worth it.

Paul sniffed, because he would never blow his nose when she asked. He didn't like tissues. Just sucked it back up into his nose like a kid. That's when everyone turned. Which was good, because at that point Daisy wasn't sure how to broach the fact that they were standing there.

No one spoke. No one even moved, like it was a television show and someone had hit the Pause button. After a few moments John stood up.

"How much did you hear?" he asked.

"All of it," Daisy said.

"Why are you here?" Hanlon asked, his face twisted in confusion.

Before Daisy could respond, Kat said, "I texted them. I told them to meet us."

Hanlon turned to her, his mouth hanging open. "Why the hell would you do that?"

"Because they deserve to be a part of it," Kat said.

Hanlon shook his head. "I should never have done this. I should have handled this myself. This is getting out of control."

Daisy stepped forward. "Wait."

She let go of Paul's hand, looked back at him, and nodded. Then she turned to the rest of the group. "We want in."

"Now hold on…" Paul said, putting his hand on Daisy's shoulder.

"He took our daughter," Daisy whispered. "Our little girl, Paul."

"This isn't the way," Paul said, shaking his head. "This isn't right."

"And what is right?" asked John, his voice thick with emotion. "That he got off on a technicality? What about when the next kid dies? Will it be right then? Because I think the next kid who dies is on us. Getting caught is just going to make him more careful."

"John's right," said Susan, looking down at her hands, wringing them together.

Hanlon exhaled. Daisy held her breath. The detective was weary, regretful. Worst of all, he looked to be reconsidering. But finally he shook his head.

"If we're going to do this, we need each other's backs," Hanlon said. "We need to be in agreement. So if anyone is having second thoughts, please say something now."

"I'm not so sure about this," Paul said, raising his hand.

Daisy cringed, and pushed her body against his, trying to get him to shut up. Once upon a time, she had appreciated that he was so thoughtful. That he was a man of high moral fiber who thought things through carefully and deliberately.

This wasn't the time for him to be such a damn bleeding heart.

There was only one heart she wanted to bleed.

Kat said, "We should tell him."

"Tell us what?" Paul asked, hesitant.

"He didn't just have pictures of the three of them," said Kat. "There was a fourth picture."

Hanlon put his hands on his hips, looked at the

floor, and sighed. "We thought it might be his next victim."

Daisy knew it was coming before Hanlon said it. The way Paul gripped her hand, squeezing it so hard it hurt, he seemed to get it, too.

"He had a picture of your son, Jian," Hanlon said. "Mei's twin brother."

Daisy felt the breath leave her body. Her head spun. She turned to her husband. Paul's mouth parted and twisted, like something terrible was about to escape. Then he clamped his lips together and nodded his head, his eyes suddenly cold.

"We're in," he said, before grabbing Daisy's hand and yanking her out of the room.

CHAPTER 8

PAUL ZHOU

PAUL TOOK THE turn at high speed, nearly sending their beige minivan skidding off the slick roadway. His stomach rocked but he didn't care. He had to get home. It was like the fog in his head had lifted and suddenly everything in front of him was clear.

He had to make sure Jian was safe.

"Let's try to get there in one piece," Daisy said from the passenger seat.

"I thought you were a thrill seeker all of a sudden," Paul said. "Plotting to kill a man and all that."

"You mean to tell me you haven't thought about killing him?"

Paul drummed his fingers on the steering wheel, waiting for a light to turn green. Of course he had. How could he not? But every time he approached the idea, it made him ill. It wasn't their job to take the law into their own hands. This wasn't the old West. There was a system in place for a reason.

Even if the system didn't always get it right...

He didn't blame Daisy for the way she felt, he would give her that. But he was worried. She'd been the rock of this relationship. He'd never felt closer to her, admiring the way she kept things together. With the house, with Jian, with him. He wanted to support her. But this felt like too much.

The light turned green and Paul pressed down on the gas. He didn't answer his wife. He didn't know what to say. He just wanted to get home.

"Just call Pammy again, okay?" he asked.

Daisy pecked at the screen of her phone and held it up to her ear. It's not even like they were far, less than three minutes now, probably.

That's why it happened. Scott must have been watching their house. Waiting until Paul was in the basement doing laundry, and Daisy was making breakfast, and the twins were playing. Finding a perfect instant when Jian wasn't paying attention, and he lured Mei out of the house. That's how he must have done it.

He thought about Mei. How she was the one with boundless energy, while Jian was quiet, more reserved. He and Daisy had wanted to pay respect to their heritage, so they gave their children traditional Chinese names. *Jian* meant "strong," and *Mei* meant "beautiful." They were an inseparable unit, the two of them.

And now, a broken one.

Paul turned onto his block and gunned the engine. A car swerved out of the way, and the driver leaned on the horn as the call connected and Daisy said, "Pammy? Are you there? Is Jian okay?" Her voice was shaking.

Paul pulled the car up to the front of the house, not even bothering to turn it off, and bounded into the house. The front door wasn't locked. That alone made him furious. Pammy was supposed to lock the door behind them. He should have done it himself.

He rushed inside and saw Pammy sitting on the couch with her phone held up to her head, a confused expression on her face, a horror movie playing on the television. He'd deal with her later.

He took the stairs two at a time and threw open the door of the twins' room, and saw just a rumple of blankets on Jian's bed.

He pulled them away, throwing them over his shoulder, and saw the boy curled up around his sister's favorite toy, a stuffed octopus she called Charlie.

Paul fell to his knees and put his hands on Jian, relief flooding him.

The boy woke up, confused, and Paul crawled onto the bed and pulled him close. Across the room, in the dim green glow of the nightlight, he could make out Mei's empty bed, still unmade, her polka-dot footie pajamas bunched up by the pillow.

He and Daisy didn't yet have the strength to move them.

Daisy appeared in the doorway. She sat on the edge of the bed and patted Jian, who had already fallen asleep again, oblivious to Paul's panic.

"Pammy is okay staying the night," she said. "I told her we're staying with friends and needed a night away. I thought I would need a better excuse, but she's okay with it."

"You need to tell her to lock the door," Paul said, brushing away a tear. "She has to lock all the doors and set the alarm. You need to tell her. I don't think I can do it without losing it."

"I'll tell her," Daisy said, and she climbed into bed behind Paul, put her arm around him and Jian. "I'll do it in a minute."

Paul couldn't help but glance up at the window. They were on the second floor, but he felt like he would see Scott standing there, staring in at them, waiting for his opportunity to strike.

He didn't see anything, of course, just the tree in the front yard, but that didn't make him feel any safer.

"You know we need to do this, right?" Daisy asked. "It's not even about revenge anymore. It's about protecting our son."

Paul nodded.

"I know," he said.

And he did. He didn't care about the legality, or the philosophical implications. None of that mattered. He would do whatever it took to keep Jian safe.

CHAPTER 9

Staten Island Register
Breaking news update
Playground Killer suspect spotted at
Rosebank liquor store

Thomas Scott, the suspected Playground Killer who was released from custody earlier today, was spotted around 6:30 p.m. at Staten Island's Best Wine & Liquor in Rosebank.

Witnesses say he was buying a bottle of alcohol and menacing the clerk, and may have assaulted a woman on his way out of the store. The police have yet to respond to a request for comment from the Register. A phone call made to the store wasn't answered.

A judge ruled earlier today that the evidence being used against Scott in the murder of three Staten Island children was inadmissible, because it was collected by someone in an illegal search, at the direction of a police officer.

Law enforcement sources say they still consider

Scott to be a suspect. The 37-year-old janitor appeared to be smiling as his lawyer led him from the courthouse to a waiting car this afternoon.

Keep an eye on the Register website for up-to-the-minute updates.

CHAPTER 10

JOHN KENNELLY

JOHN SAT SHOTGUN as Detective Hanlon drove them south on the West Shore Expressway. Through the darkness, John could make out two tanks of liquefied natural gas looming on the horizon.

Hanlon said, "Here we go."

John looked at the tanks—rusted behemoths that had been decommissioned decades ago. They were nothing but an eyesore, and for years politicians had promised to tear them down and replace them with a shopping plaza and housing, but plans never came to fruition.

The tanks just sat there, getting rustier, like sentries on the side of the highway, guarding Rossville, which was mostly auto shops, industrial sites, and the recently closed Arthur Kill Correctional Facility.

Hanlon pulled off the expressway, and after a couple of turns, maneuvered the car down the dirt pathway. The sun was dipping below the horizon, the sky cast purple. They were surrounded by high weeds on either side, and before long John couldn't even see the road behind them.

If this was the location Hanlon had in mind, it couldn't be more perfect.

Paul and Daisy had rushed out so quickly—and given the information about the new photo, he didn't blame them. The others wiped down the apartment, and Hanlon told John he had something to show him. So Kat and Susan took off for home, while Hanlon and John climbed into Hanlon's aging Buick. They hadn't spoken in the twenty minutes since they got in the car.

The whole way, John had to fight the urge to lash out, to call him an idiot, to chastise him and lecture him, even hit him. He knew it wasn't smart to hit a cop, but he didn't care. He was still angry. He couldn't not be. This man had made such a stupid mistake that had cost them justice for their children.

But he needed him to complete the plan and get his revenge. That meant he would tolerate him.

Hanlon stopped the car in front of a large warehouse sitting on the water, the building a ruin of its former self. There was a gaping hole in one wall, up near the roof, and the windows were smashed and broken. The dock sticking off the back was collapsed into the inky bay.

They climbed out, and the LNG tanks practically loomed over them.

"This is it?" John asked.

"Used to be they had security guards," Hanlon said. "But after two years, the guards hadn't seen a single person on site, so they got let go. Most folks in the neighborhood don't even know it's here, and kids can't cross the expressway to get to it."

Hanlon led him toward the front of the building. They found a gunmetal gray door with a small window crisscrossed by security wire. It was sitting ajar from the frame, the knob broken off, a rusty padlock holding it closed. John looked around and found a cinder block half buried in the dirt. He pulled it out, brought it to the door, lifted it over his head, and brought it down hard. The lock snapped and fell to the ground, the door yawning open, everything beyond that pitch black.

The two of them stepped inside. It looked like the set of a horror movie. Dim light trickled in from the windows set high in the cavernous room, which was mostly stripped bare. The floor was scuffed and the guts of old machinery were pushed up into the corners. It smelled like motor oil and mildew.

Hanlon pulled a Maglite out of his overcoat and shined it around.

"What was this place, exactly?" John asked.

"Distribution, shipping, mechanical repair," Hanlon said. "It was a multi-use facility. Too expensive to remediate, and the land is zoned industrial, so it'd be a pain in the ass to rezone it for homes. Nobody wants it."

"Okay, so we have a space," John said. "That's a good start. But how are we going to do it? Shoot him?"

"Ballistics can be a tricky bitch," said Hanlon. "I'd prefer not to. Knives are an option, but that's a little personal."

"I'd be happy to use my hands," John said.

"You say that now."

"I mean it."

"Well, before we decide anything, let's get the full lay of the land first," Hanlon said.

So they cut wide circles around the space, looking behind gutted machines and old piles of wood. Hanlon even shined his flashlight up into the wooden rafters. Looking for squatters or inspiration, John couldn't tell. But Hanlon was right. It was good to have a sense of the layout.

They reached a doorway leading to more rooms. John said, "I didn't know you lost your son."

"T-boned by a drunk driver," Hanlon said. "On the passenger side. My wife and son were killed on impact. I made it out with a titanium hip that aches when it rains."

"I'm sorry to hear that."

"It was a long time ago."

"What happened to the drunk?" John asked.

Hanlon turned and looked at him, unblinking, his face flat.

John was about to ask for clarification when he saw the answer.

Hanlon knew what it meant to take revenge outside the bounds of the law. He was the perfect man for this job, then. It almost made John respect Hanlon a little more, in the sense that they were kindred spirits. But he pushed the feeling aside. Anger, the dominant emotion of his life, took the wheel. John wondered if it would ever go away.

If killing Scott would help.

They passed into the new set of rooms, opening doors, checking in corners, scaring off rats. John wondered about the best way to do the deed.

The important thing was, he wanted Scott to suffer.

Drowning is supposed to be an incredibly painful way to die. In the days after John Junior was found, when John had stopped crying long enough to maintain his composure, he would sit in the basement with the lights off, and he would hold his breath, counting off the seconds until his lungs screamed for oxygen. His muscles tensed and body shaking.

He would breathe in, let the oxygen rush in, think about that incredible feeling of relief.

He would think about that relief never coming.

Of the pain getting worse.

And then he would cry some more, thinking about what it must have been like.

In the next room, the last one on the row, close to the bay now, both men stopped. Hanlon trained his flashlight around the room, revealing the details.

Along the far wall was exactly what they were looking for.

Perfect place. Perfect man. Perfect method.

John balled up his fists and smiled.

"Are you thinking what I'm thinking?" he asked.

"That works," Hanlon said, nodding slowly.

Hanlon's jacket vibrated. He reached into his coat and came out with his phone, pecked at the face of it. "Scott was spotted at a liquor store in Rosebank," he said.

"How do you know that?" John asked.

"I have a Google alert set up for his name," Hanlon said, placing the phone back in his pocket. He stood for a minute, looking up and away, and then raised his hand and snapped his fingers. "Staten Island Express Suites. That must be it. It's right near there."

"You think that's where he is?"

"If I was a lawyer who wanted to hide the most hated man on Staten Island, it's where I would put him. That's not the kind of place where people worry about each other's business."

"Well then," John said. "I guess that's where we're headed. I'll start texting the rest of the group."

CHAPTER 11

THOMAS SCOTT

THOMAS SAT ON the bed, numbly watching a rerun of *Friends,* still wishing the television picked up the Cartoon Network. This show was funny enough, but the colors were dull, lifeless. He liked colors. He liked the cleanliness of animation. Cartoons never looked dirty.

He picked up the container of sesame chicken next to him, used the plastic fork to skewer a gooey piece of meat. It tasted like cotton. Which wasn't an indictment of the place he'd ordered it from. It was a little different from his regular place, but not *bad* different. He just couldn't concentrate on things like flavor. There was too much to think about.

He got up, pulled aside the heavy blackout curtain and peeked into the parking lot. It looked the same as it had twenty minutes ago. And still, every time he pushed it aside, he expected to see a group of cops, dressed in armor and carrying guns, ready to cuff him and drag him away like last time.

At least this time he would know why. The first time, he had no idea what was happening. They were just there, and his instinct was to figure out what was happening, and because he kept trying to pull away to talk, one of the cops jammed a nightstick in his stomach. He doubled over in pain and didn't put up a fight after that.

Or maybe he'd look out the window and see John Junior's dad, waiting to tear him apart. He wished he could talk to him. Explain what happened. He was sure that if he got a couple of minutes, he could make him understand.

He sat on the bed again, took a long pull from a plastic bottle of water. When it was empty, he placed it carefully in the trash can, then picked up the bottle of rum, ripped off the plastic around the cap, unscrewed it, and took a sip. It stung the back of his throat, and he winced and coughed. It splashed around his throat and burned. After a few minutes he took a longer sip.

Thomas surveyed the room again. It was familiar now, but not comfortable. The smell of smoke wasn't going away. It was cramped, and occasionally he would see something flit in the corner of his vision, something he feared was a roach or a mouse. And even though he didn't have any bites or welts, he still assumed it was only a matter of time before the bed-bugs found him.

The whole place seemed to be a magnet for filth.

He thought about his apartment. Neat and tidy and clean and bug-free.

His life, nearly gone from him now.

He'd have to move. There was no way he could stay on Staten Island. And truthfully, it's not like there was a whole lot that was compelling him to stay. But he'd miss it. Staten Island was a nice little place. You got a slice of city life, and it was still quiet at night. And the rents were affordable. Not like across the bridge, where you paid several thousand dollars for the privilege of living in a shoebox. With the kind of money he made, this area was the best he could afford.

He didn't have any family. No real friends, outside some people he saw around at the local shops and at work. He'd heard nice things about Portland. The Oregon Portland. Quiet, lots of nice places to eat. And plenty far away from here.

Far was good. He needed to be someplace where he could start again. The idea terrified and excited him in equal measure. It's not like he had anything here holding him back. But he'd miss the familiarity.

He took a little sip of rum, getting used to the sharp, stinging bite of it, and put the bottle on the nightstand. He picked up his phone and opened his email. He tapped out a message:

To: Mark Amato
From: Thomas Scott
Subject line: Time?

I need to get out of here. I'm ready to leave town. Maybe you can arrange some kind of ride over to my apartment so I can get my stuff. I'd really like to figure out what's next. I can't live like this and I can't live here anymore.
Thank you. I might go for a walk in the morning but otherwise will be at the hotel all day.

Talk soon,
TS

Thomas put the phone aside and put his head in his hands. Sighed.

Through it all, the thing that hurt most was, he missed the kids. Their sweet smiles. Their laughs. Parents were rude, inattentive, unkind. Thomas wasn't a nice-looking man, and sometimes he got nervous talking to people, and he scrubbed toilets, and that made him unworthy of respect and attention. To most people, he was like those characters in the background of a cartoon that no one interacts with. Just there to fill the space.

The kids, though, they had yet to be jaded to the world. They were nice.

He got up again. Checked out the curtain. A beige minivan pulled into the lot and traveled around the building. Probably someone looking to park for the night. Or else they were looking for a little privacy and were too cheap to pay for a room.

Thomas hated this part of town.

He got himself ready for bed. Stripped down to his boxers, putting his clothes in a neat pile, so he could hop in and out of the shower quickly. He hated showering, and hated that the filthy room made him feel compelled to take another one.

It was a necessity, yes, but it was a frustrating act. He thought back to when he was a child, and he and his friend were horsing around in the backyard, and he fell into the in-ground pool. His dad, long since dead now, had already laid down a blue tarp to keep the fall leaves out.

He hit the water and the tarp wrapped around him like a giant hand, pulling him down into the water, choking him. He couldn't remember much of what happened. Just blacking out, and suddenly he was on the concrete next to the pool, sputtering and coughing, his mother hovering over him, pressing her hands into his chest.

That blue tarp had nearly killed him.

It was incredible, how something can instill a fear so deeply, that a person carries it for so long. A little water in his face, up his nose, and he flashed right back to that terrible moment.

He assembled all of his belongings on the dresser top. Belt and phone and wallet and bottle of rum. He wanted everything neat and close so that in the morning, he'd be ready to leave. Mark would have gotten back to him by then. He was sure of it. He'd go someplace where he'd be able to go to the store and not worry about being attacked by strangers.

As he crossed the room to the bathroom, there was a knock at the door.

CHAPTER 12

REX HANLON

THEY ASSEMBLED IN a parking lot, in the shadow cast by a supermarket that had closed two hours ago.

Hanlon knew this would be a good spot. There were no cameras, and the supermarket had no late-night workers. It was the kind of flaw you only learn about when you're a cop. The corner was often littered with dime bags and used condoms in the morning, but while the owner was happy to complain to police, he was too cheap to install a surveillance system.

They were blocked from view by the Zhous' mini-van. The seats had been taken out, and it was sporting a set of plates they'd pulled off a car that had been sitting on the side of the road down in Port Richmond for a couple of weeks now. Probably abandoned, and the NYPD hadn't gotten around to towing it.

The real plates were in the spare tire well, ready to go back on after the job was done. It wasn't an elegant plan, but it was easier than trying to procure some other kind of transport.

Hanlon looked at the assembled group, everyone now in dark clothing. Susan and John were eager and ready. He was a little worried about John still. The man, now wearing a Yankees hat that seemed a little too small for him, was clearly seething, holding back throughout the entire trip to the warehouse and back. He was a little surprised that John *hadn't* hit him yet.

Kat stood off to the side, her eyes vacant as she stared into the distance. She was strong, stronger than she looked, and he hoped she was up to the task.

It was Daisy and Paul who worried him. He hadn't wanted to get them involved. First, it meant there were more conspirators. Second, the two of them didn't seem particularly useful, aside from their van. Both were diminutive and reserved, not exactly the best types in a tough spot.

Meek. That's the word he would use to describe them.

Still, though, Daisy was enthusiastic, hopping on the balls of her feet. Paul still seemed hesitant. He kept looking around, nervous, like he was expecting someone to sneak up on them. That, or he was looking for an escape route.

Hanlon closed his eyes and said a quick prayer to himself. He was afraid. There were a lot of people involved now. As the saying went, too many cooks can ruin a stew. One stupid move and the plan would fall apart.

At least they seemed to have eased off him a bit. It still hurt, standing there in front of them. Bearing the scar of his failure. Knowing that he'd let them all down. Because the precinct captain was getting pressure from the mayor and the media to close the case. His need to please—and more than that, his need to stop a scumbag killer—made him too ready to bend the rules.

"So, we're going to go over it one more time," Hanlon said. "Everyone ready?"

The parents nodded in turn. Hanlon took a knee on the ground, wincing as he went down. There were three sticks laid out to look like a C—a rough approximation of the shape of the motel.

If Scott was there, he was in the room farthest from the lobby. He and John had done a quick recon on the way over, and it seemed only two rooms were occupied, based on the lights. At one room, a strange man came out, and after a few minutes, another went in. Hanlon was pretty sure Scott wouldn't be having visitors, so that narrowed it down.

He also confirmed the lot behind the hotel was empty.

There were only two other cars in the inner courtyard. Neither of them were owned by the NYPD. He knew all the undercover cars the local precinct used. Hell, he'd sat in more than half of them. And neither of the cars were nice enough that they could have belonged to the lawyer. So unless a convention suddenly came into town and the place got a rush, they had plenty of space and privacy to get in and grab Scott.

Hanlon pointed to one end of the C.

"Lobby," he said.

He pointed to the other.

"Scott," he said.

He picked up a rock and put it behind the spot where Scott was staying.

"Van goes here," he said. "You stay close to the hotel, in the shadows, where no one can see you. Stay quiet. Don't turn the headlights on, and don't draw attention."

He stood back up, feeling a twinge in his lower back. It was simplistic, maybe a little ridiculous, but he always figured people retained information better when there were visuals. And there wasn't any room for error.

"I'm going in the front," said Hanlon. "First, to see if it's him. If it is, I'll get him to open the door and get into the room. Then I load him out the back window to you, and you all put him in the van. Susan will drive, Daisy sits shotgun, Paul is in the back. Kat and John will come with me. We'll follow behind."

John threw up his hands. "Wait, wait, wait. That's not going to happen."

"Yes, it is," Hanlon said. "You all follow the rules I set out. I'm doing this for a reason."

"Why?" John asked, challenging him.

What he didn't want to say was that he couldn't trust John to not pull the van to the side of the road and kill Scott there. Call Hanlon old-fashioned, but he wanted another man in the car, hence Paul. Despite Paul's hesitancy, Hanlon figured out the fight-or-flight response would kick in and Paul would be able to keep Scott subdued in the back.

He also didn't want Paul and Daisy alone in there, because there was too much emotional baggage. If Paul got really nervous, he might try talking Daisy out of it. Susan, at least, was unfamiliar, and would probably respond less to Paul.

And Susan didn't seem to be having second thoughts, so he trusted she would keep Paul on track.

It was too much to get into.

"Because I told you, this is how it's getting done," Hanlon said. "And that's that."

He stared John down, waiting for the bigger man to protest, but John accepted it. Seemed he wanted to move along with the plan and saw no sense in stalling. That was good.

"Going through the window feels a touch complicated," Paul said.

"It's too risky to bring him out through the front," Hanlon said. "If he yells, if he puts up a struggle, if someone comes out of their room, we're going to have an issue. Has to be like this. I slip in, we get him out. Once you've got him safely in the van, I'm going to strip the room down, leave a little tip and a note on the counter, so when the maid comes through in the morning, it looks like he checked out in a rush. John and Kat, you go back to my car and wait for me. I'll only be a few minutes."

"And this is going to work?" Paul asked. Clearly not believing it was going to work.

Daisy pushed her body into him a little, an annoyed look on her face. John looked ready to say something, but Hanlon spoke first.

"This is the best plan we've got," said Hanlon. "Now, everyone take one of these and put your phone in."

He handed out small felt pouches that were rigid on the inside, and closed with a small flap and button. Susan took the stack and passed them out.

"What are these?" Daisy asked.

"It'll block the signal on your phones. This way if any kind of suspicion falls on any of you, nobody can go back and track your movements."

"Why not get burners?" Paul asked. "Like in the movies."

"One, because we don't have time," Hanlon said. "Two, because burners come with their own risks." He opened the passenger door of the van and pulled out a black messenger bag. "Now, all of them, in here."

The parents slowly followed the order, softly placing their phones in the bag. When it was Paul's turn, he paused, seeming to think too long and too hard about it. Hanlon was about to say something when John got in front of him. For a second Hanlon thought John was going to hit Paul, but he just put his hands on Paul's shoulders and looked him in the eye.

"We need you on this," he said, his voice earnest. Almost desperate. "Okay Paul? Can you do this? Please?"

Paul nodded. Dropped his phone in the bag.

They were ready to go. Hanlon climbed into the passenger seat as John got behind the wheel, doors slamming and the engine turning over.

It was time.

CHAPTER 13

SUSAN KENNELLY

JOHN REACHED INTO the open driver-side window and took Susan's hand.

"I love you," he said.

"I love you, too," she said, offering a soft smile in return.

"For John Junior," he said, squeezing her hand. He leaned in and kissed her. His stubble raked her face like sandpaper and it hurt, but when he pulled away, she kept on smiling.

She knew better than to disagree with John.

She knew better than to make him angry.

As John walked around the front of the car, Susan exhaled.

She hated this. The very idea of killing someone made her physically sick. She'd thrown up twice already, when no one was looking. But the idea of saying no to John was a nonstarter. With the state he was in, thirsty for blood, she didn't trust what he would do. So she'd be the good wife, follow along. Because it was easier.

John took his spot by the window next to Kat, peering inside, but the curtain was closed. Paul was in the back, sitting on the floor of the van, his head in his hands, holding a bundle of zip ties. John had a handful of them, too.

"Are you ready for this?" Daisy asked from the passenger seat.

"As ready as I'll ever be," Susan said, fake-smiling.

"We have to do it," Daisy said. "Knowing he had Jian's picture, I won't sleep. I'll never sleep another night that he's alive."

Susan wondered what it was like, having another child. The pain of losing one while still having to comfort and console the other. She wondered if it hurt more or less. She'd never know. John Junior was their first, and it was a difficult pregnancy. The doctor had told her having another child would be too risky, so they decided that their family was complete with the three of them.

And now it wasn't.

With John Junior in the house, John had mellowed. Not that he'd been a violent man before—he'd never raised his hands against her—but sometimes Susan thought it was only a matter of time. Sometimes he would get so angry, his voice growing so loud, Susan was amazed no one ever called the police. She imagined the neighbors turning up the volume on the television, closing the windows, figuring it would be best just to ignore it.

And it was over such little things, too. The dishes would sit in the sink for a little while, because she had errands to run or laundry to do, and suddenly John would erupt.

Things weren't perfect, but with John Junior they'd gotten notably better. Especially as John Junior got older, more engaged, understood more about what was happening around him. The boy had made her husband into a kinder, gentler man.

And now the loss of her son would make John into a murderer.

She closed her eyes, breathed in through her mouth, out through her nose, like she learned in yoga class, but it didn't help. She didn't feel any calmer. Watched as Daisy flipped down the visor and pressed her fingers to a picture held there by a rubber band. The twins, no doubt.

Susan checked the clock on the dash. Nearly midnight.

There was a flash of movement out of the corner of her eye.

The curtain pushed aside and the window opened.

John and Kat took a few steps back. Susan twisted around in her seat and saw Scott climb out the window. His hair was wild, his t-shirt put on inside out. His pants were unbuttoned, showing off plaid boxers. That sick pervert.

Just seeing him made her grip the wheel so tight her knuckles went white.

Scott fell to the ground in a heap and quickly got up. Hanlon wasn't behind him, though.

And then Susan saw that Scott was holding something in his hand. She squinted.

A gun.

He pointed it at John's chest.

CHAPTER 14

THOMAS SCOTT

WHEN THOMAS SAW Hanlon, he knew he was in trouble.

After the knock, Thomas peeked out the window, and he saw the detective, hands behind his back, glancing around the parking lot.

In that moment he knew there was no way he was making it out of the room alive.

Not after the threat from the cops. Not after the way Hanlon had treated him in the interrogation room. Screaming at him, telling him it was only a matter of time before he cracked, pushing the pictures of those poor, dead children into Thomas's face. All Thomas had wanted to do was not look at them. But Hanlon made him look anyway, and the images haunted him.

Hanlon banged his fist against the door.

"Police, open up," he said.

Thomas didn't often get angry. But this made him angry. And it was just enough to kick his survival instinct into gear.

After the way he'd been treated, he wasn't going to roll over and play dead.

So Thomas came up with a plan.

It wasn't a great one, but it was a plan.

He just had to get the timing right.

Thomas picked up his belt from the dresser, opened the door a crack, just enough so Hanlon would think he was being welcomed inside.

The detective pushed his way in, looking around. He seemed confused to be facing an empty room. Thomas had backed out of his line of sight, into the jumble of curtains, his heart beating furiously in his chest.

As soon as the door closed, Thomas whipped his belt around the detective and shoved him into the wall, pressing his body hard against him.

Hanlon struggled, sputtering and yelling, but Thomas was stronger. He grabbed the two ends of the belt and cinched them together, so Hanlon's arms would be pressed to his side.

"Get the hell off me, you sick bastard," Hanlon yelled, throwing his body back, trying to gain the upper hand.

Thomas used his foot to close the door and shoved the detective down onto the floor, so that he would be wedged between the bed and the wall. Then he grabbed one of his socks, and he felt a little bad because the sock was a day old now, but he had to work with what was on hand.

"You have no idea what you're…" Hanlon started.

The rest of what Hanlon had to say was cut off as Thomas crammed the sock into his mouth. He took off Hanlon's belt—the detective's eyes went wide and he bucked harder, like some terrible sexual violation was about to happen, which made Thomas sick to his stomach—and he wrapped up Hanlon's legs.

Then he sat on the bed.

Hanlon kicked and squirmed like a fish on the deck of a boat. Trying to free himself, screaming in the back of his throat. The sound wasn't loud enough to penetrate the walls.

Thomas's mind went blank.

Then he got up. Paced the room.

Okay. He had a cop tied up in his motel room. A cop who was probably here to do very bad things to him. That had to be the case. Otherwise he would have shown up with more cops, right? For a second Thomas thought maybe he was here to apologize, but given how angry Hanlon looked, that he'd called Thomas a "sick bastard" right off the bat, that probably wasn't the case.

He checked the window again. There was no police car in the lot.

A thought seized him: What if he had backup?

What if he had someone to check in with?

Thomas knelt down and went through Hanlon's pockets while the detective screamed into the sock. Hanlon had nothing in his coat or pants, but Thomas found a small ankle holster holding a compact, silver six-shooter.

Thomas pulled it out and lifted it up to the light. He'd never held a gun before.

It was heavier than he thought it would be.

And much, much scarier.

He didn't want to take it, but didn't want to risk Hanlon getting free and shooting him as he climbed out the window. So, resolving to toss the gun as soon as he got outside, he pulled on his suit and shoes, minus one sock, as he crossed to the bathroom, not wanting to wait any longer.

He pulled up the window and swung a leg out,

the frame cutting into his stomach, then squirmed through and fell to the ground.

When he got up, he saw John Junior's father.

And he looked ready for round two.

Thomas was suddenly relieved to have the gun.

CHAPTER 15

JOHN KENNELLY

IT WAS ALL John could do to keep himself from diving at Scott.

Intellectually, he knew the man had a gun. And he knew the gun was pointed at his chest. But a big part of him simply did not care. His son's killer was standing there—right there, in front of him, no more than a few yards away. Without even thinking about it, he tensed his calves and rolled his weight onto his toes, ready to propel forward.

Luckily, sense prevailed.

He took a deep breath. Tried to calm the adrenaline raging through his body like a river.

"How about you put away the gun?" John asked through gritted teeth. "You owe me for what you did to my son. So let's make this a fair fight. More fair than the chance you gave him."

Scott was panicked. Sweating, breathing fast, eyes darting between the parents assembled in the dark parking lot. He seemed unsure of what to do. John was a little surprised, and thankful, that Scott hadn't pulled the trigger yet.

And he knew he shouldn't goad him, but he couldn't help it.

"Listen, just listen…" Scott said, his voice shaking. He sounded so much like a child, his voice contrasting starkly with his heavy brow and his rough appearance.

Screw it. Scott didn't seem all together anyway. The guy was definitely a few cards short of a full deck. Maybe he was too afraid to fire. John took a step forward, the asphalt crunching under his foot.

Scott whipped the gun up and leaned forward, pointing the gun square between John's eyes. John put his hands up and took a step back, hoping it would calm the man, but it didn't seem to help. He glanced back to make sure no one else was in the line of fire. Susan and Daisy were still in the van with Paul, and Kat had moved a little behind the van, out of view.

"I did not kill your children," Scott said.

That was enough to brush away the fear and bring the anger back to the forefront.

"What?" John asked, a little surprised by the boldness of the claim.

"I did not kill your children," Scott said. He sounded so much surer of himself the second time.

"You're going to lie to my face?" John asked. "To all of us? The cops had you dead to rights."

"I did not kill them," Scott said, a tinge of sadness in his voice. "I would never kill them. They were nice, and sweet. They were kind, and, and beautiful—"

"Listen to yourself," John said, his voice booming. He didn't care who heard him. "Grown men don't talk like that! You know who talks like that? Freaks."

"I am not a *freak*," Scott said, stabbing the gun forward in the air to punctuate each word. John's heart skipped a few beats.

This was getting out of hand. He needed to de-escalate. He looked around, and the rest of the parents were frozen. Paul hadn't even left the van. He seemed to be watching through the window. The coward. Leaving him alone to deal with this madman.

Stall. That's what he would do. He would stall. He would talk as long as he could, keep Scott placated and confused, until he found his opening.

And then he'd exploit it, in the bloodiest way possible.

He'd do it right here. Forget the warehouse. He would gladly pay whatever the price was. If that meant spending the rest of his life in jail, so be it. He had no more children. There was only Susan, and she'd survive without him.

Maybe she'd even be better off.

It would be worth it, to see this man extinguished from the earth.

"Where's Hanlon?" John asked. "Is he hurt? Does he need help?"

"He's not hurt," Scott said, glancing back to the window. "He's just tied up. I don't hurt people. I wouldn't hurt him."

John believed Hanlon was probably okay. He hadn't heard any gunshots. And if he wasn't okay, then it wasn't some great loss to the world. He was a mediocre cop who screwed up and put them all into this mess. They didn't need him to finish it.

"Okay, it's good that he's not hurt," John said. "Listen, we can solve this. I'm willing to hear you out. But first, you have to put down the gun."

"As soon as I put down the gun, you're going to come after me," Scott said.

"That's not true." John tried to sound convincing.

"Yes, it is," Scott said. "I see it. You're lying. You're just telling me what I want to hear."

Okay, so maybe this guy wasn't a complete idiot.

John wasn't sure what to do. But Scott didn't seem to know what to do, either.

One thing was for sure: John didn't know how much longer they could stand here like this, out in the open. Surely, someone would be by soon and stumble across this scene, a wild-looking man holding a gun on a bunch of people standing around a minivan.

John tried to think of another way to stall, another question to ask, when Scott waved the gun like he was trying to bat away a fly. "Get away from the van."

"I can't do that," John said.

Scott took a step forward, held the gun up. "Yes, you can. Get away from the van. All of you. Leave the keys."

John shook his head. "Now wait—"

"Now!" Scott yelled, his voice again taking on the shrill tone of a child.

John didn't want to get shot today. Then he'd lose his chance for revenge.

Lose the battle. Win the war.

John put his hand up and waved at Kat to move away from her place behind the van. He turned to Susan and Daisy, and found them frozen in fright.

And he got an idea.

"Susan, Daisy, the two of you, get out of the car now," he said, purposely leaving out Paul.

He hoped Paul would be smart enough to get the message, and stay hidden in the back. He hoped Susan and Daisy were smart enough to get out of the car without saying anything, without alerting or pointing out Paul. It was their one last chance to maintain the upper hand.

And it worked.

Because when Susan and Daisy opened the doors, the interior lights popping on, Paul's face had disappeared from the window. There wasn't much space to hide in the back, with the seats taken out, but maybe there had been something he could throw over himself.

Or maybe Scott was in too much of a panic to notice.

Or maybe Scott would turn and shoot Paul, and that would give John the opening he needed.

Any of those options worked. He honestly did not care. Whatever path put his hands around the throat of his son's killer was an acceptable one.

The women got behind John, and he put his arms up, like he could block Scott from getting to them. The group cut a wide circle around him, away from the van and toward the back wall of the motel. Still no movement from the van.

Scott's eyes seemed to soften now that things were going his way. He stepped toward the van and closed the sliding door, then walked around to the driver's side, never taking his eyes off them for too long, never bringing the gun down.

He stopped as he reached the door and looked at the assembly of parents.

"I did not do it," he said. "I did not kill them. I couldn't have killed them. I would never—I would *never*—do something like that. I hope you find out who did. I'm sorry. But I'm leaving. I can't be here anymore."

Scott climbed into the car. John considered rushing it, but saw that Scott didn't take his hand off the gun. He just moved it to his left hand and placed it on the steering wheel as he turned the key in the ignition with his right hand.

Then he backed the van toward the parking lot, whipped it around, and drove off, tires squealing and throwing up bits of loose asphalt. They watched in silence as it turned the corner and disappeared.

John cursed silently to himself and adjusted his son's Yankees hat.

It was up to Paul now.

The one person in this group John had the least faith in.

CHAPTER 16

PAUL ZHOU

PAUL PEEKED OUT from under the blanket and watched as Scott started the van and pulled out of the lot.

Scott had glanced back, barely, but didn't seem to notice the rumpled blanket, which Paul had managed to get over himself after John made it clear he should stay in the back. Not that he had any idea why this was a good plan. The truth was, he was too scared to try and get out.

Paul's heart beat in his chest with the speed of a hummingbird's wings. He wasn't sure what to do. He couldn't just rush him. The man had a gun, and Paul didn't have a death wish.

So he watched. After a couple of turns, Scott placed the gun on the passenger seat. Okay, that was a start. If he was fast, maybe he could get to Scott before Scott could get to the gun.

But did he want to?

He'd heard the man say he didn't kill their children.

What if that was true?

Maybe Scott was innocent of all this. If so, this entire plan was a terrible mistake. Cops got things wrong sometimes. There had just been a whole series on Netflix about police officers screwing some guy who was falsely arrested for a crime, from years before, that he didn't commit. Paul hadn't watched it yet, but everyone was talking about it. Maybe Hanlon was off about the whole thing.

Though that didn't explain the pictures Scott had in his apartment.

He could be lying. What did Paul know of killers? Psychopaths are supposed to do things without any sort of feeling for consequences, without understanding of human emotion. If he'd really killed their children, then lying about it would be a lot easier than the act of taking a life.

This wasn't some late-night movie. It was real life, where things weren't laid out so clearly. Where bad guys didn't give eloquent soliloquies about their crimes.

Paul wished it were a late-night movie. That he was an action hero, with the strength and courage to subdue the man. But he couldn't get himself to move out from under the blanket. Maybe he could get to Scott in time. But even if Scott wasn't able to get the gun, he could still crash the car. Scott was buckled in. Paul wasn't. He'd go flying through the windshield and would end up a smear on the pavement.

No, right now he had to focus on staying alive. Hope that Daisy and the others were following closely behind, formulating some kind of plan.

So he waited, keeping the blanket just high enough that he could keep an eye on Scott. Waiting for something to happen.

Scott drove, and stopped, and drove and stopped again, muttering to himself. Paul listened hard but couldn't make out what he was saying over the sound of the engine and the tires on the road.

What if they weren't following? What if he was all alone? That meant sooner or later, he'd have to act. He just had to wait for the perfect moment.

And with the car moving, that probably wouldn't happen anytime soon.

Paul focused on staying as still as possible and slowed his breathing. The rough carpet on the floor of the van scratched his cheek. He prayed that Scott wouldn't glance in the rear-view mirror and get curious about the blanket.

CHAPTER 17

DAISY ZHOU

DAISY RAN PAST the others, watching the van as it cut around the corner and disappeared from view.

She turned to John, Susan, and Kat, the three of them dumbfounded. She couldn't believe that they were standing there like that. It had been scary enough when Scott was holding a gun on them. It made her blood run cold and her body seize up, to see that monster wielding the power of life and death over them.

But now he was gone. And Paul was with him.

For as much as she wanted to put faith in her husband, she found that faith flagging. Paul wasn't a man of action. He was a man of thoughtfulness. And thoughtfulness didn't mean much against a loaded weapon, or a man desperate enough to use it.

She hated thinking that. She hated doubting her husband. But she couldn't help herself. Every second the van got further away, it made her feel more and more like she might not see him again. At least, not alive.

Daisy put her hands up in the air, trying to snap the other parents out of their stupor. "We have to do something!"

"Okay, okay, let's check on Hanlon first," John said. "I'll do it. The rest of you stay here."

John ran around the side of the building as Daisy stood there, bouncing on the toes of her feet. She didn't know what to do. Her van was gone. Her husband was gone. She felt empty.

All that doubt and uncertainty about her marriage were suddenly erased. She couldn't lose Paul, too. She wouldn't know what to do. She couldn't bear the prospect of raising Jian by herself.

She went over to the other women. Kat was shaking her head, clearly frustrated, while Susan had wrapped her arms around herself, sobbing silently. It seemed like the gravity of the situation was pulling them apart.

Maybe Paul was right. Maybe this wasn't the right thing to do.

Kat put her hand on Daisy's arm. "It's going to be okay," she said.

"How do you know that?" Daisy asked. "How could you possibly know that?"

"Because Paul is a smart man. He's a cautious man. He won't do anything that's going to get himself killed."

Daisy nodded. Kat was right. Maybe the thoughtfulness would save him.

Then she got an idea. She reached around to her back pocket, thinking maybe she would text Paul, try to communicate with him some way, find out where the van was.

But the phone was in the bag, with all the rest.

The bag was in the van.

So Scott had the van, her husband, and all their cell phones.

She wanted to scream.

John and Hanlon reappeared, jogging around the side of the building. Hanlon was huffing, his hair unkempt, his clothes ruffled. And more than that, he looked pissed. John was running him through what happened, about Scott taking off.

As soon as they got close, Daisy dove forward and slapped Hanlon hard across the face. Her hand stung from the impact. The blow seemed to stun him. He staggered back and hit the wall, putting one hand to his cheek, eyes wide.

"What the hell happened in there?" Daisy asked. "Can't you do anything right?"

"Now hold on," Hanlon said, rubbing his face.

"No, no holding on," Daisy said. "We have to go after them right now. You have to call the police. Let them know."

"That's not going to happen," John said.

Hanlon nodded. "Do you know what kind of hell we'd be in?"

"My *husband* is in the *van*," Daisy said. "I don't know how to make it clearer."

"And I can't make this any more clear," John said, talking slowly, like she was a child. "Now shut up and let's go get into Hanlon's car. We'll go after them and we'll fix this."

"But—" Daisy said.

John drew himself up so that he seemed a few inches taller. He stepped toward Daisy, his face suddenly set in stone. The words that came out of him bubbled from someplace deep and scary.

"No more *but*s," he said. "Get moving."

Daisy tried to hold his gaze, but his eyes were like chips of granite. John was an angry man, and the way he directed his anger at her shook her to her core. She looked over to Susan, thinking his wife would support him, but she was looking down at the pavement.

Their relationship seemed suddenly cast in a new, disturbing light.

Daisy couldn't believe it. She wanted to reach up and slap John, too, but in that terrible moment, she got the feeling like he might hit her back.

"Okay, fine, let's go to the car," she said, not wanting to waste any more time.

They ran for the parking lot, making their way to Hanlon's car. The wide bench seats gave them enough room—Hanlon driving, John up front, and the women in the back. Kat in the center, with Susan on one side and Daisy on the other. They barely had the doors closed before Hanlon started the engine and whipped the car out of the parking lot.

He seemed to be driving with a purpose, and before Daisy could ask where he was going, John did it for her. "What's the plan?"

"He said he was leaving, right?" Hanlon asked. "He said that?"

"Yes."

"He's panicking," Hanlon said. "He knows he's not safe here. I bet he's aiming for the expressway. There's a ramp not too far from here. It'll be the first thing he comes across, and it's going to look awful inviting."

"And what do we do when we catch up to him?" Susan asked.

"We're playing this one by ear," Hanlon said.

Daisy tried to formulate a plan on her own, the whole time staring at the back of John's head. What kind of man was this? And what path had he put them on?

CHAPTER 18

THOMAS SCOTT

THOMAS TURNED THE car onto the entrance ramp of the Staten Island Expressway and merged into traffic. It was light, though it was after midnight, and more people were out than he would have expected.

Exhaustion suddenly overwhelmed him. He was tired. So tired.

And he didn't have any idea what he was doing.

He was in a stolen van with a gun. A van that was no doubt getting reported to the police right now, and a gun that would land him in jail for a very long time. He'd assaulted a cop and stolen the gun from him.

That was serious. Super serious.

His first experience with the justice system had not been a good one. He had a feeling that no matter how much he explained the circumstances of what happened, no one was going to believe him. It would be his word against theirs, and right now, his word didn't seem to be worth anything.

Seeing all the parents together like that just about killed him. The pain and the suffering they were going through. He almost didn't blame them for coming after him like that. He couldn't imagine what loss like that must do.

He just wished their anger wasn't directed at him.

He thought he could reason with them, but clearly he couldn't, so it was best to get out of there. He figured he could drive a little while until he got an idea.

He had no friends. No one in his life who cared about him or knew where he was. He couldn't go to his apartment. There wasn't anyone he knew who could bail him out of this. All he could do was keep driving—until when? The expressway would eventually split off. And both directions led to New Jersey.

That seemed like a good enough idea. If he was over state lines, didn't it mean that the cops couldn't come after him or something? They'd have the get the police in New Jersey involved, and that would waste even more time.

Okay then. He could drive to Jersey. Ditch the car and the gun as soon as he could. Maybe he could find a train or a bus and just go south. Forget Portland— getting all the way across the country suddenly seemed like too much. But in Jersey he could get a train. He'd taken it before, down to Florida once, to visit a cousin.

The visit hadn't gone so well, but Florida was okay. He didn't mind the heat, and he'd always wanted to visit Disney World. Not that he had any idea what to do down there, other than that. The cousin had passed, years ago. Thomas didn't know anyone else. He wouldn't even have a place to stay. All he had was the clothes on his back, the small amount of cash Amato had given him, and the modest savings in his bank account.

But no matter where you went in the world, people needed things cleaned. It would be easy enough to find a job, and maybe a small apartment. It didn't seem so impossible, and it felt more possible with every inch of roadway he put underneath the tires of the van.

It suddenly felt like this terrible episode of his life was slipping away. Like maybe he'd have a chance to start new. He looked around at the outlines of the trees against the night sky, at the lights of the businesses that flashed by. He'd miss this place. Deep down, he really, truly loved it. It was his home.

But there wasn't anything he was leaving behind.

He could make this work.

But as Thomas drove, something struck him as not right. There was something off that he couldn't quite place his finger on. He became so panicked that it was hard to focus. But after a few moments, he realized what it was: traffic seemed to be slowing down.

He had been intent on keeping the car under the speed limit, turning on his blinker, and carefully changing lanes. He didn't want to draw any undue attention. But there were suddenly more brake lights up ahead. The outlines of the trees and the lights of the businesses weren't whipping by as fast.

His newfound sense of relief slowly slipped away as he realized there were flashing lights up ahead.

An accident. He could make out the police car and the ambulance and the tow truck, sitting there in the middle of the road.

He was stuck in the left lane as traffic came to a dead stop.

CHAPTER 19

PAUL ZHOU

WITH THE WAY the van was moving, Paul was sure they were on the expressway. Scott had been driving fast for a long time, and Paul could hear the sound of cars whipping past them.

This wasn't great. He had no idea which way Scott was headed—to Brooklyn or to New Jersey—but figured that either way, this wasn't going to end well. He might be fleeing the island, and Paul was stuck.

Worse than that, Scott would be very unhappy to find he had a guest along for the ride.

Paul tried to come up with a plan. Scott didn't look back, not in any of the time Paul was looking, so it seemed Scott had pretty much completely written off the back. There was some space to cover between the two of them, but with the gun possibly out of Scott's reach, that put Paul at an advantage.

He could dive forward, grab the gun, and stay on the floor. Point the gun up at Scott. Even if the car came to a short stop, he could wedge himself behind the passenger seat so he wouldn't be thrown through the windshield.

The prospect of grabbing the gun scared Paul.

He'd never held one. Never even seen one in real life, outside the occasional gun holstered at the side of a policeman. What if the safety was on? Scott was a killer—he'd know whether he'd left the safety on. He'd know in an instant that Paul had no clue what he was doing.

Or maybe not. Maybe he really wasn't that smart, which is what everyone had been saying. Maybe Paul just needed the gun in his hand and that would end it.

He breathed deep, in the process inhaling the warm, musty scent of the blanket, which made him think of his son and daughter. This was the blanket they kept in the back of the car for impromptu picnics. Driving past Clove Lakes Park or Silver Lake Park, they would pull it out and sit on the grass with the kids. Sometimes with snacks, sometimes reading books, and sometimes they'd sit there just to sit.

What if Scott was going to their house?

If he was on the expressway, then all he had to do was take it to the Arden Avenue exit, and it wouldn't be long until they were in his neighborhood. What if Scott was planning to drive up to their door and finish what he had started? After all, he'd had that picture of Jian in his apartment. *Why?*

He wanted to climb up to his knees and peek out the window, see if he could figure out where they were. What direction they were headed in. And he knew that if Scott went anywhere near the Arden Avenue exit, Paul would get that gun and fire it without a second thought.

He would cross that line if it meant protecting his son.

He was just about to push himself up, try and catch a glimpse of the surroundings, when the car was filled with swinging red lights. It wasn't accompanied by sirens, so it couldn't be that they were getting pulled over. The cops would have put their sirens on.

And then Paul realized that it must be a car accident. Something jamming up the expressway. Even in the middle of the night, it was so easy to shut this entire thing down.

The car came to a stop, and Scott slammed his fist on the steering wheel.

This was Paul's chance.

CHAPTER 20

DAISY ZHOU

DAISY TAPPED HER foot as Hanlon guided the car down the expressway. She couldn't know if they were going the right way, but something down in her gut told her they were. That Paul was just up ahead.

The problem was that traffic seemed to be slowing down. It was late now, so there shouldn't be this much traffic on the expressway. Maybe there was an accident ahead. She wanted to ask Hanlon if he had a radio he could check, but found herself unable to form the words.

She was still so angry at him.

And at John now, for trying to impose his will on them. She felt the need for revenge. To make Scott pay for what he did. But that need didn't outweigh the life of her husband. She didn't need to ask John how he felt—clearly he didn't care. The only thing that mattered to him was ending Scott.

This whole thing was coming apart at the seams. She'd gone along with it because she felt this burning anger in her stomach, like a flame she thought she could snuff out if Scott were dead. But she was starting to understand how Paul felt. Why he was so unsure about this whole thing.

Who were they to be judge, jury, and executioner?

The plan didn't matter to her anymore. All she wanted to do was find her husband.

But with the way the cars were slowing down now and boxing them in, it was seeming a lot less likely to happen anytime soon.

Hanlon reached down toward the radio and flicked a switch. A waterfall of static filled the inside of the car, and then a male voice broke through.

"Central, we've got a 10-53 between Slosson and Bradley. Victim likely, bus dispatched and arrived on scene. Send AIS. Repeat, send AIS."

"What's all that supposed to mean?" John asked.

"Car accident up ahead," Hanlon said, pointing forward with his chin as the car came to a stop, stuck behind a sea of red brake lights. "'Bus' is an ambulance. 'Likely' means the victim is likely to die. They want the Accident Investigation Squad to come out."

"What if it was them?" Daisy asked, her blood running cold.

"They'd be asking for a hell of a lot more than AIS," Hanlon said. "Remember, Scott has a gun."

"Yeah, your gun," Daisy said, hoping the words would sting.

Given the look Hanlon shot her in the rear view, it seemed like she'd accomplished that mission.

"So, can't you just radio in ahead?" Daisy asked. "They might be stuck in the same thing. The cops might have him boxed in. They could get him."

"No way," John said. "We do that, we have to call the whole thing off. We'll never explain it away."

"He's right," Hanlon said. "Better to wait. Scott may not be the smartest guy I've ever tangled with, but he has to know he can only get himself in more trouble. I'm sure this will open up in a minute."

Daisy scoffed. She couldn't believe they'd gamble with the life of her husband. She looked at Susan, who was staring vacantly out the window. She looked like a mouse, so timid and afraid. It made her angry. So she turned to Kat.

"I can't leave him out there like that," Daisy said.

"Better to just listen to what they said," Kat responded.

"Forget this," Daisy said. She opened the door and jumped out. She was running as soon as her feet hit the pavement, cutting a path down the shoulder of the expressway. Cars whipped past on the other side of the concrete divider. Hanlon and John were calling for her, but she couldn't hear what they were saying, and she didn't really give a damn.

She ran as fast as she could in the direction of the accident.

And, hopefully, her husband.

CHAPTER 21

THOMAS SCOTT

THOMAS LOOKED AT the line of brake lights in front of him. The way was completely blocked. In the distance, it looked like there were police officers trying to clear room so traffic could start moving through a free lane.

Thomas's heart was slamming against the inside of his rib cage.

He, the most wanted man on Staten Island, was in a stolen car, and suddenly he was a sitting duck. He looked at the cars around him. Already, people were shuffling, craning their necks, a few leaning on their horns.

No one was looking into the van.

But it was only a matter of time.

What if someone recognized him? Would a mob of people drag him from the car and beat him to death? Would they bring him over to the cops, who would find the stolen car and the gun and the cop tied up in the motel room, and then toss him right back in jail? He kept thinking back to the liquor store. The way people looked at him with disgust, like he had come there on purpose to hurt someone.

He considered hopping onto the shoulder, but there was construction, so it was closed. He couldn't back the car up—there were too many cars behind him now, and anyway, the nearest exit was too far away.

He fantasized about driving one of those monster trucks that could jump up and roll over an entire line of cars. How easy it would be then, just to ride across this mess and speed away. But that wasn't real. He was in a minivan, and although it had some nice features—GPS and satellite radio and heated seats— it wasn't exactly built for what he had in mind.

"Damnit damnit damnit," Thomas said, looking around, trying to decide the best course of action.

He looked to his right. On the other side of the three lanes of traffic, there was a grass-covered embankment. It wasn't too steep and looked easy enough to climb. With traffic at a dead standstill, it would be easy enough to make his way across.

No, the real problem was that big stone wall at the top of the embankment.

Thomas knew that on the other side there was a line of quiet homes, and the wall was to drown out the never-ending hum of the highway. He looked to the left, across the opposite three lanes of traffic, up the other embankment, and there was no wall. The problem was, the cars on that side were whipping by at top speed.

Traffic was slow up in the distance, rubberneckers slowing down to look, but as soon as drivers passed the wreck, they pressed down hard on their gas pedals, racing each other to make up for the time they'd lost. There were enough cars moving just fast enough that Thomas knew his chances of getting all the way across without getting smashed to bits were low.

He looked at the wall to his right, wondered if it

was low enough that he could climb over it, or if he could backtrack to the last exit.

And then he saw it.

About a hundred yards ahead, there was a gap. He could just make out a little bit of light streaming from the other side. If he could make it there, he could probably squeeze through.

He had no idea what he'd do when he made it there, but it was better than sitting here. Better than driving past some cops who might recognize him, or might get curious and run his plate, and then he'd be in the same position as before.

He thought back to his filthy cell at Rikers. All the people lined up outside it who wanted to do him harm. He didn't want to go back.

He was preparing to exit the car when he glimpsed movement in the rear-view mirror. He turned to check what it was, and suddenly something slipped over his head, cinched around his throat, and pulled him back into the seat. The flow of oxygen to his lungs was immediately cut off.

CHAPTER 22

PAUL ZHOU

SCOTT WAS MUTTERING curses under his breath. Paul knew that if he was going to do something, this was his chance.

But he remained frozen under the blanket. He wasn't a killer. He wasn't even a fighter. He'd never been in a fight in his life.

He wondered if he could signal to someone outside the car, but wasn't sure how to do that without attracting Scott's attention. He thought about opening the back door of the van. He could just reach the handle. But he wasn't sure if it was locked. The doors usually locked after the car was started. If he made too much noise trying to open it, Scott could turn around and make short work of him with the gun.

He paused, breathed in the smell of the blanket.

They'd spent so many beautiful afternoons sitting on it. He ran through them in his head, highlights of Mei's short life. He focused in on one of the earlier memories. She took her first steps off this blanket, into the freshly mowed grass of Silver Lake Park.

He would carry the memory of that day with him for the rest of his life. The way she tentatively propped herself up, standing and laughing and swaying with a newfound sense of power. She did that occasionally, but couldn't seem to muster the courage to take a step, and would inevitably plop down on her butt.

But this time, she smiled like she'd been let in on a secret, and she stumbled forward. It was only three or four steps before she went down, and Paul scooped her up and rocked her in his arms, brushing her black hair out of her face as she cried little crocodile tears, less hurt and more looking for Father's attention.

Paul saw a grass stain up on the edge of the blanket and had to fight back his own tears.

The memory of his daughter and what he lost filled him with rage. The thought of that most perfect piece of him, which he'd created, gone before she had a chance to fall in love or join a team or stay up late or any of the other things kids are supposed to do—it was too much.

Paul may not have been a man of action, but the adrenaline was pumping. The anger was giving him strength. It was pushing him to remember that this was the man who had killed his daughter.

Scott was a big man. Paul wasn't as strong as Scott, but he was smart. He reached his hand around, as slowly as possible so as not to disturb the blanket, and came across Mei's sparkly purple jump rope, wedged into the corner. Something he had forgotten to clear out of the car the last time he cleaned.

Any other time he would have been annoyed at the oversight.

Right now it was perfect. Fitting that this was the way Scott would die.

Because even though Scott was a big man, as long as Paul had a little leverage, things could be made a little more even.

What would it take? Three minutes? Four?

Suddenly he understood what was driving John so hard. What made Daisy light up so much. For as detestable as this whole thing was, it was *something*. And doing something made him feel so much less helpless. Like he wasn't just tumbling through a void.

He threw the blanket aside, charged forward, threw the jump rope over Scott's head, making sure to loop it around his neck, and leaned back with all his weight. Scott thrashed and drew both hands to his throat, desperately trying to free himself.

Paul looked up, saw Scott's frightened eyes in the rear-view mirror, and locked on to them. He wanted to see the life leave them.

He wasn't afraid anymore.

CHAPTER 23

THOMAS SCOTT

DARKNESS DANCED AROUND the edges of Thomas's vision. Something hard and tight was cutting into his throat. He scratched at it, but couldn't get a finger underneath it. He flailed his arms, desperately trying to reach for something, but there was nothing close. The gun might as well have been a million miles away, out of his reach on the passenger seat.

Someone must have been in the car with him. When Thomas had gotten in, he hadn't seen anything but a dirty old blanket. But he was sure no one had come in since. The doors hadn't opened, the lights hadn't gone on. Someone had been waiting.

All he could see in the rear-view mirror was a pair of furious eyes.

He tried to cough, to choke, to call out for help, but all he could do was feel his lungs screaming for air, and the thing cutting into his throat, crushing his trachea.

Then he realized his foot was still pressed firmly on the brake pedal.

He picked it up and pushed it down hard on the gas. The van leapt forward and collided with the car in front of it. It wasn't much of an impact, but it was enough that whoever was behind him seemed to falter. The thing around his neck loosened just enough that he could slip a hand under, creating some relief for his throat. Thomas took a greedy gasp of air, savoring the feeling of his lungs filling back up, nearly crying from relief.

He turned and saw someone moving, pushing toward the front seat.

Going for the gun.

Thomas threw his elbow back and it smacked off something hard. The person yelped in pain and fell back as a bolt shot up Thomas's arm. He slammed the car into Park and reached for the gun, but only succeeded in knocking it away. It fell somewhere between the passenger door and the seat, out of reach.

He was about to climb over when he noticed the driver of the car in front of him stalking toward the van. He was a big man, better than six feet tall and wide across the shoulders. He had big glasses and a bushy mustache and his face was twisted in anger. He was yelling something, and even with the window closed Thomas could tell it wasn't going to be good.

So Thomas threw himself into the back, figuring he'd push past the person in the back and escape through the rear of the van, which would be clear now that they'd moved forward.

But as he scrambled around the seat and onto the floor, someone jumped onto his back and wrapped an arm around his throat, screaming into his ear, "You killed my daughter!"

Once again, he couldn't breathe.

CHAPTER 24

PAUL ZHOU

PAUL THREW HIMSELF on top of Scott. Driving the car forward might have been enough for Scott to distract him, but it would also piss off the other drivers and alert the police.

All he had to do was hold him.

But the man was strong. He was bucking and fighting, trying to get away, moving toward the back of the car. And meanwhile, someone was smacking the car window, trying see what was going on. Probably the person in front of them who they'd hit.

"Someone help!" Paul yelled out, gripping the man tighter, wrapping one arm around Scott's neck, and the other around his own wrist, trying to keep ahold of Scott.

The front driver-side door opened, the interior flooding with yellow light, and a male voice asked, "What the hell is going on in there?"

Paul was about to answer when he felt the body under him shift. Scott was getting his feet underneath him, and Paul couldn't do much more than go along for the ride, as the bigger man threw him back into the wall of the van. Paul's head smacked on the glass, and he saw stars, loosening his grip enough that Scott was able to move toward the back.

He fiddled with the door and found the button. The door slowly rose and Paul got a good look at Scott's face. He looked so much more sinister in the harsh interior light.

Scott stepped one foot out of the van, looked back, and paused.

"You're Mei's father," Scott said.

Paul felt a white-hot explosion spark in the center of him. "Don't you dare say her name," he said, choking back tears. He scrambled to get out of the van as Scott backed up and put his hand in the air.

"I did not kill your daughter," he said.

And then he ran off.

Paul tried to follow and stumbled out of the back. Just as he was about to turn and see if anyone could help him find the direction Scott ran, someone pushed him back against the hood of an idling car.

He turned and found a huge man with glasses and a mustache, his face red. "What the hell is wrong with you, you idiot?" he asked. "You smashed into me. I guess it's true that Asians can't drive."

Paul was about to say something when Daisy appeared. She shouted "Hey," threw her hand out, and struck the man across the face.

"That's racist," she said. "My husband is an excellent driver."

It took a second for Paul to process the sight of his petite wife appearing out of nowhere like that. He didn't know what to do, and watched as the man stumbled for a moment then reached back his hand to smack Daisy.

That white-hot point of rage in Paul's stomach grew bigger. He stepped forward and threw out his fist, jabbing the man's nose. It opened like a faucet, spouting blood. The man staggered back, holding his face.

The quickness and brutality of it shocked Paul. But his wife was in danger. One member of his family was dead. He wouldn't allow another to be hurt.

It didn't take long for the big man to regain his composure. He balled his fists and set himself, preparing to launch forward. Paul knew this was not a fight he was going to win, but he had to do everything he could to protect his wife.

He braced himself.

CHAPTER 25

REX HANLON

HANLON CUT THROUGH the cars on foot just as traffic was starting to pick up. He had no idea what was happening up ahead, but knew there was a very real chance things had just gone south.

He hated leaving his own car, but if there were cops, he might be able to handle it. If those cops saw Scott, then the game would be up. There'd be no explaining that. He might even be in a lot of trouble. Scott could tell them everything that happened at the motel, and the pieces would fall into place fairly quick.

It'd be his word against a kid killer, sure. But there were enough parties in play now that there was no outcome that didn't end with him losing his career, his pension—probably his freedom.

He ducked to the side and jogged on the shoulder, drivers honking their horns at him. He held his badge up over his shoulder, hoping it would catch the light and shut them up.

He wondered if John would think to put the car on the shoulder and wait. Hanlon should have told him to do that. John had insisted on coming, of course, but Hanlon thought it was better to leave him with Susan and Kat.

He was getting tired of this. Part of him just wanted to put a bullet in Scott's skull. Let those parents rest, knowing the man was dead. His career was over anyway. May as well end it with a bang.

Up in the distance, Hanlon saw another car pulled off to the side of the road. The shoulder was blocked because of construction, so it was cutting off a full lane, but cars were able to stream around it.

As he got closer, he recognized the van.

He broke into a run, his knee and hip immediately screaming in protest. Damnit, his age was catching up with him, and he hated it. Hated how he used to be able to run like this and barely break a sweat. Now he would feel some serious pain in the morning. Probably the next day, too.

As he approached the van, it took him a second to figure out what was going on. Daisy was behind Paul, the two of them standing in front of a bigger man with his fists clenched and blood on his face. Hanlon threw himself between them, and held up his badge.

"NYPD," Hanlon said, sucking in air, trying to catch his breath. "What the hell is going on here?"

The man put his hand up, pointing past Hanlon. "This idiot drove his car into mine. Then this bitch slapped me in the face, and he punched me. I want you to arrest them right now."

Paul and Daisy started to protest, but Hanlon gently pushed the man farther away from the two of them. Right off the bat he could see the man's eyes were a little glassy, and upon stepping closer could smell the thick scent of beer on him.

"Sir, have you been drinking tonight?" Hanlon asked.

The man went white. "Uh…"

"Come with me," Hanlon said.

He walked toward where the van and the car were pressed up against each other. The man was docile now, his face drenched in fear. Hanlon took a look at the bumpers of the two vehicles and found the car's was a little loose and some of the paint had been sheared off, but otherwise, it didn't look too bad.

"That's a pretty easy repair," Hanlon said, standing up and looking the man dead in the eye. "Few hundred bucks, I figure. If I told you that you could go home and handle it yourself, would that be preferable to a DUI?"

The man seemed to think about it.

The plan to capture and kill Thomas Scott now rested on this guy's shoulders—and he didn't even know it. Hanlon looked around him, down the expressway, at the cop car that was still lingering. Any moment they could notice what was going on here and come down to investigate.

Hanlon held his breath.

The man's shoulders slumped, and Hanlon exhaled. Defeated, the guy stalked off, got back in the car, and slowly pulled into traffic. Hanlon smiled and turned to the Zhous. The two of them were too far away to have heard the exchange, so they were both incredibly confused.

"Lucky for us, he had a couple of drinks tonight," Hanlon said. "Now, what the hell happened?"

As cars picked up speed, the occasional driver leaning on the horn, Paul ran him through the events in the minivan, stumbling over his words: staying hidden, attacking Scott when the car stopped, Scott's escape, and the altercation with the other driver.

Good on Paul, Hanlon thought. Here he'd thought

the man was a sissy. At least he'd stepped up to defend his wife. He couldn't help but notice that Daisy was throwing the stray grin at him as he told the story.

"So," Hanlon said. "Bad news, Scott got away. Good news, the other officers didn't see you or him, so this is still in play."

"He says he didn't kill our children," Paul said.

"He's lying."

"I know."

Hanlon was shocked. Paul had been the weakest link in the chain, and was suddenly resolute. He wondered what had changed, but then realized it didn't matter.

"So, what's next?" Daisy asked. "How do we find him?"

Hanlon stared off, watching the cars speeding past them. At the big, open expanse of night sky.

Scott was on foot. He was afraid and alone and not all that clever. But Staten Island was more than a hundred square miles, home to a half a million people. A mix of homes and apartments and parks and businesses. And unlike the rest of New York City, this was the borough that gladly went to bed early. If Scott wanted to stay hidden, this place was just dense and quiet enough that it wouldn't be hard at all.

The trick was figuring out where he would go next.

CHAPTER 26

THOMAS SCOTT

THOMAS GLANCED BEHIND him and saw a car approaching. He was pretty sure he wasn't visible, with the way the tree over his head was blocking the streetlight, creating a deep pool of black. But he ran up a driveway between two darkened homes, just to be safe.

He peeked around the corner from his spot of safety and saw it was a police cruiser, driving slowly down the street, the officers craning their necks.

He waited until the car made it to the corner and turned before he headed back down to the sidewalk. His mind raced. He had no idea where to go next. But he knew the hotel wasn't safe.

He sighed and looked around at the quiet residential block. A long row of houses on one side, the noise-dampening wall on the other.

He felt trapped between the two.

For one brief moment, Thomas thought of walking over to the expressway overpass, climbing up the guardrail, and jumping into traffic. The fall might not be enough to end things, but the speeding cars would handle the rest.

The pit in his stomach was so dark and so deep he didn't think he'd ever be able to climb out. What did he have to live for? He was one man against the world, and it didn't seem like anything would convince these people he'd had nothing to do with the death of their children.

No. He didn't do anything wrong.

He wouldn't surrender to that feeling.

But he couldn't stay, either.

He walked to the corner to get his bearings and then realized where he was: a couple of blocks from the nursing home where he'd done some part-time work a few years back. He headed down the block, sticking to the shadows, watching every car that passed him to make sure that it wasn't a cop or one of the parents.

Now that he was on foot and felt relatively safe, it finally hit him. The utter disbelief that Hanlon had talked the parents into coming after him. They were all in on it—Mei's dad and mom, Billy's mom, John Junior's parents. He didn't know them by their names, just the names of their children.

For a second he thought about calling the cops. Hanlon was clearly taking the law into his own hands. But then he realized: The cops still thought he was guilty. Why would they believe him over one of their own?

The brown brick of the nursing home rose in the distance.

He knew there was a nurse at a desk out front, and there'd be a guard doing rounds of the property after midnight, so he cut through the driveway, doing his best to stay out of sight, toward the back door that was sometimes kept propped open with a cinder block, so staff could sneak outside for cigarettes without getting locked out.

He just had to hope the cinder block system was still in place.

As he approached, it looked like the door was closed, but upon closer inspection he realized there was a small piece of wood holding it. He eased the door open and peered into the darkened hallway. There was no movement on either end. He waited a moment and ducked in, cutting across the squeaky floor to the storage closet.

As he reached for the handle, a yellow beam of light flitted across the darkness. He listened, and heard footfalls coming down the hallway. Must be the security guard. He reached forward and grasped the knob.

Finally, something went his way.

The door wasn't locked.

He ducked in and closed the door as quietly as he could, leaned against the door and listened to the footsteps get louder, then softer, and finally disappear.

He flicked on the light, squinting in the harsh white glow, to take stock of his surroundings. This was an overflow room for extra supplies, and it was barely used, because there was another storage closet closer to the nurses' station and therefore more convenient. He just hoped that was still the case and no one wandered down here for anything.

He was so desperate for sleep his eyes hurt. His arm ached from where he slammed it into Mei's father's head. All he wanted to do was lie down. The idea of being in this place made him sick, hiding like this. But he had no other options.

In the morning, he would see Amato. And this would all be over.

He pulled some towels and blankets off a rack and

arranged them on the floor, turned off the light, felt his way to the makeshift bed, and curled up.

The floor was hard and smelled antiseptic. After Rikers and then the hotel, this just felt like another place he was trapped, with no safe route of escape. Within moments he was softly weeping.

CHAPTER 27

Staten Island Register
Breaking news update
Suspected Playground Killer breaks
into Willowbrook nursing home

Thomas Scott, the man suspected to be the Playground Killer and released from custody by police yesterday, was found early this morning sleeping in Sweet Acres Nursing Home in Willowbrook.

According to an employee who wished to remain anonymous, Scott was discovered by a nurse sleeping in a storage room. He reportedly threw her into a wall before fleeing the scene.

A judge ruled that the evidence being used against Scott in the murder of three Staten Island children was inadmissible, because it was collected by someone in an illegal search, at the direction of a police officer.

Scott was also involved in an altercation at a Rosebank liquor store last night, where he reportedly threw another woman to the ground.

Law enforcement sources say they still consider Scott to be a suspect and are currently searching for him in Willowbrook.

Keep an eye on the Register website for up-to-the-minute updates.

CHAPTER 28
THOMAS SCOTT

THOMAS STOOD AT the far end of the strip mall, his cell phone pressed to his ear. The phone kept ringing. Maybe Amato wasn't in yet. He considered going to the Dunkin' Donuts across the street. The pink and orange colors were electric and inviting against the overcast sky.

He'd slept poorly on the floor of the storage room, maybe a few hours at most. It didn't help that he woke up to the sound of someone screaming.

The nurse, a young black woman with a shaved head, was holding a roll of toilet paper and shrieking. He immediately jumped to his feet and tried to get past her, but in his sleepy-headed haste, he bumped her shoulder and she fell to the ground. He paused for a moment to make sure she was okay.

As soon as she got a good look at his face, she pushed away, screaming harder, her sneakers squeaking on the floor.

So Thomas ran.

The bus he caught was empty, and the driver barely glanced in his direction as he slid his Metro-Card into the slot. The whole ride he stayed in the back, his head down, glad that it was still before rush hour.

And here he was. Outside Amato's office. Waiting for his lawyer to show up so he could settle things up and get the hell out of Dodge.

His brain felt thick and muddy. A cup of coffee would set him right. But he knew that if he went inside the Dunkin' Donuts, he ran the risk of another situation like at the liquor store. He could see through the big plate-glass windows that the place was crowded. All it would take was for someone to recognize him. A lot of those people probably had newspapers with his face on them.

Thomas had passed a bodega on the walk over from the bus. As Amato had predicted, all the front pages featured pictures of him outside the courthouse.

And the headlines turned his stomach.

'PLAYGROUND KILLER' SUSPECT BACK ON THE STREET RUMBLE AT THE COURTHOUSE AS SUSPECTED KILLER WALKS

The worst one was:

KIDDIE KILLER SUSPECT GOES SCOT-FREE

Thomas thought you were supposed to be innocent until proven guilty. But it seems the newspapers were already convinced of his guilt.

All it would take was for one person to look up from their paper, and Thomas wouldn't leave that Dunkin' Donuts alive.

So he crossed the parking lot to Amato's storefront.

Thomas peered through the window. Inside there was a room with an empty desk for Amato's secretary and a door leading to Amato's office, which seemed to be ajar. Thomas entered.

Amato was probably in the bathroom or something. That's why he didn't answer the phone. Thomas was flooded with relief to be here, on the verge of escape. Finally, he could settle up and get the hell off Staten Island.

Thomas crossed the silent office and pushed the door open.

But instead of Amato, he saw Hanlon.

The cop was standing next to Amato's desk, holding the gun from last night at his side. He lifted it up and pointed it at Thomas.

"Shut the door," Hanlon said.

CHAPTER 29

PAUL ZHOU

PAUL KICKED A small gray rock. It skipped across a patch of drying mud outside the warehouse. He looked up and watched as the sun peeked through the clouds. He was so full of nervous energy and anticipation he felt like he was floating above the ground.

John, Susan, and Kat were inside. Daisy was with Hanlon. It was an arrangement Paul wasn't thrilled about—he'd rather have gone himself—but Hanlon was pretty adamant, and anyway, Daisy would only be driving. Hanlon insisted that, this time, he wouldn't let Scott get away.

Hanlon's thinking, at least, was sound. Scott had to know he couldn't go home. He would feel cornered. He didn't have any family and didn't seem to have any friends. It made sense he would go to the lawyer's office, looking for a way out.

They'd get the drop on him, get him in the van, and come here.

And this nightmare would be over.

Paul walked across the front of the warehouse, running his hand along the crumbling façade. There were no sounds but the rustling of the high grass and the lapping of the waves in the Arthur Kill, the narrow body of water separating Staten Island from New Jersey.

Across the water was a collection of refineries. Hanlon had picked a great spot. This didn't feel anything like the most populous city in America. It felt like the middle of nowhere. The kind of place you could scream your head off and no one would come along to help you.

He sighed. Closed his eyes. One moment he was sure they were doing the right thing. After being stuck in the car with Scott, being so close to him, he felt it down to his DNA. This man needed to pay. But in the harsh light of day, free from the adrenaline, his brain fuzzy from lack of sleep, he wasn't so sure anymore.

There was only one thing he was sure about: Something terrible was about to happen, and it would happen whether he wanted it to or not. So maybe best to just go along with it. The only thing that mattered was getting home to Jian. Pammy had reluctantly agreed to stay through the day, but by dinnertime, she needed to leave for her study group.

He wondered what Jian was doing. Reading, hopefully. He preferred Pammy read to his son rather than watch television, though he was sure she sneaked in some cartoons here and there. It made him ashamed, thinking about his son while he stood in a field preparing to kill someone. He'd tried to be a good father.

Did this make him a bad one?

Paul didn't have time to dwell on that, because he heard a crunching sound in the distance, and then the whir of an engine. The van appeared from the high grass bordering the muddy roadway. Daisy was driving and Hanlon was sitting shotgun.

Immediately Paul knew something was wrong. Even this far away, even with the sunlight glinting off the glass, there was something about the expression on her face. It was the same look of concern she got when one of the kids talked back or there was something around the house that Paul had forgotten to fix.

The van pulled in next to Hanlon's car and the pair got out. Daisy moved quickly toward Paul, clearly wanting to tell him something. They were about a hundred feet apart and she waved at him to come closer as Hanlon walked around to the side and opened the sliding door. Paul jogged to meet her.

"Paul—" Daisy said.

There was a banging sound behind them. John came out of the warehouse, swinging the door a little too hard against the brick wall. His sleeves were rolled halfway up his thick arms and he was wiping the sweat off his forehead with a handkerchief.

And he was smiling.

The smile of a man without a care in the world.

Paul turned back to Daisy. Hanlon had already pulled out Scott. The man was kneeling in the mud, his hands bound behind his back with white plastic zip ties. Strips of white cloth were tied around his head, constricting his mouth.

"I didn't think he was going to do it," said Daisy.

"Do what?" Paul asked.

Hanlon pulled another body out of the car, dragging him down into the mud. It was Amato, in a pink dress shirt, navy pants, and expensive brown shoes. He was trussed up the same as Scott. Hands behind back, gag in mouth, his perfect hair askew.

"He said we had to take the lawyer, too," Daisy said, her voice heavy with concern.

Paul stepped around her, putting his hand on

her shoulder as he passed, and approached Hanlon. "What the hell are you doing? This isn't what we agreed on."

"Shut up," Hanlon said, his voice calm as he held his revolver in his right hand. Not pointing it, not even lifting it, but clearly meant to keep Scott and Amato docile. Scott was shaking and Amato's eyes were rimmed in red, like he'd been crying.

Paul got the sense that maybe the gun was meant to keep him docile, too.

Amato looked up at Paul and tried to speak through the cloth binding his mouth, but before Paul could make anything out, Hanlon yelled, *"Hey!"* The lawyer immediately fell quiet. Hanlon looked past Paul to John. "Help me with them?"

"No, first we have to talk about this," Paul said.

"Nothing to discuss," John said, gripping Amato under the arm and pulling him to his feet. "This man was going to enrich himself personally and professionally by helping a child-killer get out of jail. To my mind, that makes him just as bad."

Paul didn't know what to say. He stood between everyone, shocked at what he was seeing. That Hanlon and John were so callously preparing to kill a man who'd done a bad thing, but not a thing in the same league as what Scott did.

"We need to talk about this," Paul said.

"It's too late," John said, shaking his head, speaking to Paul like he was a child. "He's a witness now. What are we going to do, leave him here and hope he doesn't tell anyone? He'll go straight to the cops and we'll all go to jail. Try being a father to your kid behind bars."

Hanlon nodded and tightened his grip on the gun. It made a little clicking noise, metal on metal. Whatever the sound was, it made the point.

So it's like that, Paul thought.

All that doubt and fear that Paul had felt at the beginning, inside Scott's apartment, came rushing back. It was like someone had turned on a light switch and he could finally see the entirety of what they were doing.

This was wrong.

Hanlon and John led the two bound men toward the warehouse. Paul put his hand on Daisy's arm and pulled her away. He lowered his voice. "We can't do this."

She nodded, her eyes vacant. "I don't know what to do."

"I know what we can do," Paul said. "We go in and try to talk some sense into everyone. And if things go south, you run. Get in the car and drive away. You will not look back. I will take the fall for this and I will swear you had nothing to do with it. If anyone names you, we'll both say I forced you into it."

"Paul…"

"No. Jian lost his sister. He is not losing both of us, too." Paul felt a lump in his throat. "We're too far into this now. I will do whatever it takes to protect this family. To protect you."

Daisy looked at him and smiled. Tears cut down her cheeks. She lifted her chin up. She was six inches shorter than him, and this had always been her sign that she wanted a kiss. Paul obliged, lowering his head down and pressing his lips on hers. He savored it, afraid that it might be the last time he'd have the opportunity.

"I love you, Paul," she said.

"I love you, too, Daisy," he replied. "Now let's get in there and fix this."

CHAPTER 30

THOMAS SCOTT

IT WAS SO bright outside and so dark inside that, as soon as Thomas crossed the threshold into the warehouse, it was like he'd gone blind. He blinked, waiting for his eyes to adjust to the dim light that was spilling in narrow beams through dirty windows near the ceiling.

As his vision grew sharper, he realized just how filthy the inside of the warehouse was. It made his shoulders tense. Dirt and dust and oil and mildew, everywhere. Probably other, worse things. Excrement. Dead animals.

He imagined what it would take to get this place clean: Weeks of labor, truckloads of supplies. He would start with the walls. A good brushing and a scrubbing, to get all the grit and gunk off. Doing the walls first meant not having to do the floors twice.

It was a ridiculous thing to think about, but it was distracting him from the current situation.

Hanlon was holding his arm tight, marching him right behind Amato and John Junior's dad. Their feet scraped in the dirt on the concrete floor.

At the end of this walk he was going to die.

And he was a little surprised—a thing like that ought to upset him. Scare him more than anything had ever scared him before. Yet this entire ordeal had been so terrible, he was ready for it to end. If anything, he was annoyed at himself. He should have been smarter than to go to Amato's office. Of course that's where they would look for him, because of course it was the most sensible place for him to go.

Maybe he deserved this.

He felt bad about getting Amato involved. He hoped, at least, they would let him speak long enough he could convince them to let Amato go. Maybe Amato would be smart enough to swear to not go to the police. Thomas would gladly allow him that— tell Amato he didn't want revenge, he didn't want anyone else to suffer. He wanted to go to his death knowing he hadn't inadvertently condemned someone else.

But he felt like it wasn't going to work out that way.

They approached a door and Thomas felt dread bubbling in his stomach, hot and thick. That terrible feeling of anticipation over what was next. Were they going to shoot him? Stab him?

Would it hurt?

He hoped it wouldn't hurt too much. He hoped it would be quick.

John Junior's dad pushed the door open and led them through.

The first thing Thomas noticed was the two women standing off to the side—Billy's and John Junior's moms. It was a big room, with a staircase and a platform and what looked like a big pane of glass. There was something strange about the glass. Some kind of visual distortion. A stray sunbeam hit it and seemed to break apart and scatter across the room. It took a second for Thomas to figure out what he was looking at.

When the realization hit, he screamed hard into the gag.

It was a tank full of water.

And he knew what form of death they had chosen for him.

He threw himself backward, trying with every ounce of strength to get away. This only caused Hanlon to push him into John Junior's dad, who grabbed him by both arms and nearly lifted him off his feet before slamming him into the ground.

John Junior's dad climbed on top of him and drove the flat of his fist into Thomas's nose. Thomas felt something shift in his face. His head shot back and cracked against the concrete. Once, twice, three times, until the pain was so great it overwhelmed every other sense and his body gave up, falling flat against the floor. He tasted copper in his mouth.

"That's right," said John Junior's dad. "You're going to suffer like my son suffered."

CHAPTER 31

DAISY ZHOU

DAISY PUSHED THROUGH the door to find John straddling Scott, pounding his fists into the man's face, then leaning down and whispering something into the bloody mess that remained.

There was a wild energy in the room, like at any moment someone might scream, but everyone was holding back. Susan was off to the side, her eyes darting around, her hand at her mouth. Amato was on his knees with Hanlon standing behind him, clutching his gun in his hand.

Daisy felt Paul come up alongside her. She was struck by how comforted she felt by his presence, and that made her angry—but only at herself, for doubting him and their relationship. Paul was a good man, and he had been right from the beginning.

"Wait," she said.

Everyone paused and looked up at her.

"We need…we just…" she said, struggling to find the right words.

"With all due respect, shut up," Hanlon said. "Right now, we're going to finish this. You all signed on. You all knew you were going to get your hands dirty. So let's get it over with."

As Hanlon spoke, John climbed off Scott, crossed the room, and picked up a cinder block and a length of chain. Scott scrambled away, his sobs filling the room and stabbing at Daisy. It was the sobbing of a child, and her maternal instinct made her want to cradle him and comfort him, no matter how much it made her sick to think that.

She couldn't help it. There was something so pathetic about him.

About all of this.

"Hanlon, we did not agree to kill an innocent person," Paul said, raising his voice. "But I forced Daisy to be here, so the first thing we should do is let her leave."

Hanlon made a confused face, but realization slowly dawned on him. "Oh, I get it. Working your defense. Nobody is leaving right now, so just be quiet and let us work."

John had looped the chain around the cinder block and started on Scott's legs. The man was still struggling, but had backed up into the brick wall. With his hands bound and no place to go, he tried twisting away, but didn't have any leverage.

Daisy's mouth was dry. Paul was already crossing the room to Hanlon, like he wanted to get in between the cop and the lawyer.

"I can't let you do this," Paul said.

Hanlon raised the gun and aimed it at Paul's chest.

Daisy's heart skipped a beat.

"You're not 'letting' me do anything," Hanlon said.

Paul slowly raised his hands until they were up by his shoulders. Amato yelled into the gag.

"You can't be serious," Paul said.

"I am very serious," Hanlon said. "Do you know how many lawyers I have watched get guilty men back onto the street? And how many of those guilty men who have gone on to rape and kill again? And for what? The assholes play the system. It's all loopholes and technicalities, even when the evidence is screaming in your face."

Amato was still yelling, trying to say something.

"That doesn't give you the right..." Paul said.

"Don't you tell me about rights," Hanlon said, his voice taking on a sharp, dangerous edge. "Do you know what it was like, watching a jury acquit the man who killed my wife and son? He blew so high on the breathalyzer he should have been dead. He should have spent the rest of his life in jail. But he had money. And his high-priced lawyer managed to convince a jury that the breathalyzer was faulty. The man who killed my family walked, because of men like him."

To punctuate the point, Hanlon put his foot on Amato's back and kicked him over. The lawyer's face smacked against the floor. He rolled over and groaned.

"My family had rights, until a drunk driver and a lawyer told me they didn't," Hanlon said. "Now stand over in the corner with your wife. This will all be over soon."

Paul stepped back slowly.

Daisy considered reaching out to him, but the tension in the room was so heavy, she was afraid any sudden movement might cause Hanlon to panic and fire. She finally recognized him for what he was: twisted and deranged by the tragedy of his past.

John, meanwhile, was holding Thomas under the armpits, dragging him toward the tank.

CHAPTER 32

JOHN KENNELLY

SCOTT WAS HEAVY, and it would be a tough job getting him up the metal staircase, and onto the platform at the lip of the tank. John couldn't ask Paul or Daisy for help. Hanlon was busy keeping things under control. Susan and Kat were too slight for this kind of work.

It was up to John.

Ultimately, it would be worth the effort.

Every waking moment since John Junior died had been consumed by an emotion too simple to peg as "anger." It was a blackness that opened up in the center of him, a vacuum that consumed and destroyed everything, until there was only empty space left behind.

And now, nearly at the end of this, a calm washed over him.

The tank couldn't have been more perfect. He wondered, vaguely, what it was for, but decided he didn't care. All that mattered is that it would serve the purpose he wanted it to. They'd gotten lucky—and not for the first time. As soon as he saw it, he knew that's how he wanted Scott to die. As chance would have it, there was a working firehose nearby, wrapped up behind glass near the tank, which made short work of filling it.

John pegged the water level at about eight feet. The cinder block and chain would keep Thomas below the surface. And since it was constructed mostly of glass, they'd have a clear view of him as he struggled and died.

John would be able to stand there and press his face against the glass and stare Scott in the eyes the entire time. He felt good. He wanted to cry. It wasn't sad or happy crying. Just all the emotion that had built up, ready to spill out. He looked down at this mess of a man, struggling but unable to get away. Soon he would be gone. It wouldn't bring back John Junior, but it would sure as hell make John feel a lot better.

He was so at peace that, as he reached the steps and dragged Scott up the stairs, one by one, he was only vaguely aware of the voices in the room, still arguing. The Zhous, unable to accept reality, those cowards.

But as he reached the platform, as Scott renewed his struggle and John kicked him in the head to calm him down, he heard another voice cut through the din.

"John!" Susan called.

He turned to find his wife diving past Hanlon, pulling the gag out of Amato's mouth. The lawyer coughed as John dropped Scott and yelled, "What the hell are you doing?"

CHAPTER 33
SUSAN KENNELLY

SUSAN KNEW JOHN was in pain, and she knew he needed this, and she told herself she could live with what they planned to do to Scott. She wasn't happy about it, but she'd find a way.

Still, despite all of Hanlon's bluster, she didn't believe Amato should die.

And the lawyer was so desperately trying to say something. She couldn't help herself. She yelled for her husband to stop and ran to Amato, hoping Hanlon wouldn't fire the gun, and yanked the gag away. He coughed hard, like he was trying to clear a heavy cold from his lungs.

John was yelling at her but she wasn't listening. She knew there'd be consequences and she didn't care. She was done standing by and letting things happen.

"You're making a mistake," Amato said, the words coming out heavy and scattered.

"Shut up," Hanlon said, whipping the gun against the side of Amato's head with a sharp crack. The lawyer went down hard. Susan yelped and jumped back. She looked up at her husband, whose face had gone beet red. Scott was cowering at his feet.

"Susan, I want you to listen to me…" John started.

"No," Susan said, a little shocked at the force of the word and the volume of her voice. "You listen to me. I have been afraid of you for a very long time but I will not let that overshadow the fact that we're about to kill an innocent person."

John's face fell. The anger replaced by sadness. It wasn't her defiance that hurt him. She could see the thing that cut him deepest was the admission that she was afraid of him. And the worst part was, he seemed to understand what she meant almost instantly.

"Two innocent men," Amato said from the floor, a smear of blood across his cheek.

"What?" Susan asked.

"We're both innocent," Amato said. "Has no one noticed the way he's freaking out? The way he's shaking? Scott has a major phobia of water. The guy has a hard time taking a shower. You think he drowned those kids?"

"What the hell are you talking about?" Hanlon asked.

"I'm saying that the evidence was planted," Amato said. He smiled, showing off pearly white teeth now stained with blood. "Who knows? Maybe by you, Detective Hanlon."

CHAPTER 34

REX HANLON

HANLON FELT HIS skin burning as every eye in the room settled on him.

That bastard lawyer and his silver tongue. Hanlon had known the gag would be necessary. He was afraid that given the freedom to speak, Amato would try to turn them on each other. And now it was happening.

The gun was heavy in his hand. He hadn't fired it in ten years. A liquor store robbery. He wasn't even on duty. The revolver was his backup piece. He was picking up something to chase the nightmares away, that recurring dream of his family's car, the metal twisted and coming apart like tissue paper. As Hanlon approached the counter, a man took out a gun and tried to hold the place up. Hanlon shot him. He never gave it a second thought.

Amato was doing something bad, too. Protecting a guilty man. Playing head games with them. He should shoot him. Not give it a second thought. All it would take would be to lift his arm and squeeze the trigger. Barely more effort than it would take to brush his teeth in the morning.

And yet, something was wrong. Something in the cop part of his brain, waving a hand at him, trying to get his attention.

Did Scott have a fear of water? He seemed to remember the lawyer mentioning something about it, but Hanlon had brushed it off as a Hail Mary attempt. Watching Scott cower like a frightened child put it in a new context.

And if it were true, why would he use water—drowning—as the murder weapon? There was something about it that didn't track. Unless it was the perfect murder weapon, given how much he feared it…

He suddenly felt torn in two directions.

Barely more effort than it would take to brush his teeth.

The gun was heavy in his hand.

Amato perked up again.

"Or, you know, a guy whose own wife is afraid of him, I would wonder what he was capable of," he said.

The gazes turned away from Hanlon and swung up to the platform, where John's mouth was hanging open.

"How dare you…." he said.

"I'm just saying what everyone is thinking," Amato said.

"Forget this," John said. "He's first. Then you. I'll do it myself."

Hanlon watched as John put his foot on Scott's back and shoved, sending the man tumbling into the water with a loud splash.

CHAPTER 35

THOMAS SCOTT

AS SOON AS Thomas hit the cold water, he was right back in that pool. The one that had almost killed him as a child.

Instead of the dark, dirty ceiling of the warehouse, he saw the sunlight slicing through the canopy. Felt the blue tarp reaching up and wrapping around him, dragging him under.

His muscles tensed so tightly he was afraid they would tear. His sinus cavity burned as it filled with water. He tried to fight, kick his feet, move his arms, but with everything bound, all he could do was sway back and forth as he looked up at the surface of the water, only a foot or two above him.

He screamed, but the only thing that escaped was a stream of bubbles, and then water filled his mouth, choking him.

CHAPTER 36

PAUL ZHOU

WATER SLOSHED OVER the lip of the tank and spilled onto the floor. Amato struggled to get to his feet, a difficult task considering his arms were still behind his back. Paul rushed to him and pulled him up.

Hanlon asked, "What the hell are you doing?"

"You're not going to shoot me," Paul said, hoping his gamble would pay off, that Hanlon's hesitation before meant he was having second thoughts.

The detective didn't say anything back, just shook his head in confusion.

Paul rushed for the staircase but felt the floor disappear out from underneath him as John slammed him into the wall. The air was forced from his lungs as the bigger man pressed him up against the brick, the rough surface pressing against his face.

"Don't you dare interfere with this," John said. Paul felt flecks of spit slapping the side of his face. "You will not take this from me."

Paul struggled but John was nearly twice his size. He tried to twist, away or down, but couldn't. He worked his legs up, trying to get some leverage on the wall, when he felt John back off a little.

He turned to see Susan hitting her husband's back, drawing his attention away. John turned and she smacked him across the face, hard. Paul took his opening and bounded up the stairs. There was a scuffle behind him but he didn't turn back to look, just got onto the platform and threw himself into the water.

It was so cold he tensed up immediately. He kicked down hard, trying to get to the bottom, to the cinder block, so he could lift it out of the water, enough that Scott would be able to get his head above the surface.

He could barely see, the way the water was stinging his eyes, but managed to grip it with both hands and swam up, into Scott, pushing him up, too, trying to get them toward the side of the tank.

Paul couldn't lift the cinder block and get Thomas out of the tank at the same time, so when he broke the surface he was relieved to see Daisy on her knees, reaching down into the water. She grabbed Scott's shirt and held him in place, the man sputtering and coughing and crying, as Paul heaved the cinder block onto the platform.

He crawled out of the water and onto the cold platform, lying on his back and staring at the ceiling, listening to Scott weep as he tried to pull himself up with Daisy's help, when there was a deafening crashing sound from somewhere in the warehouse.

Paul climbed to his feet and looked around the room.

"What the hell was that?" he asked.

But John was already crossing to the door where they had entered the room. He tried to open it, but the door wouldn't budge. He pressed his face to the small square window.

"Something fell in front of the door," he said. "It's blocked."

"Does anyone smell smoke?" Susan asked.

It took a second, but Paul noticed it, too. The acrid stench sneaking into the air.

"Where the hell is Kat?" Hanlon asked.

CHAPTER 37

KAT TAYLOR

KAT OPENED HER purse and removed the slim leather wallet. She undid the button holding it closed, revealing the picture of her son, Billy. His black hair perfectly combed, eating an ice pop, so his mouth and lips were rimmed in cherry red. It was from the annual block party. A candid shot taken by her neighbor, slipped into the mailbox a few days after the event.

Looking at it now, though, she couldn't remember the picnic. Only that terrible morning when she thought Billy was watching television while she made breakfast, but instead had decided he wanted to go for a swim in the pool. Even though he wasn't allowed to go in by himself.

He slipped out and closed the door behind him, so she never heard him calling for help, thrashing to keep himself above water. Instead she found him floating face down, and his lips were already blue by the time she pulled him out.

Her vision grew blurry with tears and she shivered, running her finger down the picture.

"I'm so sorry, Billy," she said, her voice shaking. "I'm so sorry I wasn't paying attention."

She knew she should call the police, but what then? They'd take Billy to a lab and poke and prod him and put him in the deep, dark ground. And Billy was so afraid of the dark. That wasn't where he was supposed to be. So she dressed him and brought him to his favorite playground.

It hurt like hell to leave him there, and she hoped that's where his soul would stay. The police would show up eventually, yes, but maybe he'd be tethered to that playground.

It was a comforting thought.

But it wasn't long before she realized her son would be alone. It would be a very long time before all his friends caught up with him in heaven.

And Billy's father had gone in the opposite direction. Kat was sure of that.

The thought ate at her. Billy on a swing by himself, with no one to push. Climbing up the slide and coming down with no one to cheer him on. She thought of killing herself so she could join him, but realized that first he would need some friends his own age.

Jian, Mei, and John Junior had been good friends of Billy in day care. And Kat could see their families were falling apart. Susan was terrified of John. Daisy was drifting away from Paul. The four of them such a mess, and wouldn't their children's lives be so much better on an eternal playground, free from worry and pain?

It wasn't easy, holding Mei and John Junior under the water in her tub. And dragging them to different playgrounds—Kat knew going to the same one would be a sure way of getting caught. She was sure they'd find each other. Staten Island was an island, after all.

She was preparing to send Jian to them when Hanlon came sniffing around.

Kat was indifferent about spending the rest of her

life in jail—she was going to kill herself at the first opportunity anyway—but she didn't want to leave the job undone. Mei, surely, would want her brother to join them.

So she went with Hanlon to Scott's apartment, and she planted—then "found"—the pictures there. They'd been easy enough to get. It took less than a half-hour of clicking around on Facebook, where private grief was now a matter of public record. She needed more time, and she knew Scott would be the perfect suspect. He had no friends or family, he looked a little creepy, and he had odd fascinations with children and cartoons.

It was easy enough, making Hanlon think it was his idea for her to break into Scott's apartment. She didn't anticipate they'd be caught, so when John attacked Scott outside court, she knew the best thing to do next was to turn their anger onto Scott.

Everyone was in such desperate need for an outlet, it blinded them and kept them from thinking critically. Paul was a problem, but even he fell in line. Honestly, with so many moving parts, she was a little surprised that it worked.

Until it didn't.

So while they argued with each other, she sneaked out, toppled some industrial shelving in front of the door to block their exit, and lit a fire. It wasn't elegant, but it would give her enough time to finish with Jian. She would follow right after him.

She turned the key in the ignition, and the Zhous' van roared to life. She yanked the car into drive and maneuvered it away from the warehouse and toward the road.

"All your friends will be with you soon, Billy," Kat said, hoping her son could hear her.

CHAPTER 38

THOMAS SCOTT

THOMAS HUFFED, TRYING to get the water out of his nose. He could smell the smoke, too, growing thicker as the seconds passed. He looked around the room from his vantage point, on the platform over the tank.

John Junior's dad was throwing his shoulder into the door. Hanlon ran to help him. Mei's mom was checking on Mei's dad, who was sitting on the staircase, while John Junior's mom was helping Amato up, getting him free from the zip ties.

Everyone was talking at once, words stumbling over each other, but Thomas could make out one phrase from Hanlon, as he and John Junior's dad took turns throwing themselves into the door.

"It was her," he said.

The "her" was Billy's mom. She'd disappeared, and someone had set them up to die. He had no idea why, and he didn't even care. He was just glad to be out of the water.

"Will someone just call the police or the fire department?" John Junior's mom yelled.

"We can't do that," Mei's mom yelled back. "All

the cell phones are in the car. Another brilliant idea from Hanlon."

"Hey, I had no idea something like this was going to happen," Hanlon said.

"Well, maybe you should have been paying more attention," John Junior's dad said, before throwing himself into the door again, wincing as it barely budged.

Thomas reached for his phone, before realizing it was gone; Hanlon had taken it from him back at Amato's office, wiped it down, and tossed it in the dumpster.

The smoke was getting thicker. Thomas could feel it in his lungs now. He coughed once, twice. Looked around. No one was paying attention to him anymore.

He rolled onto his side, and then his stomach, to push himself up, see if he could help with the door, when he noticed something built into the wall under the platform. He crawled to the edge and peeked over and saw an old vent. It looked just about person-sized, and where it led had to be better than here.

His body ached, but he managed to roll onto the floor and duck-walk under the platform to the vent. It didn't take too much effort to wrench free. After he did, he was glad his pants were wet, so he was able to wipe away the black streaks of dirt the vent left behind on his palms.

He stepped out from under the staircase, the room now hazy. Amato and John Junior's mom were coughing hard. John Junior's dad was on his knees, panting. Hanlon was trying to get him back up. Mei's dad, meanwhile, was screaming "Jian!" and kicking the door.

Thomas coughed, said, "Hey."

Paul kept kicking, kept screaming.

"Hey!" Thomas yelled.

Everyone turned and looked at him, like they'd forgotten he was there.

"I found a way out," he said.

He ducked under the staircase and got to the mouth of the vent. It was black beyond the opening, with nothing to light the way. No telling what kind of terrible things were in there. Living things. Dead things. Filthy things. And with his clothes wet like this he'd be like a mop, picking everything up along the way.

He shuddered, took a deep breath, and started crawling.

Luckily, the trip didn't last long, and as he moved toward a square of gray light, the smoke seemed to lessen. He came up on another vent. He put his shoulder into it and it collapsed forward, rattling to the floor.

Thomas climbed into the main room of the warehouse, near where they had come in. Flames were licking up the walls, up into the wooden rafters. His chest and knees were nearly black. He wiped his hands off the best he could and tried not to think about it as he felt something pushing him.

Thomas moved forward, and John Junior's mom was behind him, climbing out of the vent.

She stood up, stared at him for a moment, and said, "We were wrong."

Thomas looked down and saw that Daisy was next, with someone behind her.

"I just…" Susan said.

Thomas smiled. Tried to make it seem nice, even though he didn't have a very nice smile. "Let's get out of here first."

They ran through the door, the others behind them. The sky was draped in a heavy blanket of dark clouds, but the air was clean. Thomas took deep, greedy breaths of oxygen. He fell to his hands and knees, happy to be alive. He leaned back and felt raindrops smacking his face.

Mei's dad dashed past him, to Hanlon's car, and screamed out, kicking the tire, pounding his fist on the hood. Thomas crawled a few feet forward to get a better look, to see what the problem was.

The tire was flat, and there was a screwdriver sticking out of the side.

CHAPTER 39

DAISY ZHOU

KAT, OF ALL people! Daisy's stomach twisted into a knot. She had told Kat so many intimate things. Living without her daughter while still caring for her son. The way she felt about her husband. That one night she spent too long looking at bottles of vodka and sleeping pills, sitting next to each other on the counter.

She had trusted Kat.

And the entire time, Kat had been the one who'd killed her daughter.

It made her dizzy to think about it, so she pushed the thought away and focused on the task at hand. Everyone had made it out and was standing around the car. The warehouse was spitting black smoke from the windows, though how long it would take to attract the attention of the FDNY, she had no idea. This far back, it might be mistaken for something coming off a refinery in New Jersey.

Paul had climbed into the car, opening and throwing things into the back seat.

"There has to be a radio, something," he said. "She might be going after my *son*."

"There's not, just the scanner," Hanlon said. "It doesn't do outgoing."

Daisy pointed to Hanlon. "Tire, now."

He nodded and ran to the back, throwing open the trunk. John and Scott rushed over to help. The two of them reached the trunk at the same time, and for a moment, paused, staring at each other.

Scott reached into the trunk and came out with the tire iron gripped in his meaty hand. Daisy thought he might swing it at John, who seemed to think the same thing, and took a few steps back.

"Get the jack," Scott said, turning to the flat tire and getting to work, loosening the nuts.

The tire was changed with the speed of a NASCAR pit crew. John pumping the jack, Scott working the tire iron, Hanlon swapping the bad tire for the donut. Still, it felt like a million years. Daisy knew every second that passed was a second Kat got closer to her son.

The job done, everyone threw their tools to the ground and piled into the car. Hanlon and Paul in the front, John and Susan and Daisy in the back. Amato and Scott climbed into the open trunk to hitch a ride, and the car began maneuvering the bumpy, uneven road.

They neared Arthur Kill Road and the car slowed. Amato and Scott jumped off. John and Susan climbed out, too.

"We'll find a phone or flag down a car and call the police," John said, leading Susan away, toward a cluster of buildings farther down the road.

Daisy rolled down the window and looked at Amato and Scott. The two of them stood there, still bloodied, sticking out like sore thumbs.

"I'm sorry," she said.

It made her feel stupid saying it. That such a common, five-letter word could possibly undo everything that had happened in the past twenty-four hours. But with her son's life hanging in the balance, it would have to do.

Hanlon slammed his foot on the gas, and the car leapt onto the road.

As they made their way to the overpass that would lead over the expressway, Daisy said, "Maybe we should stop and try to call someone, too."

"We need to trust that John and Susan will find a phone," Paul said.

"And what about Thomas and the lawyer?"

She was met with silence from the front. Just the sound of the tires on the road and the rain, growing in intensity, smacking on the windshield.

They'd been discovered. They'd plotted to kill both men. Nearly accomplished it, in the case of Scott. And while Paul had saved him, that would only go so far. She couldn't help but think of her husband's proposal: That he would take the fall, try to make it so she would stay out of prison.

She didn't want to leave him, but she couldn't leave Jian, either. They didn't have any other family. There was no one to take him.

He'd be alone. She couldn't think of anything in this world worse than a child left alone.

Hanlon whipped the car around, leaning on the horn, running red lights. The roadway was getting slick and there were moments where it almost felt like the tires were coming off the surface.

They weren't even that far from the house. Another couple of minutes, tops. Less, with the way Hanlon was driving. For once, the usually brutal Staten Island traffic wasn't too bad.

Daisy pressed her hands over her chest, closed her eyes, breathed in deep, tried to calm herself.

And that's when she was thrown against the side of the car.

There was an explosion of glass and metal. Something cut her scalp, pain screaming through her skull. She opened her eyes, only for them to fill with blood as they spun in a circle and the car twisted around her.

CHAPTER 40

Staten Island Register Twitter account
    -BREAKING TRAFFIC ALERT, Eltingville: Accident w/multiple injuries, caused by car speeding @ Katan & Wainwright. Advise detour via Richmond.

CHAPTER 41

KAT TAYLOR

KAT CROSSED THE porch and knocked on the door. There was no sound from inside. She checked behind her and found the street to be quiet. It was just before 5 p.m., so a lot of people weren't home from work yet, and anyone home would have been sent inside by the rain.

She knocked again and rang the doorbell.

There was a sound of a lock unclasping, and the door, chained to the jamb, opened a few inches. She couldn't really make out who was behind it—just a brush of blond hair and a big blue eye with thick eyelashes. It was a young woman's voice that asked, "Yes?"

"Hi, I'm a friend of Daisy and Paul," she said. "They asked me to come over and relieve you. They got held up."

The blue eye stared at her for a couple of seconds, not moving, not blinking, and Kat wondered if maybe she had said the wrong thing, or if the girl was too suspicious to let her in.

The door closed, there was a sound of metal sliding on metal, and the door swung open. Kat was faced with a petite, perky blond girl with curly hair. "Hi, I recognize you. Why don't you come in?"

Kat smiled, happy she didn't have to work any harder to get inside. The others had taken so much planning, luring the kids away, convincing them that she was allowed to give them a bath.

The girl would be a problem, but one she could solve for good when she was finished with Jian. Right now she just needed to buy a little time.

The whole thing was a little more slapdash than she would like, but at least there was a playground just down the street.

She stepped over the threshold, closed the door behind her, and kicked off her muddy shoes, not wanting to dirty the house. She asked, "Where's Jian?"

"He's upstairs napping," the girl said. "Actually, this would be a good time to see if he's awake. Want to come up with me?"

"That'd be great," Kat said. "You lead the way."

The girl turned. Just inside the entry to the house was a table holding a glass vase full of flowers. Kat picked it up and swung it at the girl's head as hard as she could.

CHAPTER 42

JOHN KENNELLY

JOHN HATED RUNNING. Ever since John Junior died, he'd been eating more, drinking more, packing on extra pounds. Suddenly he was cutting a new notch at the very end of his belt and finding some of his dress shirts didn't exactly fit anymore. Susan had been gently goading him into getting back to the gym, or at least thinking more about what he ate.

And he had ignored her.

Now he wished he hadn't. His chest was constricted and he was already sweating, despite the cool rain that was now coming down harder. He glanced back and saw that Susan was keeping up as they reached the end of the road, a big gray building looming on the other side.

It looked abandoned, but as they turned the corner they found an open garage door and a red sports car inside. A young skinny guy in coveralls, listening to a large pair of headphones, was doing something to the engine with a wrench. John called out, "Hey, you, hey!"

The man didn't even look over. The music must be too loud. John swore and ran harder, pumping his legs, muscles burning. The man finally noticed him and pulled off his headphones. John reached him and spoke between gasps. "I need...to use...your phone."

"Whoa, what's going on?" the man said.

"If I don't use your phone right now, someone is going to die."

The man's eyes went wide and he pointed to the wall, to an ancient plastic phone with a curly cord that probably had started out white and had turned yellow with age. "Okay okay, right there. No long distance."

John called 911 and as soon as the operator picked up, he gave her the Zhous' address. "Do you have that?" he asked.

"Yes, sir, I do," said the woman on the other end, taking on an annoyed tone. "But what exactly is the nature of your emergency?"

"Just send someone there right now," he said. "Right now. Someone's life is in danger."

"Sir, can you tell me your—"

John hung up the phone and turned to find Susan staring at him.

Her hair plastered to her face. Her clothes soaked. Just as beautiful as the day he met her. More so, probably.

He remembered that first time, at the St. Patrick's Day parade on Forest Avenue. She was the friend of a friend, and luminous. Sparkling as much as the shamrock sticker on her cheek. The second he saw her, all he wanted was to know everything about her.

She was a slight woman, and yet in that moment, it felt like she was so much taller than him. All that anger he'd felt turned inward, and it felt like the ground dropped out from under him. He couldn't believe how selfish and blind he'd been. Susan deserved so much better than this.

So much better than *him*.

He crossed to her and took her hands and said, "I don't know what to say right now. I just…I am so sorry. For everything."

"We have some things we need to work on," she said.

"We do. And I want to work on them. I promise."

"Okay."

She was looking at him with a mix of emotion—concern, disappointment. She let him hold her hands, but didn't seem to want to get any closer. He dipped his head down and pecked her forehead. For a second it seemed like she was going to move away, but then she let him do it.

"C'mon, let's go," he said.

"Where are we going?" she asked.

"We have to see this through."

CHAPTER 43

PAUL ZHOU

PAUL THREW HIS shoulder into the door three times before it finally gave way. The momentum sent him tumbling onto the asphalt.

They were in the middle of the intersection, cars stopped all around them. The front end of Hanlon's car was smashed, and steam was rising from the hood. The side was collapsed against a telephone pole, which was now pushed to an odd angle. The side of the silver Prius they hit had crumpled, but the driver was pulling himself out of the mangled wreck, and seemed more angry than hurt.

Paul stood and felt dizzy. He grabbed the door for support and looked into the back seat and saw Daisy was moving. There was a heavy gash across her head, bleeding freely.

"Are you okay?" he asked.

"Yes, yes…"

Paul looked across to the front. Hanlon's head was thrown back. It looked like he was napping. Daisy reached over and pressed her fingers to his exposed neck.

"He has a pulse," she said. "Go."

Paul turned and ran. His shoes, still soaked through

from his dive into the tank, were heavy. It was only a few blocks and he cleared it quickly, dodging the tangle of cars that had built up around the accident, throwing himself forward and trying not to slip on the slick surfaces.

He had never run so fast in his life.

He could hear sirens in the distance. Hopefully headed his way. When he reached the house he ran up the porch and grabbed the doorknob, throwing it open and nearly stumbling into the foyer.

Pammy was sprawled on the stairs, flowers and water and shattered glass scattered on the floor around her. Her hands were zip-tied behind her back. He knelt down and saw she was wincing and groaning.

It made him feel terrible to do it, but he vaulted over her and ran up the stairs toward the bathroom. The door was closed and locked. He kicked at the doorknob till the flimsy plywood gave way, and found Kat on her knees, the faucet running, the tub full of water. She was holding something below the surface.

Something that was thrashing and fighting back.

He grabbed her and pulled her away. She screamed and fought, but Paul lifted her clean off her feet and threw her into the wall, bringing down shelving that sent towels and knickknacks scattering across the floor. Kat left a dent in the sheetrock and hit the ground with a thud.

Paul fell to his knees and reached in, pulling out Jian. The boy was dressed in his navy dinosaur pajamas, sobbing and choking on water, his hair flat and plastered to his forehead.

When he saw Jian was breathing, Paul held the boy to his chest.

"It's okay, Jian," he said. "I'm right here."

Paul looked over his shoulder and realized Kat was gone.

CHAPTER 44

DAISY ZHOU

DAISY WAS PRETTY sure her wrist was broken.

It felt like it was on fire, and when she wiggled her fingers, the pain only got worse. She was still bleeding from the wound on her head, but she didn't care. Hanlon was alive and she saw an ambulance fighting its way through the crowd, and that was enough for her.

Some people tried to stop her from leaving—yes, she was bleeding, and yes, she was leaving the scene of an accident—but she didn't care about that, either.

She made her way for the house, hoping Paul had been fast enough.

Hoping she hadn't just lost her second child.

As she turned the corner of her block, she nearly ran into someone. She stumbled and stepped back, instinct kicking in, telling her to say she was sorry.

That is, until she realized it was Kat.

The woman was drenched, and her eyes were wide and wild. She was breathing heavily. This calm, kind woman now looked completely the part of the deranged killer that she had been hiding from them for so long.

The two women stared at each other for a few moments, nothing but silence and a massive amount of hatred between them.

"You're a mother," Kat said. "You have to understand. I just couldn't leave him all alone like that. I just wanted his friends to be with him."

Daisy inhaled hard and held her breath.

So that was it. The reason this woman had killed Daisy's daughter.

So her son wouldn't be lonely.

For a second, Daisy felt pity for this woman. That the loss of her son had twisted her so badly she was broken in two, her psyche shattered until the most terrible thought possible would seem like a logical choice.

Then, making sure to use the wrist that wasn't broken, she made a tight fist, reared back, and punched Kat as hard as she could.

CHAPTER 45

JOHN KENNELLY

THEY HAD BEEN lucky. A cab passed by, headed back to a nearby dispatch garage, and John flagged it down. Even though cabs weren't supposed to pick up street hails, the guy's eyes lit up when John whipped out a thick stack of 20s and waved it at him.

The rest of the ride, he didn't feel so lucky. The space between him and his wife seemed huge. He put his hand in the empty seat between them, hoping she would take it.

After a few miles, she did.

That gave him some hope.

This was his road to Damascus. The scales had fallen from his eyes, and suddenly the world looked entirely different. He saw what his anger had twisted him into. And not just the anger after John Junior's death. The anger that had always been a part of him, that he had chosen to bury.

He had no idea what would come next, but he made himself a promise: He would be a better husband. He wouldn't follow in the footsteps of Hanlon, who had let his grief twist him so sharply that he would actually put his life and career at risk.

And for what?

It wouldn't have changed anything. Killing Scott—or in this case now, Kat—wouldn't bring back John Junior.

Blood didn't wash out blood.

The cab turned the corner on the Zhous' block, and they were met by a cavalcade of police cars and ambulances. A fire truck was pulling up from the other direction.

"Right here is good," John said.

They got out of the car, the rain tapering off, and crossed through the maze of vehicles, making it to the house just in time to see a police car pulling away with Kat looking out the rear window, her left eye bruised and nearly swollen shut.

John caught her good eye for a moment and felt that surge of hatred come back, hard and fast, but he took a deep breath and let it dissipate.

Kat going to jail would be justice. Maybe not the exact kind of justice he wanted, but at least it would be the right kind of justice.

Daisy was sitting on the back of an ambulance, Jian next to her, a paramedic looking them over. Paul hovered nearby and turned to face John and Susan as they approached. He smiled and nodded, assuring them that everything was okay.

John looked around. "Hanlon?"

"We got in a car accident," Paul said. "Banged up pretty bad, but they're taking him to University Hospital now. Should be okay."

Then Paul stepped forward and embraced John.

John was a little taken aback, but he hugged back. He felt terrible for the way he'd treated Paul. After all, Paul had been right all along.

"I should have listened," John said.

"Let's not worry about that right now," Paul said. "We've got some other problems to address."

John looked up and saw a familiar pair of figures across the street.

"Yes, we do," John said.

Amato and Scott were standing together on the sidewalk, watching them, their faces flat and unreadable. After a few moments Scott exchanged some heated words with Amato and then walked toward them.

This was it.

John looked around at the police officers milling about. Even if he tried to run, there was no place to go. He wondered if there was any way to keep Susan out of it, to make sure he got the blame for their part in it.

He deserved the blame. He had to save her. She deserved that.

More than that, actually. She deserved the world and everything else he had promised her on the day they got married. But right now, he figured he could manage at least this.

John turned and looked at Paul, who wore a look of concerned panic John figured was pretty similar to his own. They nodded to each other, understanding that there was only one thing left to do: protect the shattered remains of their families.

CHAPTER 46

THOMAS SCOTT

IT WAS A little incredible, how persuasive Amato could be. He employed his way with words to convince an older gentleman heading to the grocery store to give them a lift in the direction of the Zhous.

Before getting in the car, Amato turned to Thomas and said, "Keep quiet."

Thomas nodded and followed the order as Amato spun a tale about how they were driving and the car broke down and thank you so much for picking them up and they just had to get home because their mother was sick and they called a cab and it never showed up…

Thomas just looked out the window and stared at the island flashing by.

It didn't seem like such a scary place anymore.

A lot of people like to knock Staten Island. But for Thomas, it was perfect: Not too busy, not too quiet. Just right.

And even when he was a stranger, he felt like he belonged. He hated the thought of losing that, of his life changing so drastically that it would suddenly become unrecognizable. Now he was innocent. For sure innocent.

He could stay, and without a cloud of suspicion hanging over his head. He could go into stores without being treated like scum.

The relief he felt at that—he didn't even know how to describe it. It was the best thing he'd ever felt.

As they got close to the Zhous' house, the car moved slower and slower. After two blocks they saw flashing lights and emergency vehicles. A police car drove past them, and Thomas thought he saw Billy's mom's face flash in the window before the car turned the corner. Amato had the driver duck down a side street to avoid the mess.

The rain tapered off and Thomas smiled. The air had never tasted so sweet.

"So, I guess we'll just talk to the cops who are already there," Amato said. "I don't even know where to start with all of this."

Thomas didn't say anything. He didn't know what to say. He knew he should be angry. Those people had tried to kill him. All he ever tried to do was be nice to those children, to give them a nice and clean place to play. And his reward was being hunted like an animal, nearly driven from the place he'd called home his entire life.

And yet, he was so happy to be alive, so happy this was over, he couldn't be upset.

Instead he thought about what that must be like—to lose a child. Thomas didn't have children, but he saw the bond that existed between parents and children. The way a mother's face would brighten when she picked up her baby from day care. The pride a father would take in learning his son had stood up or taken a step.

It's a hurt he would never know, but the more he thought about it, the more he realized it was probably worse than whatever he'd been through.

It made him think about his own parents, and how

much he missed them after they were gone. The hole it had left in the center of him, but even then, it fit within a natural order to things.

People died every day. Parents and loved ones and friends and strangers.

But parents shouldn't have to bury their children.

They reached the Zhous' house and saw the parents assembled around an ambulance.

"Time to get started," Amato said. "I'm going to look for the officer in charge. Do you need me to get you a paramedic?"

"No cops," Thomas said.

Amato put his hand on his shoulder and arched his eyebrow. "What? They tried to kill you. They tried to kill *me*."

"Can you blame them?"

Amato's eyes went wide. "Yes, I can blame them!"

"I'm not splitting up a family," he said. "I don't want to press charges."

"Now wait a minute—"

"And you shouldn't, either. We can live with this. Look at what they have to live with."

Thomas held up his hand, gesturing across the street, at John Junior's mom and dad. At Mei's mom and dad. Jian was there now, holding tight to his mother, hiding his face, sobbing.

Thomas watched as John Junior's dad and Mei's dad hugged. Two men who could barely stand each other a short while ago, come together now.

And yet, despite the resolution they had reached, they all still looked so sad.

Everything that had happened here—it seemed to make them realize some things they needed to realize. And that was a good thing. But it would never take away the hurt and emptiness.

Amato shook his head and started to say something, but John Junior's dad had noticed them. Thomas didn't wait to hear what Amato had to say. He crossed the street, cutting between police officers and neighbors, until he reached the parents.

They looked up at him, their eyes filled with terror and regret.

John and Paul stopped a few feet away from Thomas.

"I know what we did was wrong," John Junior's dad said, putting his hands up. "I can never...I just...I don't know what to say. But please, our wives—"

"Please say it was just us," Mei's dad said. "I'm begging you. *We're* begging you. It has to be us."

"We should pay the price," John Junior's dad said, tears forming in his eyes and rolling down his face. "They shouldn't. We don't deserve your mercy. We really don't. But we have to ask for it."

Thomas's throat grew thick, his breath catching in his chest.

He looked at the two desperate men, and past them, at their wives, their faces drenched in terror. Realizing that this was the moment when everything would change.

These men were so broken, he wasn't even afraid of them anymore.

Thomas raised his hand and John Junior's dad winced, but Thomas just held his hand out, palm and fingers straight. After a moment John Junior's dad reached out and took his hand, shaking it cautiously, completely unsure of what was happening.

"I am so sorry about what happened to your children," Thomas said. "I can't imagine what that must be like."

John Junior's dad's face spread into a wide smile

and he fell into Thomas, wrapping his arms around him, pulling him close. The man was shaking, and Thomas couldn't tell if he was laughing or crying, but he held tight, and then Mei's dad joined them, throwing his arms around them and saying "Thank you, thank you," over and over.

The three of them stood there, in the middle of the street, their fractured existence slowly knitting back together, destined to remain heavily scarred but at least with the possibility of healing on the horizon.

And as they stood there, his face buried in John Junior's dad's shoulder, Thomas could feel the warmth of the sun on his back.

ABOUT THE AUTHORS

James Patterson is the world's bestselling author and most trusted storyteller. He has created many enduring fictional characters and series, including Alex Cross, the Women's Murder Club, Michael Bennett, Maximum Ride, Middle School, and I Funny. Among his notable literary collaborations are *The President Is Missing*, with President Bill Clinton, and the Max Einstein series, produced in partnership with the Albert Einstein estate. Patterson's writing career is characterized by a single mission: to prove that there is no such thing as a person who "doesn't like to read," only people who haven't found the right book. He's given over three million books to schoolkids and the military, donated more than seventy million dollars to support education, and endowed over five thousand college scholarships for teachers. For his prodigious imagination and championship of literacy in America, Patterson was awarded the 2019 National Humanities Medal. The National Book Foundation presented him with the Literarian Award for Outstanding Service to the American Literary Community, and he is also the recipient of an Edgar Award and nine Emmy Awards. He lives in Florida with his family.

Rob Hart is the author of *New Yorked*, nominated for an Anthony Award for Best First Novel, among others. He is the former publisher at MysteriousPress.com and class director at LitReactor.

ALEX CROSS ENTERS THE
FINAL SHOWDOWN WITH THE
RELENTLESS KILLER WHO HAS
STALKED HIM AND HIS FAMILY
FOR YEARS.

TURN THE PAGE FOR A
PREVIEW OF THE NEWEST
ALEX CROSS THRILLER

FEAR NO EVIL

COMING IN NOVEMBER 2021.

CHAPTER

Washington, DC
Late June

MATTHEW BUTLER COCKED HIS HEAD to one side, considering the big-boned blonde in front of him. She was handcuffed and shackled to a heavy oak chair bolted into the concrete floor beneath bright fluorescent lights.

If the woman was anxious about her predicament, she wasn't showing it in the least. She was as chill as the yoga outfit she wore. No sweat on her pale brow. Beneath her warm-up hoodie, her chest rose and fell calmly, each breath measured. Her shoulders were relaxed. Even her eyes looked soft.

Butler adjusted the strap of his shoulder holster.

"I know they've trained you for this sort of thing," he said in a voice with the slightest of Western twangs. "But your training won't work against me, Catherine. It never does."

A fit, balding man with a hawkish nose, Butler had workman's hands and wore black jeans, Nike running shoes, and a dark blue polo shirt. He crossed his thick forearms when she smiled back at him with brilliant white teeth.

"Whoever you are, you are going to be destroyed for what you're doing," Catherine Hingham said. "When they find out—"

Butler cut her off. "You know, in my many years as a professional, Catherine, I have come to rather enjoy the delicate process of breaking into hearts and minds. They are very much interlinked, you know—hearts and minds—and I have found that one is almost always the key to the other."

"Langley will annihilate you," Hingham said, studying Butler as if she wanted to remember every line in his face.

"Your operators won't help you today," Butler said, gesturing at a pile of blank paper and a pen on the table before her. "Tell me the truth and we can all move on with our lives."

"I'll say it again: You have no jurisdiction over me."

Butler chuckled, gestured around the room. "Oh, but in here, I do."

"I want to see a lawyer, then."

"I'm sure," he said, sobering. "But we're talking about a serious threat to our national security, Catherine. A few rules of engagement can and will be broken in order to thwart that threat."

"I am not a national security threat," she said evenly. "I work for the Central Intelligence Agency, with the highest clearances, in support of my country's freedoms. Your freedoms as well."

"That's what makes your traitorous actions so hard to understand, Catherine."

Her face reddened and she shifted in her chair. "I am no traitor."

Butler took a step toward her. "The hell you're not. We know about the Maldives."

Hingham blinked, furrowed her brow. "The Maldives? Like, the islands in the Indian Ocean?"

"The same."

"I have no idea what you're talking about. I have never been to the Maldives. I've never even been to India."

"No?"

"Never. You can talk to my case officers about it."

"I plan to at some point," Butler said, taking another step toward her. He reached down to touch the back of her left hand before letting his finger trail across her wedding band and modest engagement ring. "Does he know? Your husband?"

"That I work for the CIA?" she said. "Yes. But he has zero idea what I actually do. Those are the rules. We play by them."

Butler sighed as he gently took hold of her left pinkie with his leathery hand, thumb on top.

"Do you know the surest way to sever the connection between the body and mind, and therefore the heart?"

"No," she said.

"Pain," Butler said. He gripped her little finger tight and levered his thumb sharply downward until he heard a bone snap.

CHAPTER

CATHERINE HINGHAM SCREAMED IN AGONY, fighting against her restraints, then yelled at him, "You cannot do this! This is the United States of America and I'm a sworn officer of the Central—"

Butler broke her ring finger, then waited for her to stop screaming and crying.

"You have eight fingers left, Catherine," Butler said calmly. "I will break them all and if you still do not tell me what I want to know, I will have your five-year-old daughter brought here and I will begin breaking *her* tiny fingers one by one until you confess."

The CIA officer stared at him in disgust and horror. "Emily has cerebral palsy."

"I know."

"You wouldn't. It's…monstrous."

"It is," he said and sighed again. "And yet, because there is so much at stake, Catherine, I will break your little girl's fingers. But only if you make it necessary."

The CIA officer continued to stare at him for several moments. He gazed back at her evenly until her lower lip trembled and she hung her head.

"The costs," Hingham whispered hoarsely. "You have no idea what a child like Em..." She could not go on and broke down sobbing.

"The heart wins again," Butler said. He pushed the pile of blank pages in front of her. "Start writing. The Maldives. The numbered accounts. Their connections. All of it."

After a few moments, Catherine Hingham calmed enough to raise her head. "I need witness protection."

"I'll see what I can do," Butler said and held out the pen to her. "Now write."

The CIA officer reached out with both handcuffed hands shaking. She took the pen. "Please," she said. "My family doesn't deserve what will happen if—"

"Write," he said firmly. "And I'll see what I can do."

The CIA officer reluctantly began to scribble names, addresses, account numbers, and more. When she'd moved to a second page, Butler had seen enough to be satisfied.

He walked behind the CIA officer and nodded to a small camera mounted high in the corner of the room.

A gravelly male voice came through the tiny earbud Butler wore in his left ear. "Mmmm. Well done. When you have what we need, end the interview and file your report, please."

Butler nodded again before moving in front of Catherine Hingham. She set her pen down and pushed the pages across the table at him.

"That's it," she said in a hoarse voice. "Everything I know."

"Unlikely," Butler said, using the nail of his index finger to lift up the first sheet so he could scan the information she'd provided on page two. "But this looks useful enough for now. It will give us leverage. Was that so hard, Catherine?"

She relaxed a little and said, "Okay, then, I've given you what you wanted. Now I need a doctor to fix my hand. I need witness protection."

With his fingernail, Butler scooted the confession pages to the far right of the table. "You're a smart woman, Catherine. Well educated. Yale, if I remember. You should know your history better. We don't protect traitors in the United States of America. From Benedict Arnold on, they've all had to pay the price. And now, so will you."

The CIA officer looked confused and then terrified when Butler took a step back and drew a stubby pistol with a sound suppressor from his shoulder holster.

"No, please, my kids are—" she managed before he took aim and shot her between the eyes.

CHAPTER

3

FROM THE TIME WE'D MET as ten-year-olds, John Sampson, my best friend and long-term DC Metro Police partner, had been stoic, quiet, observant. Since his wife, Billie, had died, he'd become even more reserved and was now given to long bouts of brooding silence. I knew he was still wrestling with grief.

But that late-June morning, Big John was acting as wound up as a kid about to hit the front gates of Disney World as he bopped around my front room, where we'd laid out all our gear for a trip we'd been talking about taking for years.

"You think we'll see a grizzly?" Sampson asked, grinning at me.

"I'm hoping not," I said. "At least, not up close."

"They're in there, big-time. And wolves."

"And deer, elk, and cutthroat trout," I said. "I've been studying the brochure too."

Nana Mama, my ninety-something grandmother, came in wringing her hands and asked with worry in her voice, "Did I hear you say grizzly bears?"

Sampson glowed with excitement. "Nana, the Bob Marshall Wilderness has one of the densest concentrations of grizzlies in the lower forty-eight states. But don't worry. We'll have bear spray and sidearms. And cameras."

"I don't know why you couldn't choose a safer place to go on your manly trip."

"If it was safer, it wouldn't be manly," I said. "There's got to be a challenge."

"Glad I'm an old lady, then. Breakfast in five minutes." Nana Mama turned and shuffled away, shaking her head.

"Checklist?" Sampson said.

"I'm ready if you are."

We started going through every item we'd thought necessary for the twenty-nine-mile horseback trip deep into one of the last great wildernesses on earth and for the five-day raft ride we'd take out of the Bob Marshall on the South Fork of the Flathead River. An outfitter was providing the rafts, tents, food, and bear-proof storage equipment. Everything else had to fit into four rubberized dry bags we'd use on the river after he dropped us off.

We could have signed up for a fully guided affair, but Sampson wanted us to do a good part of the trip alone, and after some thought, I'd agreed. Six days deep in the backcountry of Montana would give Big John many chances to open up and talk, which is critical to the process of coping with tragic loss.

"How's Willow feeling about our little trip?" I asked.

Sampson smiled. "She doesn't like the idea of grizzly bears any more than Nana does, but she knows it will make me happy."

"Your little girl's always been wise beyond her years."

"Truth. Bree liking her job?"

Thinking of my smart, beautiful, and independent wife, I said, "She loves it. Got up early to be at the office. Something about a possible assignment in Paris."

"Paris! What a difference a career change makes."

"No kidding. It was like the gig was tailor-made for her."

"Maybe we should think about going into private-sector investigations too."

"Pay's better, for sure," I allowed.

Before he could reply, my seventeen-year-old daughter, Jannie, poked her head in and said, "Nana says your eggs are getting cold."

I put down my dry bag and went to the kitchen, where I found my youngest child, Ali, already finishing up his plate.

"Morning, sunshine," I said, giving him a hug. He ignored it, so I tickled him.

"C'mon, Dad!" He laughed, then groaned. "Why can't I go with you?"

"Because you're a kid and we don't know what we'll be facing."

"I can do it," he insisted.

Sampson said, "Ali, let your dad and me scope it out this year. If we think you're up to it, we'll bring you along on the next trip. Deal?"

Ali scrunched up his face and shrugged. "I guess. When do you leave?"

"First thing in the—"

My cell phone began to ring at the same time Sampson's chimed.

"No," John protested. "Don't answer that, Alex. We're supposed to be gone already!"

But when I saw the caller ID, I grimaced and knew I had to answer. "Commissioner Dennison," I said.

"John Sampson and I were just heading out the door on vacation."

"Cancel it," said the commissioner of the Metro DC Police Department. "We've got a dead female, gunshot wound to the head, dumped in the garage under the International Spy Museum on L'Enfant Plaza. Her ID says she's—"

"Commissioner, with all due respect," I said, "we've been planning this trip for—"

"I don't care, Cross," he snapped. "Her ID says she's CIA. If you want to continue your contract with Metro, you'll get down there. And if Sampson wants to keep his job, he'll be with you."

I stared at the ceiling a second, looked at John, and shook my head.

"Okay, Commissioner. We're on our way."

JAMES
PATTERSON
RECOMMENDS

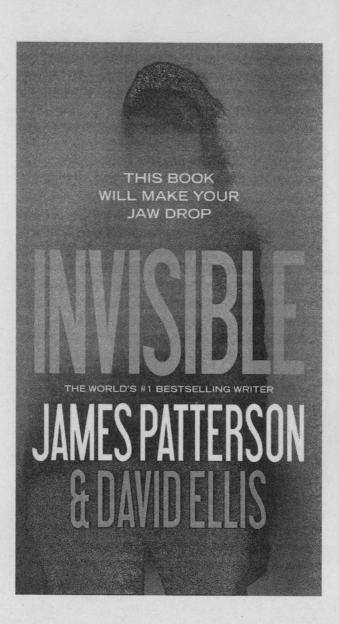

THIS BOOK
WILL MAKE YOUR
JAW DROP

INVISIBLE

THE WORLD'S #1 BESTSELLING WRITER

JAMES PATTERSON
& DAVID ELLIS

INVISIBLE

When I started writing *Invisible,* it seemed like every other TV network was telling the same kind of police stories, robberies, and crime twists. So I wanted to tell a different kind of suspense story, one that would really make your jaw drop. In the novel, Emmy Dockery is a researcher for the FBI who believes she has stumbled on one of the deadliest serial killers in history. There's only one problem—he's invisible. The mysterious killer leaves no trace. There are no weapons, no evidence, no motive. But when the killer strikes close to home, she must crack an impossible case before anyone else dies. Prepare to be blindsided because the most terrifying threat is the one you don't see coming—the one that's invisible.

And don't miss Emmy Dockery's second mystery, *Unsolved,* available now.

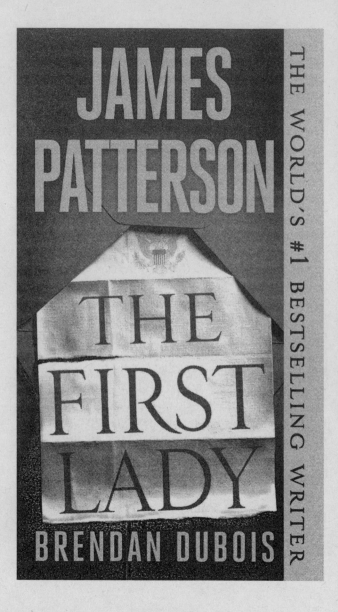

JAMES PATTERSON

THE FIRST LADY

BRENDAN DUBOIS

THE FIRST LADY

The US government is at the forefront of everyone's mind these days and I've become incredibly fascinated by the idea that one secret can bring it all down. What if that secret is a US President's affair that results in a nightmarish outcome? Sally Grissom, leader of the Presidential Protection Division, is summoned to a private meeting with the President and his chief of staff to discuss the disappearance of the First lady. What at first seemed an escape to a safe haven to get away from the revelation of her husband's indiscretion turns into a kidnapping when a ransom note arrives along with what could be the First Lady's finger. It's a race against the clock to collect the evidence that all leads to one troubling question: Could the kidnappers be from inside the White House?

THE CORNWALLS VANISH

There's nothing more terrifying than coming home and knowing that something is wrong. Army intelligence officer Amy Cornwall experiences that when she finishes a tour filled with haunting sites and she walks in the front door to find her home empty. She receives a phone with very specific instructions and failure to complete them will mean the death of her husband and ten-year-old daughter. Now Amy has to defy Army Command and use every lethal skill they've taught her to save her family. There's no boundary that she won't cross in order to find them because without her family, she might as well be dead.

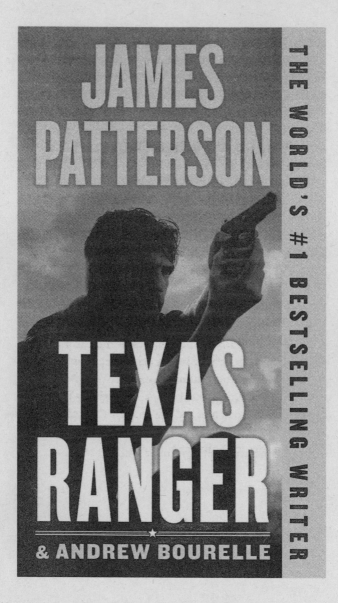

JAMES
PATTERSON

TEXAS
RANGER

& ANDREW BOURELLE

THE WORLD'S #1 BESTSELLING WRITER

TEXAS RANGER

So many of my detectives are dark and gritty and deal with crimes in some of our grimmest cities. That's why I'm thrilled to bring you Detective Rory Yates, my most honorable detective yet.

As a Texas Ranger, he has a code that he lives and works by. But when he comes home for a much-needed break, he walks into a crime scene where the victim is none other than his ex-wife—*and* he's the prime suspect. Yates has to risk everything in order to clear his name, and he dives into the inferno of the most twisted mind I've ever created. Can his code bring him back out alive?

For a complete list of books by

JAMES PATTERSON

VISIT
JamesPatterson.com

 Follow James Patterson on Facebook
@JamesPatterson

 Follow James Patterson on Twitter
@JP_Books

 Follow James Patterson on Instagram
@jamespattersonbooks